# A Christmas to Remember

# A Christmas to Remember

ANTON DU BEKE, household name and all-round entertainer, brings the charm and style he's famous for to this, his third novel. He is also the author of *Sunday Times* bestseller *One Enchanting Evening* and *Moonlight Over Mayfair*.

Anton is one of the most instantly recognisable TV personalities today, best known for his role on the BBC's *Strictly Come Dancing*, which he has featured on since its inception in 2004. His debut album reached the Top 20, and his annual sell-out tours have been thrilling dance fans in theatres nationwide for over a decade.

www.antondubeke.tv
 @TheAntonDuBeke
 @Mrantondubeke
 www.facebook.com/antondubeke

# ANTON DU BEKE

## A Christmas to Remember

ZAFFRE

First published in the UK in 2020 by
ZAFFRE
An imprint of Bonnier Books UK
80–81 Wimpole St, London W1G 9RE
Owned by Bonnier Books
Sveavägen 56, Stockholm, Sweden

A CIP catalogue record for this book is
available from the British Library.

ISBN: 978–1–83877–192–8
Special edition ISBN: 978–1–83877–416–5

*Also available as an ebook*

1 3 5 7 9 10 8 6 4 2

Typeset by IDSUK (Data Connection) Ltd
Printed and bound in Great Britain by Clays Ltd, Elcograf S.p.A.

Zaffre is an imprint of Bonnier Books UK
www.bonnierbooks.co.uk

# List of Characters

**Ruth** – a chambermaid

**Gene Sheldon** – a demonstration dancer

**Mathilde Bourchier** – a demonstration dancer

**Diego** – the head cocktail waiter

**Mr Bosanquet** – the head concierge

**Mrs Farrier** – head of the hotel post room

**Karina Kainz** – a visiting demonstration dancer

**Jonas Holler** – a visiting demonstration dancer

**Ansel Albrecht** – a visiting demonstration dancer

**Tobias Bauer** – a guest at the Buckingham

*Beyond the Buckingham:*

**Arthur 'Artie' Cohen** – Raymond's younger brother

**Alma Cohen** – Raymond and Artie's mother

**Georges de la Motte** – Raymond's former dancing mentor and friend

**Sidney Archer** – Hélène's late husband and Sybil's father

**Sybil Archer** – Sidney and Hélène's daughter

**Noelle Archer** – Sidney's mother

**Maurice Archer** – Sidney's father

**Sir Derek Marchmont** – Hélène's father

**Lady Marie Marchmont** – Hélène's mother

**Lucy Marchmont** – Hélène's aunt

**Mary Burdett** – the matron of the Daughters of Salvation

**Warren Peel** – a patron of the Daughters of Salvation

**Malcolm Brody** – an Australian airman

**Mr Moorcock** – an MI5 agent

*For Hannah, George and Henrietta,*
*my whole reason for being*

Together with our families,

# MISS NANCY NETTLETON

and

# MR RAYMOND DE GUISE

are pleased to invite you to join us for our wedding ceremony

Saturday 10th December 1938
Marylebone Town Hall
London

followed by dinner and dancing at

The Grand Ballroom
Buckingham Hotel
Berkeley Square

*Let's dance . . .*

# Prologue

## September 1938

# *The Housekeeping Lounge, the Buckingham Hotel*

T HE KNOCK AT THE DOOR is not unexpected.

But the face behind it is.

Mrs Emmeline Moffatt, Head of Housekeeping at the Buckingham Hotel – the most prestigious of London's luxurious hotels, a place that lords and ladies, dukes and duchesses, dignitaries from near and far away, have always called home – opens the door to the housekeeping lounge, and the surprise that blossoms on her face is swiftly swept away by a matronly concern. She cuts a forlorn figure, this unexpected guest. It is late at night, the very last day of September, but that does not account for the weariness in the girl's eyes.

'My dear,' Mrs Moffatt begins. 'Oh, my dear.' She steps back, inviting the visitor in. 'Quickly now, before anybody sees.'

The girl says little as Mrs Moffatt arranges one of the house chairs with cushions and sits her down. She says even less as Mrs Moffatt busies herself with a pot of tea. Whether you are lord or lady or chambermaid, nothing helps you face disaster better than a cup of Mrs Moffatt's finest tea.

'Now, my dear, shall we begin?' Mrs Moffatt is approaching sixty years old, though you wouldn't know it by the rigour with which she whips her legion of loyal chambermaids into shape. She settles herself in the chair beside her guest and takes her hand. The fact is, she's had the most life-changing day herself; it's knocked all the wind out of her sails – and, if nothing else, she would like to hear about somebody else's woes. It might help her let go of some of her own. 'You'll have to tell me what's wrong, dear. I can't see inside that head of yours. But whatever it is, we'll put it right. You can count on me for that.'

'I'm going to have a baby.'

There is a stillness in the housekeeping lounge. Mrs Moffatt has a rule: in times of consternation, in times of distress or surprise, take a deep breath, take a sip of tea, and do absolutely nothing. The stillness centres her.

She sets her tea down, reaches for the girl and takes her hand. With the other hand, she brushes the hair away from her eyes. This girl is, and always has been, beautiful – though there have been times when she wouldn't know it. Now, though, her face begins to crumple. She's held it in for so long. The wall is finally crumbling and the girl has started to cry.

'You're not the first, my dear. Believe me. I've sat here with girls just like you, more than I care to remember, and told them what I'm going to tell you right now: everything is going to be all right.'

'How can you know that? Look at me. I'm three months down. It's going to start showing soon. How can I possibly . . . ?'

Mrs Moffatt shuffles the chair closer. This time, she puts an arm around the girl.

'First things first,' she says. 'Have you seen a doctor?'

'How can I? If people were to find out . . . And my work, Mrs Moffatt, the hotel, my home.'

'All in good time, my dear.' Mrs Moffatt smiles. It's one of her sincere, soft smiles, and something in it begins to put the girl at ease. This, after all, is why she came. Mrs Moffatt, Head of Housekeeping, is mother to them all, here in this hotel. 'But before we go any further . . .' She crosses to her desk, where she opens a drawer and returns to the table with her hands full of little candies wrapped in colourful wax paper. 'My barley sugars. Well, they'll keep our spirits up as we work this out, won't they? You and me, my girl. We'll work out a plan together. You might think Mr Charles, our esteemed hotel director, is the only one adept at tidying up the little dramas of our fine establishment – but you'd be wrong. I'm a dab hand at sorting out our little mysteries myself. Well, I might even have one or two of my own!' Mrs Moffatt beams. 'So let's begin at the beginning, shall we? That's the only way to get to the end, you see. Why don't you tell me where it all began?'

Five Months Earlier . . .

April 1938

# Chapter One

'SHOW HIM IN, BILLY.'

Billy Brogan gave an ostentatious bow and backed out of Maynard Charles's office, leaving the door ajar as he scurried back to the mahogany reception desks of the Buckingham Hotel. Sitting at his desk, where his morning had so far been spent immersed in the hotel accountants' forecast of the year ahead, Maynard Charles rolled his eyes. He'd been telling young Brogan, the Buckingham's most junior – and most ambitious – concierge, that he didn't need to bow for nearly a year, but the boy never listened. In fact, he seemed to enjoy the pomp with which he inhabited his role. Deference like that could help a boy go places, especially in an establishment like the Buckingham Hotel – there was nothing the European gentry liked more than to be assured of their superiority – so Maynard had never been too insistent with the boy. He might have looked foolish, but his heart was in the right place.

A few moments later, Billy Brogan's knuckles rapped at the door again.

'Come in, Mr Brogan,' Maynard intoned – and, when the door drew back, there stood the gangly, red-headed Brogan at the side of a much older and more esteemed gentleman, his face framed in coils of grey hair and a neatly trimmed silvery moustache poised delicately on top of his red lips.

'Mr Charles,' Billy began, 'may I introduce Mr Tobias Bauer.'

Tobias Bauer was a small man, slight in stature, and walked with the aid of a cane, whose head was carved into the shape of an otter. As he came forward – oblivious of Billy giving another flowery bow at his side – he teetered slightly on his heels. Maynard, already on his feet, stepped around the edge of his desk and pulled out the seat. With whispered thanks, Tobias Bauer sank down.

'That will be all, Billy.'

'At your service, Mr Charles.'

Then, with another well-practised bow, Billy retreated.

After he had gone, Bauer ventured, 'Your young man is a credit to you all.'

Tobias Bauer was a regular visitor to English shores, but he had never lost the cadences of his Austrian homeland. He was softly spoken, but there was a quavering in his voice as well. As Maynard already knew, it was born of real fear.

'I'm given to understand you have a problem, Herr Bauer.'

'Well, quite,' Bauer began. Maynard saw how he caressed the head of his walking cane, as though it might help him find the confidence to say what he had to say next. 'It all began with that damn vote, you see. From that moment on, I knew I would never be able to go home. All the lies and counter-lies of those damned politicians! Well, it's a story as old as time, isn't it? And here I am – stranded. Yes, quite stranded!'

Maynard knew a little of Bauer's story already. As hotel director, his job was not only the management of the twelve hundred staff who made up his retinue at the Buckingham

Hotel. His days and nights might have been filled with the affairs of concierges and chambermaids, desk clerks and seamstresses, kitchen porters and pages, and all the musicians and dancers who lent the Buckingham their glamour. That was all the work of an expert at management and organisation. But there was an artistry to Maynard's role as well, and part of this involved knowing the daily comings and goings of all his manifold guests, being able to foresee pitfalls and disasters and head them off. Tobias Bauer had taken up residence at the Buckingham at the end of February – and now, six weeks later, here he remained. There was a reason for that, and its name was *Anschluss*.

'Yes,' Bauer went on, 'I'm afraid Herr Hitler has had his sights on my homeland for all his days on this good green Earth. And now it's his – a part of his Reich, for now and ever more.'

Scarcely a season passed in an establishment as finely tuned as the Buckingham without its director needing to manage some scandal, or contain some everyday disaster. But that did not mean Maynard Charles had neglected to follow the news of the outer world – and, in particular, the mounting dramas on the Continent. Soon after Bauer's arrival at the Buckingham, news had reached London of Nazi Germany's intention to annex Austria. They might claim it was to reunite its German citizenry with the mother country they had lost, but Maynard knew it for what it was: the march of a conqueror, pure and simple. Europe had seen enough of those before.

'So Herr Schuschnigg – our Chancellor, you understand – declared a vote would be held, to support our independence. That was a grave mistake, Mr Charles. Hitler could never allow that to happen. And that, sir, is why there are Nazi thugs marching through the streets of old Vienna, my home town. That, sir, is why my nation no longer exists.'

Bauer was shaking, and in the silence that followed he struggled to regain his composure.

'In my home country,' he went on, 'I have something of a reputation for speaking my mind. It has always served me well in business, but in this age it has become my curse. You see, I have not been silent about my loathing of Mr Hitler and all that he stands for. It has seen me branded as many things across the years – I have even been accused of being a Soviet, which I assure you I am not. I am simply a decent man who enjoys and respects the freedoms of the world. And now my reputation – well, it undoes me. Six weeks ago, I received word that Nazi soldiers had arrived at my country residence, asking after me.' At this, Bauer's emotions seemed to get the better of him. In his face was such a mixture of rage and terror and helplessness that even Maynard Charles, famed up and down the Buckingham halls for a cool head in a crisis, felt his heart begin to thunder. 'I'm sorry, Mr Charles, but perhaps now you understand the predicament in which I find myself. My country house has been requisitioned and, I understand, has become a regional base for the very same thugs who are turning my country to ruin. My brother is trying to flee. He warns me that I must not – that I *cannot* – go home.'

Throughout, Maynard had listened intently. Now that Tobias Bauer's words had petered into silence, he found himself staring out of the window, into the darkness of the courtyard at the rear of the Buckingham. In his mind's eye he could see the military transports that must have brought the Nazi soldiery into Vienna, their open backs packed with storm troopers. He'd known too many soldiers in his lifetime. The Great War was twenty years in the past, but there were still moments when, if his concentration lapsed for a second, he was back there, listening to the shrill whistles as he and his fellows piled over the top and marched directly into the Kaiser's guns.

War was coming again. He'd known it for long months. Tried to pretend he was wrong. Tried to pretend there was hope. But hope was dying every day in Europe. Maynard's faith was gone.

Coming back to the present, he reached for the brandy decanter on his desk, beside his Olympia Elite typewriter, and poured two stiff measures. The first was for Tobias Bauer, and was received with a look of sincere gratitude. The second was for Maynard himself. It warmed him through and through.

'Herr Bauer,' he said, 'what's happening in your country is a stain that besmirches humanity, and I am glad that you came to me in your hour of need. The Buckingham Hotel has been grateful for your custom these past weeks. We have always taken pride in making our longer term guests feel most at home – and I hope, in this, we have succeeded.'

'Oh, but you have, Mr Charles. You most certainly have.'

'Am I given to understand that you would like to extend your stay?'

'Indeed.'

'And that you do not know how long you might need to stay with us?'

Bauer nodded. 'Well, if this year has taught me anything, it's that not one of us can tell which way the world is going to turn next.'

'Then we come to the thorny question, Herr Bauer.'

'Were I able to continue in my current suite, I should do so, Mr Charles. But my funds are limited on English shores, and I was today informed, by my man at Lloyds, that the funds I have in my bank at home are . . . no longer at my disposal. Well, I suppose I should be thankful. A frozen bank account is, perhaps, the least of the evils being perpetrated on my countrymen, even now.' He hesitated, exchanging a knowing look with Maynard Charles. It was ungentlemanly to speak so brazenly of money, but there were darker things in the world this year. 'I am not a penny-pinching man, Mr Charles, but I have limited resources and know not how long I must make them last. So I come to you to ask if we might come to some arrangement that might suit both of us? Long-lasting residency in one of your lesser suites might be profitable for the Buckingham Hotel, perhaps?'

Maynard was finishing his brandy when inspiration seemed to strike him.

It was not uncommon for Maynard to contort the movements of the entire hotel to suit its guests. A hotel was, after all, nothing without its residents. But rarely had he felt that he wanted to bend the rules of the hotel more than now.

'We do have a suite, Herr Bauer. It has been out of service for many long years, but in the past month we have been dusting it down, ready for service once again. You would find it a little stark, at present. A little out of the way, as well – being hidden around a corner on our uppermost storey. But it has its charms. A little privacy. A homely atmosphere. And one of the better views of Berkeley Square that the hotel frontage allows. It's called the Park Suite – and, if you like, I could have our young friend Billy Brogan show you there right now.'

After Billy had taken Tobias Bauer through the doors of the hotel's golden lift, Maynard Charles poured himself another stiff measure of brandy. This one he savoured as a just reward for helping a man in his hour of need. Such things were good for the soul, but Maynard knew he would have to do it a thousand times over if he was to guide the Buckingham through the months and years ahead. The copy of the *Daily Mail* lying open on his desk – among all the other newspapers delivered daily to the tradesman's door– was just another in a long litany of reminders that Europe teetered on the brink of something calamitous – and that Great Britain, though she stood alone, was separated by a mere sliver of water from the Continent's unrest.

GERMAN JEWS POURING INTO THIS COUNTRY

'The way stateless Jews and Germans are pouring in from every port of this country is becoming an outrage. I intend to enforce the law to its fullest!' In these words, Mr Herbert Metcalfe, the Old Street Magistrate, yesterday referred to the number of aliens entering this country through the 'back door' – a problem to which the *Daily Mail* has repeatedly pointed . . .

Less of a problem, thought Maynard Charles, for this mighty island nation than for the poor wretches forced out of the only homes and lives they'd ever known. Were it up to him, he'd take the whole damn lot of them – and to hell with the British Union of Fascists and their like, who had marched through London only two years ago, demonstrating against kindness and generosity. To hell, too, with Lord Edgerton and the various other members of the hotel board, who proudly stood shoulder to shoulder with those fascists at their garden parties or moonlit Mayfair soireés. To hell, thought Maynard, with every last one of them who courted the murderers and demagogues rising to the top in Nazi Germany.

Then he stopped and stared into his glass. With a wry smile, he set it down – and, though there was no denying the hunger he felt for another measure, he delicately patted his lips dry on his crimson silk handkerchief and told himself that enough was enough. A drunken hotel director speaking his mind was a scandal Maynard Charles could not afford.

With this in mind, he left the office behind and ventured out, past the gleaming mahogany reception desks, across the black and white chequers of the reception hall, beyond the tall black obelisk, down which water coursed in a constant cascade. He headed along the arched hallway that sloped towards the doors of the Buckingham's most feted attraction: the Grand Ballroom itself.

As he stepped in, he heard the sounds of the legion of carpenters, joiners and other tradesmen who were, even now, finessing the ballroom's features for reopening night. Standing on the threshold, he surveyed the entirety of the ballroom, from the dance floor doors from which the hotel dancers and musicians would proudly announce themselves, to the sweeping curved bar that, after two months of hard work, was almost ready to accept paying customers again.

For a whole season, now, the Grand Ballroom had heard neither the music of its resident Archie Adams Orchestra, nor the applause that ordinarily resounded whenever the hotel's elite dancers took to the floor, led by the enigmatic Raymond de Guise and his partner Hélène Marchmont. Christmas had been and gone, one year had rolled into the next, and the Buckingham ballroom's lordly patrons had been seeking their entertainment elsewhere while Maynard's phalanx of loyal tradesmen worked, day and night, to refit and prepare the ballroom for reopening. The inferno that had torn through here last year had laid the place to ruin, but by good grace – and thanks to the leadership and investment of the newest board member, the American industrialist John Hastings – Maynard was sure that the Grand would quickly recapture its reputation as the jewel in London's crown. But in the pit of his stomach the fear remained: lords and ladies were a notoriously fickle species; if their loyalties had gone to the ballroom at the Savoy – or even, God forbid, the Imperial – then the Buckingham's fortunes would surely falter. And with war on the horizon, this was something Maynard would rather avoid at all costs.

His eyes turned to the dance floor, and its newly laid tiles of interlocking ebony and oak. There, in the space where tradesmen were not on their knees, polishing the boards to a dazzling shine, Hélène Marchmont waltzed in the arms of Raymond de Guise.

This was the reason the ballroom was the beating heart of the Buckingham Hotel. The music came only from a tinny gramophone, but the way Raymond and Hélène danced was enough to make Maynard look upon them alone. There was a time, not too far gone, when he had not truly understood the magic of the ballroom. How strange that seemed, looking out upon it now.

He was not the only one watching. As he approached the oak balustrade that ran around the dance floor, he saw that the hotel page, Frank Nettleton, was tapping his feet along to the music with his sweetheart, the chambermaid Rosa, at his side. Frank was small and wiry, his tousled hazel curls in desperate need of a visit to the hotel barber, but Maynard knew he had a good heart. As he watched, Frank took Rosa in his arms and, laughing uproariously, began to imitate Raymond de Guise. Rosa was no match for the elegant Hélène Marchmont, but Frank held himself with the grace of an accomplished dancer. Music was in the boy's veins; even an old curmudgeon like Maynard, more concerned with books and balance sheets than the intricacies of the Viennese waltz, could see that.

Even so, Maynard barked out, 'Nettleton, you know the ballroom's closed until further notice,' as he passed – and Frank, startled as if out of a dream, quickly ceased his dance, rambled an incoherent apology, and scurried with Rosa out through the ballroom doors.

'Go easy on the boy, Mr Charles.' Raymond stepped out of Hélène's arms and grinned as he approached. 'He's just starting out. Rough around the edges, yes, but you've a diamond there, if you encourage him. If only we were all as passionate as young Frank Nettleton.'

Maynard took Hélène by the hand in greeting.

'Miss Marchmont, four months away from the ballroom floor hasn't dulled your instincts, nor your artistry, I see. Are you ready for opening night?'

'We'll be ready, Mr Charles.' Hélène might have looked demure and coquettish to some – at least, that was the way the photographers had tried to capture her, back in the days when she'd graced the covers of *Vogue* and *Harper's Bazaar* – but the way she spoke now betrayed the aspect of her character that all those close to her understood: her steeliness, and inner strength. 'I've been rehearsing with Mathilde daily. She'll second Raymond and me, along with Gene Sheldon. She's got everything, Mr Charles. She's your future star.'

Maynard nodded, sagely. This was good news indeed.

'And the dance floor – how does it feel?'

'Freshly sprung,' Raymond replied. At over six feet in height, he stood a head taller than Maynard, and his crest of windswept black hair made him seem taller still. He was the hotel's Hercules of the ballroom, and Maynard trusted him above all else. 'She's still settling in, Mr Charles, but we'll have the troupe out here as soon as the finishing touches are done. We still have two weeks. By then, we'll know the floor again – all its little kinks and nuances.' He leaned forward, gripped the balustrade, and looked directly into Maynard's eyes. 'Mr Charles, we're in this together. All of us in the dance troupe. Archie Adams and all his orchestra. Oh, they might be scattered across London town, moonlighting in the clubs while they wait for the ballroom to open again. But don't think for a second that their hearts don't remain with us, right here.'

'And it's not just the ballroom,' Hélène interjected. Her crystalline eyes, too, had settled on Maynard. He might have read them each the Riot Act on occasion, but there was no one – outside this hotel or within it – that either of them would rather have followed into war. 'You hear it up and down the halls. Concierges and kitchen hands, chambermaids and pages and waiting staff. Even Mrs Farrier, down in the hotel post room! Every last one of us, here at the Buckingham, we're all in it together. We're going to make the Grand's reopening the talk of the society pages. We'll be back on top, Mr Charles. I know we will.'

There was something about Hélène's conviction that stilled Maynard's nerves. He turned again to survey the ballroom. *Yes*, he thought, *here is a place to be proud of*. A place of magic and enchantment. A place where love stories could unfold and guests

21

could, for a few fleeting hours, pretend that the world outside was not going to touch them, that a place where war was brewing, where politicians fought daily, where dark clouds gathered and grew yet darker, did not exist at all.

*We'll be ready*, Hélène Marchmont had said.

And Maynard Charles thought: *yes, I believe it at last.*

# Chapter Two

FROM THE GROUNDS OF THE Buckingham Hotel on Berkeley Square, to the Limehouse docks and the rooftops of Whitechapel, rain was sweeping London in great sheets of grey. As Raymond de Guise stepped out of a taxicab on the Whitechapel Road and felt the full force of the storm, only his dancer's feet kept him from losing his balance and tumbling into the heaps of refuse piled up at the side of the road. Thanking the driver and asking him to wait, he tightened his gaberdine overcoat and turned up his collar against the driving rain, then made haste between the awnings into a narrow cobbled alley. Halfway along, where light spilled out of the doors of a red brick chapel, he turned to climb the steps. Already, he was drenched to the skin.

So too was the man who stood at the top of those steps, keeping guard at the doors, his face hidden beneath the peaks of a tricorn hat, as if he'd stepped directly out of some bygone age.

'Ray Cohen, come at last!'

Raymond de Guise in the ballroom; good, old-fashioned Ray Cohen here in the streets of his native Whitechapel. There was a time that he'd guarded the secret of his true identity with the zealousness of an undercover spy – but no longer. Now Raymond lived with one foot in the world of the ballroom, and one foot in the streets where he was born. So far, it seemed to be working.

'Artie!' He took his brother by the hand. 'You'd think they could afford you an umbrella.'

Artie grinned. 'Go on, get yourself inside. Nancy don't know you're coming. Me and Viv, we kept it a secret, just like we promised. She'll be surprised to see you.'

*Viv?* thought Raymond, as he stepped through the doors.

They called this place the Daughters of Salvation, and for close to a year it had occupied these premises – once a derelict chapel, abandoned to vagrant sleepers. Now, when Raymond looked around, it was unrecognisable as the place he'd first seen a year before. The renovation work over the past months had transformed the shabby interior into a collection of rooms every bit as worthy as a church hospice.

It was a hive of activity. The body of the old chapel was a semi-circular reception area, at which Mary Burdett – the founder of the organisation – talked with one of her volunteers. Around her, doors led into private rooms, some dormitories and some with single beds where guests recuperated. Through one door, a small office was home to the visiting physician, one of several doctors from local surgeries who gave up their evenings to come and minister for the needy – and to help patients overcoming their opiate addictions, the very reason the Daughters was first founded. Through another door, volunteers were busily bulking out the evening soup – and the cold breeze coming in from the back of the kitchen area told Raymond that the doors had been opened to the courtyard at the back, and here the vagabond people of London's East End were being welcomed in for hot tea and food. Old loaves were bought up from the Whitechapel bakeries, bad apples and bruised potatoes taken in from the grocers' refuse, pared down and put to use. Not a scrap was wasted at the Daughters of Salvation.

Nodding at Mary Burdett, Raymond crossed the chapel floor, then slipped through the door at the very back.

The Salvation Office, as this corner had come to be called, was tiny – just a desk and a few cabinets, loaned by the charity's benefactor George Peel. Peel's was old money, inherited from his forebears who had owned the blacking factories in Charing Cross, but at least it was being put to good use. As Raymond hovered in the office door, he could hear the voice of Warren Peel, George's son – once an opiate addict himself, and now an integral member of the Daughters of Salvation itself. As he stepped inside, he saw that Warren – slight and boyish, with hair the colour of a cornfield in summer – was bent over the table with Vivienne Edgerton. And there, hidden behind them, sitting at the desk, was his own Nancy Nettleton.

The Daughters of Salvation might have been founded by Mary Burdett, but it was Vivienne and her investment of time and energy – and the allowance her stepfather gave her – that had first begun to transform it. And it was Vivienne, too, who had convinced Warren Peel's father to give generously to the charity, allowing for its further expansion. For several years, Vivienne had lived, at her stepfather's instruction, at the Buckingham Hotel instead of the family home, and she had once been the kind of girl who needed the intervention of a charity like this herself. Spoilt and lost, she'd found solace in opiates. But at twenty years old – still with her striking red hair, but holding herself more confidently than ever – Vivienne was a changed woman. Raymond had barely seen her at the Buckingham in the last months, for she'd sequestered herself here, driving the Daughters of Salvation onward. She intended it to be an empire.

Raymond coughed to announce his appearance. Both Vivienne and Warren looked up, but Nancy remained bent over the desk, working through the ledgers that she kept for the organisation.

'Sorry, Mr de Guise!' Vivienne laughed, her thick New York accent filled with mirth. 'Miss Nettleton's far too important for the likes of you now. Who needs a debonair dancer when they've got columns and figures to be working through?'

'It's time to put the pen and paper down, Nance. I'm here to take you out.'

Nancy finally looked up. As she took in his face, his coiffured black hair, and that look in his eyes he saved for her alone – the look that no guest dancing with him in the Buckingham ball-room ever saw – something inside her soared.

'Raymond,' she smiled – and, for a moment, in spite of the hustle and bustle through the partition walls, it was as if there was no one else in the world.

At twenty-five years old, Nancy Nettleton was eight years Raymond's junior. She'd taken on so much in the last year and become so adept at organising the Daughters of Salvation, all the time fulfilling her duties as a chambermaid at the Buckingham. Raymond was quite sure she could, one day, be as adept as Maynard Charles at keeping an organisation as big as the hotel going.

Nancy never ceased to amaze him, and his heart beat hard at the thought of tonight.

It was going to be the most special night of their lives.

'Warren,' Vivienne said, beaming, 'let's leave these lovebirds to get their things together. We'll be needed out back.'

'At your service, Miss Edgerton!'

'Oh, do stop calling me that!' Vivienne laughed as she and Warren strode off. 'I've told you – you may call me *Viv.*'

Watching them leave, Raymond said, 'Those two seem to be becoming firm friends. You don't think, perhaps, that there might be . . . more love in the air?'

'Anything's possible.' Nancy shrugged. She'd come to the Daughters straight from her morning shift at the Buckingham, and her mind had been lost in the balance sheets ever since. Nancy had kept her father's household finances in order from the age of nine until the day that he'd died. Mathematics, she sometimes thought, was as artful as dance. But right now she knew where she'd rather be.

She snapped the balance book shut. It could wait for another day.

'Shall we?' she asked.

Raymond beamed. 'We shall!'

By the time Nancy had packed her books away and joined Raymond out in the main hall, Vivienne Edgerton was standing with Artie at the front door. As Raymond linked his arm with Nancy, they heard Vivienne explode with laughter. He looked back at his brother and Vivienne over his shoulder, before glancing sidelong at Nancy.

Nancy shrugged. 'This is a world away from the ballroom, Raymond,' she whispered. 'Miss Edgerton might be blue blood, but the truth is, she's happier with the likes of Artie and Mary than she is with the lordlings and Right Honourables she used to consort with.'

'Yes, but *Artie.*'

'Artie's charming, Raymond.'

*Yes*, thought Raymond, wryly.

27

There was a time his brother Artie had been pretty adept at charming the locks off back gates, or the seals from the windows of the rich families. He'd been pretty good at charming necklaces from around the necks of pretty ladies too.

'You two have a glorious night!' Artie chortled as Raymond and Nancy stepped back into the veil of rain.

'I've never seen Artie so chirpy before,' said Raymond as he helped Nancy into the taxicab, still idling out on Whitechapel Road. 'Not since before Pentonville. Not since we were small.'

'Well, your little brother's a changed man. A steady salary can do that. Three square meals a day. It's knowing where he is in the world, not wondering where the next penny's coming from. He's got something to depend on.'

Raymond nodded. He still felt guilty about all the years he'd been off chasing his own dream of ballroom stardom while his family made ends meet however they could.

'Your Daughters of Salvation turns out to be about helping more people than just the homeless, Nancy, or the opiate addicts.'

'Nobody's beyond hope,' Nancy smiled, 'and for every life we can change, even just a little, a dozen more can eventually be touched. It's like ripples – every little good thing you do, rippling out into the world.'

There were other things like that, thought Raymond. He'd seen the newspapers this morning, and the reports of the demonstrations down on the Horse Guards Parade: London's malcontents, stirred up by the idea that too many refugees from Europe were somehow pouring, unchecked, into the country. It was those headlines that stirred it up. Ripples of hatred and bigotry, just like Nancy's ripples of charity and light, could echo out into the world as well.

'So where's it to be?' grinned Nancy as the taxicab wheeled away. 'Kettner's again? Simpson's on the Strand?'

In the last months, with the ballroom out of commission, Raymond had been free to indulge his sweetheart, whisking her off on a tour of London restaurants. The Cornish steak at Simpson's had been a delight, the sea bass at Rules in Covent Garden delicate and refined – and though sometimes Nancy hungered for nothing more than the Lancashire hotpot of her childhood, she had to admit that the taste explosions at Veeraswamy on Regent Street had been an experience she would never forget.

Which made it all the more surprising when the taxicab took them a mere mile deeper into the East End terraces, and deposited them outside a taproom in Stepney Green, barely a stone's throw from the house where Raymond and Artie Cohen had been brought up.

Nancy stepped out into the swirling rain. The taproom in front of her was called the Oak Tree, but it was to a side door and its staircase that Raymond pointed. With a knowing smile, he took her by the hand and led her in. Nancy's leg was aching today – it was an old injury, from the polio of her childhood, and on damp days it pained her still – but, when they reached the top of the stairs and stepped into a quaint little dining room, the pain seemed to evaporate away. It was cosy here, with a dog curled up on the fireside hearth and only a handful of tables around which locals were dining. A waiter took their coats and, soon after, came back to lead them to a table in the window. There, by the light of a single candle, Raymond said, 'Well, what do you think?'

Rain was pouring in sheets down the window. Outside, night was coming on – but, inside, Nancy could not have felt finer.

'Why here?'

Raymond tried hard to suppress his smile. 'My mother knows the cook here. I've put in a special request. Lancashire hotpot.'

Nancy's eyes opened wide. 'Raymond, you old fool!'

But she was delighted, all the same.

'I know you love the Buckingham almost as much as I do. I know what it means to you, being in that world. But I know what it means to you to be in this world too. So tonight was simply to say, I look at you, Nancy, at the Daughters of Salvation, and I see someone doing more good for the world than I've ever done, waltzing in my ballroom.'

'I think you underestimate yourself, Raymond. The joy, the enchantment you bring.' She thought of the first time she'd seen him, in those early days after she'd just started at the Buckingham: how he'd been gliding across the dance floor, and how her heart had started hammering when he first spoke her name. 'The world needs a little of that magic this year.'

'I've been thinking about it a lot. Every newspaper I look at. Every time I hear the wireless crackling out the BBC *News*. Jewish refugees flocking into the country. People just like me, Nancy. Like Artie. Oh, perhaps we're not the most observant family. We never were! But it's only by an accident of where I was born that it's not me uncertain of my future, not knowing if I even have a place in the world. And now, all these refugees flooding into London.'

Nancy nodded. One of the chambermaids, Ruth, had been near the Horse Guards Parade when the demonstrations began. She'd come back to the staff kitchenette in the chambermaids' quarters filled with the tension of it. All that hatred in the air – and from the very same Englishmen whom they passed on the streets each day. *There is such goodness in the world*, thought Nancy, *but there is such disquiet too.* The eternal battle was for which would win through: the darkness, or the light.

'Nancy, about the magic . . .'

Before Raymond could go on, the waiter appeared and deposited two bubbling Lancashire hotpots in front of them, their caramelised crusts erupting with geysers of steam.

Nancy didn't know where to turn. All of her senses had been set on fire.

'Oh, Raymond!' She beamed, and took a deep breath. 'More magical than anything on the menu at Kettner's.'

'There's something else,' he said – and, for the first time, Nancy sensed some real trepidation in his tone. She reached across the table and took him by the hand. Finding his nerve, he said, 'There's something I'm going to ask you. I wanted to do it here – right here in Stepney Green, so that you know it's the real me, not the King of the Ballroom, who's asking it.'

He looked across the table at her. He held her eyes.

*There's the look*, thought Nancy. *The look that can take a girl out of her body. The look that can make her feel like she's floating on air.*

'Will you marry me, Nancy Nettleton?'

In that same moment, Raymond flourished his other hand up from below the table, and in it he revealed a small box lined with velvet. Sitting in it was a simple silver band crowned with a single small diamond.

Not for the first time that evening, the rest of the world faded out of Nancy's understanding – and there she was, in a hazy little bubble, just her and Raymond, cocooned from the world. She looked into his eyes. How long had she known him? Two years? Well, it felt like a lifetime.

'Oh, Raymond,' she began, looking at the ring in its little velvet case.

What thoughts tumbled through her head then? What visions of the life she would one day lead? For a time, there was only one image in her mind and, in it, she and Raymond stood at the door of their own little London home, his music playing on a gramophone inside the open window, the sounds of happy cheer and chatter coming from the children inside.

It was Raymond's words that brought her back from the vision.

'We've been through so much in two short years, Nancy. And time is marching on. All this talk of appeasement. All this talk of war in the air . . .'

'There won't be war, Raymond. How could men ever be so foolish again? The people wouldn't countenance it – not after they've already lost so much. Mr Chamberlain says he's finding a way, that there'll be peace.'

'It's the uncertainty,' said Raymond, looking deep into her eyes. 'It's hardened my resolve. I know what I want. I know the future I want to lie in front of me, the future it's in my power to make happen. I want you, Nancy. I want you to be my wife.'

Nancy was the sort of girl who knew what she wanted as well. It hadn't been a husband – not before she met Raymond. That wasn't what she'd come to London for. Her head was full of dreams, yes, but not a dream like this. But it was strange how your dreams transformed.

Disentangling her hand from Raymond's, she lunged for her fork and took her first taste of Lancashire hotpot. Its taste was as divine as anything she'd had in the fancy restaurants they'd been frequenting. She'd almost forgotten the taste of good, old-fashioned lamb.

She still wasn't able to suppress the smile on her lips, and now she started laughing too.

'Why are you laughing, Nance?'

'Well . . .' She grinned. 'It's like this . . . It's a good job you asked, Raymond, because I've been thinking about it too.'

'About the future?'

She slapped him on the back of the wrist. 'About asking *you* to marry *me*! You're right. We've come so far. Who knows where we'll be in a year's time? Who knows where the world will be? It's all I've been thinking of, Raymond – you have to take your chances, whenever they come. You have to be ready to seize the things you want. So I was thinking of a way I might ask you. How I might get down on one knee and ask you to be my husband.'

Perhaps any other man would have balked at the idea, but not Raymond de Guise – and not for Nancy Nettleton. Conventions be damned! Hadn't Nancy already shown him that life can be lived however you want to live it? Hadn't she already taught him a little about not letting society hold you back, about following your heart, about always striving to do the next right thing?

'Well,' Raymond said, grinning, 'what's your answer?'

Nancy finished her forkful of hotpot. 'Well,' she said, 'what's yours?'

Then, in unison – as they would now be here and for evermore – they held hands across the dining room table and said, 'Yes!'

The feeling of the ring, when he slipped it onto her finger, was crisp and clear, and held in it all the promises of their future to come. Her ring, a perfect gift from a perfect man.

A new chapter in their story was about to begin.

# Chapter Three

T HE DARKNESS OPENED UP. Lightning split the sky. On the beach below the old manor house at Rye, waves crashed against the cliff face and outcrops of stone.

But in the old manor house itself, a storm of an altogether different nature was being played out.

The doctor had made haste by bicycle along the country lane out of town, up into the rocky heights where, once upon a time, the medieval fortifications used to stand. Now, drenched to the skin, he was following the homeowner's unmarried sister up the stairs, passing portraits of the family from times gone by, heading towards the master bedroom at the end of the landing. The big windows here overlooked the rolling green splendour of the Sussex Weald – but all of that was invisible tonight, lost beneath the churning storm.

In the bedroom, an old man lay in bed, his wife in a wicker chair by his side. The coughing that racked his chest was not the only sign that something was terribly wrong in this room. The smell hit the doctor as soon as he entered the chamber, and it was one he knew well. He'd been around death since he was himself a young man.

'Sir Derek, you old devil, what have you been playing at?'

The doctor wore his most fraudulent smile as he came to his patient's side, and began to listen to his breast with the stethoscope around his neck. Pulses were checked, tiny torchlights shone into eyes, a little thermometer tucked beneath the tongue – drawn back, some moments later, with a muttered oath.

'Sir Derek, can you hear me?'

'By God, I can!' the old man seethed. 'I'm not gone yet, Ignatius.'

'I'm glad to hear it. You're a lion, sir.' He paused. 'But even lions get infections, and I'm afraid this one has taken hold. And you haven't yet shaken the pneumonia, I'm afraid. These are the perils of a life well lived, Sir Derek. How old are you now?'

'I'm seventy-eight, but I'll live to see a hundred.'

At this, the doctor remained silent. Then, he said, briskly, 'There's something new we can look to. It's one of the "sulphonamides", but this one's barely been used as yet. M&B 693 – that's the scientific classification. But what you need to know is it's an antibiotic drug – it can help you beat this infection.'

'I don't need drugs,' the old man wheezed.

'That's as may be, but your dear wife here might like to be indulged. Mightn't you, Lady Marchmont?'

The lady at the old man's bedside nodded. She was younger than her husband by a quarter of a century at least.

'Come,' the doctor said. 'I left my case downstairs.'

In the shadowy hall, with the old man still straining for breath in the bedroom above, the doctor rifled through his valise and produced a small pot of pills, which he placed carefully on the sideboard. Nervously, Sir Derek Marchmont's wife, Marie, and his sister, Lucy, ten years his junior, looked on – neither one of them yet daring to ask the question on their lips.

'Doctor,' Marie began, 'what hope is there?'

The doctor steeled himself. 'Only God may tell when he is calling each of us forth,' he said, with the gravity that the occasion demanded. 'Lady Marchmont, he is old. His body fails him. It isn't one thing. It's many. What takes him, when it comes, will be incidental to the cause of his death.'

'And that is?'

The doctor shrugged, not unkindly. 'A life lived to the fullest, and a handsome number of years.' He sighed. 'I'm sorry, Lady Marchmont. It will be over all too soon. Treasure what days you have left.' There came a deep rumbling from upstairs, and the ringing of a bedside bell. 'If the old devil permits you to, of course!'

After the doctor was gone, Marie put one foot back on the stairs, the little phial of pills in her hand.

'Pray for him, Lucy,' she said. 'If he's to leave us soon, pray for the Lord's forgiveness.'

'It isn't God who ought to be forgiving him, is it, Marie?'

Marie's face, creased with lines already, hardened further.

'Not now, Lucy!' Then she disappeared, up the darkened stair.

Alone at the bottom of the steps, Lucy watched her sister-in-law vanish. For some time, she simply stared. *So*, she thought, *there is to be another death in the family manor.* How many of her ancestors had lived and died here? All of them leaving their memories behind. All of them leaving their regrets. All of them, their ghosts.

And this one more so than any.

Something took hold of her. Anger, a hunger to set things straight. What did it matter if Marie disapproved? What did it matter if the old man, her brother, would rant and rave when he found out? By God, he'd hardly have the breath to barrack her.

Yes, thought Lucy, she was going to do this. The fact was, she wouldn't be able to live with herself if the old man passed on and she hadn't at least *tried*.

She marched down the hallway and into her brother's study. It hadn't been used in months and, when she lit the lamps, the shadows unnerved her. So too did sitting at the old man's desk. It dwarfed her as she reached for his ink pots. She thought she heard the scurrying of mice as she found a leaf of paper, headed with the manor's own crest. Now all she had to find were the words. The words to put right a terrible wrong . . .

But Lucy was good with words.

So she started to write.

In the morning, if the storm had passed, she would head down into Rye and deliver it directly to the hands of the postmaster. Then Lucy would pray her words got through.

Watch that letter . . .

Delivered to the postmaster in Rye, bundled up with half a hundred others in a sack bound for the Sussex sorting offices; soon it finds itself in a postal truck heading north, into the outer sprawl of London. There, in another sorting office, it is shuffled along the long trestle tables – until, at last, it is dropped into a postman's sack for delivery on the morn. Up and down the streets of Mayfair it goes. Into every arcade along Regent Street, around the town houses of Berkeley Square– until, at last, it is clasped in the hands of Mrs Farrier, head of the post room at the Buckingham Hotel.

It was Frank Nettleton's job, every morning, to collect letters from Mrs Farrier and deliver them diligently around the hotel.

This morning, as every morning, the pile he took from her was heavy with communications for Mr Charles, and these he delivered promptly to the hotel director's office. There were scattered other communiques for Mr Bosanquet, the head concierge, and for Archie Adams – who often received enquiries from budding musicians – and, this morning, a most unusual occurrence, one for Mrs Moffatt, down in Housekeeping. By the time Frank arrived, the chambermaids were already gathering for breakfast, and he had to keep himself from blushing when some of Rosa's friends started whispering and pointing as he stole into the lounge. His sister Nancy was nowhere to be seen – off-shift, Frank thought, and probably in the company of Raymond de Guise – but he hurried through the bustling lounge and delivered the letter personally to Mrs Moffatt's hands.

He wasn't there to see her open it. By that time, he'd already hurried on. But the girls in the housekeeping lounge would later remark that they had never seen Mrs Moffatt look as pale as she did, in the moment she opened that letter. Not one of them had ever seen her blanch and tremble, nor have to reach out and steady herself against the wall as she took in the letter's contents. Nor had any of them ever seen her drink her morning tea with quite so many lumps of sugar. It was unlike her. Mrs Moffatt was almost sixty years old, but she was still as strong as ever. What she'd read in that letter, not one of them could say.

Finally, Frank arrived at the Grand Ballroom – where the finishing touches were being made in preparation for reopening night. He entered by the ornate ballroom doors and box-stepped a little as he crossed the freshly sprung dance floor, making for the archway by the stage. Some of the carpenters looked up from their work and gave him quizzical stares – but if Frank noticed at all, he didn't mind. He was far too lost in imagining a world in which he, humble Frank Nettleton, might tango across the ballroom floor to care what the gruff tradesmen had to think of him.

Frank crossed the dressing rooms, and sneaked through the back doors into the rebuilt studio – the same studio where he took his lessons with Raymond de Guise. The music coming from the new gramophone in the corner was not one of Frank's favourites, but he had always appreciated its stately elegance: 'The Kiss Waltz', that the American sweetheart Ruth Etting first made famous in 1930. Frank himself preferred the modern music, the jives and jitterbugs that were coming out of the New York Bowery. They were faster and looser and altogether more *untamed* than the older waltzes like this. Frank could *feel* music like that. But as he stepped into the studio and saw the graceful Hélène Marchmont tutoring her protégé, Mathilde, in the finer points of this piece, he knew he could appreciate the classics as well. All dances had one thing in common: you had to let the music live in you.

Mathilde was elegant, but Miss Marchmont was positively angelic as she danced. If he was honest, Frank felt nervous just standing here – he always did – and, for a moment, he was certain that the stutter he'd been plagued with since birth was sure to come back. Miss Marchmont was thirty years old, but something in her seemed timeless; her white-blonde hair was cropped short in the modern style, revealing her swan-like neck and accentuating the glacial beauty of her eyes. Mathilde, too, had a grace about her, but there was nervousness in her too. And no wonder, thought Frank, for she was only eighteen, scarcely Frank's own age – and, although she was the winner of last summer's junior championship at Brighton, her new career at the Buckingham Hotel was daunting still.

Hélène's eyes fell on Frank. Instantly, his cheeks flushed crimson. Perhaps he'd been staring too long. Eyes nervously darting around, he rushed forward, handed Hélène the letter, and scurried off, back into the wide open expanse of the Grand.

He did not see the look of absolute horror that sapped Hélène of all strength, that caused her to tell Mathilde to take a break from their rehearsals, that sent her hurrying for the dressing room. Frank Nettleton was far too lost in grand daydreams of his own to realise that, all around him, with the letters he'd helped deliver, lives were being undone.

Late that night, Hélène Marchmont waited at the Ambergris under Charing Cross station, as the little dance hall emptied of all its revellers. She hadn't come for the music, though tonight she'd liked it well enough. The band, an eleven-piece orchestra with too many trombones, led by the infamous Amor Whitehall had played a set of swing standards, livened up by blasting trumpets, striking French horns, and the sound of a single saxophonist. Amor Whitehall's was the only orchestra in London populated entirely by black musicians but, as remarkable as this was, it was the daring and originality of that saxophonist that the reviewers wrote about in the *Evening News* and *Melody Maker*. His name was Louis Kildare, and at the end of the night, he sashayed across the bar to where Hélène was sitting.

'Hélène Marchmont.' He grinned. 'To what do I owe the pleasure?'

'Louis, I need your help.'

It was the severity of her voice that stopped him in his tracks. Theirs was a friendship that stretched back years – for Louis Kildare was, by profession, the starring saxophonist of the Archie Adams Orchestra. His stint at the Ambergris was nothing more than a way to bide the time, and fill his pockets, while the work on the Grand was completed. But Louis knew Hélène better than any, and the tone of her voice filled him with disquiet. In the Buckingham, the chambermaids and younger concierges called Hélène Marchmont the Ice Queen, but the truth was much richer than any of them understood. Louis had never met a woman as strong and capable as Hélène. To see her trembling now, her hands kneading an envelope inscribed with her name, set his mind racing.

'Read it,' she said, and thrust the letter into his hands.

*Dearest Hélène,*

*Perhaps you will not welcome this letter, but I fear I must take that risk and send it regardless. Hélène, your father lies dying. His doctor instructs us that the remainder of his life is to be counted in months, not years. How long precisely, he will not say. Your father is an ox and has defied his naysayers throughout his life. But no Christian soul defies his Lord and God for long. He is soon to embark on his final adventure.*

*He is too stubborn to reach for you himself, so I am reaching for you with this letter. Let him not go to his end under the shadow of what he has lost. Let him not breathe his last breath without laying eyes on his only daughter once more. The past is the past. But your father is not to have a future.*

*Come home, Hélène.*

*Your loving aunt, always,*

*Lucy*

Louis must have read the letter three times before he dared look at Hélène. Now he knew why she was so pale.

'Hélène, what can I do?'

'I don't know, Louis,' she said, and as she stood all the fury she'd been holding within seemed to be unleashed. She turned in a circle, like a trapped animal. 'Sir Derek Marchmont, on his deathbed and summoning me for forgiveness. Well, Louis, what am I to think? What's supposed to be in my head, my heart, right now? You tell me, because I can't, by God above, hear my own thoughts.'

'When did the letter come?'

'I've had it in my hands scarcely twelve hours.'

'Well, perhaps that's it, Hélène. It's so fresh. You don't have to do anything right now.'

'Don't I? Because that's what she's asking, isn't it?' Hélène sank back into her seat. 'I loved Aunt Lucy.' She sighed. 'It would have to be her who wrote, wouldn't it? Knowing I couldn't just . . . ignore her.' She shook her head sadly. 'Aunt Lucy never had children of her own. She used to come to the manor twice a week. She'd take me picking apples. We picnicked on the lawns. She made an amazing high tea – for me and my bears . . .' All at once, Hélène seemed a little girl, and Louis could quite imagine how she'd been, back before the world had taught her she had to be strong. 'I miss her the most, I think. But . . . she went along with them, didn't she? When they told me I wasn't their daughter anymore, that there'd be no inheritance, that I'd brought shame to the Marchmont name.'

Louis stepped forward, then faltered. He wanted, more than anything else, to put his arms around his old friend.

'What do you want to do, Hélène? What does it say in your heart?'

'My heart says they can go to hell.'

For a time, Louis was silent. Then:

'Truly, Hélène?'

'They disowned me, Louis, and all because I fell in love with a black man. Because their grandchild' – she cupped her hand around her belly – 'was going to be born black. They threw me out and, when they found out my new husband had died and it was just me and my daughter left in the world, did they come and find me? Did they ask me to come home? No, Louis. There was only silence, long and empty and lonely while I found a way to make life work, to provide for Sybil. All their money, all their influence, all their *time* – was I worth any of that, to them? Was my daughter? No. So I kept dancing for my weekly crust. I kept doing whatever Maynard Charles asked of me, just so I could put a roof over Sybil's head. And now they come to me, after all of that, and ask me to go to his bedside, just so he can die a happy man?'

'Hélène, forgive me for what I'm about to say. You're my closest friend. Sidney was like a brother to me. You've honoured his memory in everything you've done for Sybil. He would have been proud beyond measure. But . . . if your heart's truly telling you they're dead to you, like they once said *you* were dead to *them*, then tell me, Hélène, why can I still see the torment on your face? What are you doing here if your mind's already made up?'

For the longest time, Hélène remained silent. Sybil lived with her husband's family now. For three years, Hélène's daughter had called their little terrace in Brixton home, seeing her true mother only when her schedule at the Buckingham allowed. The cost of keeping a secret this vast was severe. It coloured everything Hélène did. Every word she spoke. Every thought that flitted through her mind. That was life, now, and Hélène had long ago come to terms with it. Sybil: the centre of her world, the anchor that held her in place, the thing that gave every dance she danced real *meaning*. Her mother and father hadn't wanted any of that. The shame of their daughter being touched by a black man had been too much to bear. So Hélène had built a different life. Flawed and compromised, yes – but it was *hers*, and she was proud of it. No mother in London could have done more.

And yet . . .

She thought of Aunt Lucy, and those picnics in the grounds of the old manor house.

She thought of the day trips to London with her mother and their housekeeper, clinging to her mama's hand as she trotted from one department store to the next.

She thought of sitting on her father's knee when she wasn't much older than Sybil, listening to the old man tell stories of his time in India. All those fanciful tales of faraway places, keeping her rapt long after bedtime.

It was then that she crumpled.

'Damn it, Louis, why is it never so simple?' she whispered. 'I thought I was done with them. I thought I knew what life was.'

'Life always hits an off-note, once in a while.' Louis hesitated. 'The only question is: what can you do to put things right, to make the melody sing true? Answer that, Hélène, and all of life's mysteries will suddenly be solved.'

# Chapter Four

By Invitation Alone
The Buckingham Hotel invites you to the

HASTINGS BALL
In celebration of the reopening of the Grand Ballroom
The Society Event of the Season
RSVP, via Mr William Brogan, Buckingham Hotel

IN THE DRESSING ROOMS BEHIND the Grand Ballroom, the
dancers gathered. Out in the ballroom, the applause was
reverberating around the refashioned hall as Archie Adams
and his orchestra took to the stage. Archie Adams – he'd done
so much to cultivate and grow the legend of the Buckingham
ballroom, and the applause that filled the Grand was recognition
that here was one of London's finest bandleaders, coming back
to claim his throne. Raymond de Guise stood at the head of the
dancers, Hélène Marchmont at his side, and beamed at them all.

'We've come a long way together,' he began.

In moments, the doors would open and the dancers would fan
out onto the ballroom floor to demonstrate for every lord and
lady, every knight of the realm, every industrialist and dignitary

from home and abroad, that the Buckingham might have been cowed by the arson attack of last year, but it was never defeated.

'Through fair weather and foul, through triumph and disaster,' Raymond continued. 'And I'm proud to stand here – not as your leader, but as your friend – so that, together, we can return to triumph again. There might be dark days coming, my friends, but here, tonight, we can make our own light.'

Simple words, but what an effect they had. The way Raymond spoke drew all the dancers in.

Next it was Hélène's turn.

'There's nothing I can say to you, here, that isn't already in your hearts.'

Outside the dressing rooms, the applause had died down. Archie Adams had announced their first number, a fast, frenetic version of the old standard, 'Happy Days Are Here Again', with one of the night's guest vocalists about to join in. Any moment now, that would be their cue.

'Go out there,' Hélène continued, 'and let the music pour through you.'

'We're ready,' said Raymond, with one ear to the door.

Raymond and Hélène took each other's hands and the dancers fell in line behind them. As they waited for the doors to open, Hélène tightened her fingers around him.

'Something's wrong,' Raymond whispered. 'You haven't been yourself for days. Are you all right, Hélène?'

'I am,' she said.

'Not nervous?'

'It's nothing, Raymond. I promise.'

'Is it Sybil?' he whispered – for Raymond was one of the very few to keep Hélène's secret.

46

'She's well. It's . . . nothing, Raymond.'

She was lying. Raymond could tell. You didn't spend years of your life dancing in somebody's arms and not get to know the measure of their hearts. But before he could probe her further, she said, 'Am I to understand congratulations are in order, Raymond?'

It was the only thing that could divert Raymond's attention from whatever was plaguing Hélène.

'How did you . . . ?' He paused, unable to keep the smile from his face. 'We haven't told anybody yet. Nancy's nervous of what the management might think. And Mrs Moffatt—'

'Oh, Raymond.' She laughed. 'You'd better start telling people soon. It's written all over you. You've been giddy as a schoolboy. And the way she holds her hand, as if she can feel the ring on it, even though she takes it off every morning. If I can guess, why, anybody can.'

At that moment, the dressing room doors opened. Waves of music and applause crashed over them, sweeping down from the edges of the dance floor where all the lords and ladies, politicians and dignitaries of London gathered. For now, the dance floor itself was an empty expanse – the freshly sprung eye of the storm.

But all of that was about to change, for Raymond and Hélène were waltzing their troops out to battle.

At the balustrade above the dance floor, Maynard Charles was gripped by a strange feeling. He had to drain his glass of brandy, a 1920 vintage Albert Simpère, before he understood what it was.

It was his nervousness draining away.

47

How could it not? The opening performance was a fantasia magical enough for him to believe, for a moment, that the world outside the Grand did not exist. Hélène was turning in Raymond's arms, then she was gliding around him as he lifted her from the ground. The other dancers in the troupe parted every time the King and Queen of the Ballroom waltzed through, until finally, when the music came to its climax, it seemed that the whole dance floor was for Hélène and Raymond alone.

Conversations had died all around him. Every eye was on the two dancers as the music came to its final, long note, and Raymond and Hélène – lost in a world of their own – turned and turned again in each other's arms.

Then, as the music came to an end, roars of applause filled the ballroom. It was a sound more magnificent than any Maynard had heard in an age. He steadied himself on the balustrade.

*If I were a different man*, he thought with a wry smile, *perhaps I might shed a tear.*

'Ladies and gentlemen,' came the voice of Archie Adams himself, 'please welcome to the stage Mr John Hastings!'

The dancers had parted, forming a narrow aisle down the middle of the dance floor, and into it walked the American industrialist, John Hastings. He did not look like a significant man. He was of distinctly average build, with a round face and spectacles that hid his eyes, but the way he approached the stage – bouncing on the heels of his feet, hands continually clenching and unclenching into fists – gave the impression of somebody sprightly and full of mischief. Scarcely thirty-six years of age, he had the boyish face of someone much younger. The whole Grand applauded him onto the stage.

Maynard felt figures crowding his shoulder. He drew himself upright, only to find himself standing among the other members of the hotel board, which John Hastings had joined only a few short months ago. He'd brought with him the sizeable fortune that had rescued the Grand, and provided the Buckingham itself with the ballast it needed for the difficult months ahead. While the applause continued, Maynard looked each of the board in the eye. If Uriah Bell, who'd made his millions as a financier for the Limehouse docks, looked pained to be here, that was nothing compared to Lord Edgerton, whose dispassionate face had been without expression all evening. Alone among them, only Sir Peter Merriweather – whose family controlled so much of the farming land in the Yorkshire wolds – looked enamoured by the evening. Maynard Charles tried to gravitate towards him, but Lord Edgerton had already fixed him with his eye. Six feet and seven inches tall, with jet-black hair and a striking jawline that, people said, gave him the look of a Roman general, he was an imposing figure.

'I see we haven't yet taught our new American compatriot the benefits of English modesty and restraint,' Lord Edgerton intoned, 'so let's leave him to play the peacock up on stage. I should appreciate a word, Maynard.'

Maynard Charles began, 'My lord, might I—'

'It is about my stepdaughter.'

*It always is*, thought Maynard ruefully. He was dog-tired of playing nursemaid to Vivienne Edgerton.

'If I may, my lord, I—'

In the end, Maynard was saved by John Hastings himself. Up on stage, the American had found the microphone belonging to the ballroom's roster of special guest singers, and began to speak.

'My Lords, ladies and gentlemen, friends from home and far away.'

'He thinks he's Caesar,' muttered Lord Edgerton, barely bothering to conceal his indignation. 'Friends, Romans, countrymen . . .'

Maynard Charles thought: *that wasn't Caesar, you fool; it was Mark Antony.* But he kept the smile inward. Like every man of good standing, he knew his place.

'. . . lend me your ears!' finished John Hastings, up on stage – and laughter rippled around the Grand. 'First of all, let me say, on this very special night, how honoured I am to be standing here with you, alongside my wonderful wife Sarah. There she is, folks – the reason I'm here with you now.'

All of the eyes in the ballroom turned to seek out a petite American lady at the edge of the dance floor, wearing a Parisian gown of chiffon and lace. Sarah Hastings was obviously nervous of the attention.

'It was Sarah who first convinced me – a man of arithmetic and balance books – of the beauty of dance and song. My darling Sarah – with a little help, I have to say, from your own prince of the ballroom, Raymond de Guise – who convinced me that, in the Buckingham Hotel, my family and I could have a new home away from home. I am proud to be here with you tonight as your newest investor. I am beyond proud that the Grand Ballroom has been reopened, so that once again London can experience its magic. I welcome you all here with that thought alone: we all need a little magic in our lives.' Here Hastings's voice darkened. He lifted the glasses from his nose and rubbed his eyes, thoughtfully. 'Ladies and gentlemen, let me not besmirch this occasion with talk of what is going on outside these walls. The world can wait. But one thing I will say is this: let's seize the moment while we can. Let's take every ounce of happiness our short lives allow. And let's . . .' He grinned, putting his glasses back on again. 'Let's dance.'

A mighty cheer rose up, shepherding Hastings down from the stage and into the waiting arms of his wife Sarah. Back on his stool at his gleaming ivory white grand piano, Archie Adams counted the band in for another number – the fiery bombast of Benny Goodman's 'Sing, Sing, Sing' – and the dance floor opened for all and sundry to come.

'The man doesn't know the meaning of class,' Uriah Bell was muttering. 'He doesn't know the true costs of elegance and reputation. Americans never do.'

*No*, thought Maynard Charles bitterly – though, as always, he was wise enough to keep such thoughts to himself. *But at least he knows the perils of privation. At least he knows the true cost of a shilling.*

Hastings's family company had somehow survived the Wall Street Crash when so many others didn't. When the world was collapsing around them, the Hastingses were finding a way to safeguard all their many thousands of employees. Reputation and elegance were vital to an establishment like the Buckingham Hotel – but Hastings's were the kinds of talents that were going to be indispensable in the months and years to come.

Maynard Charles looked around the swarming ballroom. Tobias Bauer was stepping into the arms of Hélène Marchmont, and she was performing the enchantment she always did – making an amateur dancer, lacking in confidence, feel like a star as she let him lead her around the dance floor. All of the hotel dancers were doing the same, accepting the hands of guests and marching off, with them, into the music.

Raymond de Guise was accepting the hand of none other than Vivienne Edgerton, here tonight at her stepfather's behest. Vivienne's mother, Madeleine, who'd moved from New York to be with her new husband and promptly forgotten about her daughter, was here as well, being escorted onto the dance floor by the suave Gene Sheldon. It was a relief, thought Maynard, that Vivienne had condescended to appear at all. Once upon a time, young Miss Edgerton had been unable to ignore the lure of a party; champagne, and worse, had called out to her each and every night. But this year, Vivienne seemed to get her excitement elsewhere – and chief among them was showing her lordly step-father how little he was needed, nor wanted, in her life. It would have been just like her to dismiss his invitation out of hand, and take joy in the opprobrium that followed.

'My daughter, Maynard. I see her dancing now, but it's the first I've seen of her in months.'

Maynard had been gazing over the spectacle of the dance floor so intently that he'd quite forgotten Lord Edgerton was looming over him. He turned, forcing himself to keep an emotionless face, and nodded. The fact was, though she might have been a resident in this hotel, Maynard had seen little of her either. It wasn't that he hadn't wondered why; he knew all about the nights she spent away from the hotel, the odd hours she returned, the new sense of purpose and direction with which she walked. He knew, in short, that she was no longer the lost little sot who'd been washed up here, desperate for attention, desperate for release. He just hadn't found out why, because some secrets are better left uncovered.

'She's . . . different,' seethed Lord Edgerton. 'She even looks different, Maynard. I want to know what's going on with her.

There's been quite enough disturbance to this hotel, courtesy of that girl, and if—'

'Perhaps she's simply growing up, my lord. It's a problem youth seems to have.'

Lord Edgerton was still puzzling over this, trying to decide whether he'd been subtly scolded, when a slight, shaggy-haired boy, covered in freckles, appeared between them and tugged on Maynard Charles's sleeve.

Maynard looked round. There was little Frank Nettleton, his eyes pleading.

'Nettleton.' Maynard sighed. Gathering himself, he looked back at Lord Edgerton and the other members of the accumulated board, said, 'One moment, gentlemen', and swiftly ushered Frank back into the throng.

'Frank, I've been too lenient with you. The ballroom's out of bounds tonight. I know how much you want to dance here, but . . . you're a hotel page. I can't have you scuttling around the ballroom, least of all when Lord Edgerton and—'

'Mr Charles!' Frank piped up, trying hard to keep control of his stutter. 'You have it wrong, sir. I didn't come for the d-d-dancing – I came because . . .'

Maynard's face blanched. 'What is it, Frank?'

'You have a visitor, Mr Charles. One of your . . . associates. I'm sorry, Mr Charles. He said it couldn't wait.'

The ballroom could fend for itself.

The moment Maynard Charles stepped out of it, back to the reality of the hotel reception, he felt the magic dissipate. *Back to business*, he thought, as he marched gravely behind the concierge desks, down to his office at the end of the hall.

He had not seen the man lurking in the darkness there in some months – and, in truth, he had hoped never to see him again. Mr Moorcock looked significantly older than his middle years. He looked thinner, too, than the last time Maynard had seen him. His grey woollen suit dwarfed him, and the white hair was ragged at the edges. The dark Bollman trilby he ordinarily wore was nowhere to be seen, and in its place was a flat cap of indeterminate design. He was smoking a White Owl cigar.

'Mr Moorcock, you seem to be sitting at my desk.'

'I hadn't noticed,' the man said, with a gravelly drawl.

Even his perfect King's English seemed ragged, thought Maynard. The years did that to a man. But so too did Moorcock's profession.

Ignoring the slight, Maynard drew up another chair and sat down.

'You'll have to make this quick. We reopened the ballroom tonight, after last year's little incident. I shouldn't be missed.'

'I picked my night carefully, old boy. With so much going on in this hotel, nobody will notice you're gone.'

Maynard permitted himself a laugh. 'I can hardly credit how you call yourself a spy at all, with logic as broken as that.'

Moorcock opened his cigar case, offered Maynard one of his White Owls, and shrugged when he refused.

'Mr Charles, I'm aware that our arrangement has faltered of late. I'm here to discuss—'

'Arrangement?' muttered Maynard. 'You mean to say, the way you blackmailed me into spying on guests in my hotel?'

Moorcock only rolled his eyes in return.

'We've been over this, Maynard. Too many times, as I recall. What you did in your private life is not my concern. But in my profession, one needs . . . insurance. We simply had insurance, so that you would help us in our endeavours. And, as I recall, you became a truly willing participant. This hotel of yours, a hotbed of aristocratic gossip – what better place to learn secrets? What better place than this to try and waylay a war?' He stopped, stood, stared down at Maynard Charles. 'I'm sorry we held leverage over you, Maynard. It was distasteful. Should it count for anything, I argued vehemently against it. But I'm afraid I am not a superior in my service. I am a journeyman, and so I shall remain. What you did for us here has added invaluable intelligence to the way we understand England's gentry and their connections with that monster on the Continent. Your efforts have been noted and appreciated. And I come to you now—'

'You want me to play again. To spy, again, on guests at this hotel.'

'The world is changing, Mr Charles. The way to war is accelerating. This business in Austria. Mr Chamberlain's conviction that Herr Hitler will remain true to his words. The complexion of this game we play is constantly shifting. We at the Office fear the tide is turning.'

The Office: that indeterminate name that truly meant Section 5, that branch of military intelligence concerned with affairs at home.

'The Office is chronically unprepared for what's coming. If war comes, it will fall to us to round up the enemy agents already seated in our midst. But we've barely begun to understand the scale of this thing. I'm speaking the truth to you, Mr Charles, because I need your help. The waves are crashing over us – and you, Maynard, are a good man.'

'My mind is on other things, Mr Moorcock. My heart as well. You're not the only ones unprepared for this thing. The

Buckingham was nearly on its knees. It's only the investment of Mr Hastings that keeps us alive. The Grand is reopening, and perhaps that will help. But my people need me here. We have a dance troupe coming in from Vienna – the Winter Hollers, resident with us for the autumn season. There's Christmas to start thinking about, though we're not yet in May. I have twelve hundred people here, and all of their families depend upon me to keep the Buckingham alive. I'm old, Mr Moorcock. I feel it, for the very first time. If war's inevitable, if it cannot be averted, I want to look close to home, to look after the people I love.'

'The very best way you can do that is by accepting that dance and music, and the trials and tribulations of bed linen, are for a lower caste of mind.' For the first time, Moorcock's frustration bubbled over. 'Let me speak to you plainly – and in the strictest confidence. Whitehall has lost control over proceedings. They no longer understand the gravity of what's happening on the Continent. Mr Chamberlain's insistence that there can be an agreed peace with Nazi Germany is the greatest fiction of our time. The recent plebiscite in Austria has proven this beyond doubt. And yet Whitehall remains stubbornly committed to brokering a peace with Herr Hitler. It is a peace that will not last. You'll have read Mr Churchill's opinions on the matter, of course. Our own analysis says the same: every agreement we make with Herr Hitler, now, only strengthens his hand. We willingly embolden him, under the pretence it will be the last time. But it will never be the last time.' Mr Moorcock paused. 'Were you ever bullied as a child, Mr Charles?'

'I had big fists,' Maynard replied. 'I was a stout little fellow. They left me alone.'

'Well, then,' he smiled, 'you understand our principle. When you give ground to a bully, it doesn't satisfy him. Let him punch you once, and soon he wants to punch you again – only, this time, twice as hard. Give him your pocket money one day, you'll be giving him your inheritance the next.'

'What has this to do with me, Mr Moorcock?'

'There can be a different future.'

Maynard arched a single eyebrow, inviting him to go on.

'We are not the only ones who doubt the sagacity of Mr Chamberlain's methods. Lord Halifax, our esteemed Foreign Secretary, is erring to our own line of thinking: that too many concessions are being made. And, believe it or not, there are voices on the Continent who would agree. Elements in Nazi Germany itself who would rather Britain put its boxing gloves on, rather than its mittens.' Moorcock paused, as if steeling himself for the next secrets he had to spill. 'Herr Hitler has been supportive, until now, of High German gentry. He sees them as the avatars of his Golden Germanic Age. But they are not all so adoring of him. We believe that some among them can see the writing on the wall – that, soon, the old dynasties will have to fall, so that Herr Hitler's power can never be challenged. And they would rather he was deposed before this came to pass. Mr Charles, it has become paramount to the work of the Office that we identify such sympathetic voices, so that we might help forge the connections between them and us. There might yet be a way to change history for the better – but I'm afraid we need a little help.'

'I'm a hotel director, Mr Moorcock. To think that I can—'

Moorcock waved his hand airily, parting the reef of cigar smoke.

'Your hotel has long been a home away from home for the fascists across the Continent. I happen to know that you have Graf and Gräfin Schect back for the entirety of the summer season. German dignitaries come and go. That little Napoleon from the

Italian embassy dines here in your Queen Mary every Wednesday evening. Your own Lord Edgerton counts himself a member of the British Union of Fascists, and would welcome Herr Hitler with open arms if he was to take his supper upstairs in your Candlelight Club. I am not asking you to change history, Mr Charles. But I'm asking you to listen again. I'm asking you to probe. The hour might already be past to avoid the coming of war. But we can, at least, help the Powers That Be make the right decision about when and where that war is announced. To do that we need those sympathetic voices. To identify them, I need a place like this. I need a man like you.'

Moorcock stood up, grabbed his flat cap, squashed it onto his head and marched past Maynard.

'It is time for you to come back to work, Mr Charles. Your country is waiting for you. You say you want to look after the people who work for you here, in this hotel. Well, here's your chance.'

After Mr Moorcock was gone, Maynard made haste back to the Grand Ballroom. There, the Archie Adams Orchestra and its guest singers were in the middle of a set of Cab Calloway's greatest hits (a tribute to the American businessman who'd helped them resurrect the Grand). Raymond de Guise, Hélène Marchmont and all the wonderful dancers of the Buckingham Hotel were keeping the guests spellbound.

Everybody was dancing, thought Maynard. And perhaps Moorcock was right: it was time that Maynard Charles himself went back to the dance floor, and turned a waltz of his own.

# Chapter Five

'WHAT DO YOU MEAN, *you* were going to ask *him?*'
Rosa's shriek was so loud that it might easily
have been heard all the way down in the Grand
Ballroom, where London's lords and ladies danced. Here, in
the chambermaids' kitchenette, it drowned out the sound of the
BBC *News*, which played over the wireless radio in the corner.

'And why not?' Ruth chipped in, from her armchair in the corner. She was busily knitting the jumpers she'd give to her legion
of nephews and nieces next Christmas. 'A woman ought to be
able to do anything a man can. We've got the vote, haven't we?
Fought for it, tooth and nail. So if a woman wants to propose,
then—'

'I heard a girl can only pop the question in a leap year,' said
Rosa. 'But Nance, you'll make a beautiful bride.'

'Or groom,' grinned Ruth, half-hidden behind her knitting
needles.

The kitchenette was busy with the clinking of crockery as the
girls got ready their suppers of teacakes and toast, clotted cream
and Cornish butter salvaged from the kitchens. All eyes turned
to Ruth. Nancy had to admit she was relieved: she'd been clinging on to the secret of Raymond's proposal for so many days,

building up to the moment she told Rosa and Ruth, that the attention was almost unbearable. All Rosa seemed to be able to talk about was the wedding: the dress, the guests, the flowers, whether Mr Charles might – on account of the groom being his head dancer – lend them the Grand Ballroom for their first dance together as husband and wife.

'And, of course,' said Nancy, 'there are bridesmaids to be thinking about.'

It was the only thing that could silence the girls in the kitchenette.

'Well, I've already asked my Frank to be the one who gives me away. The question is, who else might be helping me down the aisle?'

Nancy knew she was playing with them, but she enjoyed the look like adulation that had come across Rosa's face in particular.

'Of course,' she said, 'you'll be getting formal invitations soon, but I'd love it if you two could be my bridesmaids—'

She might have said more, then, if Rosa hadn't flung her arms around her and the whole kitchenette erupted in squeals of delight.

The truth was, Rosa and Ruth weren't the first she'd asked. She'd been at the Daughters two nights ago and, telling Vivienne the good news, had asked the very same question – but the look that had flickered across Vivienne's face was not the delight that had erupted on Rosa's, but a kind of shock and fear.

'Oh, Nancy,' she'd finally said, catching her breath. 'After everything we've done together, I would be honoured, but . . .'

She'd trailed off. Catching the anxiety in her voice, Nancy had said quickly, 'Of course, I understand if it would cause trouble for you at the hotel, or with your stepfather. I wouldn't want to put you in a difficult position.'

Vivienne had hesitated. 'I'm sure some of your chambermaid friends would love to be your bridesmaids,' she had said at last.

At least the sting of it was gone, now that Rosa was dangling from her with such excitement. Sometimes, when she was with Miss Edgerton, Nancy quite forgot that there were *rules* to life – that those a cut above shouldn't really mix with those 'down below', that there were conventions you had to observe. Nancy knew that Vivienne didn't think like that anymore, but her family did, and that was enough.

Nancy was pleased to be able to forget about it now.

'Have you picked a church?' Rosa asked.

'We're thinking of the town hall, in Marylebone. Well, Raymond's from a Jewish family, and my father was a Presbyterian. But with the town hall, we could do it the way *we* wanted.'

'Not a church?' gasped Rosa.

'Good for you, Nance,' Ruth chipped in. 'Sticking it to tradition again!'

'Our Ruth here,' said Rosa to Nancy, 'is one of these that hate tradition. As for me, I'd be perfectly happy if my Frank got down on one knee one day! But Ruth, you've hardly even looked at a boy since we've been working here, have you?'

Ruth shrugged, refocusing on the half-jumper in her hands. 'I got better things to think about than boys.'

Rosa rolled her eyes – as if to say that there wasn't a better thing to think about in all of the world.

'Nancy, we've been dancing, we've been picnicking in Hyde Park, we've been all over – and every time a boy makes eyes at her, she goes all cold. Nobody's good enough for Ruth!'

'Well, not all of us can fall into the arms of Raymond de Guise!'

If Ruth was trying to deflect the attention by invoking his name, it did the trick perfectly. Rosa immediately flashed back to Nancy and the simple ring on her finger. Nancy blushed, and busied herself pouring tea.

'Oh, balderdash!' Rosa exclaimed. 'You don't need a debonair dancer to fall in love. You barely even need to go dancing or picnicking, or strolling around London town. There's plenty of eligible young bachelors right here in this hotel.' She paused, her eyes revolving to the kitchenette door. 'Look, here comes one of them now!'

Standing in the doorway was the concierge Billy Brogan, with his mop of wiry red hair and his face spotted in freckles. Gangly and lean, Billy was a couple of years Nancy's junior and, however hard he tried to brush up smartly in his uniform of ebony waistcoat and crimson bow tie, he never quite managed to look like anything other than a member of the Brogan family. He stood slightly crookedly, with one hand stuffed in a pocket. The watch dangling from a chain on his lapel was an affectation, intended to make him seem a cut above – only Billy hadn't noticed it was back to front and, besides, it had stopped working last summer and had never been repaired.

Another figure waited behind Billy. Rosa bustled past him, out into the hallway, and came back with Frank Nettleton on her arm.

'Sit yourself down, Frankie, we've got tea and toast coming.'

'Not like that lot have down there,' said Billy, sashaying past Frank and Rosa and, oblivious, taking the seat Rosa had intended for her sweetheart. 'They've got caviar on little biscuits. Chicken livers crowned with little sprigs of parsley.' Billy reached up and grinned when Nancy appeared with a plate of toast and butter.

'But this will suit me just fine. How many chicken livers do you need just to feel full?'

'I been down in the Grand, Nancy,' said Frank.

Rosa looked up. 'Well, go on! What's it like?'

Ruth simply settled down with her knitting – hardly interested in the Grand Ballroom, or the boys, at all.

'Frankie's a Nettleton through and through,' declared Rosa, with pride. 'You were one for sneaking down into the Grand Ballroom when you first arrived, wasn't you, Nance?'

Nancy nodded. 'An adventure I never intend to repeat.'

'Well, go on, Frank! What was it like, this opening night of yours?'

'You shouldn't be sneaking around, Frankie,' whispered Nancy.

'Oh, I wasn't, Nance, I promise. I had a message for Mr Charles. Couldn't wait, could it, Billy?'

Billy, his face stuffed full of toast, spluttered out an answer that nobody could understand. On the other side of the kitchenette, Ruth looked up from her knitting, saw the toast crumbs showering out of Billy's bristly lips, and shook her head, as if to say that here was the reason she wasn't in any rush to find herself a gentleman friend.

'Well,' Frank went on, 'it was another world, Rosa. Even more splendid than it used to be. You think the rest of the Buckingham's beautiful? Just take a sneaky peek around the doors of the Grand Ballroom. Even the chandeliers are new! And the dance floor, it's been sprung by a team that came from Paris especially for it. And the orchestra, and all the dancers, they've been doing nothing but practise for months – so you should have seen the way they turned, and—'

'You want to take me down there for a dance, Frankie?'

'You'll have to show him that ring on your finger first, Nance!'
Ruth called out.

Nancy came and put her arms around Frank.

'He already knows, silly.'

'Gerroff me!' Frank said, wriggling out of her embrace. Then
he cocked his head to one side and said, not for the first time,
'I'm pleased as punch for you, Nance. Now we'll have *two* dancers in the family.'

'Only one a hotel dancer,' said Ruth. 'You remember that,
Frank.'

'For now,' Frank said, 'but maybe I'll get my chance. It's been
done before. Raymond told me himself. There was a porter,
Simon Carpenter – he got his break in the Grand three years
ago, all courtesy of Mr de Guise. Now he dances at the Imperial
Hotel. Calls himself Simon le Strange—'

'He sounds like a conjuror!' Rosa said, laughing. 'And a traitor,
to go to the Imperial like that.'

'Well, all I got to do is practise, and maybe I can get a chance
too. Raymond's been giving me lessons, hasn't he, Nance? I even
got to dance with Miss Marchmont's new understudy, Mathilde!
Of course, all that's going to stop now the Grand's open again.
They won't want to dance with a hotel page now the demonstration dances are starting again. So . . .' Frank paused. 'Stand up,
Billy. Go on!'

Billy, who had finished his toast but remained sprinkled in
its crumbs, took his cue and leaped readily to his feet. It was as
if, thought Nancy, he was standing to attention, her own little
brother his sergeant major.

'The thing is, without a chance to practise dancing in the hotel
anymore, I got to thinking we should plan another trip. All of

us here, and whoever else we can rustle up from the kitchens or the porters or . . . why, anyone who wants to come! Mrs Moffatt and Mr Charles himself – the more, the merrier!' Frank waited for the laughter to ebb away. 'Me and Rosa, we went down to the Starlight Lounge just behind Oxford Street one night. I thought we could go back. A little adventure of our own. I could do with the practice.'

Rosa gripped Frank fiercely – 'Don't be silly, you're a natural!' – and let him spin her around, right there in the kitchenette.

'Well,' Nancy ventured, 'I reckon that's settled! Raymond won't be able to come, though, so I'll be in want of a partner of my own.' She sidled over to Billy playfully, and put an arm around his shoulder. 'Well, Billy, what do you say? You're my oldest friend here in the hotel. It only seems right that you and I . . .'

There was something awkward about Billy Brogan today. He felt stiff and ungainly and, when he shook off Nancy's arm and coughed to clear his throat, his eyes darting nervously into every corner of the kitchenette, Nancy was quite sure that something was wrong.

'Sorry, Nance. You see, that's the reason I come up here with Frankie. Me and Frank was talking about the Starlight Lounge, as we do, and I thought I might like to ask' – his eyes roamed over the kitchenette, until they landed on the corner – 'you, Ruth, if you'd like to step out with me. Just to go dancing, o' course.'

Rosa revolved towards Ruth, her eyes wide with excitement.

'Oh, give over, Billy Brogan!' Ruth said, waving her hand in dismissal. 'That smart tongue of yours is going to get you into trouble one day.'

Silence fell.

'Well, why not, Ruth?' Billy gave a little example of his footwork, describing a solo box-step on the threadbare rug, but this only confused things further – for, before he'd finished, he'd stumbled and had to steady himself by grasping Frank's shoulder. 'You could do worse than me. I scrub up smart.'

Ruth, who was feeling the pressure of a dozen sets of eyes boring into her, had started to flush a deep shade of red.

'Billy, you're not serious . . .'

The silence had deepened. Nobody else dared breathe a word. In the end, it was Rosa who broke the silence.

'Go on, Ruthie.'

But Ruth wasn't the only one burning a brilliant shade of red. Billy himself had started to go purple and, before Ruth could open her mouth to reply, he said, 'No, it's all right, it's . . . good. I was only joking around. I don't need a girl to go dancing with. We're all going, aren't we? All of us, together. Doesn't mean we have to have . . .'

By then, the sentence had died, because Billy had turned and loped hurriedly out of the room.

'Go on, after him, Frankie!' Rosa cried, half-pushing Frank towards the door before rounding on Ruth. 'Well, that was charming, wasn't it? Ruth Attercliffe, you mean-spirited—' She caught herself before she said worse. 'Did you have to make a total fool of the boy? Couldn't you see he was wearing his heart on his sleeve?'

Evidently, Ruth could – because the colour had drained from her cheeks and, where once she'd been embarrassed, now she was battling back tears.

'I didn't mean to make him feel silly.'

'Couldn't you have just danced with him?' Rosa softened. 'Oh, Ruthie,' she said, rushing to her friend's side and putting her arms around her, 'you're your own worst enemy. Billy Brogan's not that bad.'

'He just . . . isn't my type.'

'He's handsome enough.'

'I know.'

'He's charming, too,' interjected Nancy. 'And his heart's in the right place – even if, every now and again, it doesn't seem quite connected with his head. Billy's got to be worth a shot, hasn't he?'

'Nance is right,' said Rosa. 'Maybe you just don't know what your type is. You need to try things! Maybe you'll kiss a few frogs along the way, but—'

'It just doesn't feel right,' said Ruth. 'It doesn't feel magical. And . . . I deserve something magical, don't I? Just like the two of you.'

Rosa beamed and, settling on the arm of Ruth's armchair, draped herself around her friend like a fur stole.

'Oh, Ruth, you silly girl! You find magic in the most extraordinary places.'

And Ruth, whose tears were seeping back into her eyes, felt a weight lift off her for the first time that evening.

'The most ordinary places too,' she whispered.

Billy was already back at the concierge desk when Frank caught up with him. He was so busy, flicking through the guest book and making notes on an adjacent leaf of headed notepaper, that he barely registered as Frank scurried over. It was only when Frank – who saw soon enough that the book Billy was diligently focusing on was upside down – reached out and turned it around that he looked up.

'You got out of there sharpish, Billy.'

'Ah, well, you know how it is. All you lovebirds talking dancing and weddings. That's not for the likes of me. See, I got a business head on these shoulders, Frank. Having a sweetheart would only drag me down. I got important work to do for Mr Charles and—'

'Oh, Billy,' Frank said solemnly. 'You weren't joking at all, were you, when you asked about the Starlight Lounge?'

Billy's eyes returned to the guest book. For a moment, he pretended to peruse it again, mouthing numbers to himself as if he was performing elaborate calculations in his head. But his heart wasn't in the charade and, soon, he looked up.

'I just thought, what with you and Rosa, and Nance and Raymond, that . . . well, it'd be nice, you know. To have someone to love and spoil and . . . talk to. Really talk to. And Ruth, well, she's always had a way about her. She don't put up with any nonsense, not like the rest of the chambermaids.' Billy caught himself and added, 'Your Rosa and Nancy excepted, o' course.'

'Billy, I thought you were just playing with her.'

'That's what everyone thinks,' said Billy. 'Billy Brogan, good for a laugh but not much else. Well, Frankie, I've got a lot to offer a girl. I've got a—'

'Billy, you're . . . shy!'

Billy drew himself up to his full height, filled his chest as if it might make him feel braver.

'Well, take a look at you, Frank Nettleton. When you turned up at this hotel last year, you could hardly speak for that stutter of yours! And now, here you stand, thinking you might even get a chance in the hotel ballroom. It's funny how the world turns.

And me, well—' He paused, finally feeling his courage return. 'But I'm a social climber, Frankie. I always have been. That's why I'm a concierge and you're a hotel page. I embrace change. And . . .' He grew softer, all the courage draining away. '. . . maybe Ruth does too.'

The sounds coming up from the Grand Ballroom were glorious. Frank listened to the Archie Adams Orchestra reaching the climax of one of their own hit records, 'The Lovers in Lambeth', and thought, dreamily, of what it might be like to be down there now.

Then, snapping back to reality, he reached out and clapped Billy on the shoulder.

'I'll have a chat with Rosa. We'll get her there, Billy, I promise. You and Ruth, dancing in the Starlight Lounge – just a bit of magic in the air. Well, you never know what might happen! In times like these, we've all got to seize the day.'

May 1938

# Chapter Six

ALL OF THE OLD CLICHÉS *are true*, thought Hélène as she stepped through the back door of the little Brixton terrace and saw Sybil standing on a wooden stool, stirring cake mixture at the kitchen counter.

*My, how she's grown.*

'Mama! Mama!'

Sybil dropped her spoon, smearing cake batter all down the cupboard door, and tumbled off the stool to reach her. At three years old, with her father's eyes and her mother's smile, she was steady on her feet, but still plummeted and plunged in moments of high excitement.

'Mama, I'm making cake!'

The figure standing at the stove, who had been watching Sybil erupt with excitement with a smile on her own face, was Noelle Archer – Sybil's grandmother. Nearly sixty years old, she was settling into her elder years with a dignity Hélène rarely saw among the lords and ladies of the Buckingham – who, more often than not, refused to accept the limitations of their bodies, eating and drinking themselves into corpulence and disease. Noelle had tight white curls and a kindly smile, and the lines that were deepening around her eyes were more the result of a lifetime of laughter than the signs of a woman past her prime.

*Besides*, thought Hélène, *Noelle is in the second prime of her life.*

Having raised three children of her own, she had spent the last three years devoted to the little girl who was now scrambling into Hélène's arms, leaving dollops of cake batter all up her green woollen coat. At first, Hélène had worried that she was asking too much of the Archer family. But the love of a child brings out the very best in people – and Hélène had seen for herself how Sybil had brought the light back into Noelle and Maurice's eyes, how caring for her went some way to healing the wound of Sidney's sudden demise. They said that the Grand Ballroom was a place of starlight and love, but you didn't need expensive chandeliers and a resident orchestra for that. Here in this cramped Brixton terrace, love was all around.

'I keep thinking she'll forget about me.' Hélène laughed, straining to keep hands covered with cake mixture out of her hair. 'But every time I arrive—'

'A daughter never forgets her mama, Hélène. She talks about you every day. Come on, come through. I've a pot of tea already made.'

The narrow kitchen opened up into the Archers' living room, where a fire crackled in the grate and the radio was buzzing with the BBC *News*: more talk coming out of Austria; Mr Hitler on a tour of the Italian provinces, being met everywhere with rapturous applause. The world was such a divided mess, thought Hélène – and sometimes, she feared, it was the same in her own life as well.

Noelle helped her out of her coat, promising to brush it once the smears of batter were dry, and settled her at the table in front of the fire, where the Archers ordinarily took their meals. The tea was still hot, so Noelle poured it into cups, setting a glass of milk aside for Sybil, and left mother and daughter to get reacquainted while she busied herself in the kitchen.

It was good to have some time alone with Sybil. Hélène craved it, all week long. She supposed that there were mothers out there who'd tell her she was abominable for leaving her daughter to the care of somebody else, but none of those mothers would ever understand the sacrifice she'd had to make. How else was she to provide for Sybil, if she gave up the dance floor?

'Have you missed your mama, Sybil?'

'I made biscuits.'

She reached for one now, from the plate by the teapot. Ugly and misshapen, and yet each one concocted with a child's love. Hélène accepted one. Dunked in tea, it was a chewy, over-treacled delight.

'I danced with a prince this week, Sybil. Prince Gustav, son of the Crown Prince of Sweden. Also named Gustav.' Hélène whispered into Sybil's ear, 'It gets confusing with princes.'

'Are you a princess, Mama?'

'Not quite, little one. But you – you're *my* princess.'

'No!'

Hélène's fingers were creeping under Sybil's arms, and the fits of laughter that filled the room were a music so much more enchanting than anything the Archie Adams Orchestra could ever create.

Sybil was laughing, still, when Noelle returned, poured herself a cup of tea, and sat down. By the look on her face, she was grateful to be off her feet – and, in this, she and Hélène completely agreed.

'It's getting harder,' she said.

'Rushed off your feet again, are you?'

'Not that,' said Hélène – though she was; ever since the Grand had reopened, Maynard Charles had been exacting in his demands from his dancers. There was time to make up for. Profits to recoup. 'I meant . . . this.'

Sybil, who had stopped laughing and was only now gathering her composure, dived back for another biscuit and proceeded to make a calamitous mess as she dunked it in her glass of milk.

'I don't know why,' said Hélène, 'and it's nothing you've done. You're doing everything right. I just think it's that, now that she can speak, now that she's – why, now that she's a *person* . . .' It seemed ridiculous to express it like this, and yet somehow it fitted. 'It feels like I'm missing so much more. She's taking in so much more of the world around her. The world that, day after day, I'm not in.'

'Many mothers see their children less, Hélène. The folks you'll dance with, up at the Buckingham Hotel. They don't put their children to bed at night. They're not the ones their children run to when they graze their knees. They have nursemaids and governesses.'

A look ghosted across Hélène's face. 'Nursemaids and governesses,' she said. 'That's what it was like when I was a girl.'

*It's time*, she thought. There were no secrets between her and Noelle – so she set Sybil down on the floor and produced from her clutch bag the letter that she'd returned to, time and again, in the past days.

Noelle read it carefully.

'I remember you speaking of your Aunt Lucy,' she finally said.

'She's the only one I remember with fondness in my heart. Oh, Noelle, it's been eating me up. I've put pen to paper three times, thinking I'd write back – but not once having anything to say. Louis said that, if I was truly finished with them, I'd have shredded the letter already. And maybe I would have done, if it was anyone but her. But Aunt Lucy . . . She's the one who was there for me, every night, while my parents were off gallivanting. We wrote to each other, back and forth, for a little while after my parents . . .' She did not finish that sentence, and Noelle did not ask her to, for the pain was written in lines across her face. 'I can still smell Aunt Lucy. She smelled of apples and blackberries, from when she took me picnicking in the orchards on my father's estate. I always felt terrible that I'd—'

'Walked out on her?' asked Noelle, with an air of incredulity.

Hélène nodded. 'But she didn't follow, did she? When it came to it, she needed my father – or, more properly, she needed his money. Being disowned was all right for me, but not Aunt Lucy. She was too scared.'

She slumped in her seat and sighed. It was so unusual to see Hélène losing her elegant posture that it nearly broke Noelle's heart.

'What do you want to do, Hélène?'

'I think . . .' She reached down and hoisted Sybil back onto her lap. 'I think that to go back there now would be a betrayal.'

She'd said it with such fire that Noelle rocked back in her seat. Even Sybil must have felt it, for she strained to wriggle out of Hélène's arms, then came on hands and knees across the table, sending biscuits and sugar cubes clattering all over, until she plopped onto Noelle's own lap.

'Sybil has but one family, Noelle.'

For the first time, Hélène was speaking with passion, certain at last of the words to which she gave voice. She did not take a breath, not even as the door opened into the kitchen and the sound of tramping feet announced the arrival of Maurice Archer, Noelle's husband.

'She has me, and she has you, Noelle – and you too, Maurice,' she added as he appeared from the kitchen door. 'She needs no other family. They had their chance, four years ago. To go to them now? Why, Noelle, it would be to betray everything you did for her. Everything you did for me.'

Maurice, whose face had fallen to confusion and concern, tramped a little further into the room. When Noelle realised he was leaving muddy boot prints behind him, she leaped up to lay down a trail of newspapers over which he might walk. This he followed to the table, where, sitting down – and blowing a raspberry at Sybil, who took joy in blowing one in return – he read Aunt Lucy's letter.

After some time, Maurice brandished the note aloft and said, 'This is a love letter.'

Hélène stared at him.

'Well, it is, isn't it, Noelle?'

Noelle came to his shoulder.

'It's an act of love,' Maurice declared. 'I know why they denounced you, Hélène. I know they couldn't stand the thought of their perfect daughter being sullied by the likes of us. By the good Lord above, I've been hearing such things half of my life. I still do. I was in the Coach and Horses, right now, on Coldharbour Lane and there were boys in the corner, kept looking at me like I ought to have been doffing my cap and shining their shoes. I feel all that, and it hurts – yes, it still hurts, even now. But, Hélène, this is a message from the other side. This is somebody's hand, reaching out for yours from some dark and lonely place. Death is coming. What's to say your Aunt Lucy hasn't been waiting for a chance, any chance, to cry out for you? If there wasn't love in it, why, she'd hardly have written at all.'

'So what am I to do? Go to them and put my arms around them and tell them I . . . forgive them? Or, worse, ask *them* to forgive *me* – when there's not a thing I've done on this earth that I'd take back? When there's not a thing I've done wrong? Only to fall in love and have a beautiful baby and—'

'Oh, Hélène!' Maurice laughed. 'I'm not saying go there and grovel. What I'm saying is Death's riding in. I've seen enough of it. We all have.'

He closed his fists and she imagined, in that moment, that he was not only thinking of Sidney – but of all the many deaths of his life: the deaths he'd seen at sea in the Merchant Navy, and the deaths that stalked the land in those first years after they came to England, with the Great War just gone and the Spanish Influenza striking down so many.

'I'm not thinking of them, Hélène. I'm thinking of you, and what it might feel like to wake up one morning and receive a telegram to tell you your father's passed away – and to know, in your heart, that you might have given him one more chance, one last chance, to put right what he did so wrong. I'm thinking about regret, Hélène, about that kind of regret that can last a lifetime.'

For a time after that, they sat together. Noelle came to pour more tea, Sybil came to help – and then, once she'd finished tidying up the not inconsiderable spillage her daughter had made, Hélène whispered, 'You wouldn't be angry, if I was to see them?'

'Hélène.' Maurice laughed. 'You'd have to hardly know us at all, to ask such a question! Our love for you is not conditional. We wouldn't dream of asking you not to go. It's a question for your heart alone – and we'll be here, right where we are now, whatever you decide.'

'I'm not sure I could go back to Rye. The streets are too full of ghosts.'

'Then don't,' said Noelle. 'Write to them. Tell them you'll meet them, but not in Rye. Your mother and aunt could come to you – it's the least they owe you. Dinner at the Buckingham. Or, better yet, somewhere else in London. A café. A restaurant. Somewhere you can leave any second, if it gets too much for you.'

Hélène exhaled. Somewhere in the midst of the conversation, a decision had been made.

That night, back in her quarters at the Buckingham, Hélène could still taste the vanilla of her daughter's cake. She breathed it in, remembered its textures, the way it had ended up smeared all around Sybil's face, and somehow found the courage to put pen to paper for the final time. Then, before her courage deserted her, she took the service lift down into the Buckingham basements, and into the post room itself.

After that, though the tension did not leave her, somehow Hélène felt in control. This thing that was happening in her life, she was the one in command of it – and, wherever it took her, whatever happened next, it would not be done with bitterness and regret hanging over her. It would be done with decency and poise – and yes, even elegance. The world could throw all manner of madnesses at you, but if you had your poise – well, perhaps things would turn out right.

# Chapter Seven

THROUGH THE DARK FOREST, the king and his liegemen rode. All around them stretched the deep entangled woodland, the sun reaching only through gaps in the canopy above.

Men rushed out of the trees, bows and arrows held aloft. In a chaos of whinnying horses, the procession that had been advancing through the forest stopped. These brigands, dressed in green and flashing pearly white smiles, were suddenly all around them.

'I suppose you realise the penalty for killing a king's deer is . . . death?'

In the shadows of the new Odeon cinema on Leicester Square, Nancy Nettleton curled into Raymond de Guise. Up above them, across a sea of countless heads, the scene was being played out in glorious Technicolor. Robin Hood himself – the dashing figure of Errol Flynn, flashing his trademark smile – seemed as tall as the Buckingham Hotel.

'Do you know,' whispered Raymond, 'I've always liked the name Errol—'

The laugh that burst out of Nancy's lips was quite unladylike, and attracted the attention of the cinemagoers in the row directly behind. Some moments later, she settled into the crook of his arm and whispered, 'I prefer a good, solid name. A name my father would have been proud of. Edward, perhaps. Teddy. Ted.'

'If we *were* to have a son,' Raymond grinned, 'I was thinking of naming him Raymond.'

'You're not serious.' Nancy stopped. Up on the screen, Errol Flynn was whistling past. 'Raymond?'

Raymond fixed her with a forlorn look, as if in one single word and its grave intonation she'd destroyed the dream of a lifetime. Then, unable to keep up the pretence any longer, he chortled.

'One day, Nancy. One day. We've a wedding to think about first.'

A wedding. *Their* wedding. Nancy had known girls who'd grown up dreaming of nothing else but walking down the aisle, all of their family and friends looking on – and, though this was not her, she had to admit that, now that she was wearing Raymond's ring, the thought of her wedding day kept popping into her mind at the most inopportune moments. She'd be changing grotty bed sheets in the Grand Colonial Suite and, all of a sudden, she'd be picturing a dress, or remembering a beautiful line of poetry that she imagined someone might recite as Raymond led the toasts.

Later, as the film finished and they joined the crowds tramping out of the picture house, she was thinking of it still. Evidently, so was Raymond.

'I wrote and told Georges,' he said. 'He must have written back instantly, because I received a reply this morning. Georges says he wouldn't miss it for the world.'

Georges de la Motte: Raymond's benefactor and, once upon a time, his ballroom tutor – and the very man who had been responsible for lifting Ray Cohen out of the dance halls of the East End and turning him into the darling of high society. Georges was out in California now, pursuing his own stardom on the silver screen. Perhaps, some day soon, his face would be projected into the cavernous interior of the new Odeon cinema. Nancy liked the thought of that.

They were slow to leave the cinema. Conversations buzzed all around them. Into the chorus of voices, Raymond said, 'I wonder if Georges should be my best man. Artie would only make a mess of it.'

'You do him a disservice, Raymond!' she chided him, grinning. 'Your brother's a transformed man. You ought to see the pride he takes in his work, down at the Daughters of Salvation.'

'Have you thought, perhaps, about bridesmaids?'

Nancy said, 'Rosa, and Ruth, of course, but you know Ruth – she's a stick in the mud. She won't even tolerate the idea of a dance with Billy, so the thought of getting her into a bridesmaid's dress is . . .' She faltered. 'The truth is, I already broached it with Miss Edgerton, but . . . she seemed uncertain, somehow. I may have made a mistake there, Raymond. Sometimes, I forget that Miss Edgerton's a cut above. The last two years . . . I know she loves me, she's said as much – but, I don't know, perhaps something of the old feeling still lingers. Doing the *proper* thing.' She paused. 'Or maybe I'm complicating it. Maybe she just has something else on her mind. I suppose she thinks I'll be walking out on the Daughters of Salvation, as soon as I'm Mrs de Guise. But . . .'

Her thoughts had taken her this way a few times over the past few weeks. Every time she got carried away, picturing life as the new Mrs de Guise, a little voice whispered in her ear: *a married woman, at work changing beds by day and in the East End by night? Will the world even allow it?* The voices became strongest when she wasn't with Raymond; at least when he was here, she could breathe him in, picture vividly the future she held in her hands.

The night was still young when Nancy and Raymond emerged, arm in arm, out of the cinema and took in the starry vaults above Leicester Square. As the other cinemagoers fanned out around them, hailing passing taxicabs or scurrying for the sanctuary of the last Underground trains, they wandered past the Regent Street arcades and through the grand town houses of Mayfair's outermost edges. It took them an age, or so it seemed, to reach the open expanse of Berkeley Square, where the balmy spring night was filled with the scents of crocuses opening up – but that was only because they wandered so aimlessly, walked so slowly, so that the night didn't have to end.

There was the Buckingham hanging above them, its grand white façade like a shimmering beacon in the night. The great copper crown that sat between the hotel's pavilion roofs glittered where the moonlight spilled across it.

They stopped in the heart of the square and, quite unprompted, Raymond turned on his heel, opening his arms as if the whole of Berkeley Square belonged to him. Up above, somebody angrily closed their curtains and snuffed their bedchamber light; evidently, they were sick to death of seeing young lovers profess their undying affection on Berkeley Square.

'Raymond,' Nancy ventured, as he gazed at the stars above. 'Raymond?'

Raymond's turn came to a halt. 'Nancy?'

'What we said before. About children and . . .'

He rushed to her. 'Don't fear, those days are some time off yet. I mean to say, I dream of it, of course I dream, but . . .' He was stumbling over his own words. Debonair Raymond de Guise, the King of the Ballroom – and yet, far too often, Nancy Nettleton turned him into a lovesick fool. 'But, Nancy, don't you?'

The earnestness in his voice prompted her to reach out for his hand.

'Oh, Raymond, you old fool, of course I do! But I suppose there are things I haven't thought about. Like . . . what *does* happen after? After we're married, well, what does life look like? Will they even want me here, at the hotel? We'll need to find a home, somewhere to call our own, and – well, none of the other chambermaids are married, are they?' She paused. 'Will they even let me stay? I'm not sure I'm ready for home life, Raymond.'

Raymond's heart stilled. 'Not ready?' he whispered.

'Raymond!' She flung herself into his arms and he, in turn, waltzed her around the square. 'I'm ready for a life with you. I am. I'm dreaming of it. But I suppose I haven't thought about what comes next. I look ten years into the future and I see our children running around us, growing up loyal and decent and full of love. But when I think about next year . . .'

Together, they stopped and turned to the gleaming face of the hotel. There it was: the only home they knew.

'Have you thought about where we might live?' Nancy asked.

Raymond nodded. 'It will feel strange not to live at the Buckingham – but Mr Charles said—'

'The board wouldn't allow it?'

He nodded. 'Along those lines. It's not considered appropriate for married men to live on site.' He grinned. 'We'll work it out. Here or there. There or . . . anywhere. As long as we're together.

We have time to work it out. And . . . perhaps none of us should think too far ahead.'

In that moment, he was thinking of all the conversations he'd had with Maynard Charles, all the voices on the radio, the headlines from the Continent.

'Come on, Nancy,' he finally ventured. 'It's late already.'

Together, they approached the sweeping marble stairs, where the hotel doorman stood proudly in front of its great revolving brass doors. Hand in hand, they banked away from the grand entrance and strolled into the narrow darkness of Michaelmas Mews. One of the hotel pages was asleep at the tradesman's entrance. Raymond gently roused him as they walked past.

'Don't let Mr Charles catch you sleeping on the job, young sir!'

As they waited for the service lift that would ferry them upwards, Raymond bent his lips close to Nancy's ear and whispered, 'Whatever happens next, it will all be worth it. I know that, in my heart.'

They were talking about the wedding in the chambermaids' kitchenette when Nancy awoke, later than she'd meant to, and reeled out to meet the other girls. They were talking about it still, as they rode the service lift down to the ground storey and bustled, together, into the housekeeping lounge – where the chambermaids were busily bickering about who should lay which table, who should brew the tea, and who should man the banks of toasters busy churning out teacakes.

'She says it's going to be a registry office affair,' one of the girls was saying.

'A registry office? But that's hardly the dream, is it?'

'Well, Raymond's Jewish, they say. But who'd have known? What, with a name like de Guise . . .'

'But Mr Charles has promised you the Grand, hasn't he, Nance?' one of the girls chipped in – though Nancy, oblivious to it all, had hardly heard a thing. Her eyes kept flitting, instead, to the door which opened up onto Mrs Moffatt's own little study. 'Well, Nance, it'll be as grand and romantic as any church, if they pull out all the stops for the Grand, won't it? And they won't be shy about spending the pennies, will they? Not with it being Raymond de Guise—'

'It's Nancy's wedding too, you girls!' Rosa snapped. 'Raymond's not a god, you know. He's just a man. And he's not a patch on our Nance.' Suddenly, she caught herself and clapped a hand over her own mouth. 'Sorry, Nance. He's a good sort, and all, but it's *him* who's the lucky one here – not you.'

Nancy still didn't seem to hear. The girls were all seated now, but she was still on her feet – and, leaving the chattering girls behind, she hurried to the door of Mrs Moffatt's office.

Nancy's fingers, delicately rapping on the door as she pulled it closed behind her, were hardly enough to rouse Mrs Moffatt from what she was doing. Mrs Moffatt was of the opinion that the Head of Housekeeping had to lead by example, and this meant everything from loading the laundry wagons to brewing the breakfast tea, so it was a quite unusual state of affairs to find her here at breakfast, immersed in her papers. As Nancy approached, she found herself prickling with a peculiar sense of foreboding. This only intensified as she crossed the small study and realised that one of the papers on the top of Mrs Moffatt's desk had been torn into pieces, and left in shreds scattered there.

All of a sudden, Mrs Moffatt looked up and said, 'Sit down, dear Nancy. I've been wondering how long it might be before we had our little chat.'

Nancy, even more perplexed, said, 'Mrs Moffatt?'

Mrs Moffatt was smiling – but, if Nancy was right, it was taking her a great effort to do so. The smile had not reached her eyes. With her own face creasing in concern, Nancy took the chair, facing Mrs Moffatt across the desk.

'Dear Nancy,' Mrs Moffatt began, 'I understand congratulations are in order.'

Nancy said, 'So you heard, Mrs Moffatt.'

'Oh, you know this old place. A girl can hardly wash her hair in the Buckingham without the kitchen porters hearing about it, then telling the concierges, who let it slip to the pages. I heard it from Harrison, the barber. By chance, he heard it from . . .' Mrs Moffatt beamed. 'I'm teasing you, Nancy. The girls haven't stopped chattering about it ever since they heard. I've been waiting for the right moment to tell you I wish you all the love and luck in the world.'

The words settled something in Nancy's stomach. This, at least, was something. It gave her the courage to carry on.

'My head's been a whirlwind. I love Raymond. More than I thought possible. And Raymond, like he always does, is getting caught up in the romance of it. Don't misunderstand – it's what I love him for. I need a man like that. But you know me, Mrs Moffatt. I'm a good country girl. I like my feet on the ground. And—'

'It's usual to be nervous, my dear.'

'I'm not nervous about Raymond. He's the love of my life. And the way he thinks of us, his *grand romance*, that's a part of him I'll always treasure. It's what happens *next* that's been bothering me. We're all dreaming of the wedding day and the dances in the Grand Ballroom, but . . . what happens the day after that, and the day after that? Nothing has to change for Raymond. He might not live at the Buckingham anymore, but when it comes to his work, he can carry on as it was before, always dancing. But as for me . . .'

Mrs Moffatt left aside what she was about to say: that, judging by the bluster on the Continent, things might change for all of them at any moment. Instead she said, consolingly, 'You're worried about your work – as a married woman.'

'I'm worried about *me*, Mrs Moffatt. Oh Lord, it must sound so foolish! Foolish and . . . selfish, even. But I've been working, one way or another, since I was nine years old. Coming to London was never about finding a husband, not for me. I know other girls dream of those things, and I'm not saying they weren't sometimes in my thoughts too, but I wanted to – why, I wanted to change the world! Raymond's the best thing that's ever happened to me, but it wasn't part of my plan. And I feel I've made my contributions – right here at the hotel, and everything I've been helping Miss Edgerton do with the Daughters of Salvation, too. Does it all have to end, Mrs Moffatt?'

For a time, Mrs Moffatt was silent. But there was not judgement in her eyes. There was only love.

'These are difficult questions, and ones we all have to face.' She paused and, reaching into a drawer of her desk, produced a handful of orange barley sugars, which she unwrapped from their wax papers and handed to Nancy. 'I should like to tell you a story, Nancy – a story of a married woman who has worked all of her life.' She paused. 'Here I am.'

'I'm not sure I understand.'

'You're too young to remember anything, I should hazard to guess, of the Great War. But those years are forever stained upon my memory. I daresay you'll find it difficult to imagine, but there was a time, in an age long ago, when I wasn't your Mrs Moffatt at all. My name was Emmeline Ellis until I was a fair bit older than you are, and my sweetheart Jack was the one named Moffatt. Well, we were married in 1913, scarcely a year before all the kings and emperors took it into their heads that the whole world should go to war. Jack took himself off in September that year, proud as any Englishman, and promised he'd be home by Christmas. But, of course, he wasn't. None of those brave boys were. And we women – we married women – left behind, we couldn't just put our feet up and wait, could we? No, Nancy, we had to find work. It wasn't just our households that needed us. It was our country. All the men off dying for their king, and we women left behind to keep on living. And that's what we did. As a matter of fact, that's how I came to the Buckingham itself. You'd have been barely a girl, dear Nancy, and here I was, right where you are now – a chambermaid, just starting out. I suppose I'd have asked myself the same questions you're asking yourself now, if my Jack had come home. But that wretched year of 1917 left so many of us widowed, and I had to keep on striving.' Mrs Moffatt stopped, for she was growing dewy-eyed and had to dab at the corners of her eyes with the hem of her apron. 'I'm getting away from myself. Nancy, what I'm trying to say is – the world is changing. To keep on working as a married woman would not be the conventional thing. But you are, my girl, one of this world's unconventional wonders. It has been done before and, if there is a way, I will help you find it.'

'Mrs Moffatt,' said Nancy, and already she could feel a weight lifting off her shoulders, 'I should like that very much.'

She was on her feet, and almost at the door, when something flurried up in her heart and she found herself compelled to turn around.

'I'm sorry about your husband. I should think you've heard it said too many times across the years, but it seems too cruel, the way these things went back then.'

Mrs Moffatt said, so quietly that she almost went unheard, 'It's strange how time dulls the pain. I knew my Jack scarcely five years of this lifetime. And here we are, twenty years on, speaking of him now.' She paused. 'There are longer pains in a lifetime, Nancy. Trust me. Take your happiness where you can. Have your pleasures and your joys, and never be ashamed.'

'It's why Raymond and I want to marry as soon as we can,' Nancy confessed. 'All the talk of war in the air.'

'War will have to take care of itself. But as for love – well, we only have a little time afforded to us. Go out there and make this a year you'll always remember. I envy you it, my dear. Life's too full of sadnesses we must all endure and overcome. We should each allow ourselves a little joy.'

After Nancy had gone, Mrs Moffatt remained at her desk, turning her barley sugar between her teeth. Remembering Jack made her sentimental. But it wasn't the thought of his voice, nor his touch, that weighed on her as she listened to the girls chattering in the housekeeping lounge on the other side of the door. It wasn't the memory of their wedding day, in the parish church in Pembrokeshire, nor how her father had wept when he walked her down the aisle. No – what weighed on her most was a story even older than that, one she had thought lost to the mists of time.

She reached out for the shreds of paper she'd scattered across her desk. There was a reason, she realised now, that she hadn't burned them in the grate. She was testing herself. Taunting herself, perhaps. Because, as long as these shreds of paper were still in existence, so were the words written across them in a precise and diligent hand.

One by one, Mrs Moffatt gathered the pieces of paper together. One by one, she arranged them on the empty expanse of her desk. Soon, the letter was taking form once again. Her eyes gazed over it, taking in its every declaration, its every question and hidden aside.

*One day I should like to sit with you and drink English tea, and speak of what it was like, on the beaches at Mandurah where I grew up. I would tell you about my summers there, and the wide open sands, or the first job I took on a convoy heading north, or the day my stepbrothers and I took off for the recruiting office and became Australia's newest infantrymen. I should like to tell you about Shep, my boyhood dog, who waited for me every day, all day long, at the bottom of the lane that wound its way down to my school. I should like to tell you about Rachel, my first love. I should tell you about the day I went off to Point Cook, to train with the Royal Australian Air Force. And I should like to tell you about Neville and Charlotte, my ma and pa, who raised me with the courage of their Australian ancestors — but with, I now know, a touch of English class as well. Neville and Charlotte, who looked after me — I swear to you — as if I was their own.*

*One day, I should like to hear about your life too, Emmeline. There are questions I should like to ask, yes, and perhaps there are stories you'd like to tell me too — but, most of all, I only want to look you in the eyes and know you for who you are.*

*I am going to leave this letter, now, in the way that I have long dreamt of leaving it. With these three simple words, which are the sum of a lifetime:*

*Your son,*

*Malcolm*

Little wonder that tearing it up hadn't been enough to drive it from her mind, thought Mrs Moffatt, as she scrambled in her drawers for a roll of medical tape to begin fixing it back together. She'd been tearing up this particular story for nearly thirty-three years. More than half her lifetime had been spent in stopping shreds like these from piecing themselves back together – but what use was tearing up the paper, when not even tearing up the memory itself was enough to keep the truth at bay?

Secrets always came out in the end.

# Chapter Eight

SPRING WAS IN THE AIR.

So was music.

On the north side of Oxford Street, the Starlight Lounge announced itself in a pentacle of lights around a glittering archway, designed to make its dancers feel as if they were waltzing their way into the stars themselves. As the springtime darkness settled over the streets of Fitzrovia, Frank stopped his little crowd outside the archway and said, 'It's a new club. They opened it with a dance for New Year. You won't think it's like the Grand, but it has a different kind of energy. A different feeling. Doesn't it, Rosa?'

Rosa, who had accompanied Frank to the Starlight Lounge three times already, nodded. She loved being here with Frank, even if she did sometimes find him swept away by other partners desperate to be shown the jive and jitterbug he'd been learning from Raymond de Guise. Those dances, so fresh to English shores, were alluring and freeing. They could never dance a jive in the Grand Ballroom. A dance like that was not for lords and ladies. It was for people who knew their worlds might not last forever. It was for people who didn't care for rules and decorum, for being told what to do and when to do it; dances like this freed the soul – and that, Frank had decided, was what a boy like Billy Brogan really needed.

Nancy, Rosa and Ruth were already entering through the silver arch, but Frank held Billy back with a hand on his shoulder. It had only been a short moonlit stroll from the palatial town houses of Mayfair, but Billy had been squirming every step of the way. He'd had his hands stuffed into his pockets; he'd barely spoken a word – and this was so unlike Billy Brogan that the girls had surely started to think he was sulking. Only Frank really knew what manner of malady was affecting his friend.

'It's nerves, Billy. That's all.'

'I've never heard anything so ridiculous in my life,' said Billy, drawing himself up in mock horror. 'Me, Billy Brogan . . . nervous? No, you know me, Frank. I've chinwagged with princes. I've got Mr Charles's ear. You know the kind of jobs I do for him at the hotel. By the Lord, he has me spying on ambassadors and archdukes. Every German dignitary coming into the place this year, he's got me writing down their particulars. I can hardly be nervous of a little dance hall, now, can I?'

But Billy was blathering and fell quiet when Frank took him firmly by the arm.

'We'll have a little drink. That'll give you courage.'

'You haven't been listening to one word I've said. I don't need Dutch courage. I have the courage of the Emerald Isle!'

Frank smiled, and steered him through the arch.

Inside, the Starlight Lounge was already filling up. The great expanse of the glittering dance floor was surrounded by a balustrade painted in perfect black, and the lights in the ceiling above had been arranged to look like the wheeling constellations of a night sky. Some couples were already on the dance floor, just waiting for the band to begin – but Rosa and Ruth had set up camp at one of the tables on its edge, resolving to watch the lights until the revelries really began.

'You're going to have to lighten up, Ruth.' Rosa grinned. 'It's a dance – that's all it is!'

'Then why do I feel like I've been press-ganged?'

Rosa creased her brow in a question.

'Like they used to do to sailors!' Ruth groaned. 'They'd kidnap the drunk ones from the taproom floors, and when they woke up, they'd already be at sea.'

'Ruth, you've been reading too many books! That's why it's good for you to be right here. You can get out of that head of yours. Just enjoy something for once. Trust me! I'm your friend, aren't I? I'm practically your sister. Look, all you need's a drink – and here comes Nancy now.'

Nancy, who had been threading her way back from the bar, sat down at the table with three gin cocktails, each garlanded with a twist of lemon.

'Fancy!' Rosa beamed, and winced as she took her first sip. 'Go on, Ruth, live a little!'

By now, Frank and Billy had emerged through the starlight arch and stood at the other side of the dance floor, looking out across the spectacle.

'Who're you going to dance with, Nance?'

Nancy said, 'I should think I'll enjoy just watching.'

'I'll bet you'll have gentlemen crawling all over you, a fine girl like you!' Rosa seemed to be warming to her theme with each sip. 'Will Raymond be jealous, if you're up dancing with every eligible bachelor in this place?'

Nancy grinned. 'Raymond has nothing to worry about.'

She lifted her finger to flash the engagement ring she was wearing in the spectral light. She got to wear it so rarely, up and down the Buckingham halls – and, even though she was not the sort of girl who'd grown up dreaming of diamonds, even Nancy was drawn in by the way it glittered, and all that that glittering foretold about the future of her life.

'Here, let me have another look,' said Rosa.

'Have you started thinking about a dress?' asked Ruth.

The girls were so lost in the conversation that they hardly even noticed as Frank and Billy sauntered over, rum cocktails in each hand, and deposited themselves into the seats around the table.

'How're you feeling, Ruth?' asked Billy.

Frank could tell he was trying his best, but he'd drawn his seat altogether too close to Ruth and it was plain for everyone – except Billy – that the girl was uncomfortable.

'Like a fish out of water, Billy, but I s'pose you know how that feels as well.'

'Not me, Ruth, never!' Billy exclaimed – and, to Frank's horror, he promptly drained his glass dry. 'See, a young man like me knows where to fit in almost anywhere. High or low, plush hotel or street market, it's all the same to me. I pride myself on it, see. It's how Mr Charles has been tutoring me.'

Frank felt like hanging his head in his hands. It would, he reflected, have been much more endearing if only Billy might have agreed with Ruth, and told her that he felt the same. Then, perhaps, they might have had something to talk about. And, besides, he thought, it was the truth! Billy was so uncomfortable that he could hardly sit still. He needed another drink – and fast. But no sooner had Frank got to his feet, meaning to thread his way back to the bar, than the stage doors opened and, out of a portal of bright light, the orchestra appeared.

'There he is,' said Frank, leaning close into Rosa's ear. 'That's Woodrow Lloyd. Follow his family back far enough, and they were stars of the music halls. His mother starred on Drury Lane. Showmanship runs in families.'

Woodrow Lloyd was leading an eleven-strong orchestra, with trumpeters, trombonists, three saxophonists, and a cornet player sitting at the side of the stage. As for Woodrow himself, the stage at the Starlight Lounge was dominated by his jet-black piano, across which the lights were cascading to give the impression of yet more stars. They looked classical, thought Frank, and in many ways they were – the Woodrow Lloyd Orchestra were regularly played on the radio broadcasts to which Raymond had introduced Frank – but they had the devil in them too. That was what Raymond called it: the devil. And as soon as the music began, the devil appeared.

'Come on, Rosa, let's go!'

Frank took her by the hand and, in a second, they were down on the dance floor. Most orchestras thought they needed to warm their clientele up. They would break out a couple of standards, 'Body and Soul' or 'Embraceable You', and gently up the tempo, leading the dancers on like they were puppets on strings. But not so the Woodrow Lloyd Orchestra. The first song was a veritable assault on the senses. Frank needed no other excuse to start improvising on the dance floor, leading Rosa through an energetic jive, of swinging hips, and flicks and kicks and spins. Nor was he the only one. As Nancy looked down, she could see the jive spreading, like fire, from one couple to another. Her little brother, a superstar in miniature! And what better place for a star than this?

'You fancy it then, Ruth?'

Ruth, who hadn't budged an inch, looked round at Billy.

'Perhaps in a little while, Billy. Why, someone's got to save our table, don't they?'

Billy nodded. 'That's right, and I'm happy to do it with you. It'll give us some time to get better acquainted.' He smiled. Frank had been right; this was easier than he'd thought it would be. All you had to do was *try*. Open your mouth, and sometimes the words just started flowing. 'You know, Ruth, I don't know if I remember you coming to the Buckingham. How long's it been?'

'Oh, a little while. Three years? Four? I can hardly remember.'

'It gets like that, doesn't it? The years just bluster by! Where you from?'

If she wasn't going to dance, she might talk – and this, at least, gave Billy some hope that the evening was not altogether lost. In no short order, Ruth had told him about the family home in Finchley, where she'd lived with her mother and grandmother since she was small.

'I'm not like you, Billy, with all those hundreds of brothers and sisters of yours. Me, I'm an accident, you see. My dad was away at war and . . . Well, I suppose you know how it goes. He never did come back and I never did get to meet him. Mum and Nan looked after me as best they could after that. Kept me on a tight leash, you might say. They were horrified to think of me taking work at the Buckingham. They'd be even more horrified if they could picture me here – in a dance hall, of all places!'

'It's a big wide world,' said Billy, with an air of wisdom (though, in truth, he had no idea what he was being wise about). 'They'd probably like the Buckingham. Have they ever visited?'

'Oh Lord, no! To them, London's the other side of the world. And they're only in Finchley. I think it's because of the Great War. It made them small. They don't like to think about places too far away – and, for them, that means the corner shop at the end of the street.' She paused. 'But I think they would like it in the end, wouldn't they, Nance?'

Nancy had been standing at the balustrade but, when she heard her name, came back to take her seat at the table. Billy frowned; he liked Nancy, had always liked her – perhaps at one point a little too much – but he would much rather have spoken to Ruth alone.

'For instance,' Ruth went on, 'there's a lovely old gentleman I've been taking care of, Mr Bauer. He's the one taken up residence in the old Park Suite. Such a sweet old soul, with his books and his studies and the German newspapers you concierges sort out for him. My mum and nan would approve of that sort of a man. They think the big wide world's full of blackguards, but there are gentle souls out there too. Mr Bauer's one of them. Makes me proud to do his scrubbing, if you know what I mean. He trots down to the Queen Mary every night and just likes to sit there, watching the world go by.'

'That's what you like too, is it?'

Ruth screwed up her face. 'Sorry?'

'Just watching the world go by?' Billy grinned, because he knew – he *just knew* – that this was his moment. 'That's to say, we might get down and dance, if you . . .'

Ruth had frozen and, in that same instant, Nancy – who had been politely staying out of the conversation – stood up, snatched Billy's hand and hoisted him to his feet. 'I'll dance with you, Billy.'

'Oh, that's kind, Nancy, but I was hoping that—'

'I said *I'll* dance, Mr Brogan!'

Before Billy could put up another protest, Nancy was leading him – or perhaps *hauling* him – down the steps, through the balustrade, and into the storm of dancing couples. The Woodrow Lloyd Orchestra had launched into a blistering rendition of 'May Day May', one of their own best known numbers, and as the saxophone took flight, driving Frank and Rosa – somewhere in the heart of the maelstrom – to their most energetic dancing yet, Frank putting his arms around Rosa's waist and lifting her up so that she seemed, almost, to soar with the saxophone's song, Nancy needled Billy in the side and said, 'Billy Brogan, you blunderbuss!'

'What?' he gasped, buffeted on either side by dancing couples. 'What did I do?'

'You're ruining what hopes you ever had with Ruth. You mustn't *bully* her into it. You can't bludgeon somebody into dancing with you. If she wants to dance, she'll dance.'

'Nance, you got it all wrong. It might loosen her up!'

'That's for *her* to decide, you silly boy.'

Nancy dragged him yet further into the throng, then positioned herself so that he might take her in hold. Tentatively he did it, but all the while his eyes were cast over her shoulder, at the table where Ruth now sat alone. She didn't even seem to be watching him.

'Keep your eyes off her. Goodness, you've a brain in there, Billy Brogan! Put it to work. If Ruth wants to dance with you, she'll say it. And if she doesn't . . .'

Billy froze. A terrible truth was dawning on him.

'If she doesn't, Nance, well, then what?'

'Well, then' – she smiled, blunt and simple – 'you can dance with me. I might have a gammy leg, but I daresay I can show you a thing or two.'

Even with her leg complaining as it was tonight, Nancy was a far better dancer than Billy. She could tell that Frank had shown him some steps, because at least he knew how to take her in hold and make an attempt at some simple box-stepping. But every few steps, something seemed to go wrong for him. His feet got tangled with hers, or they got entangled with each other, or he had a sudden outburst of ambition and, seeking to turn Nancy around on the spot, instead ended up with her pinned against the balustrade.

'Don't panic, Billy,' she said. 'The thing is not to panic. You've just got to let it flow. That's what Raymond says.'

'Let it flow?' Billy muttered. 'What's that even mean?'

He tried again, and wound up stranded in the middle of the dance floor, without even Nancy to hold on to. He tried again after that, and somehow found himself beached again. By the time he got back to Nancy, she had been approached by a man in a dark navy suit and silver tie, who promised her a dance of the utmost satisfaction. She politely demurred, and turned back to Billy. This time, when he took her in hold, she was determined to steer him correctly. But, half a song later, they were entangled again – and no amount of encouragement from Nancy, nor cajoling from Frank, could keep Billy on the dance floor.

'Ruth had a lucky escape,' he grunted, dusting himself down from his latest stumble. 'I'm going to sit down, have a drink, and a chinwag. That's what I'm good at. That's what—'

'Oh, Billy,' Nancy ventured. 'Billy, please.'

He turned and, with the dancers fanning out around him, gave an ostentatious little bow. *Beaten*, thought Nancy with a wry smile, *but not yet defeated – that was Billy Brogan all over*. And yet, as he tramped back through the dancing throng, she fancied she could see the gears turning in Billy's mind, churning up all sorts of troubling thoughts. No matter how charming a person was, there was one thing you truly couldn't disguise: even worse than having two left feet on the dance floor was being embarrassed about it. Being embarrassed was like poison to a dancer. And the way Billy had pushed his hands into his pockets, feigning nonchalance, told Nancy that he was embarrassed beyond measure.

By the time Billy was climbing the steps out of the dance floor, he was already rehearsing the things he'd say to Ruth.

'Better off just sitting here, I should think,' he said, under his breath. 'See, I'm used to dancing on a sprung floor – just like they have in the Grand. These ordinary floors, they don't feel right to me. My body just doesn't like them. No, only the finer things for a gentleman of my estimation.'

He was so focused on rehearsing these lines that he was almost at the table by the time he realised Ruth was no longer alone. Sitting by her side, and evidently engaged in a conversation much more riotous than any Billy had ever dredged out of her, was a petite dark-haired girl with striking blue eyes. Her dark hair was cascading around her shoulders and, in the starry lights of the club, the silver pin on her collar glittered like a cluster of diamonds. Billy saw, with some surprise, that her fingernails were painted with tiny scenic landscapes. Evidently, this girl had some elegance of her own.

'Oh, Billy,' Ruth began, on seeing him approach, 'meet Martha. Martha's like me – not much for dancing.'

'Oh Lord, no!' Martha crowed. Her Estuary accent was even stronger than Rosa's. 'My husband drags me along, of course, but we have to bring my sister with us. They're dancing down there right now.' And she lifted her dainty hand to wave at him, somewhere below.

'Oh, stop it, Martha!' Ruth cried, throwing her head back to laugh. 'You're distracting them!'

Billy had never heard Ruth laugh so uproariously before. It was a beautiful sound. He took his seat and picked up one of the glasses left there. It was probably Frank's, but that didn't matter; Billy drained it in one.

'You should try it,' he began. 'Dancing, I mean.'

'Oh, I've tried it,' Martha returned. 'It's just not for me, and there's not a thing in the world that's going to change that.'

'Oh, I don't know,' said Ruth. 'Sometimes I think, if I had a little more confidence, it's the sort of thing I might like.' She gave a non-committal shrug. 'Well, maybe one day. Right now, I'm glad there's others like me in these clubs.'

And she reached out and squeezed Martha by the hand.

'It's not so hard if you do want to try it, Ruth,' said Billy. 'It's just about . . . letting go.'

'Letting go?'

Billy floundered as he searched for the next words. What was it Frank had tried to tell him? That dancing wasn't about being so studied and practised that things never went wrong. That dancing was about . . . the experience, not the art. Was that it?

'Well, you know, it's all about the heart,' he said, and clutched two hands over his chest. 'It all happens in here.'

That was the thing about conversation, the thing at which Billy truly excelled: if you had enough confidence, you could make the world believe almost anything at all.

'The heart?' Martha said, squinting up at him.

'That's right.' Billy slipped into the seat beside Ruth. 'You've just got to let go and find a way to love it. Now, Ruth, I know that sounds frightening – but it's nothing of the sort. You've just got to . . .' He sent his mind cartwheeling backwards, searching for something affecting and profound that he might say. 'You've got to lose your fear. Shed your inhibitions. The music wants to get into your body, you see. You've just got to give yourself over to it. Let it flow . . .'

Billy smiled to himself. It was good to feel confident again. Dancing might not have come easily to him, but bluster most certainly did.

And then Martha spluttered with sudden laughter.

'That's what you were doing down there, was it? Giving yourself to the music! Well, now I've heard everything! Now, even *I* want to dance!' Her eyes fell on the dance floor, picking out her husband and sister in the throng. 'Hugo! Hugo, get up here!'

Down on the dance floor, the man named Hugo let go of his partner and picked his way through the dancers to meet his wife.

'Here – Billy, is it? – tell my Hugo what you just told me. Tell him all about the way to dance.'

But Billy, who knew he was being made a fool of, simply said, 'I'll leave you to it, shall I? There's things more important in this world than dancing, you know. Don't you know a war's coming?'

105

He was purpling with indignation as he marched away. He scarcely even heard Ruth calling after him, nor the apology she was trying to make as he scythed his way back through the dancers and inveigled his way directly between Rosa and Frank, reaching the height of their dance.

'Bill,' Frank began, seeing the way he was holding himself so rigidly, 'what's happened?'

'I got a proposition for you, Frank Nettleton.' Taking Frank by the arm, he hauled him to the edge of the dance floor. 'You want to become a hotel dancer, don't you? You want to start doing the demonstrations in the Grand, and maybe even one day dance with the guests at the balls as well? Well, don't you?'

'You know I do, Billy, but what's this . . . ?'

'Well, see.' Billy's words were coming out like artillery fire, such was the power of his indignation. 'I'm a social climber, aren't I? I'm a confidant of Mr Charles. I'm going places at that hotel – you see if I don't! And maybe there's ways I can help you. A word in Mr Charles's ear, perhaps. A favour for a favour – that's how it works at the Buckingham. So, listen here, Frank. If I help you get a try-out in the Grand, you help me do some dancing of my own.'

'I already showed you a few steps.'

'Not just a few steps!' Billy declared. 'I want you to teach me, just like Raymond de Guise has been teaching you. Now, I know I'll never be a master – I know that – but if you can teach me a tenth of what Raymond's teaching you, well, I'll be able to hold my own in a place like this. And Ruth up there, she says . . . Well, she says all she needs is a bit of confidence, and then maybe she'll dance too. So that's the deal – you'll give me that confidence, and I'll pass it on to Ruth, and then we'll all come back here, all of us, and dance the night away – and I won't once end up flat on my face and, who knows, maybe, *maybe* then, Ruth might want to go for a Sunday stroll with me, or . . .'

Billy had quite run out of steam. His words petered into nothingness, and for a time both he and Frank stood there, with the light of the stars cascading over them and the music of a strident Argentine tango filling the air. Rosa backed away, hiding a smile.

'So that's the deal, Frank. Shake on it?'

Frank clasped Billy's hand in his own and shook it firmly.

It was the very first time he'd felt Billy Brogan trembling, or seen him afraid.

June 1938

# Chapter Nine

IDSUMMER'S NIGHT WAS A LONG time in coming. Hélène danced with guests in the ballroom. She put on the show, as always she did, making them feel talented and proud, able – by tricks of posture and bearing – to make it seem as if even the decrepit old Graf König, visiting from his Bavarian estates, was gliding on air. She did it all with a smile, because that was what she'd been practising her whole life.

But, by midsummer's night, Hélène was tired, more tired than she'd ever been before.

Today, when the demonstration dances were done for the afternoon, she retreated to a corner of the dressing rooms and took from her clutch bag the letter she'd been clinging to all week. It was a short thing, perhaps abrupt, the culmination of weeks of courage and self-control. As the girls fanned out around them, Hélène dared to lift the letter to her lips and breathe in its musty pinewood scent. No doubt the girls around her thought she was breathing in the scent of some lover. None among them knew it was a letter from home, with all the scents of her childhood kneaded into its grain. Nobody here knew it came from her Aunt Lucy, telling her that they accepted her invitation; that tonight she and Hélène's own mother would visit the Buckingham Hotel and dine in the Candlelight Club. The thought was so fragile that she hadn't even confided in Louis Kildare.

Presently, Raymond appeared. He'd taken off the charcoal-grey tail-suit jacket he'd worn earlier and, with his collar undone, he looked almost as if he didn't belong here. Yet, even as relaxed as he was, there was something effortless about Raymond's elegance. Hélène wondered if the man had ever felt as knotted inside as she did now. Everyone had secrets to preserve, but tonight she felt hers more keenly than ever.

'Perhaps we should rehearse again, Miss Marchmont,' he said, with a courteous smile that drew the attention of the other girls instead. Honestly, the way they made eyes at him! Hélène had a mind to grab hold of them and tell them that there was a world beyond the ballroom, that they ought to go out and live, live, live, before something came in to sweep it all away.

She had already crammed the letter back into her clutch bag and was up on her feet by the time she replied. It was, she admitted to herself – and she chastened herself immediately for being so unkind – difficult to see Raymond floating on air, his head full of thoughts of his wedding, when everything inside her was hardening to stone.

'Raymond, we'll work wonders tonight – but I can't rehearse, not again. I need to rest. I can feel it in my body.'

The smile left Raymond's face. 'Hélène, are you . . . ?'

'I'm fine,' she promised him, and laughed. 'We're just not as young as we used to be.'

'Oh, Hélène, we're in the prime of our lives!'

She grinned. 'You'll always be in your prime. Won't he, girls?'

And as Mathilde and the other girls gathered around, each wondering if they might take Hélène's place and rehearse with him this afternoon instead, Hélène quietly slipped away. From now, until the twilight settled over Berkeley Square, there would just be Hélène and her letter. Sometimes, all you really needed was a few quiet hours where you didn't have to pretend.

Hélène's mother and aunt were already in the Candlelight Club when she arrived, just as the afternoon was paling towards night. The doors of the Candlelight Terrace were still open, the balcony gardens heady with the scent of the summer blossoms. And there they were, sitting at a table by the open terrace doors.

Hélène stilled, lingering in the shadows where she might not immediately be seen. The Candlelight Club was both a cosy spot for an evening aperitif, complete with private booths and cubbyholes where guests could gather, and a stylish modern lounge, with a smooth mahogany bar that ran around the room's circumference. Hélène's heart had constricted as soon as she saw them sitting there, for she'd asked Ramon, the head waiter, to reserve one of the candlelit cubbyholes instead, some place where their conversation might go on undisturbed. And yet, there they were, in the heart of the club itself.

Marie looked smaller, somehow, than Hélène remembered. She was quite certain that four years could not do that to a woman, so perhaps it was some trick of her imagination, making her remember her mother as she'd seen her when she was a girl – for that was the only way she liked to remember her at all, back before recrimination and regret.

At Marie's side was Aunt Lucy and, to Hélène, she looked the same as ever she had. Lucy had the same white-blonde hair that Hélène had been fortunate enough to inherit but, where Hélène wore hers short, Lucy's was a waterfall reaching the small of her back. Hélène had inherited the same regal height as Lucy too. They had the same slender wrists, the same dazzling eyes. Lucy had been beautiful, once. That she'd remained unmarried was an oddity that nobody in the family had ever been able to understand.

Hélène reached the table and waited, nervously, until they looked up.

'Hélène,' Lucy stuttered, as soon as she saw her. 'Oh, my dear Hélène . . .'

That was the thing that made Hélène crumble – Aunt Lucy's voice; she hadn't heard it in years. You could only keep voices in your memory for so long. After that, they fluttered away. Hearing it now, she realised how much she'd forgotten. That fragility in the way the voice wavered; that strength in the way it held true: was ever a thing more of a Marchmont trait than this?

'Aunt Lucy,' she said, formally – and though Lucy seemed ready to take her niece in her arms, the brittle way Hélène held herself kept her at bay. 'Mother,' she said, turning.

'Hélène,' her mother ventured, in a tone so much more measured than Lucy's, a voice uncertain of what it was going to say, and how. 'You look well, my dear.'

'Isn't it beautiful here?' Lucy went on, if only to fill the silence that threatened to envelop them all. By now, Marie had risen to her feet too, and together the three women stood around the table, facing the darkening light over Berkeley Square. 'All these flowers, I've never seen the like!' Lucy continued. 'Do you remember, Hélène, how your mother and father stayed here once? I've been longing to come here ever since – and now, here I am.'

It was a legend in the family, Hélène remembered. Her father had stayed at luxurious hotels all over the Continent – and, indeed, had taken his young wife (his second, after his first died young), to the Paris Ritz on the first night of their honeymoon. But, in those days, he'd kept a pied-à-terre on Baker Street and the thought of staying in a London hotel had always seemed a decadence too far. The night they'd stayed at the Buckingham had, Hélène recalled, been the night of Marie's birthday, when Hélène was younger than Sybil was now. It held such a special place in their memories that, when Hélène first announced she was to join the new Grand Ballroom there, it had seemed the most perfect synchronicity of their lives.

*But of course*, thought Hélène, *they could have come at any time in the last few years.*

Sir Derek and Lady Marchmont had more than enough social standing to have graced the Grand on a Saturday night, or to have dined in the Queen Mary Restaurant. That they hadn't done so was deliberate. Every day was just another decision to stay away.

'Why don't we sit?' Lucy asked.

'Tell me,' Hélène began, 'how did you come to be seated here? I'd reserved one of the corners, where we could—'

'Oh, Hélène,' Marie chimed in. 'Why a dark corner when there's the beauty of the terrace to look out on? I sat here with your father, you know. Why come at all, if we're just to sit in a corner?'

*Why indeed?* thought Hélène – and the idea crept into her head that they'd have been better off at Simpson's in the Strand. The strength she'd sought to draw from being here, in her own world, seemed suddenly lacking.

So she sat down.

It was tentative at first. There was so much that could not be said that the silences stretched long. Avoiding any mention of Sir Derek, they spoke about the Candlelight Club itself. They talked their way through the cocktail menu, as if this was the most important thing on earth. The conversation wandered to the Grand, and the stories Lucy had read in the society pages about the debonair dancing star Raymond de Guise, still being courted – or so the tittle-tattle said – to go to California and become a star of the silver screen.

When Hélène told them that Raymond had resolved to remain at the Buckingham, and that he was doing it all in the name of true love – for he'd lost his heart to a chambermaid, and asked her to be his wife – Marie arched one of her eyebrows and said, 'Well, love will make a man do the most foolish things. You'd have thought a man like this Mr de Guise might have found a chambermaid a bit beneath him, don't you think?'

'Is that so?' said Hélène.

She hadn't meant to say it so severely, but by the looks of the couple on one of the neighbouring tables, she'd spoken louder than she'd thought.

She lowered her voice. 'Do you know, Mother, I sometimes wonder what a person with an attitude like that can know about love at all. Deference, yes, and obligation, certainly. But love? It crosses boundaries, doesn't it? It crosses worlds. And isn't that how it's meant to be?'

'Hélène, my dear,' her mother began, 'I know how angry you must be. That isn't why we came. We don't want anger. We just want . . .'

It was on the tip of Hélène's tongue to start talking about Sidney, and all that she'd sacrificed to be with him. Not her inheritance, but the love of her family, the love of her father, the sense of belonging and home that she used to have – all of it, she'd given away freely, so that she could be with him. Everywhere she looked, people were swooning over Raymond de Guise. How wonderful it was, they all said, that he'd given up the chance of a life in the sun, Hollywood glamour and style, for Nancy Nettleton. Well, what did they know of sacrifice? When you scarcely saw your daughter so that you could pay for her to live a good life, when you'd forsaken the very family that reared you because they couldn't stoop to give the man you loved a chance – Hélène knew about 'sacrifice' all too well.

She was growing too hard. Very consciously, she tried to settle herself. But the clock on the wall was ticking, counting down the hour until she had to return to the Grand, and there was still so much she wanted to say.

She reached into her clutch bag and brought out a small leather folder. Unbuckling the clasp, she set it down on the table and opened it up, to reveal within a little book of portraits, taken by the photographer at his studio on Clapham Common. They were nearly a year old now – how quickly the time flew by! – but, in each of them, Sybil sat delicately in Hélène's lap, against a succession of backdrops depicting Venice, London, and a beautiful glittering seaside cove.

'Mother, this is your granddaughter.'

Marie produced a pair of spectacles – she'd never worn spectacles before – and balanced them on her nose. Then, with an impassive face, she looked over the pictures.

'She looks like you, Hélène,' she finally said.

'She does not.' Hélène smiled. 'She looks like Sidney.'

There was stony silence.

'And how are you finding motherhood?'

'I can't lie to you both. It hasn't been easy. A pregnancy in secret. A life lived the same way. After Sidney died, I thought – how easily one falls from grace. There was I, one year, dancing in the Grand

Ballroom and holidaying with you each summer in Nice. And by New Year – pregnant and alone, and faced with—' She stopped, if only to gather herself. 'I'd thought to take lodgings in Lambeth. Somewhere to have my baby alone. But I hadn't counted on the kindness of Noelle and Maurice. They're Sidney's parents. They gave me a home, while I had my daughter. Mr Charles was convinced easily enough. I made it known I'd been invited to California, to audition for the screen – and the chance of this hotel having given rise to a new star, what that might do for the ball-room's reputation, was too much for him to ignore. But I wasn't in California. I was on Brixton Hill, giving birth to my Sybil.' She stopped. 'I wrote to you, of course. You never replied.'

'Hélène, you must know it hasn't been easy for us either—'

'Easy for you?' Hélène seethed. 'Look at her! She's your . . .' Remembering herself and where she was, she brought her voice down to a low whisper. She'd been a fool, to bring them here. But everywhere else – Simpson's or Kettner's, the places they used to go – spoke of them; here, at the Buckingham, was Hélène's alone. 'She's beautiful, and she's funny, and she deserves so much more than I've been able to give her.'

She trembled. Lucy reached across to take her hand and, although some instinct told Hélène to wrench it away, she let her. Always, inside her, those two forces: to cling on, or to simply let go.

'How is my father?' she finally whispered.

'He's surviving,' Marie replied. She said it with a ferocity that was not meant for Hélène, but only in defiance of the forces that were snatching her husband away from her, one day at a time. 'His lungs are old. His heart is strong, as yours is, Hélène, but it beats too slowly now. The pneumonia he lived through, but

118

the damage is done. Parts of him are giving up. Some days, he gets out of bed. Others, we take him soup and read to him. He's dying, Hélène. There's no defeating what's coming.'

Silence, all around. Hélène did not know how to feel, and this was the most perplexing thing of all – because neither sadness, nor relief, swept over her now; just a long, echoing emptiness, like the Grand Ballroom after the last waltzes were danced.

'Does he know you're here?' she finally asked.

'Not yet, Hélène,' said Lucy, with a more consoling tone. 'We thought – perhaps you didn't want to see us. Or perhaps, when you did, you'd realise you never wanted to again. His heart is old, and we did not think it could take the disappointment.'

'Disappointment?' Hélène breathed. '*His* disappointment?'

'I meant to say, if you didn't want to visit him one last time, before he—'

'So it's all on me,' Hélène laughed, with a bitter tone. 'All these years, every day a chance to come and see me, to come and make up for what he did. And yet it's all up to *me* whether he gets to die forgiven or—'

'Hélène,' Lucy began, when her mother turned her face away, brittle with tears, 'we didn't want to upset you. Look at you. Look what a life you've made! It must have been so hard, doing it alone.'

'I haven't done it alone,' she said. 'Sybil *does* have a family who love her. Her father's family.'

'Hélène Marchmont,' her mother interjected. 'That was poisonous.'

*It really wasn't*, thought Hélène. Acknowledging the love Sidney's parents had shown her, while acknowledging the love she'd lacked from her own, wasn't an attack; it was only an observation.

'What do you want from us, Hélène?'

'Want?' snapped Hélène. 'Mother, I gave up wanting years ago.'

'Well, what would you have me do? He's an old man. He deserves his fitting end, doesn't he? To go off into the great unknown, having seen you one last time. He *cherished* you, Hélène. Don't you remember that?'

'I do,' she whispered, 'and that's why it hurts. That's why it hurts more than you can know. That you all – all three of you' – and she turned her shoulder on even Lucy – 'locked the door on us. She was an unborn child.'

'Hélène, you're painting it all wrong. We came here to put all this behind us, not to dredge it up. We all deserve that chance, don't we?'

'Not if you can't face it, Mother.'

'You were raised in a good Christian household, Hélène. You were raised to understand forgiveness. And don't you dare tell me it's only us who need forgiving. You played your part in it too, as I remember. So we can let bygones be bygones and you can come and do this service for your dying father, or we can—'

'Service?' Hélène gasped.

'Now, Marie,' Lucy interjected, placing a hand on both of their forearms, 'that wasn't what we said, was it? Hélène, we didn't come to force you. You're a strong woman, and you're not to be forced. We came only to see if there was some crack left open, a place where the light might get in, somewhere that there might be just a little hope that some good might come out of this, after all this time.'

Even now, Lucy looked hopeful.

'I would have thought it might begin with an apology,' said Hélène – and, feeling sure of herself now, feeling certain what she wanted, she drew herself up high. 'An apology for throwing out your only daughter, for no sin other than that she'd fallen in love. An apology for disowning your unborn grandchild, and all because—'

'Oh, Hélène!' screamed Lady Marchmont, and as she turned suddenly in her seat, her cuff caught her cocktail glass and sent gin and vermouth splashing over the table. 'Listen to yourself! You're as sanctimonious as you used to be precocious! Your father didn't disown you because he's an evil man. He's a good man. He's the very best of us. He loved you, Hélène, more than you could ever know. But you broke his heart, you sorry girl. You broke his heart on the day you came home to tell him you were having a black man's baby!'

Silence.

There was silence in the Candlelight Club.

Every eye was on them. Every guest, every drinker, every waiter. Up at the bar, Ramon and Diego, the cocktail waiter, stared. Aunt Lucy stared. And Hélène Marchmont herself, feeling the pressure of countless eyes boring into her, stared on in silence, as her mother's exclamation echoed all around.

In the emptiness, Hélène's eyes lifted to the clock hanging above the terrace door.

'Mother, I am needed in the ballroom,' she said with breathless eloquence.

Then she was up and on her heels, marching back across the silence of the Candlelight Club, down, down, down through the Buckingham's layers, and across the black and white chequers of the reception hall – where Billy, who had once learned the very same secret rippling out across the hotel, watched with a curious gaze as she disappeared around the back of the ballroom and into the dressing rooms.

The troupe was already gathered for the evening's delights. Hélène had wanted to find Louis Kildare, but she had come too late, for the Archie Adams Orchestra had already taken their places on stage. Quickly she began to get changed.

As soon as she was done, Raymond rushed up to her and took her by the hand.

'Thank goodness. I was beginning to think I'd have to ask Mathilde to step into the breach.' He paused, sensing her rigidity. All elegance, all poise, had seemingly deserted Hélène Marchmont. 'Are you unwell?'

Out in the Grand Ballroom, the band had struck up, a fervent blast of piano and trombone.

'It's nothing,' she said, as, statuesque, she walked with Raymond to the head of the column of dancers, ready to go through the doors.

'Something's wrong. I know that there is. I can feel it in your body. Whatever it is, you're holding it in. Hélène? You've got to let it out—'

She shook her head, squeezed his hand, commanded him to stop asking by the tear-filled look of her eyes.

'Let's dance,' she said – and, in that same moment, the doors opened up, the ballroom crowd put up a roar of applause, and out they twirled, Raymond de Guise and Hélène Marchmont, gliding out across the gilded dance floor as if that was the only thing that mattered in all of the world.

# Chapter Ten

T HERE WAS SOMETHING ABOUT RETURNING to the Daughters of Salvation that restored Nancy's sense of equilibrium, her certainty about her purpose in life. As she stepped out of the taxicab and vanished into the alley off Whitechapel Road, she felt her heart soaring. It wasn't that all the excitement about the wedding wasn't real; it was only that, sometimes – just sometimes – the chatter in the chambermaids' kitchenette, or the way the girls wanted to look at her engagement ring, or to talk about what dress she might want to wear, got too much, and she needed reminding – as, she told herself, everyone does – that there are scales in the world: that one person's day of joy was somebody else's black night of despair.

There was a time when she'd come here three times a week, snatching what little sleep she could between her late night returns to the Buckingham and the pre-dawn breakfasts in the housekeeping lounge. Now that George Peel's investment had afforded Miss Edgerton the means to employ a host of other helpers and attendants, Nancy frequented the Daughters of Salvation less often, arriving only at the end of each month to balance the ledger books, or perhaps on an off-day – when Raymond had not planned some wonderful excursion for them, cruising along the river into Kingston, or to visit the Royal Observatory in Greenwich – to muck in with the rest. She stopped to look up at the frontage of the building. The gutters had been replaced since she'd last come here, and the window frames, which had been rotting, were new as well. Artie Cohen stood there, as he always did, at the top of the steps – and even the clothes he was wearing looked new. There was no other word for it: clean-shaven and with his hair shorn short, Artie Cohen looked *smart*.

'There she is!' Artie declared, and rampaged down the steps to meet her. 'My very own sister!'

'Oh, do stop it, Artie!' Nancy laughed. 'I've had quite enough of that at the hotel.'

'You're the gossip of the hour, are you?'

'The day, the week, the month . . .'

Artie rolled his eyes. 'I'll bet Ray's lapping it up.'

It would have been a lie to say that the excitement wasn't constantly bubbling up in Nancy as well. Sometimes, when she awoke, she caught herself thinking: *this time next year, I'll be Mrs Nancy de Guise* – and the idea still had the power to perplex her. On the mornings when their schedules aligned and she was able to spend the night with Raymond, she would wake and realise: this is going to be my life.

'Raymond's got me dancing again,' Nancy said. She could still feel the persistent niggle in her leg, but when she was in his hold it didn't seem to matter. He had her soaring. 'You'll have to learn a few steps too, Artie, if you're to be . . .' Her words faltered.

Artie shrugged. 'He hasn't asked me to be his best man,' he said awkwardly, shuffling from side to side. 'I s'pose he's just biding his time. Either that or he's already got his old man de la Motte signed up.'

Nancy touched him on the forearm. 'I'm sorry, Artie.'

'Well, he ought to know which side his bread's buttered on, oughtn't he? A man like Georges de la Motte won't give Ray the kind of send-off he really deserves. It'd be canapés and champagne and dinner at the Academy, I should think. As for me, I'd throw him a night like the Cohen boys used to have . . .' He spluttered to a stop. 'All in good taste, o' course, Nancy. I wouldn't want to damage the groom before the wedding, would I?'

Although Nancy didn't think he had already asked his old mentor to be his best man, something in the pit of her stomach told her it was a decision Raymond was deliberately not making.

'Come on, Nance, there's lots of work in there to keep you busy tonight. I'll show you through.'

Artie put one hand in the small of her back, as if he might propel her through the chapel doors, and with the other he pushed them open, revealing the half-moon hall at the head of the Daughters of Salvation.

In a horseshoe around the edge of the hall, all the volunteers and attendants of the charity were gathered. The moment they saw her, a great cheer rose up, echoing in the rafters high above.

Nancy staggered.

'Fooled you, Miss Nettleton!' Artie crowed. 'I'm pleased as punch with how that went. Give them a tap on the window, make sure they get themselves in position, keep you nattering until it's time to go through.'

'Congratulations, Nancy!'

There were two dozen volunteers and paid attendants gathered in the reception hall, and out of the heart of them strode Vivienne Edgerton. Tonight she looked positively dowdy – and this, Nancy knew, was deliberate, for she had long ago sold all the ball gowns and nearly all the day dresses she used to buy with her stepfather's allowance. In a brown Mother Hubbard dress, with a high neck and loose-fitting sleeves, she looked almost Victorian. Her hair, still the colour of vibrant flame, was tied up in a bun and netted as well; evidently, Vivienne had been working in the kitchens tonight.

'Nancy,' she said, as she presented her with a bouquet of pink peonies, crowned with a card. 'From all of us, with love.'

Nancy could not deny the beauty of the bouquet. A gift like this from the staff at the Daughters of Salvation meant everything to her. She opened the card, saw the dozens of signatures written there and realised that this gift was not only from the staff but from the various patients and other derelicts who relied on the Daughters for so much of their daily sustenance. This made her heart soar even higher – to think that so many people who had come and gone through these doors remembered her. She pressed it to her breast.

'Thank you,' she announced.

She was about to walk through, when Vivienne put a hand on her arm and held her back.

'Not so fast, Miss Nettleton.' She smiled and, unfurling a leaf of paper, she began to read aloud. 'The Daughters of Salvation, our beloved home and the cause to which each of us here are devoting our lives, predates the appearance of myself and our dear Miss Nettleton, standing here at my side.' She looked sidelong at Nancy, her eyes twinkling. 'Our beloved Mary Burdett is the one who gave birth to our proud organisation, and deserves all the thanks in the world for originating something so special, so splendid, here in Whitechapel's heart. But I want to talk a little, tonight, about my own introduction to the Daughters of

Salvation – and how this would never have happened without the woman standing at my side, Miss Nancy Nettleton, soon to become Mrs Nancy de Guise.'

Across the hall, the cheers went up again.

'You see, there was a time, not so very long ago, when I myself was enslaved to the scourge of opiates. I lived from day to day, spending my stepfather's money, caring only for myself, in a spiral of self-destruction so steep and sheer that there was no hope that I would ever come out of it.' She paused. 'Then along came Nancy Nettleton. It was Nancy who picked me up and set me back on my feet. It was Nancy who, when I declared my intention to support the Daughters of Salvation with what income I could provide, accompanied me here on so many lonely nights. Put simply, the Daughters of Salvation as we know it would not exist without the estimable lady at my side – and, I remain quite certain, neither would I.' Vivienne's voice had dropped to a reverential tone, but in her next words she exploded with pride and excitement once more. 'If ever a soul should deserve good fortune, good health and love in this life, it is this one. Nancy,' she said, turning directly to her, 'we, all of us here – but especially me – wish you and Raymond all the love in the world. Ladies and gentlemen, Nancy Nettleton!'

The cheering erupted for a final time. In the chaos, Nancy saw Warren Peel lifting his hands up high to applaud. She saw Mary Burdett and her young crowd, aprons on and sleeves rolled up, grinning from ear to ear. She saw Artie putting his fingers to his lips to let out a shrill whistle. She let it crash over her and thought: *well, maybe it's all right to be the centre of attention, just for once.*

'Nancy,' Vivienne said, when the cheering had started to fade, 'there'll be no champagne corks being popped tonight. Our work goes on, as it must. But there are pots of tea, and there are cakes galore. And there's fresh cream and strawberries – and all the good wishes in the world!'

The Daughters of Salvation was busy long into the night. Wedding festivities or not, the good work went on. Nancy, who spent the first hour in the back office with Vivienne, listened to the hum of activity through the walls and felt the thrill of it, just like she had in the organisation's first tentative months. Now, volunteers flitted in and out, voices called out in celebration, and Warren made two appearances, seeking Vivienne's advice about the renovation they were making to the back storeroom.

'But of course,' Vivienne said, when Warren had taken his instructions and hurried on, 'in the longer term, it's bigger premises we'll need. Do you remember the Rowton House we visited, on the Camden Road?' Nancy did; it had been one of their first ports of call when Vivienne had decided she would invest in a charitable concern. 'We might not be nearly as big as that sprawling place, but imagine if we had its resources. All the good we could do.'

Nancy said, 'Warren's making a place for himself here.' She remembered when he'd been found, lying bootless and blue in the cold, robbed by the same men who plied him with the opiates he craved. 'Is he working every week?'

'Every *night*,' said Vivienne – and Nancy believed she could even see a smile playing in the corners of Miss Edgerton's lips.

'*Every* night?'

Vivienne shrugged. 'I can only presume he enjoys the company.'

After the month's books were balanced, Nancy drifted on, taking in first the bedrooms behind the partitions in the main hall, then the kitchens, where a team of young women were hard at work, chopping onions, peeling potatoes, and rendering down the bacon fat donated by the local butcher. Finally, she passed out of the back of the old chapel into the courtyard garden at its rear. It was here that Mary Burdett presided over the wood-burning range, with two other girls attending her, and one of Artie's friends standing sentry – an old ne'er-do-well from his Pentonville days, who went by the improbable name of Fletcher Crook. The back courtyard wall was open to the alley behind it, and through the old oaken doors tramped a motley collection of the hungry and destitute.

As the line moved on, Mary left her girls at the range and joined Nancy on the steps overlooking the yard.

'So how do you like your party, Nancy?'

There was bunting strung up around the courtyard. Mary and the others had stitched it themselves. To OUR ONE AND ONLY NANCY NETTLETON it read, the letters surrounded by embroidered flowers and stars. Underneath, the line of derelicts and down-and-outs snaked around the yard. Little groups had gathered around its edges, partaking of strawberries and cake as if they were gifts from Heaven itself.

'It's exactly my kind of party.' She smiled. 'May I?'

She gestured to the range, as if she was eager to take her place among the other girls – and Mary, who had never been known to say 'no' to Nancy Nettleton, sent the others back to the kitchens for more supplies, so that she and Nancy could work together.

'It feels like we've been here an age,' said Nancy, 'though it's scarcely been a year. Vivienne's looking for new premises. You and she must have talked about that.'

'We have,' said Mary. 'Too many times to count. She's right, of course. But I'm old, and I get sentimental about this place. If it has to move on – well, that's what happens in life. But it doesn't mean you can't feel a little heartache over it.' She paused, filling another bowl with carrot and potato soup and passing it to one of the eager guests. 'What about you, Nancy? Is it . . . time to move on for you as well?'

Nancy, who was busy carving up loaves of yesterday's bread, paused.

'Mary, I don't intend to go anywhere.'

'Things will change, you know.'

The next vagrant in the queue opened his lips in a toothless smile when he saw Nancy, and blathered out congratulations of his own.

'Thank you, Hamish,' she said, ladling an extra carrot into his bowl. 'And God bless you, sir.' Then she turned back to Mary. 'People keep saying that to me. I'm in love, Mary. I'm getting married. But that doesn't mean I have to stop being me.'

'You'd be a fool to think things won't change, though. That's just a fact of life. I never had that problem, of course, on account of never meeting the right gentleman. But, Nancy, it wouldn't be right to think things can just carry on as they've been. You'll have a different kind of life. Different needs. A young mother can't be on the streets of Whitechapel after dark like this. A young mother ought to be at home, looking after her dearest, making them a fine home, filling them with love – so they don't end up like young Warren in there, neglected and looking for love in some opium den.'

Nancy said nothing, only continued to serve the soup.

'Nancy,' Mary whispered, her voice laced with regret. 'I can tell I've upset you. Nancy?'

'Let's not speak about this.'

'I know how much you love this place, my girl. I can feel it in your every breath. But we've got to be realistic. You'll have other priorities. Looking after your young ones. The Daughters will need to make other arrangements, my dear, if—'

The ladle clattered out of Nancy's hands, ringing as it struck the stones at her feet.

'Whoever said I was going to have a baby straight away?' she demanded. 'I'm not a prude, Mary.' She lowered her voice. 'Raymond and I are careful. There are ways . . .'

'You'll make such a good mother,' one of the girls chipped in, arriving from the kitchen with a tureen full of fresh soup.

'Isn't anyone listening to me?' Nancy gasped, as the girl trotted back into the chapel. 'Anyone would think I was being sent to the country to recuperate from ill health. I'm getting married. It's a joyous thing. It doesn't mean I'm becoming Raymond's personal chambermaid, does it? It doesn't mean I have to give up everything I've been working for, everything I've dreamed about, to make him dinner and have his babies as soon as the ring's on my finger.' Realising she was speaking too loudly, Nancy composed herself, served another visitor, and whispered, 'I see all that in my future, Mary. I see me and Raymond with our own little dance troupe, two boys and two girls, and a house in the country, but . . . not yet.'

For a time, they simply served soup together – until, at last, Mary said, 'Nancy, my dear – are you sure you're ready to be married at all?'

'I am!' Nancy proclaimed. 'But it's because I love him, Mary, and because he loves me. Not because he wants to lock me up and throw away the key. Not because he wants to be a father by next summer, and a father twice over by the summer after that. Not because he wants to stop me coming here, or working at the Buckingham, or – why, doing all the things that make me *me*. It's *me* he fell in love with, isn't it? He doesn't want to change all that, now, does he?'

But long into the night, as she served the last guests at the Daughters of Salvation, as she shared a taxicab back to the Buckingham with Vivienne, as she crept up the service stairs and slipped into her quarters behind the chambermaids' kitchenette, that simple question replayed itself in her mind. Because, if that was what married life had to be like, if there really was no other way, then perhaps Nancy really wasn't ready for marriage at all . . .

# Chapter Eleven

'SIT DOWN, MISS MARCHMONT. We have much to discuss.'
Hélène lingered in the doorway of the hotel director's office, listening to Billy Brogan's nervous footfalls retreating along the corridor. It seemed fitting that Billy had been the one sent to fetch her; he had known about her secret for two years already and, in all that time, had never breathed a word. You did not shoot the messenger, not if you had any honour left within you – and, if she was to lose everything tonight, Hélène meant, at least, to maintain her honour. She stepped into the office and closed the door behind her.

'Mr Charles, I mustn't stay long. I'm due to take to the dance floor in half an hour.'

'I'm afraid this can't wait, Miss Marchmont. Perhaps you might take a seat?'

There was an anxious cast to Maynard Charles's face. The decanter of brandy was open on the desk, and evidently he'd already drunk a stiff measure because a crystal tumbler was sitting empty by its side.

'You understand, of course, why you're here.'

'Mr Charles, let me begin by saying—'

'That you lied to me, Hélène?'

133

Hélène had no reply to that. She let it wash over her instead, and waited until Mr Charles continued. The old man had been kind to her in the past, but it occurred to her now, watching him pace the windowed wall with his hands folded in the small of his back, that he was only ever at his kindest when he was doing what was right for the hotel. To Maynard Charles, the Buckingham mattered above all other things: keep it in good health, and you were on his right side; besmirch its reputation, and he was no longer the genial hotel director, obsessing over the Housekeeping logistics or the night managers' schedule, but a tyrant instead. Suddenly, Hélène remembered the other times she'd been summoned to this office, and told that her weekend leave was to be cancelled, that she was obliged to stay and dance at the request of some valued guest. She'd missed out on so many evenings with Sybil because of that.

Three days had passed since that moment in the Candlelight Club. They had lasted a lifetime. She'd left after the final dance that night, taken a taxicab she could hardly afford all the way to Lambeth, and spent the night at the Archers' on Brixton Hill, with Sybil sleeping in the crook of her arm.

The sense of restoration it brought her did not last long. The next day, at the demonstration dances, every hope she'd had that her mother's vitriolic outburst might, by some strange mercy, have gone unheard, were dashed. It was Louis Kildare who took her to one side and told her that the musicians *knew*; that they'd heard it from the dancers, who'd heard it from the pages, who'd heard it from the porters and the lift attendants, the cocktail waiters and head concierge. She'd strode into the dressing rooms with her head held high, holding it together as she and Mathilde helped each other into their gowns, and it wasn't until she saw Raymond that all the pain and anger she was trying to keep within came spilling out.

In the corner, he took her in his arms and said, 'Hélène, I'm sorry.'

His words disintegrated into silence. Hélène extracted herself from his arms, dried her eyes, and out they went to dance.

They were speaking of it in the ballroom. She didn't need to hear the voices to understand that. She sensed it in the eyes of the waiters who sashayed from table to table, skirting the edge of the dance floor itself. She felt it in the way the musicians watched her between numbers. She fancied she could even feel it in the way the aged Graf König declined to dance with her, and instead passed her off to one of his nephews.

*At least Maynard Charles is not sneering*, she thought now, though the look on his face was hardly any better.

'I trusted you, Hélène. You were my star. So precious to the Buckingham that, when you petitioned me for a six-month sabbatical, time to explore your opportunities across the Atlantic, I went in front of the board for you. That was a battle hard fought, but I won it in the end. I did it for you. And now . . .'

Hélène thought: *you didn't do it for me. You did it for the hotel. To keep me on a leash, or to have something to boast about, to forge a reputation for the ages.*

But the vitriol she felt as those thoughts formed vanished as quickly as it had appeared – because everything he was saying was true. She'd told a lie, and she'd been living one for four long years.

'Do the board know?'

'Hélène.' Maynard sighed, and for the first time she understood there was genuine regret underpinning everything he said.

'I told them myself. I had to. They have eyes and ears in this hotel. Had I not gone to them, it would have trickled to them all the same – and then where would I be? So, yes, the hotel board know. That's why you're here, my dear.'

*My dear.* It took only those two words for Hélène to understand how this conversation was going to play out. And yet there she remained, cloaked in silence.

'You know how this world works, Hélène. You *know* it. You're not blinkered to what I have to do to keep this hotel alive. Every day, some new scandal to control and contort. A concierge stealing from guests. A chambermaid bedded by some lord, left sobbing in some corner. The arson attack last Christmas. Everything Miss Edgerton used to get up to, before she straightened out her ways. By the Lord above, I've been putting out fires in this hotel for nearly twenty years. That's what I'm here for. But, Hélène, there are some scandals too big to—'

'What would you have had me do?' Hélène suddenly snapped. She hadn't meant to, but the words burst out of her with a savage force. 'Mr Charles, allow me to explain.'

'I don't need an explanation.'

'You're not in possession of the facts. Or . . . you're not in possession of a heart. I'd have left, gracefully, if Sidney hadn't been struck down by that bus. I'd have retired and you'd never have heard of me again. I'd have been off, having my baby, and to hell with the lot of you.'

Maynard's face turned as purple as a bruise, but his hands still strained in the small of his back.

'But then he died, and what was I to do next? Throw myself on the charity of the parish? Mr Charles, try and see it from my perspective. Sidney was dead, and his child was growing within me. My own mother and father exiled me from their estate. I didn't have a choice. I did the only thing I could to look after that little girl – and I certainly won't apologise for it now. She's healthy and she's happy and I did every last thing I could to make that happen. Give me my time again, and I wouldn't have it any other way.'

'You should have come to me, Hélène,' he murmured. 'Believe it or not, I know a thing or two about forbidden love.'

Hélène stared at him. 'Mr Charles?'

'If I'd known what you were going through, I'd have . . . found a way.'

'A way to what?'

'To help, Hélène. I'd have *helped* . . .' He sighed. 'You've been a fool.'

'I've been a mother.'

'And a damn fine one, I shouldn't wonder. But to bring them here, to welcome them into the Candlelight Club and just—'

Hélène softened. 'I wanted to meet them in a place that was mine. Surely you can understand.'

Maynard nodded. 'I've kept other secrets in this hotel, Hélène. I should have liked the opportunity to do it for you as well.'

For the longest time, she simply sat in her seat, face creasing in confusion, until finally Maynard went on, his voice scarcely a whisper now.

'I could have controlled it.' He was quaking. 'I spend my days controlling scandals.'

'Not ones like this,' Hélène whispered, and she saw real tenderness in Maynard Charles's eyes. 'A black man having a child with your principal dancer? No, Mr Charles, if I'd come to you, I'd have made you a part of it. After Sidney died, there was only one person in this hotel who could control this scandal. Me. So I set about it, in the only way I knew how.' She paused, but when he said nothing, she went on. 'Please believe me – I didn't want to mislead you. I didn't want to live this lie.'

Maynard took a deep breath, drawing himself upright once more.

'Hélène, I really am sorry. I don't want to do what I'm about to do either.'

The colour had drained from his face. Hélène parted her lips to speak, but he lifted a hand, begging for her silence. What he was about to say was obviously causing deep distress. He was not an inconsiderable man, but in that moment it seemed he could be pushed over by a stiff breeze.

'I'm to go before the board in the morning and tell them how this happened. I'm to tell them, too, what I'm doing to stem this tide. The recoil from this could be severe, but I need to show them it can be contained, that there's life in the ever-after. If I can do that . . .' He stared at her, not unkindly, and went on. 'The Buckingham Hotel depends on the reputation of the ballroom. That ballroom dragged this hotel up out of the Depression. It's the ballroom that brings the high and mighty to us. It's why kings and crown princes call the Buckingham suites their home away from home. The board will want to see me protecting that reputation, Hélène.' He hesitated. 'At all costs.'

'Mr Charles, please.' Suddenly, Hélène was on her feet. She reached out, as if she might take his hand, but the chasm between them was too vast. 'My daughter needs the ballroom too. *I* need it. There has to be a way—'

'I'm suspending you from dancing in the Grand Ballroom for a minimum of two weeks. In that time, you are not to remain inside the hotel. I've arranged for Billy Brogan to pack you a bag from your quarters while we've been speaking, but you have my permission to return there and collect any important possessions he's overlooked. You're to leave a forwarding address with the concierge desk, so that I might summon you in due course, and so that we might – if there's a way – come to some better resolution.'

It was the formality of it that stung her the most. How could he go from such understanding – such depth of feeling and emotion – to this, in only a few fleeting seconds? She supposed it was what he had to do. The stiff upper lip, the decorum of it – Hélène knew more than most about putting on a brave face.

Maynard reached for the telephone on his desk and dialled a single number.

'Send Billy Brogan in,' he said, and promptly put the receiver back down. 'I'm going to do my best for you, Hélène. That's my promise to you.'

'Mr Charles, you can't do this to me. I'm lost without it. Sybil and her grandparents, they depend on me to . . .'

He could hardly look her in the eye – but, by sheer power of will, he forced himself to meet her gaze. His own eyes were glistening now.

Fingers rapped at the office door and, when it swung open, there stood Billy, with a leather bag at his heel.

'I think I collected everything, Miss Marchmont.'

Hélène said nothing. Refusing to let Billy carry the bag one more step, she hoisted it up and marched along the corridor, out across the black and white chequered tiles of the hotel reception, past the obelisk where the waters still cascaded down, and out through the revolving brass doors, into the Mayfair night.

This time, as she marched, her head was not held high.

This time, she let it hang low, the better to hide the tears.

At the bottom of the sweeping marble steps, a taxicab was waiting. The hotel doorman, dutifully not acknowledging that this was Hélène Marchmont, star of the Grand Ballroom – and just as dutifully not noticing the sobs she was trying to keep in – opened up the door for her.

There was one thing to say for Maynard Charles. Good or bad, angel or devil, on her side or standing shoulder to shoulder with the hotel board, he had planned her exit to perfection.

July 1938

# Chapter Twelve

SUMMER HAD BROUGHT FRESH COLOUR to Berkeley Square. Behind the railings of the town houses, terracotta pots erupted with carnations and marigolds in a myriad colours. The manicured lawn of the square was a verdant dell, across which the midday sun shone like molten gold – and, twice a day, the Regency Florists sent their finest artists up from the Regent Street arcades to furnish the Buckingham suites and restaurants with bouquets of wild indulgence.

But none of that compared to the riot of colour exploding in Mrs Emmeline Moffatt's heart as, begging reprieve from her duties for the day, she crossed London by Underground train, emerging to stand at the bustling ticket desk tucked inside King's Cross Station.

'Madam?' the ticket clerk ventured, when she finally reached the head of the queue.

Mrs Moffatt shook herself out of her thoughts. The ticket clerk was a young man, still carrying the gangliness of his youth. She looked at his face, framed in curls of red hair, and thought: *you're half as young as he'll be. You're a babe in arms. The years of my life have been flickering by, all bound up in the Buckingham Hotel, and I've been letting them go, one by one . . .*

'Where can we send you, madam? What train are you boarding?'

Here it was. She took a deep breath.

'I'd like a ticket to Mildenhall, please.'

The ticket clerk screwed up his face, then consulted a chart on the wall behind him.

'You'll have to change at Cambridge. Single journey, is it?'

Time seemed to stand still. All the hustle and bustle of the busy concourse faded into silence, until finally she stuttered, 'Return, please. Yes, yes, I'll need to return.'

She might have been coming back on the evening train, she realised, but that was the only way in which this journey could ever be called a 'return'. For what she was about do was not something that could be undone. Once she stepped onto that train, there would be no turning around.

It took over three hours for her to reach the station at Mildenhall. As she stepped down from the train platform, Mrs Moffatt nervously asked one of the porters, 'The air base, sir. Is it far?'

The porter gave her a look of surprise. 'I should think it's a couple of miles at least, love. There's a bus service, but that's just to ferry the lads in and out.' He stopped. 'You looking for somebody, are you?'

Mrs Moffatt clutched her bag tight to her chest.

'I am not,' she declared, and hurried fitfully out of the station.

It took her a little time to orient herself. Mildenhall was a small parish, sprung up around the grounds of an old manor house, but she soon understood its true purpose. The village square was full not only with shoppers and market tradesmen, but men in the blue-grey uniform of the Royal Air Force. Mildenhall market was not as vast as the markets she'd visited in London but this far from the Buckingham Hotel, she felt quite untethered. She needed something to anchor her.

A nice pot of tea might do.

There were cafés aplenty on the corners of the market square. She chose the quietest one, and took a seat in the window, where a waitress brought her a scone with clotted cream and jam of such tartness that it startled her back into life. She sat there, watching the market go by, until the tea was cold, then ordered another pot, with a cosy in case she wanted to linger even longer.

Then she opened her bag, and took out the sheaf of letters she'd folded within.

*Dear Emmeline,*

said the first.

*Dear Mrs Moffatt,*

said another.

*I have not heard from you, but perhaps it does no harm for me to continue to write, all the same. I have always liked writing letters. I believe I wrote my first to you when I was twelve years old, and kept it under my pillow for I knew not where to send it, nor even your name.*

She kept having to stop. When she could not read on, the tea sustained her until she could turn back.

*Your son, Malcolm*

the letters ended –

*or, Yours, in hope, Malcolm Brody*

All in all, there were eight of them now. Each one of them written with painstaking care – she could tell in the quality of the penmanship – with each word laboured over lovingly, as if the writer was some poet of great renown and not a simple, solid airman, stationed here in this unassuming country town.

He had written:

*Please write back, if only to tell me you would like me to desist. I am a grown man now, nearly thirty-three years of age, and I am happy. How few of us can say that, in this day and age? I have health and I have heart. I have had two parents who loved me. The hole in my life is you and, should you not wish to fill it, you can rest assured that I shall carry on with my head held high, and make the mother and father who raised me proud, and serve my king and country. But write to me and tell me, so that I might carry on. The years of our life are so fleeting, and I am in England, I fear, in preparation for a war to come. I should not like to waste any more of this passing time.*

It was these last words that had made her get on the train. Mrs Moffatt, too, could feel the years slipping through her fingers. It was twenty-one years since her husband had died. One war was slowly being forgotten, even as the spectre of another reared its ugly head. She was being given a chance, wasn't she? A chance to reclaim some of those lost years?

A bell rang, and Mrs Moffatt started.

A blast of warm summer air told her the door was open and, when she looked that way, three airmen in their navy-grey uniforms walked in. Each one of them was tall and lean, with perfectly cropped hair – two of them chestnut brown, one a copper blond – and each smiling from ear to ear. Casually, they walked up to the counter, talked quickly with the waitress, and then sauntered back to the door, meaning to take one of the tables on the pavement outside.

Mrs Moffatt's heart skipped a beat. The teacup, which she'd been clinging to, rattled so fiercely that tea sloshed over its rim, staining the letters on the tabletop underneath – and drawing the attention of the airmen standing in the door.

'Georgia,' the copper-blond one called out, 'fetch us a cloth, won't you?'

'Are you all right, love?' asked the second.

'Let me assist,' said the third, as he took a dishcloth from the waitress and set about cleaning the table.

Just in time, Mrs Moffatt scrabbled her letters together and folded them safely inside her magazine.

'Just a bit of a wobble,' she said, not catching the airmen's eyes. 'It happens now and again.'

'Georgia,' the copper-blond man called out, once everything was clean, 'get a new pot, won't you?' He smiled, sweetly. 'These are on us, love. Why don't you get yourself an apple tart too? Georgia's mum out back – she makes the best apple tarts.'

For the first time, Mrs Moffatt dared to look up. The three airmen were looking at her sympathetically, like they might an out-of-sorts grandmother, and she flashed them a smile in return.

'Thank you so much, dears,' she said – but this time she didn't stutter at all. As each of them had spoken, a revelation had hit her, and all the panic she'd been feeling had fluttered instantly away.

The three airmen – they were all Englishmen, through and through. Not one of them spoke with an Australian accent.

Mrs Moffatt didn't stay for her final pot of tea, though she was grateful to take a slice of apple tart away with her, wrapped in a piece of greaseproof paper. She nibbled at it as the train chugged her slowly back into London. By the time she'd arrived at King's Cross, there was only a crust of pastry left, and this she broke into pieces and ate on the Underground train that took her back to Oxford Circus.

It was six o' clock. By rights, she ought to have only just been boarding the train. By rights, she ought to have pottered out to the airbase itself, asked somebody where she might find a Mr Malcolm Brody, or at least watched from afar until she heard Australian voices.

But her heart was simply not ready for it.

She started to feel restored as soon as she came to the oasis of Berkeley Square, where the grand white façade of the Buckingham looked down upon her like a long lost friend. Entering by the tradesman's door on Michaelmas Mews, she wended her way through storerooms and back corridors until, at last, she approached the hotel director's office. She'd listened to Maynard Charles so many nights across the years. She'd borne his secrets and carried them with her. And tonight the thing she needed more than anything else was somebody to listen.

She knocked on the door.

'Enter,' came Maynard's grave voice.

Inside, he presided over a desk strewn with papers, while Billy stood to attention, like a soldier on parade.

'Off with you then, Brogan. I'll speak with you later.'

'Yes, Mr Charles.'

The young concierge nodded, seemingly dropping his voice an octave to match the old hotel director. Then, he slipped past Mrs Moffatt and into the corridor beyond.

As soon as he was gone, Maynard looked around, distracted.

'Emmeline, you look like you've seen a ghost. Are you quite well?'

'Maynard.' She trembled, eyeing the decanter among the papers on his desk. 'Might you pour me a glass?'

Maynard's eyes opened fractionally wider, for this was a sentence he had rarely heard from Mrs Moffatt's lips. More often, she'd been known to put the stopper back in the decanter, to repeat her mother's favourite mantra, that 'moderation made men magnificent'.

'Emmeline, I can't stop. I've a situation in the Queen Mary. The Hamburg Schechts are checked in to the Atlantic Suite, but I'm afraid they've rather caught me on the hop. I hadn't known, until right now, that they're dining with Lord Adlington. He'd normally be staying with us, but for a reason I can't quite fathom he's up at the Imperial. Were I a suspicious man, I might suggest I'd been tricked.'

Mrs Moffatt nodded. Lord Adlington was cousin to the Lord Lieutenant of Cornwall and, as such, had been schooled with King George himself.

'You know what this means,' said Maynard wearily.

She supposed she did. Those Nazi sycophants, creeping closer to the good King George. She knew there were games at play, here in the Buckingham Hotel, of which she had no part. Quite frankly, that was the way she liked it. The games and counter-games of politicians and kings were not for her. And yet she needed him tonight. She needed *someone*, just to listen.

'Maynard, there's something I've got to . . . That is to say, something weighing on me. I'm afraid I find myself in a bit of a pickle and – oh dear, I hardly know where to begin, but . . . I'm a good person, Maynard. You, of all people, know I'm a good person, don't you?'

But Maynard Charles was straightening his waistcoat and manoeuvring past her, out into the hall.

'Emmeline, I'll find you soon. I promise. It's the Schechts, my dear. You understand, I have to be there for the Schechts.'

What a faraway feeling this was, to be standing on her own, wanting only to talk. She tried to follow, crossing the reception hall and watching him vanish through the Queen Mary doors. Maynard Charles had a role to play in all of this that was so much greater than hers. He served unknown men – she understood this, at least – and the imperious faces of the hotel board, and sometimes, as he navigated his way between them, he could forget that other worlds revolved around him as well.

Through the restaurant doors, she saw the Austrian exile, Tobias Bauer, sitting at a table on his own, reading one of his pocket novels, and the loneliness of it struck her, deep inside. The world was too full of lonesome people.

*Hundreds of us*, she thought, *right here in this hotel – and not one of us daring to reach out for another.*

*No matter*, she thought. She'd been keeping this secret alone for half of her life. It shamed her to acknowledge, even now, that not even Jack had known. She wondered if she'd have told him, in the end, if he had lived. She liked to think he'd have wrapped his arms around her and told her he understood, and that their love would not have been diminished, but enhanced greatly instead. Such foolish dreams! But she chose to believe in them now.

At last, she turned from the doors of the Queen Mary, meaning to make for the housekeeping lounge and catch up on all of the paperwork she'd missed out on across the day – and there she saw another lonesome soul, waiting at the concierge desk. Archie Adams was decked out in his resplendent white dinner jacket, his hair neatly trimmed and his silvery moustache waxed to perfection. They said he'd never wed for he was married to his orchestra, the real love of his life. But band members came and went and this had always seemed, to Mrs Moffatt, a peculiar kind of existence.

'No more peculiar than mine,' she muttered out loud, and tottered across the reception hall.

'Emmeline?'

It was Archie's voice. She had almost disappeared into the Housekeeping hall but, by instinct, she looked back and saw the look of concern creasing his face.

He had seen the tears glimmering in her eyes. She was certain of it.

'I'm quite well, Mr Adams. It's been a long day, that's all.'

She turned again, meaning to repair to the housekeeping lounge and compose herself, but Archie followed.

'And my day's just beginning.' His voice was light, but she knew he could be commanding when he needed. His boys in the orchestra were slavish in their loyalty; he'd brought most of them up out of nothing. 'I need to be backstage in an hour, Emmeline, but perhaps . . .'

An invitation was being proffered. She wanted, more than anything, to accept it – but another part of her, the part used to dealing with other people's problems, was suddenly flustered.

'Oh, Mr Adams,' she said, 'I'm being a silly old mare. I'm tired, that's all. I'll be—'

'Emmeline, do it for me. I'm nervous. In scarcely two hours' time, I'll be up on stage in front of every notable in Mayfair and beyond.' He smiled. 'I think I'm going to need a barley sugar to get me through.'

In the housekeeping lounge, there were barley sugars aplenty, but what Archie really had in mind was a hot toddy – and, just this once, Mrs Moffatt was happy to oblige. Without any of her girls to set a bad example to, she mixed up hot water and lemon, ginger root and whisky from the cabinet, and added a healthy teaspoon of brown sugar each. After that, they repaired to the armchairs in her office and sat in the lamplight together.

'You must think me a fool,' Mrs Moffatt began, 'to be whimpering like that.'

'Lord knows, I whimper enough!' Archie declared, though Mrs Moffatt hardly believed it. Archie Adams seemed to emanate calmness. It was, she decided, what she needed tonight. 'Something's happened?'

'It's been preying on me for weeks, Mr Adams.'

'Please,' he said, 'call me Archie.'

'My girls know it, Archie. I've been short with them – even Nancy Nettleton, and she's such a sweetheart, living out her dream. But I've been abrupt with them all and they're starting to notice.'

'I daresay not a soul among them thinks sorely of you, Emmeline. We're all entitled to an ill-tempered day here and—'

'It's more than that.'

She'd said it with such force that Archie, at first taken aback, spluttered with laughter.

'Now I see.' He smiled. 'Old Mrs Moffatt has a temper.'

152

'Less of the old!' She laughed, and Archie was pleased to see her smile. 'I must be three years your senior, if at all.'

When the laughter had subsided and an awkward silence prevailed, Archie Adams said, softly, 'Tell me, Emmeline,' but still Mrs Moffatt said nothing.

After that, the silence continued, filling the air between them, swelling and swelling further until it was almost too much to bear. Mrs Moffatt had started fidgeting in her seat and, when she reached for her toddy, her hand was trembling more violently than it had in Mildenhall that afternoon.

'I'm sorry. I don't mean to pry. I thought it might help. The old talking cure, like they said after the Great War. To keep it in, that's to bed down with the devil. When you let it all out, you let the angels in.'

Suddenly, Mrs Moffatt was on her feet. She marched to her desk, where she'd left her handbag, and from it withdrew her pile of letters. These she deposited on Archie's lap.

She couldn't say it, but Archie could read it – every last word.

'There,' she said, bringing her hand to her mouth. 'It's all there.'

Archie took the letters in, one by one. As his eyes scoured each page, Mrs Moffatt turned away, turned back again, paced one wall and then another. The clock on the wall was advancing – first five minutes, then ten – but inside her heart an ice age was thawing.

It must have taken Archie twenty minutes to finish the last letter.

'My dear Emmeline,' was all that he said.

'Aren't you going to ask me?' she whispered. 'What happened? What kind of a person I could be to have done what I did?'

153

'I should think you'd tell me, if you wanted. And I should listen, if you so desired.'

She told herself to keep quiet. But she'd been silent all of her life, and the walls were crumbling, now. Why not kick them down herself? They were her walls, after all. She was the one who'd built them. They'd been meant to protect her but, too late, she realised they'd been keeping her in. Instead of building a fortress, she'd built a prison.

'I called him Michael,' she ventured, timidly at first.

'It's a fine name.'

'But now he's Malcolm.'

Archie Adams nodded, but said nothing. This was not the sort of story you coaxed out of someone. There was a thing he had learned through all his long years playing with orchestras: sometimes, the only good thing you could do was to *listen*.

'I was twenty-three. Old enough to know better. Already an old maid, by some accounts. That's what my sisters and cousins all made of me. Still lived at home, while they were off getting married. Still took my mother strolling by the seafront each day, down there in sunny Southend. But . . .' She stopped, shaking her head sorrowfully. 'He was older. A gentleman. I wasn't the first to fall for those charms. Full of wild tales of his days in India, or of leading the charge down in the Transvaal. An old soldier, I thought. Nearly twice my age! And there was I, immature for my years. Naïve, they later said – and, what's more, they were right. He used to take me for evening strolls. Or we'd go picnicking down on the sands. And then he said, "Why, Emmeline, light of my life, you've changed my very soul."' She winced. 'I believed him. I was a romantic at heart, you see. So when we started taking hotel rooms together, well . . .' She stopped. 'I'm ashamed, Archie.'

He said, sternly now, 'You've no need to be ashamed.'

'As soon as I knew I was pregnant, I rushed to tell him. I knew there'd be obstacles. Gossip, perhaps, and rumour. But we'd spoken of being married already and I thought, if we did it there and then – eloped, even, though it would have broken my dear mother's heart – nobody need know what we'd been doing.' She hesitated. 'Only, he didn't want to marry me. After I told him, I never saw him again. The last I heard, he'd gone to Clacton and met a girl there. I'd hazard she heard all the same stories I did.'

'He was a deplorable man, Emmeline.'

'But where did that leave me? Well, I'll tell you, Archie. It left me at St Maud's. I'd confessed to my mother, eventually. Three months, I was able to keep it a secret. By the fourth, I was showing and the secret had to end. So I broke her heart after all. But she sorted things, quietly and efficiently, as was her way. A cousin had a cousin who knew about St Maud's, up on the Norfolk coast. They took in girls like me and sorted us out, and after our babies were born, they sent us back to the world, as if none of it had happened.' Her voice broke at last. The wall had crumbled to the earth. 'I saw my son for a few short hours. Then they wrapped him in his swaddling and took him away.'

Archie Adams stood, took two strides towards her and, quite unbidden, folded his arms around her.

'I'm a devil, Archie,' she wept.

'You're nothing of the sort,' he whispered in return.

'I ran away to London, after that. Wrote letters to my mother and father as if none of it had ever happened. But I do believe they stopped loving me, after everything I'd done. So after a little while, the letters just stopped. I didn't mind. I found my new family, right here in the hotel. I was happy and I was strong. And then I met Jack and . . .' She was so quiet now that Archie could hardly hear. 'I thought Jack and I might have children. I longed for it. I'd show the world what a good mother I could be. But then Jack didn't come home from that dreadful war, and I never did get a chance to show myself I could do it, that I was better than I'd been.'

Archie stepped back, braced Mrs Moffatt by the shoulders, forced her to look into his eyes.

'You've been a mother to more girls than you know, here in this hotel. They think of you like that, Emmeline. You must believe it.'

'The only chance God gave me to have a child of my own, and I gave it away. I watched them wrap him up, even though he was crying for his mama, and they put the pencil in my hands – and I signed my name on their paper. I couldn't even bring myself to read it. I already knew what it said. That he wasn't really mine. What kind of mother does that make me?'

'Mothers do the most wonderful things for their children, Emmeline. And this boy in these letters – look at the good life he's lived. Look at the love he's had, and the opportunities, and the success. An airman, come across the world to serve with the RAF. That childhood he speaks of, running wild under an Australian sun! What you did broke your heart, but it wasn't your choice – and maybe, just maybe, he got the best of it, in the end.' He stopped. 'I was thinking of Miss Marchmont, of whether she'll dance for us ever again. Louis Kildare knew, of course. He kept the secret for her. We had a drink together the other night, after the band had played, and he told me all about it. I should like to find a way of helping Hélène Marchmont. She took the hard road, the better to provide for her child – and you, Emmeline Moffatt, you did the same.'

Something in the words was drying her tears.

'I don't know what to do, Archie. I went there today, thinking I might catch just a glimpse before I said hello. But I didn't have the courage, even for that. I tried, but I failed.'

'Emmeline, I've lived an unusual life. I was there, in Flanders, like everybody else. Most of those who came home wanted nothing more than sweethearts and families of their own. Well, the war made me realise what I wanted as well. I wanted laughter. I wanted music. I wanted song. I bent my life about it. I've loved every second, but perhaps it's protected me from some of life's hardest edges. Music does break your heart' – he smiled – 'but it heals it again. There's one thing music has taught me, Emmeline, that might be useful to you now. Because when I play a bad note, when the band falls out of rhythm and we send dancers frolicking in a dozen different directions – well, I know it isn't the end of the world. We've failed, but we can always pick up our instruments and try again.'

'Archie, you're talking in riddles. I'm not sure I understand.'

'What I'm saying is that just because you lost your courage once, doesn't mean you'll lose it again. We pick ourselves up, we dust ourselves off, we march back to the music and the fray. Life isn't finished, yet. So we're past our prime! We still have hearts, don't we? We get to choose the course of our lives, take our happiness where we can.' He laughed. 'Listen to me! Maybe it's all this talk of war in the air again, addling my mind. But none of us are here forever. It's down to us to make the best of the years given to us. And I say – if your faith deserted you once, there's no reason you can't recapture it again. No reason you can't go back to Mildenhall and meet this brave, decent, happy young man who has your own blood pulsing in his veins.'

He paused, if only for breath, and was delighted to see the look of hope that had come flickering back to Mrs Moffatt's face.

'And if you like,' Archie declared, 'I shall come with you. There's courage enough between us, Emmeline – of that I'm sure.'

# Chapter Thirteen

THE HOUSE AT 62 ALBERT YARD, Lambeth, was not typically quiet – but today the silence on the landing at the top of the stairs was absolute. Seven breaths were held, seven voices reined in, seven delighted smiles restrained from becoming deep, belly laughs. The only sound at all was a gentle tapping and a whispered voice from beyond the bedroom door.

On the other side of that door, Billy Brogan tapped the four sides of a simple box on the floorboards with his feet, counting under his breath with every step – 'One, two, three, four . . . One, two, three, four . . .' – while Frank Nettleton perched on the edge of the bed and watched.

'Oh, Billy, you're *thinking* too much!'

Billy, who had his arms open and held in a frame, as if enveloping some elegant dancer, froze. The scowl deepened on his face.

'Thinking's what I'm good at, Frank. How am I going to put my feet in the right spot if I don't think?' He returned to his counting. 'One, two, three . . . One, two, three . . .'

'Oh, for heaven's sake!' Frank chortled. 'Let me show you!' And in a second he had taken Billy in his own arms, leading him in a box-step around the carpet they'd cleared of all his old books and toys. 'It's like this, Billy. You just have to let it go.

You don't need to think to breathe, do you? You don't need to think to walk. So why would you need to think to dance? It's just counting. Even those little scamps out there can count.'

Billy shot a look at the door. It was no secret that all of his brothers and sisters were crowded at the top of the stairs, desperate to catch a glimpse of what was happening beyond the bedroom door. Patrick and Annie, Conor and Daniel, Roisin and Holly and little Gracie May – by rights they ought to have been at the breakfast table, but apparently the idea of Billy learning a little waltzing was much more important than food.

'Come on, Billy, loosen up. You're too stiff.'

'I can't loosen up – you're holding me too tight.'

'Too tight! I barely got my hands on you.'

'Yes, well, it's giving me the creeps. You're standing too close.'

Frank laughed. 'Well, how close do you want Ruth Attercliffe to stand?'

'Not as close as this, Frank. I can feel your heart beat.'

'That's *your* heart!' Frank beamed. 'Billy, you're nervous! Look, there's only you and me here. Nobody's going to laugh at you. You get used to this, Frank, and you can get used to anything. Just follow me. And that counting – for heaven's sake, try not to do it out loud. Soon enough, you won't need to count at all.'

He tried to count in his head. *One.* But it was harder than it sounded. *Two. Three.* Soon he had started counting out loud again. *One.* And, as soon as that had happened, he was getting louder and louder – *TWO! THREE!* – focusing as much on the counting itself as he was on the placement of his feet. *ONE! TWO! THREE!*

So they stepped and they turned, and they stepped and they turned – and, somewhere along the way, Billy started to feel that he'd got the hang of this, that perhaps he might even one day be able to soar across a dance hall like all of the rest.

Until, all of a sudden, he was on the floor, with Frank entangled in his arms – and, looking up, he was startled to see that, somewhere along the way, the bedroom door had been pushed open, and a gaggle of faces had been staring at him with unadulterated delight.

Even little Gracie May – at four years old, the youngest of all the Brogan brood – was clapping in glee.

Billy rough-housed Frank away and leaped to his feet, racing at his brothers and sisters with a fist clenched tight.

'Off with you, you lot!' he cried out – but not one of the Brogan brood was afraid. They never could be – not of their big brother. Instead, all a humiliated Billy could do was carve a path through them, calling back to Frank as he loped down the stairs, 'Come on, Frankie, we got work to be doing – not like this lazy lot!'

After Billy was gone, Frank came and crouched among the overjoyed children.

'You lot'll put him off forever if you keep on laughing!'

'It was funny though, Uncle Frank!'

Frank loved it when the Brogan children called him 'uncle'. He'd been boarding with the Brogans for a year, ever since Nancy set him up at the Buckingham and wrote for him to come down from their old home in the Lancashire hills. Frank liked to think he was more of a big brother to them all – especially now that Billy had been afforded a room in the staff quarters at the Buckingham – but, either way, it meant he was part of the family, and this was a feeling quite unlike any other.

161

He grinned. 'I know it's funny,' he said quietly, so that his voice did not carry, 'but only because he's getting so cross with himself! Now, come on, it's breakfast!'

Downstairs, Mrs Brogan watched her brood tumble after Billy and Frank. Billy was scowling as he marched furiously for the front door.

'I've a lot to deal with, and I won't listen to this a moment longer. What with Miss Marchmont banished from the ballroom and all the guests scheduled to dance with her needing to know what's going on, and be found replacements, and be dealt with at the desks, I'm a wanted man.'

'Just not on the dance floor!' his little sister Annie howled from the bottom of the stairs.

'Come on, Frank,' grunted Billy. 'We've places to be.'

When they were almost at the door, Frank shaking his head ruefully at the gathered children, Mrs Brogan scurried after them.

'Is everything all right, Billy? The Buckingham's not in trouble again, is it?'

That was the perpetual fear in the Brogan household. A brood like theirs was not uncostly, and the wages William Brogan Senior brought home from Billingsgate did not always keep up with the repairs to their dilapidated old house, let alone the coal and groceries and clothes that the children needed. Bed and board from Frank went some way to offsetting those costs, but without the pay Billy sent home from the Buckingham (not to say the offcuts of venison, half-eaten jars of pickles and day-old loaves he rescued from the kitchen waste), the Brogans would soon feel the pinch.

'Nothing like that, Ma. At least, I hope not.' Billy opened the front door. Though it was early, the summer sun was in the ascendant. 'It's this business with Miss Marchmont. They say Mr Charles banished her until he could put his pleas before the board. Sometimes, if you let a fracas die down, people stop talking about it. But . . . everyone's talking about it being in the society pages. What that might do to the ballroom. And we've already got guests wondering where she's been. All it takes is one chattering chambermaid—'

Frank needled him in the ribs with the point of a finger.

'Not that all chambermaids are chattering, of course. But all it takes is one loose tongue. Now, I personally have known about Miss Marchmont's secret for two years, and I never breathed a word, so . . .'

Billy's voice petered out. What he had said wasn't strictly true, for he'd found himself coerced into telling Miss Vivienne Edgerton, back when she was spending most of her time in the cocktail lounge, or imbibing the powders the old head concierge used to get Billy to provide for her. He was truly ashamed of this, and keeping Miss Marchmont's secret since then had been the way he absolved himself. Now it was all coming crashing down.

'Miss Marchmont don't deserve it, does she, Frank? She's done the Buckingham proud. We're all standing beside her. Even Mr Charles, I should think, in his own way.'

Billy and Frank talked it through as they made the long amble up to the Buckingham, over the bridge at Westminster and through St James's Park, where the guards were on parade outside Buckingham Palace. In summer, this was the most glorious walk of all. Billy loved to saunter through the trees where, in days gone by, true princes and princesses of the realm had parleyed and played. Just being here made him feel special – and it might even have made him forget his failures on the dance floor,

if the enigmatic figure of Raymond de Guise hadn't been waiting for them the moment they slipped into the hotel through the
tradesman's entrance.

'Mr de Guise!' Frank stammered. 'I mean, Raymond. What
are you doing here?'

'Why, waiting for you, of course.'

It wasn't just that the sight of Raymond, loitering among the
dust-sheets and crates by the tradesman's entrance, was strange.
It was that he was decked out in his finest evening wear, a tailored
midnight blue suit and dress shirt, his black hair combed back
with pomade and glistening like lacquer.

'I'll leave you two to your chinwag,' Billy declared, hurrying
onwards. 'I got important things to attend to. This hotel waits for
no man.'

As Billy passed, Raymond called out, 'How are those lessons
going, Billy?'

Billy beamed. 'Mr de Guise, I'm prancing on air!' and flicked
his feet in such a fashion that the toes of the left caught the heels
of the right, sending him staggering out of the storeroom and on
up the hall.

Frank shrugged. 'Not well. Raymond, is it possible that some
people just . . . can't dance?'

'It's quite possible,' Raymond said, 'but most of those people
are cold in the ground.' It took Frank a little while to catch on
to the joke, by which time Raymond was saying, 'Frank, there's
something I thought you might like to see.'

'Why are you dressed up like that, Raymond? Breakfast can't
have been served yet. The demonstration dances aren't for hours.'

'Frank,' Raymond said with a thrill, *they're here.*

Frank didn't need to think twice to know who Raymond meant. Like the rest of the Buckingham Hotel, he'd been anticipating their arrival all season.

'The Winter Hollers.'

To Frank, even their name conjured up an air of magic and mystery.

'Fresh in off the boat. I'm to meet them in the Grand shortly, and put on my best for them. They'll want to know where Miss Marchmont is, just like everyone else. But if I can dazzle them with our ballroom, perhaps that won't matter. The whole of the dance troupe are bereft. But perhaps the Winter Hollers coming could set things right.'

'All the way from Vienna, Mr de Guise. Dancing their way across the Continent – what a life that might be . . .'

'Well, come on, Frank. Mr Charles has been introducing them to their suites – personal service, from our hotel director himself – but they'll be bound for the Grand any moment.'

Frank needed no further encouragement. He followed Raymond up, through the snaking labyrinth of service passageways unseen by the guests , and to the reception hall – where the gates of the golden lifts were already opening, revealing a collection of faces and figures he had never seen before.

'Mr de Guise, is that . . . ?'

'Jonas Holler.' Raymond nodded towards a long, lithe man with a head of jet-black hair that rivalled his own. 'Karina Kainz, his partner on the dance floor.' He indicated a statuesque blonde lady emerging from the huddle behind them. 'Oh, Frank, it takes me back – I'd meet companies like this every season when I crossed the Continent with Georges.'

The guests had all emerged from the lift now. Others were fanning into the reception hall, having descended by the palatial guest staircase tucked just behind. At once, Raymond stood to attention.

'I've got to go – put on a show of my own. But I wanted you to see them. Keep dancing like you do, smooth off those rough edges, find a little more grace, and you might be dancing in a company like this one day. I mean it, Frank.'

With those words, Raymond hurried to meet the Winter Holler Company in the reception hall. Frank supposed he should have gone his own way then, down to the hotel laundry where the other pages gathered – but he didn't want to move a muscle. He only wanted to *see*. Down there, Raymond was throwing his arms open wide and bowing to a portly middle-aged man, whose face was dominated by an enormous silver moustache, waxed into such curls that they looked like the tusks of a leopard seal. Then he was introduced, one after another, to the new faces in the crowd, and soon he was bowing graciously to Karina Kainz. Her hair was the colour of the cornfields Frank used to trundle past in the valley back home.

He was not sure why the idea of the travelling company brought such wonder to his heart. He'd seen the finest dancers in London – by God, he was going to have one as a brother! – and perhaps that ought to have dulled the awe he was feeling now. But the idea that they'd crossed a continent, simply to dance in these halls, filled him not only with wonder but with wanderlust.

*It's all just an accident of birth*, he thought. *Had I been born somewhere else, maybe I could have been one of them as well. I'm good enough, aren't I? Raymond says I am.*

Frank could never forget that Raymond, too, had come from unremarkable beginnings. On the dance floor, things like that didn't matter. On the dance floor, dreams were made.

It was thoughts like these that drew Frank along the hallway and onto the edges of the reception hall, where he lingered just outside the black and white chequers, marvelling at each new dancer in turn. Many of them seemed to be about the same age as Raymond de Guise and Hélène Marchmont, in their thirties, with all the experience of their years having shaped and strengthened their bodies to dancing perfection. But there were others here too – apprentices, Frank thought, little older than he was, and one boy, with jet-black hair in tight curls, who must have been even younger. Yes, he thrilled, there was hope here, if only he allowed himself to believe.

The dancers were moving on now, led by Raymond and Maynard Charles through the ornate silver arch, and down the gradient towards the doors of the Grand. Frank knew he ought not to follow. And yet, like a moth to a flame, he scuttled across the reception hall, slipping down the garlanded passageway to the Grand. A gramophone was playing one of his favourite songs, the 'Two Penny Tea Dance', and his feet were guiding him in little flourishes as he came down the hall.

He did not dare go in. That, he knew, would have been a step too far. But nobody could condemn him for just standing here, could they? Nobody could condemn him for having a dream.

They were all gathered on the dance floor. Gene Sheldon, Raymond's second in the troupe, was bedecked in the same dashing navy blue as Raymond. Mathilde, who had risen to principal dancer since Miss Marchmont's exile, looked angelic in white satin and lace. Archie Adams and key members of his orchestra stood shoulder to shoulder with the stars of the dance floor as, one by one, Maynard Charles introduced the members of the Winter Holler Company.

'The finest in Vienna,' Mr Charles was saying. 'Ladies and gentlemen, allow me to introduce Mr Maximilian Schank' – the rotund man with the walrus moustache, evidently their company director, appraised each of them keenly – 'Mr Jonas Holler, the troupe's principal dancer – and, last but not least, the company's shining star, Miss Karina Kainz.'

The Austrian angel beamed from ear to ear.

After that, there were too many names to remember. Raymond was walking the company around the edge of the dance floor, taking Karina Kainz into hold and turning her for a few steps as the gramophone played. Soon, the Buckingham dancers were lost in conversations of their own with the Winter Holler Company, and Maynard stepped out of the fray, filled – or so it seemed – with hope that something memorable had come to the hotel; that this might indeed be a season when the hotel's reputation truly was in the ascendant.

As he watched Jonas Holler and Karina Kainz slide effortlessly across the dance floor, getting to know its nuances and kinks in anticipation of the dances and autumn ball to come, Frank could feel the pull of the ballroom like never before. It was physical, this feeling. It was as though hands were around him, pulling him towards the centre of things, teasing him to skip down and slide in among the dancers themselves.

*One day*, he told himself. *One day soon.*

August 1938

# Chapter Fourteen

I T WAS LORD EDGERTON WHO had insisted the board meet away from the Buckingham. Ordinarily, when the hotel board congregated, they did so in the Benefactors' Study, that palatial conference room behind Maynard Charles's office. But evidently, for a matter as severe as this, a meeting at the hotel itself would simply not do. Consequently, on a bright summer's morning, Maynard stepped out of a taxicab on the Mall and, tipping the driver handsomely, warily approached the doors of Boodle's, Lord Edgerton's club.

Maynard had never held much truck with gentlemen's clubs, and Boodle's was one of the oldest around. As he was welcomed into the plush interior, the air around him was heavy with the scent of the finest continental cigars. There had been a club for fine gentlemen in this town house for nearly two hundred years. The grandfathers of those who had first congregated here had been the Cavaliers of old. Maynard was given to understand that Winston Churchill himself was one of the club's attendees. No doubt Mr Moorcock had his spies in these halls as well – but the thought brought Maynard little cheer. Today was a solemn day. The future of his hotel – and no doubt the future of his own role at the grand establishment – was suddenly in doubt.

Soon, one of the managers – a dry man in brown tweed, his blond hair trimmed back in a regimented cut – arrived and ushered him onwards, up a crooked staircase to the door of a private meeting room above.

'My apologies, sir. I'm told you require no introduction.'

Maynard watched as the day manager beat his retreat. Evidently, even he was nervous of what waited beyond those doors.

But the die had already been cast, so Maynard walked through.

Inside, the hotel board was gathered. Evidently, they'd been engaged in fierce debate for some time already, because everywhere he looked – from imperious Lord Edgerton, to the hunched-over Uriah Bell, to the obscene corpulence of Peter Merriweather – faces were etched in various different agonies. Even the lesser members of the board were here. Francis Lloyd, here representing his father, was sitting glumly in one corner, while Dickie Fletcher – the young man Lord Edgerton had once called 'an idiot with an inheritance' – sat staring at his lap. Among them all, only John Hastings seemed to have kept his pleasant demeanour. The American industrialist was half the age of the elder men in the group, and yet somehow he showed more maturity than all of them combined.

It was only Hastings who acknowledged Maynard as he closed the door behind him. Maynard inclined his head in a silent greeting, then took the last remaining seat at the table. Unlike the round table in the Benefactors' Study at the hotel, here the table came to a head – and sitting at it, as if he was the lord and master of all of the rest, Lord Edgerton reigned supreme.

'Mr Charles,' Lord Edgerton intoned, 'you join us at a most opportune moment. We've debated the history of this *incident*' – he sneered the word, as if it was an insult – 'for too long already.

It's time we made some decisions. But perhaps, first, you might appraise us of what's being done at the Buckingham to tidy up this mess?'

Maynard had been ready for this. Too often, being dragged before the hotel board felt like waiting for a caning from his old headmaster; but over the years he'd developed ways to turn these moments to his advantage. The first thing was to show the right deference. In the Buckingham halls, the chambermaids and concierges, the day managers and night managers, dancers and musicians, all paid deference to him; but, in here, it was Maynard Charles who was expected to grovel, with his cap in his hand. The trick, though, was not to grovel too much. Once they saw you had backbone, they started to respect you for it – even if they wouldn't admit it.

And Maynard had come here with only one ambition in mind: to preserve the career of Hélène Marchmont. Nothing less would do.

'Miss Marchmont has been on unpaid leave from the Grand for five weeks now. I won't pretend that the staff at the hotel don't know why. It was the rumours rippling across the hotel, of course, that forced us to take action. But our action was swift and decisive. It has killed the rumour stone dead. The gossips speak of other things in the hotel now. The Winter Holler Company has landed at last. You'd be surprised how much excitement an event like this causes in a closed establishment like ours. There are new romances to dream upon. Miss Marchmont's disgrace is forgotten, as it should be. Gentlemen, the world keeps turning, from one day to the next.'

He'd been rehearsing the speech for days and, if it hadn't come out exactly as he wanted, at least there was bite to it, at least there was passion. He waited – but into the silence that followed, Uriah Bell just laughed.

Uriah Bell: he was the one Maynard hated the most. Lord Edgerton was knowable; Lord Edgerton he understood. Bell was a man completely without vertebrae, whose only real passion in life – now that his riches amounted to untold millions – was bringing others down.

'Gone, Maynard? *Gone*, my good man? By the Lord we both love, you're a fool if you think it's so. Were she to set foot back in the hotel, it would be the talk of the ballroom again. Hélène Marchmont and her little bastard.'

'Now, Uriah!' John Hastings exclaimed. 'That's quite enough! I was always given to understand that the English comported themselves with more dignity than this. Miss Marchmont is one of ours. She deserves our respect.'

'Aye,' chipped in Peter Merriweather, in his broad Yorkshire brogue, 'and she'd have had it, too, if only she'd respected us in return. The way I see this, the girl made her choice. She made it when she climbed into bed with that black man. She made it when she lied to us and took our charity, to run away in secret, so that nobody might know of her shame. And she's been taking us for fools every day since.' He stopped. 'We're good people. Good, English people! It's bad enough London's welcomed in all sorts from everywhere. There are places it oughtn't to touch, and our ballroom's one of them.'

'Gentlemen,' Hastings broke in, 'might I remind you that we are gathered, here today, in the very same club that once counted none other than William Wilberforce among its members? How can we speak of our fellow human beings like this, in the place where he plotted and planned the abolition of slavery? We are better than this, gentlemen.'

'So was Hélène Marchmont. She ought to have stuck to her own. By God, she's a beauty. She could have married a lord! Why would she stoop to this? It must have broken her father, to denounce her like that.'

'Gentlemen!' Maynard realised he had leaped to his feet. 'You're forgetting the love our guests hold for Miss Marchmont. If I can't appeal to the decency of your hearts, then let me appeal to your pockets. Miss Marchmont is valuable to our ballroom. She's its star. How can we begin to calculate what might be lost if—'

'You can stop right there, Maynard,' Lord Edgerton seethed. 'I understand the balance books as well as any man here. I understand Miss Marchmont's monetary worth. But I also understand how little she'll be worth once our prized guests learn she allowed herself to mother a half-caste child.'

There was a sharp intake of breath. In the corner of his eye, Maynard saw John Hastings remove his spectacles and slide them into his pocket, then crack each knuckle as if getting ready for a fight.

'My lord,' Maynard began, trying desperately to seem contrite, 'we need Miss Marchmont. The Winter Holler Company have arrived for their residency, but a great part of that depends upon Miss Marchmont being there to dovetail with all they have planned. There's the Autumn Serenade to think of. And Christmas, already on the horizon. We can't be without our star.'

'The way I see it, gentlemen,' said Lord Edgerton, 'we have a viable alternative. Mathilde Bourchier is younger than Hélène. Not yet twenty years old, I understand. She is, some might say, an unsullied Marchmont. I'll grant you that she hasn't been crowned Queen of the Ballroom at the Royal Albert Hall. I'll grant you that she doesn't carry with her the glamour of *Harper's Bazaar*. But she has youth with her, and as much beauty as Hélène Marchmont bore in days gone by. Yes, Mathilde – in the arms of Raymond de Guise – might be the thing our ballroom needs. And in that case, what use have we for Miss Marchmont?'

'I'm minded to agree,' Peter Merriweather grunted. 'We've already spent hundreds, nay thousands, keeping this tittle-tattle out of the pages of *Tatler* and *The Queen*. But those vultures won't be satisfied forever. If we welcome her back to the ballroom, we're forever in their pockets.'

'It's a price worth paying!' Maynard barked. 'By God, you're men of money! Don't you see how this world works? In one column – income. In the other – expenditure. To make a profit, you have to spend! That's the way the world turns round!'

If it was the anger in Maynard's voice – unheralded, and unheard of – that brought his superiors to silence, it was, at least, the opening that John Hastings had been waiting for. Before Lord Edgerton could remind Maynard of exactly what his position was, Hastings stood up and said, 'Gentlemen, I'm going to make this decision very simple for all of us. Last year, when the Buckingham was at its lowest ebb, you reached out to me and asked me to save you from ruin by becoming your investor. Now, I understand that this provokes certain tensions in a group like this. I understand that it upsets the fine balance that you esteemed gentlemen have worked towards over a good number of years. But I did not sign up to direct a hotel where we treat our own people no better than those Nazis over the water. Consequently, gentlemen, we will act like all decent men should.

We will give Miss Hélène Marchmont a chance – and, if we do not, my company will absolve itself of its responsibilities to this group. And we shall take our money with us.'

There was silence in the room.

'So,' said John Hastings, 'we need a majority decision, based on the value of shares we each hold. Mr Lloyd, Mr Fletcher, I'm afraid this renders your own votes rather mute – though I believe that, as decent upstanding young men, you'll be voting with me. And that requires two of you gentlemen' – he turned to Lord Edgerton, Uriah Bell and Peter Merriweather, the three elder statesmen of the board – 'to make the decent choice. And, if not for decency's sake, then for the future of your hotel. Because, believe me, gentlemen, I need no further reason to remove myself from this board than the knowledge that I am seated with fascists.'

The word caused a reverberation around the table, for it was no secret that Lord Edgerton dined weekly with his friends from the British Union of Fascists.

'So, gentlemen, a show of hands?'

Dickie Fletcher's hand was the first to go up. Francis Lloyd followed soon after, though he was clever enough to look glum about it. Then, after a moment's rumination, Uriah Bell lifted his arm. When Peter Merriweather did the same, he fixed John Hastings with a look that told him that, though he might have won this one battle, the war was far from over.

'That leaves just you, Mr Edgerton,' Hastings said, 'so it seems that we're decided.' He turned to Maynard Charles. 'Have your man Mr Brogan deliver a letter in person. The Autumn Serenade is but six weeks away, and the Winter Holler Company already in our halls. She's to start rehearsing, on full pay, by tomorrow afternoon. Gentlemen, good day.'

John Hastings was almost at the door, Maynard Charles excusing himself to follow thereafter, when Lord Edgerton called him back.

'Mr Hastings,' he intoned.

John Hastings looked over his shoulder.

'Have I forgotten something, gentlemen?'

'Indeed you have. It seems, you Yankee reprobate, that you have forgotten my name.'

'Oh yes?'

'I am *Lord* Edgerton, Mr Hastings. Not 'Mr', but *Lord*. And from now on, whether inside this room or without, you will refer to me by my royally appointed title. Am I understood?'

'Oh,' said John Hastings, 'I believe I understand you very much indeed.'

There was a taxicab there to pick her up. Maynard Charles might have planned her exit to perfection, but he'd planned her return down to its most intimate detail as well.

The one thing that she wasn't expecting was Raymond de Guise.

Hélène was standing at the door of the Brixton terrace when the taxicab pulled up. Sybil, straining in her arms, barely wanted to let her go – and this was the most wonderful feeling of all. Five weeks of lounging with Sybil, going to her when she cried in the night, making her meals and getting her dressed, learning all the little things about her that she'd been missing, had been the most singular joy of her life. And if, in moments, she'd heard that little voice niggling in the back of her head – that imperious, judging voice, telling her that this was a fantasy, that it couldn't go on forever – it had not diminished the joy and warmth of it one bit.

Only now, with Sybil straining in her arms, did Hélène understand the cost of those weeks as well. For how could she leave her again, and again, and again? Each time was getting more difficult than the last, and this was the worst of them all.

The taxicab window wound down, and there was Raymond.

Hélène froze. She felt as if she was tumbling, tumbling into herself.

Raymond himself had known for two years the secret she was keeping. He was no stranger to secrets himself. She thought, suddenly, of Raymond's own past, and the lie he'd lived all those years – until the day Nancy arrived at the Buckingham and transformed his life in the most wonderful ways. Being set free from that secret had lifted him. Ever since then he'd soared on air.

But his secret – of the East End, of the Cohens, of escaping into the world of dance and changing his name – was not comparable to *her* secret. And now, of course, they all knew. She didn't doubt, for a second, that she'd been the talk of the housekeeping lounge, nor that the waiters in the Candlelight Club had made jokes at her expense. Now that she saw Raymond's face, the scale of the lie she'd been living was too real. Her body throbbed with the shame of it.

*But no*, she told herself. *I'll not be ashamed. Not of this darling girl in my arms. And no, I won't be sorry that I lied, either. Because how could any of them understand?*

So she wrapped her arms around Sybil, crossed the little brick wall that separated the terrace from the road, and approached Raymond as he stepped out of the taxicab.

'Raymond,' she said, with such fierce pride that she was almost beaming with it, 'allow me to introduce my daughter, Sybil Archer.'

Raymond extended his hand gracefully, as was his way, and took the little girl's podgy fingers in his own.

'Charmed, I'm sure.'

After they had said their farewells, and the taxicab was ferrying them back along Brixton Road, Hélène felt herself crumple in her seat. Raymond, who had been respecting her silence, reached out for her hand.

'She's beautiful, Hélène.'

*She really is*, he thought.

He'd quite forgotten the expressions Sidney used to make, the way his eyes focused so intently each time he lifted his trumpet to his lips – but Sybil had the very same expressions, the very same crinkles between her eyes. And there was so much of Hélène in her too. The perfect mingling of two loving souls, thought Raymond – and, with that thought, came the weight of what must have come after. All the grief. The uncertainty. The fear of being exposed.

'The dancers are on your side, Hélène. They wish you'd told them.'

Hélène drew herself upright. She tried to compose herself, asked the driver if he might permit her to wind the window down and let in a little of the summer air.

'I couldn't risk it.'

'You're a sister to all of us. Archie Adams most of all. He hasn't said it, but he's almost ashamed you couldn't confide in him.'

She turned to him, lolled her head upon his shoulder.

'What's it like, Raymond, at the hotel?'

There was no denying the shock and consternation that had ricocheted through the dressing rooms behind the Grand. Mathilde's panic at being told that she was suddenly to be principal dancer had been the least of it. There was disappointment and confusion, anxiety for the future. There was disbelief all over.

'But then there was the guilt,' said Raymond. 'And, in the end, the utter admiration. Because not one of us could have done it. Separated from Sybil every day, dancing for her future, and all the while keeping everything hidden. You think they're things to be ashamed of? Hélène, you ought to be proud.'

'Maybe it's that way for the dancers. Maybe for Archie and the rest of them. But they'll be gossiping about me in the housekeeping lounge. Every concierge and porter will have it out for me now.'

Raymond was silent. The way Nancy had told it, the chambermaids had spoken about little else. To some, it was a romance far greater than any novelette or short story from the *Reader's Digest*s they collected. To others, a liar was a liar, and would be a liar all of their lives. But he did not say this. He simply put his arm around her instead.

'Maynard Charles has asked to see me, before the dances tonight. Hastings forced the board to reaccept me, but I'll be watched. I don't know if I can bear it, Raymond.'

'One day at a time,' said Raymond.

'Will I be dancing at the Autumn Serenade?'

Raymond held her even more tightly. 'In my arms.'

'Look at us, Raymond. You, about to be married, about to build worlds. Me, with mine falling apart—'

'And yet, the two of us, still dancing together.'

It felt good to hear this and, as they came over the sparkling waters of the river, through the great palaces at Westminster, she began to *hope*. Hope, she'd always known, was a dangerous thing. It could be like walking along the edge of a cliff in a gale, buffeted backwards and forwards. Hope was the thing that destroyed you. Hope was what killed.

When the taxicab delivered them to Berkeley Square, they didn't have to go up the marble stairs and through the hotel's iconic revolving door, for the ballroom's exterior doors were open to the summer air – and, through them, Hélène could see the dance troupe was already gathered. There was Gene Sheldon, turning with Mathilde Bourchier in his arms. There was Archie Adams and Louis Kildare and Harry Dudgeon, the new percussionist in the orchestra. And there, all around, were dancers Hélène had never seen before.

'The Winter Hollers,' said Raymond, 'getting ready for the Autumn Serenade. They're good, Hélène. John Hastings was right. He saw them on his tour of the Continent last year. He knew they'd bring some spectacle. Some continental glamour. God knows, we need it, after all the bad news pouring out of there.'

Hélène's eyes roamed further.

'She's beautiful,' she whispered, with her eyes on Karina Kainz, tall and lithe and blonde and swooning in the arms of Jonas Holler. 'They look angelic. One of them dark, and one of them light, like in all the best stories.'

'Dancing with disaster.' Raymond smiled. 'That's what Mr Schank – he's the company director, over there – calls it. They talk about dancing at the edge of things, going as far as they can go, making people hold their breath.'

*Like walking on a clifftop in a gale*, thought Hélène.

There were others in the company too. On the other side of the dance floor, hanging from the balustrade, she saw a young man with a mop of black hair, and the soft features of somebody who ought, really, to still have been hanging from his mama's apron strings. Probably he was closer to Sybil's age than he was to Hélène's – and this made her feel truly old.

'Why's Frank Nettleton talking to that boy?'

'Oh,' said Raymond, 'that's Ansel Albrecht. The youngest of the Winter Hollers, but a boy with great talent. He had to choose between ballet and the ballroom, but ballet's loss is the ballroom's gain. Frank's adopted him. Well, it's Mr Charles's fault, really – I do believe he has a soft spot for young Frank. He's given him the responsibility of being personal page to the Winter Hollers, to run whatever errands they need running, but the truth is this normally results in young Frank loitering in the ballroom and just . . . watching. Ansel's been a good friend to him. They're . . . er . . . teaching Billy Brogan to dance.'

Hélène laughed. She couldn't help herself. It was so unexpected that it caught Raymond off guard.

'Come,' she said, 'why don't you introduce me?'

Together, they stepped into the Grand. They hadn't yet reached the edge of the balustrade, where Maximilian Schank was deep in thought, when the dancers on the floor came apart and looked up.

'Mr Schank,' Raymond began. 'Mr Holler. Miss Kainz. Mr Albrecht . . .' On the other side of the dance floor, Ansel Albrecht – who had been guffawing at something Frank said – suddenly stood to attention. 'May I introduce the one true Queen of the Grand Ballroom, Miss Hélène Marchmont?'

'Mrs Archer, don't you mean?'

The dancers were surging up to introduce themselves, but all that Hélène heard were these chuckled words, coming from one of the hotel joiners, who was fixing the hinges on the ballroom door. Her eyes flashed towards him, her skin burning scarlet – but then the dancers were all around her, smothering her with their welcoming love, and when she looked again, the joiner was gone.

It wasn't the only chuckle she'd hear. She was certain of that. She was going to have to be bold, if she was going to be here at all. She was going to have to survive. So she drew herself up, painted a new smile across her face, and said, 'So, who's going to show me what I've missed? How many weeks until the Autumn Serenade are there? People, we have work to do!'

Soon, both Mathilde and Karina Kainz were taking Hélène down onto the dance floor, while Raymond remained above with Jonas Holler and Maximilian Schank, to talk about how the entrances of both the Buckingham dancers and the Winter Holler troupe might be staged.

On the dance floor, she felt free. On the dance floor, she could almost forget. Here, three women together, there was nothing to talk about but the turns and lifts, the chassés and glides, the promenades and changes of which their performances would be comprised. And here Hélène Marchmont was in her element. Here she could be queen.

An hour later, with the ballroom being cleared for the afternoon demonstrations, Hélène took her leave and disappeared through the dressing rooms beyond. For a moment, she was grateful for the emptiness. She felt as if she'd survived a storm. Then, if only to reclaim the sense that this used to be her home, she slipped out, rode the service lift upwards, and returned to her suite.

It was here that Archie Adams was waiting.

'Archie?' she ventured, when she saw him at her door. He must have slipped out of the Grand before her. 'Archie, is everything all right?'

The elder man nodded vigorously, straightening his collar.

'Hélène, perhaps we could talk?'

She took a stride towards him, closing the gap between them by half.

'Archie, please understand, we couldn't tell a soul. It was what Sidney wanted too. If he'd told you, you'd have felt sworn to us. You'd have had to keep the secret. What might Mr Charles have thought of you, then? Or the board? Please, Archie. We didn't tell a soul, but not just for our sakes. We didn't want you to be sullied by it either.'

'Oh, my dear Hélène.' Archie shook his head sadly. 'There wasn't a thing in the world I wouldn't have done for Sidney Archer – just as for any of my boys. But you had your reasons. I respect that. I daresay I even love you for it. You've been a brave woman.'

'Then, Archie, why are you here?'

Archie gestured to the door. 'Might we talk in private? There's something I'd like to discuss with you.'

Hélène fumbled with her keys and admitted them both to the chambers she had not seen in five long weeks. What an aeon that had been! But here was everything, lying exactly the same as when she'd left it.

Quietly, she closed the door.

'What's this about, Mr Adams?'

'Hélène,' Archie began, 'I've known you for ten long years. Long before the Grand Ballroom, when I was just a bandleader and you a young dancer, moving from garden party to ball. You know me, don't you? And you know I have your best interests at heart.'

'You always have, Mr Adams. Ever since . . .'

She said no more. Archie understood what he meant to her. He'd been among the first to tell her she had talent. He'd been among the first to tell her that the world craved dancers just like her – that, with beauty and poise like Hélène had, every ballroom in the world would want her. Oh, there had been other men who came to tell her such things – there always were – but Archie was one of the few who hadn't done it with a hand on her waist, or another curling possessively around the small of her back, as if she might end up owing them something. Archie Adams: the consummate gentleman. That was why she'd followed him, when he'd asked if he might represent her interests. That was how she'd first come to the Grand, the season it opened, and in doing so had changed the story of her life.

'An opportunity has presented itself, Hélène.'

It was dark in her rooms. She flurried around, turning on the lamps, before looking back at Archie.

'An opportunity?'

'An old associate of mine. A cousin of a cousin. He leads the orchestra at the Court in Chicago. You've heard of it?'

She had not. All the stories she'd told of visiting the Americas were lies. She'd been asked before, but that had been in a different world – one where Sybil was yet to exist.

'It used to be a common hostelry, there in the heart of Chicago. But now, after years of investment, it's one of the swankiest joints in town.'

When Archie adopted an American accent for 'swankiest joints' it sounded almost indecipherable – and that, at least, made her laugh.

'Why are you telling me this, Archie?'

'Because they're to lose their lead dancer. Rachel Adams. She's fallen in love and is choosing a different life.' Archie paused. 'So could you.'

Hélène realised that she was hugging herself. She needed something on to which she could cling.

'No commissions, no contracts – not between you and me, in any case. I'm not your representative for this one, Hélène. I'm your friend. I could call them right now and they'd put you on an aeroplane to Chicago. Now, I'm not saying these things are without complications, but in Chicago they'd pay you well enough that you might even have a nanny, and live in an apartment away from the hotel, and . . . be everything you want to be. Away from all this. A fresh beginning.'

'To dance . . . *and* be a mother?' she whispered.

There were other things to think about. Suddenly, her mind was a whirlwind of them. There were Maurice and Noelle. There were her friends, right here in the hotel. There were her dying father, and her mother and aunt – the very people who had pushed her life to the precipice on which she now stood.

And then there was Sybil, who – only hours before – had said her name over and over and over again as she left: 'Mama. Mama. *Mama!*'

'You don't have to decide now. There's time. I'm told Miss Adams isn't to be wed until the spring, and she'll dance until then. But . . .' Archie stepped back, his hands folded in front of him – like a penitent, Hélène observed, when in truth he had come delivering a dream. 'Think about it, Hélène. Because, if there's one thing I've learned across all these years on God's green earth – there isn't only one way to live a life.'

# Chapter Fifteen

**M**RS AGATHA NUTTALL HAD KEPT the Regency Bridal shop on Portobello Mews for thirty years. In that time, she had seen all manner of brides-to-be come and go. There were the brides who brought their mothers and grandmothers with them, prim and proper and spending their fathers' hard-earned money as if it was their own. There were the bright young things, who'd debuted only a season before and were already embarking on the true adventure of married life. And then there were girls like the one being fawned over by her bridesmaids-to-be in the shop right now. The reluctant brides. The brides who, though they glowed with the love they had for their future husbands, shuddered at being made a fuss of. Who would have been happy enough to walk down the aisle in a nice blouse from the John Lewis department store, up on Oxford Street.

The second of the Regency Bridal's two suites was a small chamber, the shape of a piece of pie. One wall was lined with mirrors; another was a deep wardrobe, big enough for three shop girls to search through at the same time. A bank of soft furnishings ran between them, and in front of this a small pedestal on which the brides-to-be were expected to pose and turn. It was this part of the operation that Nancy seemed to be struggling with. Poor girl, thought Agatha; she was going to have to find some courage if she was going to stand in front of a crowd and make her vows.

'It's beautiful, Nancy!' Rosa was exclaiming, clapping her hands together eagerly. 'Nancy, it's the one!'

'You've said that six times,' Ruth said, her eyes glinting darkly. Agatha liked this one. She had a devilish streak in her. It probably meant she'd never get married. Yes, this one had 'maiden aunt' written all over her.

'Well, this time, I mean it. What do you think, Nance?'

Nancy, who was wearing a simple white gown with long, flowing sleeves and embroidery marking its shoulders, turned on the pedestal so that she might inspect her body from every angle. Something was sitting crookedly on her. The dress nipped at her midriff. It felt tight and flowing all at once.

'It just isn't . . . me.'

'Isn't you?' Rosa cackled. 'Oh, Nancy, it's your *big day*! You look like a princess.'

Nancy grinned. 'I don't feel like a princess.'

'No,' Rosa said – and suddenly she was on her feet, turning towards the dark expanse of the wardrobe, 'but you're going to. Next!'

And, clapping her hands, she disappeared within.

Ruth, who had been looking Nancy up and down with an unusual glint in her eyes, said, 'You know, Nancy, it does look special. So did the one before last. You're going to be a beautiful bride.'

Nancy was quite taken aback. A compliment from Ruth was a rare thing.

'Thank you.'

On the edge of the room, Vivienne said, 'You'll have to excuse me, girls,' and scuttled off, looking for the water closet.

'That's the third time,' Ruth said. 'It's those cream scones from earlier. She doesn't know what's good for her. Why'd you bring her along anyway, Nancy? I reckon she just doesn't like slumming it with us chambermaids. Little Lady Edgerton—'

Nancy gave her an admonishing look.

'She's my friend,' she said flatly. 'And she's not like that anymore. Vivienne slums it more than any of us ever do. You should come and visit the Daughters. Then you'd see. There are worlds below ours, Ruth! They'd look at you like we do the crown prince of Norway.'

Perhaps it had been wrong to invite her. The fact was, Vivienne had been glum all day. Not for the first time, Nancy mused upon the two Miss Edgertons she knew: the one who, waking up each morning at the Buckingham Hotel, was tense and coiled, living a lie; and the one who, at the Daughters of Salvation each night, came alive with purpose and ambition and *passion*. She'd been hoping for the second Vivienne today, but instead she'd spent the morning silent and far away, as if her mind was on other things.

Presently, Vivienne returned, and looked Nancy up and down for a second time.

'It's not the one, but you're getting close.' She seemed brighter now. Perhaps the fresh air had restored her. 'You're going to look beautiful.'

'That's what I keep saying' – Ruth tutted – 'but she won't listen. Practical Nancy Nettleton, won't even get excited for her own wedding day!'

Nancy was about to open her mouth in a cheerful rebuke when, all of a sudden, Rosa re-emerged from the wardrobe with three dresses draped over her arms. Here was the full range of everything the Regency Bridal had to offer: an ostentatious gown, with lace ruffs and a bouffant neckline fit for Queen Elizabeth I; an elegant, understated number of unadorned silk; and a dress with tassels and minute details etched up and down every seam, fit for some Hollywood star.

'If we can't find something for you here, Nancy, we won't find it anywhere!'

But Nancy's face only creased up. 'I think we might need a break, girls. For a pot of tea and another cream scone?'

As the groans resounded around the room – even Vivienne joining in with the titters of dismay – Agatha Nuttall looked at the girl up on the pedestal and smiled. Yes, she thought, she'd seen a lot of these sorts of girls across the years.

The *undecided* brides.

'I don't know what it is,' said Nancy, as they gathered on the tables overlooking the verdant dells of Hyde Park. They'd already walked, basking in the brilliant summer sunshine, along the banks of the Serpentine, and – after an exertion like that – there was no choice but to sustain themselves with more cakes and tea. 'It's not that I'm nervous of marrying Raymond. I'm dreaming of it! It's—'

'It's this registry office malarkey,' Rosa said. 'You want a big white wedding in the church, right there on Berkeley Square.'

Ruth spluttered, showering her cup and saucer in hot tea.

'Shows how much you know, Rosa! Nance doesn't want the fuss. That's it, isn't it? She'd be happy with a little service at the town hall, then a spot of lunch on the river, then back to changing some lordling's sheets in the Pacific Suite, or sorting out the dry-cleaning for what's-his-name, our resident refugee – Tobias Bauer.'

'A sweet old man,' chipped in Nancy.

'You don't know nothing, Ruth,' Rosa chirruped. 'It's not *true love* if you're not excited. If you're not thrilling all of the time.'

Ruth smirked. 'That's the way it is for you and little Frankie, is it?'

'As a matter of fact,' said Rosa, beaming from ear to ear, 'it's exactly like that. Pooh! What would you know about it? Ruth Attercliffe, you won't even look a boy in the eye. It's like you don't even want to.'

'You don't know what you're talking about.' Ruth had grown taut. 'As a matter of fact, I'm envious of what our Nance has with her Raymond. And I'm not the only unmarried lady out today, am I, Miss Edgerton?'

Vivienne still seemed far away, watching a mother duck lead her ducklings down to the water's edge. She took a moment too long to come out of her daydream and said, 'Well, there are more important things than romance, wouldn't you say? Besides, there's time enough for all that.'

'Not if there's a war,' said Rosa. 'That's why I'm thrilled for Nancy here. Marrying, when the time's right! Well, it'll be me and Frank next. You'll give us your blessing, won't you, Nance?'

Nancy held her hands up, as if to excuse herself from the debate.

'But I should be delighted with you as a sister, Rosa.'

'Ruth here'll have to start *trying*, though. If you're so envious of true love, Ruth, you could have it with Billy Brogan. I'm saying it for your own good. You have to give things a chance, if they're ever going to blossom. It's not all just lightning strikes and Cupid's arrow.'

Ruth folded her hands across her belly. 'How do you know I haven't already got myself a chap?' she demanded.

Rosa's shriek could be heard echoing all across Hyde Park. 'Well, have you?'

Ruth was silent.

'I should say not! Look, just give him a dance. You don't have to marry him, do you? A dance is just a dance. Then see how it goes. Billy's working so hard to try and be good enough for you. Matter of fact, I know he's doing that right now – him and Frank, and that dancer from the Winter Holler lot, Ansel, they're tutoring Billy this very second. Effort like that shouldn't go unrewarded, Ruth. He *likes* you.'

Ruth scowled. 'I didn't know I had to *reward* him for doing something I haven't even asked for.'

It was Vivienne who came to her defence.

'Ruth's right. A lady doesn't have to do anything she doesn't want to do.'

'Well,' Rosa chirped, 'we're not ladies here – none but you, if you'll pardon me, Miss Edgerton.' She sighed. 'I'll say no more, Ruth. But that boy's one of the good ones, you mark my words. Might be he can be a bit of a clown, but he's as far from a scoundrel as they come – excepting my Frank, of course – and I reckon you could be good for each other. A bit of happiness while there's still a chance, see? And, well, if you have got a gentleman friend

194

you've not been telling us about – if you *have* got some deep, dark secret you're hiding away – well, we'll find out about it soon enough.' She beamed. 'You mark my words!'

'One, two, three, four . . . One, two, three, four . . .'

Afternoon was turning to twilight and, in the little dance studio behind the Grand Ballroom, Billy Brogan's lessons went on. To the crackling tune of the gramophone, Billy box-stepped around the room in Frank's arms – while, sitting cross-legged on the floor in imitation of his own old tutor, Ansel Albrecht of the Winter Holler Company tried valiantly to control his laughter.

'You've got to stop counting,' Frank whispered. It was strange being led by Billy Brogan, but (though he'd only admit it to Nancy and Rosa), Frank rather liked being on this side of the dance. It made the most simple things feel strangely new. 'Come on now, show him what we can do. Reverse corté to the left. On my count.'

'One, two, three—'

'No Billy!' Frank urged him. 'Get that count out of your head. Listen to me count down.'

Billy whispered, 'Reverse corté, got it.'

'Now, Billy!'

But, if Billy could remember what a reverse corté was, it hardly mattered – because, in the next moment, he'd tried to close his left foot to his right, trapped Frank's ankle between his own, and sent them both sprawling to the studio floor.

Ansel could contain himself no longer.

'Bravo, bravo!' he cried out, in his Austrian-inflected English, and leaped to his feet in stupendous applause.

In seconds, Billy was back upright. Frank tried to step into his hold but Billy, humiliated for the seventh time that hour, refused to take him. Instead, he just danced around the room with a phantom partner, arms held out to hold somebody who wasn't there, still counting each step under his breath.

Frank came to sit with Ansel.

'Is it hopeless?'

Ansel, who was still beaming, said, 'It is never hopeless, Frank. Music is in everyone. That's what my old tutor, Herr Lansard, used to say. It's just that, in some people . . . it's a little more hidden than others.'

Billy heard this – Frank could tell, because his cheeks flushed scarlet – and still he danced on.

They'd been coming to the studio every spare moment across the last two weeks, every hour it wasn't in use by the Winter Hollers and the Buckingham's own dancers. At first, it had just been Frank and Billy, sneaking in here to perfect their routine, but once Ansel knew what they were up to, he became a more than willing participant in their scheme.

'It is a privilege and an honour to dance with Mr Holler and Miss Kainz, but it can be a lonely affair,' he had once confided, 'being the youngest dancer among them.'

Frank could understand that. He'd been at the Buckingham a year already, but he could still vividly remember the feeling of those first weeks and months, uncertain of how to behave or who to speak to, or even who to befriend. Ansel was like him, he thought – but, oh, what a life he was living!

At seventeen years old, Ansel was not old enough to remember the last time war ravaged his Austrian homeland, but he knew only too well the way a war that was yet to be born was destroying everything he held dear.

'My father is a policeman,' he'd told Frank, the first time they came together to try and show Billy the true way to perform a double reverse spin (and ended up, instead, holding ice cubes wrapped in a dishcloth against his sprained wrist). 'He always wanted me to follow in those footsteps. But it wasn't for me. My mother, she always understood. She trained as a ballet dancer, you see. She could have been a star. But then . . . well, love comes along and upsets the best laid plans. She had me, and I was dancing before I could walk. I don't remember a day when it wasn't in my bones. My father . . . well, he never understood. Dancing is for the girls, he'd say. Dancing is for the *effete*. But even he was pleased, in the end, that I did not become a cadet in the police. Now that the Nazis are there, every right-thinking police officer is running scared. Ever since Herr Hitler set his sights on Vienna, the police have stood up to him. Now that the Anschluss has happened . . . well, it won't be long before they pay the price for those crimes.'

'The crimes of standing up for your own countrymen?'

'For treachery against the Reich,' Ansel said, shaking his head. 'My father is keeping his head down now, hoping to go ignored. But . . . I'm scared for him, Frank, and for my sister too. And – yes, I suppose I'm guilty. That it's me who got to escape Vienna, and simply because I can dance.' He paused. 'There are some among us who plan to stay, who'll just abandon the company and remain in London when Mr Schank orders us back home. Perhaps I should do the same – the romance of a runaway dancer! – but my mother and father, my sister Lisette, they long for my return.'

In the dance studio, Billy had got confused. Somehow, he was counting *backwards*.

'Is it time we told him to stop?' Ansel whispered.

'Just a little longer,' Frank said. 'By the devil, I think he's got it!'

But he hadn't. Both his legs seemed to be dancing to rhythms of their own accord. It was like watching a marionette on strings.

'I know what will help,' said Ansel.

He was wearing the most inscrutable grin. Frank watched as he picked himself up, trotted across the room, and delved into the leather satchel he carried with him everywhere. When he came back, he was brandishing a bottle of cherry liqueur.

'From my father's drinking cabinet.' He beamed. 'Hey, Billy?'

Billy stopped in the middle of his phantom dance, and looked at them witheringly.

'It'll loosen you up,' said Ansel, with a wolfish grin. 'Get rid of those inhibitions. Come on, Billy! If you can't let the music get you in the mood, how about we do it the old-fashioned way?'

It was worth a try, Billy supposed. It was worth two tries, he supposed, once he'd drunk his first measure and felt the sweet warmth radiating about his body. When he attempted dancing, and found that he was still feeling stiff and disjointed, Ansel convinced him it was worth a third try – and then, because Frank was doing it too, he decided it was worth a fourth and a fifth. There was something in this, Billy started to think. It was no wonder all those lords and ladies quaffed so much champagne on their nights in the Grand, when it made you feel as bold and brilliant as this.

'Of course,' he hiccuped, 'you won't be able to stand your liqueur, Frank, but we Brogans have been weaned on it. Even the little ones have a snifter of brandy at Christmas, don't you know?

I been developing a refined palate for the stuff since I was knee-high. Just you watch what I can do, now I've no fear.'

'Dutch courage!' Frank chortled, as Billy turned back to the studio floor.

'*Austrian* courage!' Ansel exclaimed, clapping Frank's hand. '*Viennese* courage for a Viennese waltz! Come on, Billy, show us your stuff!'

Billy strode back to the gramophone, dropped the needle back into place, and began to waltz around the room, holding his imaginary partner close.

He lasted only seconds before he was flat on his face.

'Billy, you're like a baby deer!' Ansel laughed, rushing to help him up. 'We took it too far. Next time – only one measure for you. Just enough to take the edge off.'

Ansel had reached out his hand to help him up, but Billy, affronted, scrabbled up of his own accord.

'You two are making a mockery of me!'

Then he took off, out of the studio door.

'Come on, Ansel, after him!' Frank cried. 'If Mr Charles knows he's been drinking, he'll be for the chop.'

By the time they clattered through the door, Billy had rushed across the reception hall, around the back of the golden lift, and into the warren of passages beyond. Ansel and Frank gave chase. Past the housekeeping lounge, past the old laundry – evidently, Billy could run better than he could dance, because he barely broke stride at all, not until they'd followed him down through the tradesman's exit and out onto Michaelmas Mews.

It was a balmy summer evening, and Berkeley Square was lit up by the rectangles of light emanating from the town houses all around. In the trees, nightingales were in full song. This – combined with the cherry brandy still turning his lips sickly sweet – gave Frank the most delicious idea.

'Come on, Billy,' he said. 'The night's young. Just listen to the birdsong! Here, I'll show you.'

Frank took Billy by the hands, ducked and weaved, kicked and turned. Soon Ansel was dancing alongside him, each of them jiving alone.

'It's like this, Billy! Just let it all out. Don't focus on anything. Just . . . let it happen! You know your problem? You think everything can be mastered by *thinking*. Well, sometimes you oughtn't to think at all. Just *feel*!'

Billy could feel something. He could feel it rising up his gorge, and the taste of cherry brandy back in his throat.

But he could feel something else too. At first it seemed impossible. Could it really be that Frank was right?

He lifted himself up. He let go of Frank's hands and took hold of Ansel. He turned and he weaved, he kicked and he hopped. He spun on the spot, and then – when long moments had passed and he was quite certain he wasn't going to fall over – he let go of Ansel and turned and turned again, pirouetting out across the grasses of Berkeley Square like he was a Catherine wheel.

And it felt good. It felt ridiculous – but good! He could hear Frank cheering. He could hear Ansel shouting out, 'It's working! Frank, he's doing it!' And the feeling was insurmountable. This feeling was one of elation. He was in control of it, now. He was a master. And he decided, there and then, that he'd give them a finish they could be proud of. He closed his eyes, let the music (all of it in his head!) propel him onwards, until – in the final moment – he lifted his imaginary partner high and opened his arms with a flourish, as if it was he, Billy Brogan, who was the true King of the Ballroom, and to hell with Raymond de Guise!

Billy Brogan opened his eyes.

There were Frank and Ansel, egging him on with wild, drunken delight.

And there, beyond them, were Nancy, Vivienne, Rosa – and Ruth Attercliffe herself – all stepping out of a taxicab on the opposite side of the square.

The girls stared at him with expressions of staggered disbelief. Then, in a cacophony of titters and whispered words, they vanished into the darkness of Michaelmas Mews.

'Frank! Ansel! You blackguards! You scoundrels! Now what's she going to think of me?' Billy roared, staggering up to them – and realising, too late, how dizzy the combination of dance and drink could make a man. 'You've made me look like an absolute buffoon! Now what am I going to do?'

Neither Frank nor Ansel got the opportunity to answer that question, but in moments Billy had provided an answer himself – for, no sooner had he stopped shouting, he doubled over and vomited up a thick stream of cherry brandy, right there in the grasses of Berkeley Square.

'At least she wasn't there to see this,' said a contrite Frank.

But Billy's shame was already absolute.

September 1938

# Chapter Sixteen

T HE AUTUMN SERENADE WAS A NEW addition to the roster of balls and soirées that featured in the calendar of the Grand Ballroom – yet, to Maynard Charles's eyes, it could not come round quickly enough. Last Christmas, when fire had torn through the dance studio and dressing rooms, he'd wondered if they'd ever reach this point. He'd looked at the devastation, studied the ledger books long into the dark, lonely nights, and thought that, perhaps, the great game was finished, that the Buckingham Hotel was being consigned to history. They'd lost so much: Christmas cancelled, the New Year's Masque a non-event. Kings and queens and crown princes, lords and ladies, dukes and counts from across the Continent had chosen to spend their Christmases elsewhere instead. The Savoy, the Ritz, the Imperial – all, and more, had benefited from the disaster that was the Buckingham's last winter.

*But you wouldn't think it now*, thought Maynard Charles as he stood by the doors of the Grand Ballroom, all the great and good of London society fanning out around him, and took in the splendour that was his Autumn Serenade.

Plans had been afoot for an autumnal celebration, even before the last whisper of winter left Berkeley Square. Every ballroom had a Christmas extravaganza. Every ballroom sought to seduce the scions of society for their New Year masques. There were Summer Balls aplenty, Spring Fancies, celebrations on Midwinter's Night. But, in London this year, only the Buckingham was celebrating the way the leaves were turning to russet and red around the town houses of Mayfair; only the Buckingham would garland its hall with wreaths of crisp autumn leaves, red berries, and pine cones glittering in gold. Here the guests were now – industrialists and baronets, men from the ministries and embassies, the Duke and Duchess of Norfolk and their heir apparent, and around them a coterie of other dukes and consorts from all the English shires. The Grand Ballroom was bustling with activity – bustling with *promise* – and no sight had made Maynard happier for years.

The clock above the dance floor was counting down towards seven, and the start of the evening's festivities. Feeling the anticipation in the air, Maynard picked his way along the grand curve of the cocktail bar, towards the place where Lord Edgerton and the rest of the hotel board were waiting, partitioned off by a velvet rope. They stuck out like a sore thumb in the Grand Ballroom – *like ghosts at the feast*, thought Maynard; not one of them was truly looking forward to the dancing.

The Buckingham had spared no expense this evening. The guest singers brought in to accompany the Archie Adams Orchestra were feted across London and beyond – and the Winter Holler Company, who would soon make their long-awaited debut on the dance floor, had made such a dent in the Buckingham's finances that it had taken passion and grit to get the hotel board to sign off on them at all.

'We need glamour,' Maynard had told them, though it was an argument that had been wearing thin over the years. Every aristocratic Englishman knew the value of reputation, but with the Continent closing down, every Englishman knew the value of guarding his financial reserves closely as well. Lord Edgerton, in particular, had been like a dragon with his hoard.

*But it will all be worth it*, Maynard thought. He looked upwards, waiters waltzing around him as they delivered magnums of Moët et Chandon and vintage Veuve Clicquot to the assembled guests, and saw how the chandeliers had themselves been turned into great autumnal wreaths. It was details like this that made him the proudest of all.

Tobias Bauer shuffled past, dressed in an expensive evening suit that made him look twenty years younger, and stopped to say hello. Waylaid on his way to the members of the board, Maynard inclined his head in a greeting. The board could wait; it was guests that mattered most of all.

'You've outdone yourself, Mr Charles,' Bauer began. 'And a chance to see dancers from my very own Vienna! I feel as if it is entirely in my honour.'

The old man's cheeks flushed red.

'A happy coincidence, Herr Bauer, but the joy it brings you makes it all worthwhile.' Maynard was adept at saying exactly what his guests wanted to hear, but this time he meant every word. If the world was soon to be full of exiles like Bauer, he meant to do everything he could to help. 'I trust you will enjoy your evening.'

Maynard had only just extricated himself from the conversation when another hand clapped him on the shoulder, and he turned to see John Hastings standing there with his wife. In a gown of chiffon and lace, Sarah wore a line of simple pearls around her neck, and two smaller pearls in her ears. The ring on her finger was clasping one of the biggest single diamonds he had ever seen.

'Are we all set, Mr Charles?'

'Your fellow board members are congregated, Mr Hastings. Lord Edgerton was doing the rounds earlier.' Maynard lowered his voice. 'It's his old trick – stay aloof so that, if the night's a failure, he isn't touched by it. But, if the night's a success, he can stride out and seize it as his own.'

John Hastings grinned. 'I seem to remember him balking at the very suggestion of the Autumn Serenade. And the idea of adding to our financial disadvantages by summoning the Winter Hollers . . .' He turned to his wife. 'I came across them when I was in Vienna last year. The moment I invested here, I knew they had to be a part of it. They'll be with the hotel until the Christmas season. They'll win us guests from the Continent, you can be certain of that.'

'Darling,' Sarah began, 'might you talk business later? I want to dance.'

'As soon as the music begins, my dear!'

Maynard averted his eyes. He had always known John Hastings to be a man driven by his head over his heart, but in the presence of his wife he seemed quite the opposite. *Well*, he thought, *there are two sides to all of us. I know that more than anyone.*

A sudden silence was settling over the ballroom, like the snowfall that marks autumn's end. Maynard pivoted on his heel and looked down, beyond the balustrade, onto the dance floor.

At the back of the ballroom, the doors opened and out filed the orchestra, led by Archie Adams in his immaculate snow-white evening suit. As they filed up onto the stage, there appeared from the dressing room doors two dancing couples, hands already entwined. The first to twirl out across the floor were Jonas Holler and Karina Kainz. As Karina sallied forward, in her partner's arms, her hair streamed out behind her and it seemed, to the ballroom, as if she might even be flying.

Then, moments later – to a rising crescendo of applause – Raymond de Guise and Hélène Marchmont appeared. The whispers at Maynard's back told him that Hélène's appearance was not going to go unnoticed tonight, but whatever they were saying was drowned out by the applause that greeted her too.

'How is she faring?' John Hastings whispered.

The band had struck up their first proper number now, and the rest of the Winter Holler troupe – and the Buckingham's own dancers – were fanning out. Little Ansel Albrecht was guiding Mathilde around the edge of the dance floor, the two of them as light as fawns.

'One of my principals is riding high on the romance of his lifetime,' Maynard began. 'And the other . . .'

He stopped. There was no ignoring the trial Hélène was living through. He'd seen it etched on her face, the day he ejected her from the Buckingham. He'd seen it, too, on the evening she returned, when he'd invited her to his office to explain the terms of her readmittance. But how she was faring? Well, she was a practised liar. No matter how high she held her head, did anybody really know what she was feeling inside?

'Mr Hastings,' he went on, 'I believe we are about to find out.'

She was aware of the eyes watching her. She always was, when she stepped out onto the dance floor. But tonight the eyes were watching Hélène differently. Tonight, they studied and judged.

A fortnight of rehearsal had been too long. Hélène had been dancing since she was a girl and scarcely needed a day to learn the routines Raymond had planned. But Maximilian Schank, the director of the visiting company, was passionate in the belief that the two troupes needed to spend time together, to mingle and *know* one another, if they were to dance perfectly. He wanted rehearsals each afternoon, and dinners together each evening, drinks in the Candlelight Club and more. To his credit, he hadn't once mentioned Hélène's disgrace – but she'd fancied she could see it on him, every time he looked her up and down. The thing he would never be able to understand was that she didn't need to know her partners to create the perfect dance. That was her job: to take hotel guests in her arms each night and, no matter what their ability, weave something spectacular out of whatever was in front of her. Competitive dancers like the Winter Hollers would never be able to understand the talent that took.

The Archie Adams Orchestra were superlative tonight. Even Hélène could feel it; the music seemed to envelop her as she sailed across the dance floor, turning in Raymond's arms. She heard Louis Kildare's saxophone soaring out of the riot and, for a time, this gave her strength. She danced better when Louis played, and Raymond seemed to be sensing it too. His body relaxed, in perfect symmetry with hers, and he whispered, 'That's it, Hélène. We're here. We're on top of it now.'

*On top of it?* she thought. She was *always* on top of it. She was Hélène Marchmont. The Buckingham ballroom was hers.

Wasn't it?

The more she thought about it, the more tightly she coiled – and, the more tightly she coiled, the more she could feel Raymond's arms trying to direct her. She looked up, out of the cocoon she and

Raymond were crafting together, and saw two gentlemen staring straight at her. When they saw her looking, the first averted his gaze; the second cupped his hand around his mouth and whispered to his neighbour. They were not the only ones – she could see the scornful look on a middle-aged dowager right now.

'Hélène, you're getting away from me.'

It was not like Raymond to speak in the middle of a dance. The little whispers, the winks and nudges – these were not tricks that Raymond and Hélène had ever needed, for their bodies had always seemed to come together by instinct. But now, through pursed lips, he uttered, 'Slow down. You're losing the song.'

She tried to wrench herself back.

It had been seven nights since she last saw Sybil.

'Hélène, they're watching us.'

'They're watching *me*,' she snapped, under her breath, 'not you.'

'I'm a part of you tonight. Hélène, please.'

For a time, they danced on. She could sense his fear in her body – it was like an echo that passed between them – and, after her anger had died down, she understood it was not fear for himself, but fear for her. Not the fear that he might himself look a fool in front of so many society figures – but the fear that she might look as if she couldn't cope, the fear that she might give the board an excuse to revoke her ballroom return.

'You're too fast again. I can feel your heart. Hélène, please,' he begged, in fragments of whispers. 'You haven't got your heart in the dance.'

It was these words, gentle as they were, that floored her.

'My heart hasn't been in the dance for years,' she whispered – and realised, then, how true it was. 'I've danced a thousand nights with you, Raymond, and my heart hasn't been in a single one of them. They didn't know it then, and they won't know it now. Now dance on!'

'Mr Charles.'

The first number had come to its end, and the Buckingham dancers were fanning out to accept their allotted guests into their arms. Raymond was taking the daughter of the Marquess of Granby into his arms, while Mathilde Bourchier was bracing herself to step into hold with the Marquess's much older uncle – who, by the looks of him, could hardly walk, let alone dance. John Hastings was already leading his wife Sarah onto the dance floor, as the first of Archie Adams's guest singers – Wilf Brimble, the veteran Scottish songsmith – took the stage.

The Autumn Serenade was in full swing, and Maynard looked around to see Lord Edgerton bearing down.

'Hastings isn't going to join us, then?'

Maynard directed Lord Edgerton's gaze to the dance floor.

'I believe he had a better invitation, my lord.'

'I was watching our principal, Mr Charles. What do we think?'

Maynard – who thought, in truth, that Hélène was frayed – gave a non-committal shrug.

'These are nervous times for our dancers. An event such as this. It's to be expected that she may experience a few jitters.'

'Balderdash, Mr Charles! She's a professional. If she's letting her situation affect her, she'll need to be removed. By God, the gossip in this ballroom tonight . . .'

Maynard – who knew that sometimes, to win a war, you had to sacrifice a battle – said, 'All understood, my lord. We have contingencies in place.'

'And Miss Bourchier looks delightful.'

Lord Edgerton's eyes were roaming all over Mathilde as she led her elderly charge on a quickstep of which he was quite incapable.

'I don't see my stepdaughter in the ballroom tonight, Mr Charles.'

There was always venom in his words, even in the most innocuous of questions. Maynard braced himself.

'She rarely frequents the Grand, my lord. We've spoken of this before, but Miss Edgerton has forsaken the glitz in life.'

'I think, perhaps, you know more about my stepdaughter than you've been letting on, Mr Charles.'

Maynard bristled. *I know she's grown up fast*, he thought. *I know she's twice the person you are.*

Lord Edgerton was silent, expecting some further explanation – but then his eyes were drawn back to the dance floor, and the hotel guest who stood in the centre. Where moments before he had been cantering across the floor with Hélène in his arms, the young cousin of Captain John Manners, the 9th Duke of Rutland, was now alone.

As for Hélène, all that Maynard could see was the fleeting sight of her ball gown disappearing through the stage doors. Then, she was gone.

'She's finished, Maynard,' hissed Lord Edgerton. 'If she can't stand the pressure of one night like this, she's done. And it's for the better of all of us – no matter what our liberal American friend might think. You control this, Maynard. You seize it by the scruff of its neck. I want this scandal strangled at birth. Christmas is coming. We're supposed to be rebuilding this hotel's fortunes. Damn it, man, we deserve a return on our investment. I won't have Christmas ruined. I won't risk the New Year Masque. She's lost her poise, Maynard. She has to go.'

'I'll deal with this, my lord.'

'See that you do.'

Maynard took a step towards the dance floor, if only to shake Lord Edgerton off, and set his mind to working on the way he might navigate this next predicament. He would have to talk to Raymond de Guise.

He was trying to catch the eye of one of the other dancers, hoping they might escort the abandoned guest off the dance floor, when a figure brushed past him, stumbling over his own feet as he staggered away from the balustrade. The last thing Maynard needed was some lord's errant son making a drunken commotion, so he turned, meaning to help the young fool along – and saw Tobias Bauer, righting himself against one of the tables as he made for the exit.

'Herr Bauer?' he ventured. 'Might I offer you some assistance?'

The old man turned. The tumble he'd taken was evidently not as bad as his embarrassment, for he was flushed red all around his collar.

'Nothing a stiff brandy won't fix, Mr Charles. Oh, you've put on such a show here! Such an extravaganza! It's warming an old man's heart . . . perhaps too much!'

Maynard watched him go, and allowed a smile to creep on to his face. *There is still joy*, he thought. You could be homeless, half a world away from the people and places you loved, and you'd still find the happiness in the small moments. There was something to celebrate in that at least.

Down on the dance floor, there was another commotion. The young dancer Ansel Albrecht had broken from his partner. This solved one problem, at least, for the Duke of Rutland's young cousin had taken up with Ansel's former partner and rejoined the fray.

But the look on Ansel's face was quite the same as the look on Tobias Bauer's, as he'd staggered past. The look of being in the wrong place at the wrong time. Stranded alone among all the whirling dancers, his eyes seemed to be fixed on the space where Bauer had been. Perhaps it was only that the old man's stumble had broken the young dancer's concentration. *Yes*, thought Maynard, *it could only have been that* – because certainly there was no other reason that a guest as old and genial as Tobias Bauer could distract the young man so.

Maynard allowed himself another slight smile, and reminded himself – for the hundredth time – why he kept denying young Frank Nettleton his dream of a chance to dance right here in the Grand. Youth counted for much, in this world – but it mattered not one jot compared to experience. Experience could carry you through disaster. Experience could give you the reserves of strength to survive.

He only hoped Hélène Marchmont had deeper reserves than many, for he wasn't certain how much longer he could keep her future in the ballroom secure.

# Chapter Seventeen

ON THE PLATFORM OF KING'S CROSS STATION, Emmeline Moffatt waited in trepidation. As the doors opened and a clerk began checking the tickets of all the travellers who bustled aboard, she stood there, incessantly turning a barley sugar between her teeth, obsessively scrunching her hand around the little bundle of Manila envelopes that she'd collected all summer long. Minutes seemed to stretch into hours. More than once, her nerves failed her. More than once, she stepped backwards, as if she might turn and run away.

But each time she faltered, there was a hand in the small of her back, and a whispered word to tell her that everything was going to be all right.

'Come now, Emmeline.' Archie smiled. 'I'll be with you all the way.'

So, together, Mrs Moffatt and Archie climbed into the smoky carriage and settled down with a flask of hot tea and two cream buns.

It was Archie who had persuaded her she ought to write.

At first, Mrs Moffatt was uncertain. She had tried to put pen to paper, and found that all language failed her – though she was never lost for words in front of her girls. It was easier to imagine going back to Mildenhall and spending seven days camped in that café than to dream up the words that might follow *Dear Malcolm* . . .

But every evening, before he went out on stage, Archie took to visiting the housekeeping lounge and sat with her as she teased out her thoughts. It was Archie, too, who walked with her down to the hotel post room, who made sure her courage did not fail her before she handed her letters over to Mrs Farrier for onward delivery. Then he would waltz off, while Mrs Moffatt retreated into her inventories and lists, that safe little space where she need not think too often about the past.

But one night, as they'd parted ways, he'd said something that had stuck with her, dogging her across the days and nights to come.

'There are many things to regret in life, Emmeline. But better that we regret the things we've done, rather than the things we didn't do. I should know.' He'd paused, then, and she thought she detected in Archie, for the very first time, a kind of sadness. 'I missed my chance at a family of my own. Well, I had my music, and that was where all my passion lay. But musicians get old. They forget to have romances. They forget to have families. There's my regret. I regret that I did nothing, when I had my chance. Perhaps, my dear, you should not be the same.'

Those words, she reflected now, were the reason she was here. They were the reason he was here, too, looking at her across the table, with crumbs from his cream bun sticking in his whiskers. He'd done it deliberately to make her laugh. She had not known, until the weeks gone by, what an impish sort of humour Archie could have.

By the time the train reached Mildenhall, the morning was already old, and the nerves were coursing through her again.

'I'm going to be with you the whole time,' Archie began, taking her arm.

Out here in the countryside, September had bite. The wind flurried after them, and the high road was flecked with rain.

'I'll be right there in the café, diligently reading my magazine.' He'd brought with him three copies of *The Etude* and two of *Melody Maker*. 'All you'll need to do is call, Emmeline, and I'll come running.'

'Like a knight in armour.'

Archie grinned. 'Like a loyal servant.'

She'd chosen the same café she'd sat in last time, and they were approaching it now.

*Dear Malcolm,*

she'd written.

*Perhaps you can imagine how many times I have tried to write this letter, only for my hand to give up on me, or my mind to lose the thread of any sentence I began to compose. Please don't take my tardiness in replying as a failure of my heart, but only as the explosion of feelings that have been rocking me these past weeks and months — both good, for you, dear Malcolm, and ill, for me, your mother who abandoned you. There are bound to be ghosts at the back of your cupboard, no matter how long you live. But you, my dear boy, are a ghost I have been living with for all thirty-three of your years. You may not know this, but I was married to a wonderful man, who perished during the Great War, and though he was as close to me in heart and soul as any other human being I ever*

*met, not once did I tell him about you. So, when your first letter arrived,*
*it punctured more than three decades of silence. I was undone. But I am*
*writing to you, now, to ask for a second chance . . .*

There had been other letters, after that. He'd written back almost
straight away, filled with zeal that she'd taken the time to respond,
and reiterating that he sought nothing from her.

*You write that you are sorry, but I did not come looking for an apology.*
*That is not how my ma and pa raised me. I am grateful for what I have*
*had. But I do wish to look upon your face, and see from whom I came . . .*

Well, he'd see it soon enough. Mrs Moffatt and Archie had
reached the café windows – and there, sitting alone at a table
within, was an airman in navy uniform, with hair the colour of
sand and eyes that mirrored her own.

'Archie, I can't feel my knees. I can't go in.'

But it was too late. Through the window, the airman had
already seen them.

Almost as soon as he laid eyes on her, he got to his feet. His
eyes creased, as if to ask her a question – but, when no answer was
forthcoming, he stumbled over himself to reach the door instead.
Soon, he was pulling it open, and a voice she did not recognise, in
an accent she had so rarely heard, was saying, 'Emmeline?'

Mrs Moffatt was still. Time seemed to slow down. Or perhaps
it was only the world that was expanding, rushing away from her
in a riotous blur, so that she felt herself stranded and alone. It was
Archie, at her side, who gave her the courage to say, 'Michael?'

The airman paused. He looked her up and down. He heard
the unfamiliar name and, when it occurred to him why she

might have said it, he smiled in a way that brought both sadness and delight together. To Emmeline, the whole world was in that smile. The same smile as his father – the way it reached into his eyes, and made them glow. A smile that was both the past she had buried, the present in which she now lived – and the future it was suddenly possible to have.

'Actually,' he said, 'it's Malcolm.'

He reached out a hand and, when she was too stunned to take it, swooped to the side so that Archie could take it instead.

'G'day,' he said, 'I'm Malcolm Brody.'

He gave a mock shiver, as if the wind that whipped around him was chilling him to the bone.

'It's nicer in there,' he said. 'They have hot tea and currant buns.'

*Currant buns.* There was something magical in the way he said it.

'I like currant buns,' was all Mrs Moffatt could say.

Then she felt ridiculous, and wanted to run – but Archie's arm was around her, and he was shepherding her forward, and before she knew it they were through the doors, in the warmth of the café, and sitting down.

'I'm with you all the way,' he whispered – and he would be, she knew. She could feel it, deep in her very bones.

There was already tea at the table. Soon, there were current buns and hot buttered crumpets and a pot of gooseberry jam.

'You don't get gooseberries down under,' Malcolm began.

His voice was deep and rich – *like honey*, thought Mrs Moffatt – and his accent as bright and broad as she'd imagined. There weren't often Australians in the Buckingham Hotel.

She still hadn't taken her coat off, though she'd been sitting there for five minutes already, while Malcolm chatted with the girl at the counter and sorted out their order. Archie had taken a table in another corner, and though he'd opened his *Melody Maker* magazine, Mrs Moffatt was quite certain he wasn't actually reading. His eyes kept flitting up, to check she hadn't fainted clean away.

When Malcolm returned and settled his big, burly body into the seat opposite her, he said, 'Shall I let you into a little secret?'

Mrs Moffatt nodded, with the desperation of a baby bird.

'They let you take your coats off in here.'

It took her a second to realise he was jesting. But there was power in that joke. She briskly shook off her overcoat, draping it over the back of the chair.

'You must think me addled.'

'I didn't think you were addled,' Malcolm went on, pouring the tea – and asking, with his eyes opened mischievously, if she might like a huge dollop of thick cream stirred into the mix. She very much did. 'You look a little frightened of me, that's all.'

Frightened wasn't the right word either, but a cocktail of emotions like this had no true name.

In the end she said, 'It's all so new,' and Malcolm seemed to understand.

'I've been thinking about this for nearly two years, Emmeline. All you've had is a few weeks.'

'We should drink some tea.'

'We should,' Malcolm agreed.

So that was exactly what they did.

Tea did not just slake a thirst; tea restored the soul. She allowed its warmth to radiate inside her (the extra three spoonfuls of sugar she stirred in helped too), and somehow the silence started to seem comfortable instead of awkward – so much so that, when Malcolm said, 'You know, I'm nervous too,' she was quite startled, as if coming out of a slumber.

'Oh!' she said. 'I didn't mean to suggest that you weren't! What you must be thinking.'

Her hands had started trembling. She navigated the teacup carefully back to its saucer. She had to face this as she would any other problem, she decided. As if she was not Emmeline, anguished mother, sitting in a café in Mildenhall – but Mrs Moffatt, mother to all her girls in the housekeeping lounge at the Buckingham Hotel. That thought gave her some steel, even as it anguished her further – for this wasn't a *problem*, was it? This wasn't a scandal that had to be tidied away. This was her world.

This was her son.

She found her pluck, at last.

'Your letters caught me quite out of the blue. It's been a great many years since I held you in my arms. By the end of today, I shall have been with you much longer, even, than I was back then. I didn't get to hold you for long, Malcolm. I didn't get to feed you, or bathe you, or play with you or watch you grow. You must think I'm a very foolish old woman – and grown from a selfish, selfish girl. I suspect, in many ways, I was . . . but I want you to know. You've been in my head, every single day. You've been the voice in my ear, guiding me ever onward. You've been . . . a little spark in me, day and night, ever since the day they took you out of my arms. I've dreamt about you. You'd be four or eight or twelve years old, and I'd wake up certain you were happy in some English field – or, on my blacker nights, that you were sitting in some impoverished hovel, with parents who'd never loved you, or . . .'

Words failed her.

She drank more tea.

'I thought about looking for you so often,' she said. 'They swear you off it, of course. The Sisters tell you – you've been in a different world for nine months. Now, go back to your life. But I couldn't. They looked at me differently, after that. My mother and father. My own sister. I'd become a shadow. They didn't mention you. Didn't ask what I'd called you, or what I'd felt as they swaddled you up and took you away. Well, they don't, do they? It's like the mistress my father had, or the times he'd slap my mother. It just gets brushed under the carpet, so that life can carry on regardless. I haven't seen them in decades. Not even after my Jack passed on at Passchendaele. But I got up and got on every day – and I sometimes think the only reason I could do it was because you were there, a little flame in me, keeping me alive.' She cracked. 'Even if I knew I'd never see you again . . . And here, here you are!'

No tea could hold at bay Mrs Moffatt's emotions any longer. She stirred in more sugar, feverishly adding spoonful after spoonful, as if it might help.

'Have you been happy?' she finally whispered.

'I have,' Malcolm returned, and the breathlessness in his voice told her that even he – all six foot seven of him – was racked by emotion as well. 'I wanted you to know it, the moment my first letter landed. I don't want to see you cry. It makes me think I shouldn't have—'

'Oh, but you should!' she cried, and grappled for his hand across the table.

'Ma and Pa, they told me where I came from when I was ten. By then, we'd been living outside Perth in Western Australia for eight years. I never knew any other life. So the idea I'd come from rainy, grey England, on the other side of the world – England, with its kings and queens and castles high on the hills – well, that was an adventure to me. The other boys were playing at being bush rangers. Me, I wanted to be a knight.'

'Why did they tell you at all?' Mrs Moffatt whispered.

'Oh, gee, you don't know my ma and pa!' He paused. 'They're both gone now, of course. I think that's what set me off looking. Before Ma passed, she sat me down and said – *she*'s out there, somewhere, if that's what you want. If you want to know where you came from – deep in *here*.' He clasped his hand over his heart. 'She was just like that, my ma. The Sisters picked a good one. She'd been adopted too, you see. Having me had been like the fulfilment of her own life story, and I reckon she'd always planned on setting me on the course to find you one day. That meant something to her. She'd never found her own mother, not even after years of looking. Well, doors close, don't they? But my ma, she remembered the name of the sister at St Maud's, the one who arranged the new home for me. And when I knew I'd be coming to England on service, well, it seemed like the stars were lining up.'

He stopped. Then, with a smile, he called over his shoulder, 'Two more currant buns, please!' He turned back to her. 'I don't want anything, Emmeline. I haven't come looking for money. I'm not even sure I came looking for love – though I'd take it, if that was what I found. You can never have enough love – not in days like these! There's no hiding it – I'm in merry old England in case there's a war to come. But I don't *need* it, Emmeline. I just wanted to . . . know you, for a time.'

Mrs Moffatt said, 'I thought you might be angry.'

'Angry?' His face creased up like a crumpled newspaper. 'That's what the sister from St Maud's, when I finally found her, said as well. That *you* might be angry. People didn't like being reminded of their shame, she said. Some things were best forgotten. Dig up the past, she told me, and you'll find bodies. But, pah! Start digging, I told 'em, and you might find *gold*.'

Mrs Moffatt was caught off guard.

'I've had the best life,' Malcolm said. 'I'm living it right now. That's the life my ma and pa gave me – but it's the life you gave me too. If you hadn't have been you, if you hadn't had to do what you did, why, I'd hardly be the person I am today. And, I don't know about you, but I'm pretty happy with that person.'

With a flourish, he took a bite out of his currant bun.

'I'm pretty happy with that person too,' she whispered.

'Well, good.' Malcolm guffawed. 'Then it's set. We're all happy. The world might be about to end, there might be about to be the war to end all wars, but at least we'll die happy. Can't say fairer than that!'

Mrs Moffatt's jaw had dropped open. Startled, Malcolm took her hand.

'Sometimes I forget I'm in England,' he said. 'It was a joke.'

'Then perhaps we could . . . ?'

'Meet again?'

Mrs Moffatt nodded, over and over again.

'I should like it.'

'And write?'

Malcolm nodded. 'I've even heard about these things called telephones as well.'

Afternoon was turning to twilight when the train deposited Mrs Moffatt and Archie Adams back on the concourse at King's Cross Station. With Mrs Moffatt still stunned by the day's unfolding events, they picked up a taxi cab on the bustling pavement outside.

'I'll have to go the long way,' the driver said. 'You won't believe the roads they've got closed.'

The driver wasn't joking – but even 'the long way round' seemed to be thronged as well.

'It's all the way from Holborn into Trafalgar Square,' he said, as they wended their way through the backstreets. 'If you wanted to get to Westminster tonight, you'd be better off walking – though the streets down there are clogged just as bad as the roads.'

They'd been idling at a junction for too long, without hope of picking a way further ahead, when Archie said, 'What is all this? I'm meant to be on stage in an hour.'

'Stage, is it?' The taxi cab driver leaned back to appraise his passengers. 'I'll get you there, son. Don't worry.' Wrenching the cab around, he peeped on his horn – 'You see, I'm musical myself!' – and searched valiantly for another route ahead.

'I've never known London like it,' said Archie.

'It's these protests, that's what it is,' the driver said. 'They've congregated in Trafalgar Square, pouring all down the Horse Guards Parade. It won't make the blindest bit of difference, not to the nobs in Westminster, but they've got to do it, haven't they? The common man deserves a say.'

'But what the devil are they protesting about?' Archie asked.

'Haven't you heard?' the driver snorted. 'Lord, where have you two come from? It's Mr Chamberlain! It's all over the evening editions. Landed back from Munich today. Marched straight out of his plane at the Heston aerodrome and declared he'd done it. Shaken Mr Hitler's hand. Agreed a sworn peace. Told 'em all there'd be no war.'

'And they're protesting . . . that?'

'Aye, well, it's what he did to win the peace, isn't it? The Germans are taking half of Czechoslovakia, and we've just stood back and let them. All because of promises on a piece of paper.'

Oxford Circus was a tangle but, once they were across it, the streets of Mayfair were calm. At last, they approached Berkeley Square, and the great white face of the Buckingham Hotel hanging above.

'But . . . peace for a generation!' Mrs Moffatt finally exclaimed. 'That's good news, surely!'

She could feel the lightness of it and, as they wheeled around the square to pull up to the hotel's grand white colonnade, she realised why. Malcolm had come to Great Britain, anticipating a war. Now, though he might fly in training and on parades, he wouldn't be soaring in the skies above Berlin. How cruel the thought of losing him, having just discovered him, had been – and how beautiful the knowledge he'd be safe.

'Well, that lot out there don't think so. It's that Mr Churchill that's got 'em wound up, if you ask me. They reckon he's been outsmarted, that Mr Chamberlain doesn't have what it takes up here' – he tapped the side of his head, knowingly – 'to do His Majesty proud. Peace for a generation? Pah! I'm sorry, miss, but I'm with them marching on Downing Street right now. My lad, he was being picked on at school. Spat on. Called names.

Wasn't until he boxed one of them in the nose that they laid off the poor mite. And here's the most elevated man in Great Britain, not brave enough to do the same.' The driver stopped. Too late, he realised he'd already reached the colonnade and the Buckingham's doorman was waiting to attend to the door. 'Listen to me, prattling on! I'll stick this one on the Buckingham account, should I?'

Archie escorted Mrs Moffatt through the tradesman's entrance and to the door of the housekeeping lounge. For a time, they lingered in silence together. Her hand was on his arm, and she slid it down, gingerly, until it was almost at his hand. There, for propriety's sake, she stopped.

'Thank you, Mr Adams – Archie. You won't know how today feels. I'm not certain I'll ever have the words myself. But I know how it would have felt if I'd never done it. It would feel *grey*. And it would feel wasted, and old, and like I was just sleepwalking – sleepwalking until the end. But now . . . I don't feel any of that. And I wouldn't have dared, Archie, if you hadn't come.'

She shuffled a little closer to the tall bandleader and, rising on the tips of her toes, planted a single kiss on his whiskery cheek.

Archie was surprised. But what astounded him most was that the ballroom no longer seemed to be calling out for him as it had before. He would be quite content if he was told he was to remain in Mrs Moffatt's company all night long.

'Look at us.' She laughed. 'It's been eight years since you joined the Buckingham, eight years since the Grand opened its doors, and I must have spoken to you more in the past ten weeks than I have in all those seasons before.'

'Then perhaps,' Archie stuttered, 'I might come again soon. For a cream tea.'

Mrs Moffatt smiled. 'I should be delighted.'

After he had gone, she ducked into the housekeeping lounge and into her own darkened office. For nearly thirty years she'd been keeping this kingdom. She hadn't realised, until today, why she loved this place so much, nor why she'd thrown her heart so passionately into it. She'd needed something to love. If it wasn't to be a child, it needed to be this world.

She thought of Hélène Marchmont. She'd had so little to do with the Queen of the Ballroom over the years, but, she decided, she should seek her out soon. Every life mattered.

It was as she was pondering this thought that she heard a knocking at her door. Tentative at first, she almost mistook it for the rattling of one of the hotel's ancient pipes – but, when it came again, she knew she was not mistaken.

'One moment, dear!' she called out.

Probably it was one of her girls, with her heart broken by some young rascal. Or one of them, having grown homesick, who needed some mothering. Well, Mrs Moffatt thought, she could provide them with that. Now, perhaps, more than ever.

She opened the door.

'My dear,' she began, her eyes roaming up and down the girl who stood outside. 'Oh, my dear.' She stepped back to allow the visitor inside. 'Quickly now, before anybody sees.'

Moments later, once the tea was brewed, once the shortbread fingers had been lined up on the plate and the girl settled into a seat, Mrs Moffatt said, 'Now, my dear, shall we begin?' She settled herself down. 'You'll have to tell me what's wrong, dear. I can't see inside that head of yours. But whatever it is, we'll put it right. You can count on me for that.'

'I'm going to have a baby.'

229

If it was the first time Mrs Moffatt had heard those words, she might have been completely unprepared. But three decades in the Buckingham Hotel had presented her with more than one frightened girl bearing a child. Things barely changed, from one generation to the next.

After a day when she herself had felt so in need, it felt good to help somebody else. So she told her how it was going to be. How they weren't going to panic. How what was needed was friendship and solidarity – and, yes, a little resilience and courage along the way. How she wasn't the first and she wouldn't be the last, and how these stories sometimes ended in sadness – but how they could end in love, and hope, and good cheer, if only the will was there.

'You and me, my girl, we'll work out a plan together. You might think Mr Charles, our esteemed hotel director, is the only one adept at tidying up the little dramas of our fine establishment – but you'd be wrong. I'm a dab hand at sorting out our little mysteries myself. Well, I might even have one or two of my own!' From somewhere deep inside, Mrs Moffatt found the strength of mind to smile. 'So let's begin at the beginning, shall we? That's the only way to get to the end, you see. Why don't you tell me where it all began?'

The girl squirmed. Mrs Moffatt wanted to reach out, put her arms around the girl – but something stopped her.

This girl, after all, was not one of her own.

'I suppose I fell in love,' the girl sobbed. 'I didn't mean to. Lord knows, I didn't want to! But it happened and, Mrs Moffatt, it was like I'd been missing it all my life. Like I was suddenly whole. I haven't dared tell him yet. But he's an honourable sort – though you wouldn't believe it, not if you heard the stories about what

230

he used to be like. Well, that's how I met him, you see . . .' She stopped. 'I'm sorry. I shouldn't have come. It's just . . . I needed to tell somebody. And I thought, if anyone in this hotel might help me, it might be you, Mrs Moffatt.'

'Oh, my dear, there isn't a single soul in this hotel I wouldn't help.'

Mrs Moffatt pitched forward and, taking the hem of her dress, dried the girl's tears from her face.

'I'm here for you, and always will be.' She paused. 'That's my solemn promise to you, Miss Edgerton, and it's not ever going to change.'

October 1938

# Chapter Eighteen

ON A COLD OCTOBER MORNING, Frank was up before dawn. He had always liked this time of year, back in the north country, when the nights grew long and the morning cold made a fog of his breath each time he ventured out. London was much the same. Back home, you sensed the valleys and hills wake up by the settling of the bats in the attic, the morning song of the birds. Here, it was the dying of the street lamps, the stirring of the first buses that idled at their stops. The sounds and sensations of London, waking up.

Frank left the Brogan house when the youngest of the children were still sleeping. Roisin had been up in the night, tapping at his door and asking for a story, and consequently Frank was feeling sluggish himself. But the bracing walk along the river had roused him entirely by the time he was hurrying across the frosted green of St James's Park.

Berkeley Square, too, was bejewelled in frost. Frank had to pause, just to absorb its breathtaking beauty. On the other side of the expanse, he could see Hodgson, one of the other pages, scuttling into the opening of Michaelmas Mews, so he knew he could not dally long. But the beauty of it made him want to dance. He skipped out across the lawns, feeling the crunch of the frost beneath his feet with every little shimmy and chassé he practised – until, aware of curtains twitching in one of the town houses above, he hurried into the hotel.

The girls were already flocking into the housekeeping lounge, but Rosa was waiting where she always did, at the end of the hallway, for him to arrive. Up ahead, he saw Nancy disappear through the door. She threw him a wave and, not for the first time, Frank cursed himself that he *still* hadn't thought of what wedding gift he was going to get for her.

'It ought to be simple,' he'd lamented to Rosa, one night the previous week. 'She's my sister. I've known her all my life. But Nancy . . . she isn't the sort of girl who *wants*.'

It had started to pain him. Nancy was the one who'd cleaned his knees when he fell over as a little boy. She was the one who'd cooked his meals and tucked him up in bed. But the wedding was mere months away, and he still didn't know what to get her. Mrs Brogan was knitting them a winter blanket. Frank watched it coming together, piece by piece, each night. The girls in the chambermaids' kitchen were clubbing together for a silver tea set, something Nancy could be proud of when she and Raymond set up home. But as for Frank, his mind was as empty as his pockets.

After checking the coast was clear, Rosa put her arms around Frank, squeezed him tight, and planted a kiss on both of his cheeks.

'I've seen the continentals do it,' she explained, with a grin.

'I'm nervous, Rosa. I know I s-said I'd d-do it this m-morning, but now I'm not s-sure. . .'

'Frank, your stutter's coming back!'

'It's b-because I'm—'

236

'You've no need to be nervous, Frankie. Look, he's up there in his office now. Just go and give him a knock.'

She looked over her shoulder. The other girls were already in the housekeeping lounge. Only Ruth was still sauntering through. She smirked as Rosa leaned in to give Frank another kiss, for good luck.

'That girl doesn't know what she's missing out on. How're those dance lessons going with Billy?'

Frank's face told a story for which no words would suffice: a crooked, crumpled kind of expression that spoke of entangled legs and bruises.

'Me and Ansel had him at it last night. He's got a good little box step. Anything trickier than that and . . .' Frank shrugged.

'Well, keep at it, and I'll keep at Ruth. Those two just need a little encouragement.' She didn't sound convinced; neither was Frank. 'Chin up, Frankie. You can do this! You're a natural.'

Rosa always gave him courage. That was one of the things he liked the most about her – the ability she had to make him feel bigger, better than he thought he was. The bravery she'd given him was still pulsing in him as he hurried past the reception desks (where Billy was pontificating to some senior concierge on the best way to shine a shoe) and stole down the corridor towards Mr Charles's office.

The door was ajar, and the sounds of business within. No matter how early the pages arose, a wise man would always wager that Maynard Charles was already hard at work, his hand on the hotel tiller. Billy said he never slept.

Before Frank's courage deserted him, he tapped on the door.

Under his touch, it opened inches.

Maynard was hunched over his desk, making hurried amendments to some note he then pressed into a hotel envelope and sealed with a drop of wax, into which he pressed the signet ring he wore on his little finger. Something about the sight gave Frank a shudder, as if he'd stumbled upon some scandal being hidden away. But Frank had done jobs for Mr Charles in the past; he'd listened to Billy blather on about the 'special work' he and Mr Charles conducted. Whatever Maynard Charles was doing here, it had the air of one of these specific kinds of secret.

The hotel director's eyes shot up. Nancy said he was an old darling, really, that he and Raymond had grown close over the passing years. Well, Frank did not see it that way. Maynard had a quelling eye, and it was focused on him right now.

'Mr Nettleton, to what do I owe the pleasure?'

'M-Mr Charles,' Frank stammered, reaching deep inside himself to find his courage again. 'It's about the b-ballroom. You might think me impudent, s-sir, but I've s-something to ask.'

'Well, out with it then, boy. I've a hotel to run. You'll have errands to do yourself.'

'I want to be a . . .'

*Hotel dancer,* he wanted to say. *In the demonstrations. Just for a trial. So that, one day, I might prove myself. I might step out with Raymond de Guise and Hélène Marchmont, Mathilde Bourchier, Gene Sheldon and all of the rest.*

But words had deserted him. He'd waited too long.

Maynard shook his head and said, 'I have a job for you, Frank. Take this' – and he gave Frank the sealed letter – 'to the post room, straight away. It's to go with the morning pick-up. Well, be off with you. Time waits for no man.'

'Y-yes, sir.' Frank nodded. 'Straight away, sir.'

He cursed himself all the way down to the post room, a little office in the hotel basement, where the corridor was lined with a veritable battalion of traps designed to catch and slay the hotel's rats.

*If only the lords and ladies knew*, Frank thought. *Even the Buckingham Hotel has its rats . . .*

Mrs Farrier, the post mistress, had a soft spot for Frank. A skeletal old bird, she had worked in the hotel post room since the latter years of the previous century. Her dominion, which existed for only an hour each morning and two each night, was a second world inside the Buckingham. The little office walls were a shrine to her children and manifold grandchildren, and there was always a posy of flowers by the typewriter on her desk. Mrs Farrier might have been a strange subterranean soul, but she took her work seriously and the pride she took in it was second only to Maynard Charles's.

'All the secrets and innermost lives of our guests pass through here,' she had once told Frank, while she offered him a piece of shortbread and a glass of cordial. 'And what do I know of those lives? Not a thing! Because privacy is a guest's fundamental and absolute right. You might think my job is just to put envelopes in sacks and wait for a Royal Mail officer to pick them up – but you couldn't be more wrong. My job is nothing more than a guardian to their innermost lives.'

Today, as Frank listened to the usual spiel, he offered up Mr Charles's envelope and said, 'I'm really just here for this, Mrs Farrier. Mr Charles says it's to go with the morning pick-up.'

Mrs Farrier took the envelope, looked at the address, and added it religiously to one of her grey sacks.

'An honour, young Frank,' she said, before turning back to her work.

Sometimes – just *sometimes* – it would be nice if the folks around here didn't treat him like he was an eight-year-old scamp, getting under their feet. That was how Mr Charles thought of him, he supposed.

There was one person who understood, though. One person who had come from a beginning just as insignificant and, through hard work and determination – and no small modicum of talent – had taken a step into a different world.

*Yes*, he thought, *Raymond would understand.*


In the Buckingham Hotel, different folks had different rhythms, and the lights did not ordinarily turn on in the studio behind the Grand Ballroom until mid-morning. By then, Frank had already been sent out for fresh flowers by the hotel's visiting florist and run two errands for M. Etienne Caron, residing with them for a week to attend the Covent Garden Art Fair. Only when he got a moment to breathe did he venture to the little studio behind the Grand, where Raymond and Hélène had come together to prepare for the afternoon's demonstration.

Poor Miss Marchmont. Now that Frank knew her story, there seemed something inestimably sad about her. She carried it like a shroud. The chambermaids had been talking; they said it was like a cloud following her around the hotel.

'Infectious,' one of them had said before Rosa upbraided her, 'like a common cold.'

But Frank knew that joy was infectious, too. She only had to catch it again.

For a time, he was content to watch the rehearsal. None of the dancers minded. They were used to him lingering here. Probably half of them thought he had his head in the clouds, chasing some impossible dream. But Frank was heartened to see Ansel there, practising some move with Karina Kainz. And when Raymond wandered over to him, at a break in the rehearsal, he tried to battle back how downcast he'd become.

'I plucked up the courage, Raymond. Did what Rosa's been egging me on to do. Went to Mr Charles, thinking I might ask him for a chance in the demonstrations and—'

'He said no?'

'It's worse than that,' grumped Frank. 'I started stuttering again. Lost all my words. He sent me away with a flea in my ear. They don't take me seriously, Raymond. They think I'm . . .'

Raymond paused. A look had flickered across his face that put Frank in mind of some little victory being won, or an idea being born.

'What about this, Frank? In two months' time, when the Christmas spirit is already in the air, Nancy and I will be up in Marylebone, exchanging our vows. And after that, well . . .'

He put an arm around Frank and guided him through the studio door, up through the dressing rooms and to the doors leading out onto the Grand Ballroom itself. There, together, they looked up at the cavernous expanse of an empty ballroom. To Frank, all the music, all the promise, just throbbed in the air. If he closed his eyes, he could already see the grandeur.

'We'll be here, Frank, courtesy of Mr Charles and the board. I'm quite sure Mr Hastings had something to do with this – but, for a day, the ballroom will be ours alone. And Frank . . .' He beamed, proudly. 'You could dance.'

Frank peered up at him.

'Nancy and I will dance alone. We've already chosen the song – Archie's own 'Bride to Be'. But then, before we invite everyone to the floor, I thought there could be a show. The Winter Hollers will still be with us. Mathilde and Gene and Hélène, too. Well, what if you were to dance as well? Mr Charles wouldn't have to sanction it, not on my wedding day. If Rosa doesn't mind, you might dance with Mathilde. Everyone would see you, Frank. With a closed ballroom, we could dance to whatever music we liked – no more stately waltzes and foxtrots! You could jitterbug. You could *jive*. And when they saw you, why, there isn't a soul on earth who'd say you weren't worth a chance in this ballroom. They'd see you for what you are, Frank Nettleton – born to dance!'

Frank was still staring, goggle-eyed, into the ballroom.

'Do you really think it might work?'

'Trust me. We'd have to smarten you up a little. You're good – you know that – but in the ballroom you have to be *great*. We might have to sprinkle some stardust. But five minutes on this floor could change the course of your life.'

With his arm still around Frank's shoulders, Raymond shepherded him back to the studio. A wild tango was playing on the gramophone, as Hélène fell in and out of hold with Jonas Holler, and Mathilde was corpsing with laughter as she watched. Hélène was laughing, too. It was good, thought Frank, to see her laugh.

'You'll need to choreograph a routine, of course, Frank. I'll have a word with Mathilde.'

'Maybe I could meet her this afternoon?' said Frank, realising too late how overeager he'd become.

'She'll be rehearsing the opening number for this evening. Friday nights in the Grand – they may not be as spectacular as Saturdays, but the ballroom's going to be thronged. The Duke of Coburg and his entourage are checking in, even now. Of course, I myself have a night away from the ballroom planned. Let the Winter Hollers reign supreme for a time.' Raymond paused. 'Perhaps you should work a little out yourself, and then, when I've spoken with Mathilde, we can get things in motion. Two months, Frank, to design a dance to make your dreams come true.'

When Raymond said it, it sounded like the quest for the Holy Grail itself. Inwardly, Frank beamed. Already, his mind was blossoming with possibilities.

'Design a dance?'

The voice had come from Ansel Albrecht, who was now sitting on the edge of the studio floor. Picking himself up, he joined Frank in the doorway, as Raymond returned to the fray.

'I'm to dance at the wedding.' Frank grinned. He'd rarely felt a thrill like this. 'With Mathilde, if she'll let me. Then I can show them what I'm made of.' His voice dropped to a low whisper. 'Raymond thinks I've got a chance. That I might be like you, Ansel.'

'But, Frank!' Ansel thrilled. 'This is wonderful!'

*It's too wonderful*, thought Frank. *Too wonderful to be true.*

'And on my sister's wedding day as well.'

Ansel smothered him in his arms and Frank, laughing, squirmed until he let go.

'You could help.' Frank was grinning. 'I mean, we're not getting anywhere with poor Billy, are we? He could practise his box step in the corner, and we could be—'

'Making up a dance to change your life!'

On the studio floor, a bank of puzzled faces turned, as one, to look upon the two excitable boys in the corner. Jonas Holler and Karina Kainz shared a smile.

'Would you?' asked Frank.

Ansel barely needed to take breath before he said, 'But of course. I've been trying to lend my ideas to Mr Schank and the company ever since they brought me aboard. I was choreographing my mama in the kitchen at home since I was knee-high.' His face darkened and he screwed it up, in imitation of a little boy who's been told he must eat no more biscuits before dinner. 'Of course, it is not my place, not with the Winter Hollers. But perhaps, if they were to see *me*, choreographing something spectacular for you . . . Maybe, then, we would both get what we want!'

Both boys looked at each other with eyes opened wide and hearts beating wildly. Then, laughing with the triumphs they had not yet achieved, they shook hands.

'This afternoon?' whispered Frank. 'After the demonstrations?'

Ansel shook his head. 'I cannot. I must write to my father. It's been too long, and . . . there's news I must tell him.' The way Ansel had said the word 'news' gave it a graveness that Frank did not really understand. 'But tonight – when the ballroom is in full flow? I'm not to dance this evening. Mr Schank has me resting. He thinks I am not strong like the others – but we'll show him, Frank! I'll meet you back here, when the band starts playing. By midnight, we'll have the magic in flow.'

Frank nodded eagerly – and, with the thought of their very own quest taking shape in his head, hurried back to his work in the hotel.

By mid-afternoon, Frank's errands were done. Ordinarily, he and Rosa would go for a stroll along Regent Street – but today, with winter approaching and twilight already threatening by three o'clock, they buried themselves in the big armchairs of the chambermaids' kitchenette, dreaming up what present they might get for Nancy.

'Of course, she *still* hasn't settled on her dress. Raymond said he would buy her anything she wanted from the boutiques we visited. But your sister, she doesn't know what she wants.'

All of a sudden, Frank had an idea.

'Maybe that's what I could get her, Rosa – a wedding dress!'

Rosa's eyes goggled. 'Frank, you wouldn't know where to start!'

But he did.

'Back at the Brogans . . . Mrs Gable sent down my old trunk, from back home. All my books and toys and . . .' He had flushed red, because he certainly did not want Rosa thinking of him as a little boy, like the rest in the Buckingham. 'There's a lining in that old trunk. Silk. Silk from my mother's old wedding dress.'

Rosa's face lit up. 'Well, that would be wonderful, Frank – trust you to think of something like that! She'd love that, our Nance. We've had her trekking round the boutiques, but no matter how fancy the dress, it's never quite the one. But something with all that history, with all that meaning.'

Frank felt full to bursting. This day, which had started so badly, was somehow overflowing with possibilities.

'I'm going to take a look, as soon as I'm back tonight. I could ask Mrs Moffatt to help me with a seamstress. She's bound to want to help.'

Rosa made tea and toast, and soon the other girls were coming back in, wearied from their day in and out of the hotel suites.

'Hey, look, Frank,' Rosa said, and pointed at the clock on the wall. 'Hadn't you better get going? You don't want to keep Ansel waiting. He'll think you've stood him up.'

The clock was already inching towards seven. Downstairs, the Grand would be coming alive. To think that, one day soon, he too might be striding out onto the dance floor, perhaps even taking some lady or crown princess in his arms. What was it Raymond had said? Nobody could deny him a chance, not when they saw him on the ballroom floor.

He leaned over and gave Rosa a peck on the cheek, to shrieks of delight from the other girls. Then he loped out of the kitchenette, buzzing with the promise of everything to come. Was it really only last year that he'd got off the train at Euston, to be dazzled by the sights and sounds of the Buckingham Hotel? Could it really be *him*, Frank Nettleton, who'd just walked away from his sweetheart, off to divine a dance that might change the future of his life? It was mysterious the way the world kept turning.

And what was more, in all of this talk of the future, he hadn't once thought of the Continent. He hadn't once thought of war. This alone was cause for celebration.

Frank came helter-skelter down the service stairs, too impatient to wait for a lift. If he'd been any more giddy, he might have leaped onto one of the banisters and tried to sail his way down. In mere moments, he had reached the bottom, and was about to scuttle down to the studio doors when a commotion from the reception hall drew his eye.

Guests were cascading down into the Grand Ballroom. Maynard Charles stood at the desk, with a look like pure thunder in his eyes. But among the men in their evening jackets and the ladies in their long, flowing gowns, Frank saw others: an ambulance man, dressed in his blue wool uniform and cap; a much older man, whom Frank recognised as the Buckingham's visiting physician, Dr Evelyn Moore.

Billy was there too. He appeared at the reception desk, opened his eyes wide in a silent plea to Frank, and marched purposefully off, around the golden guest lift and towards the guest stairs.

Frank followed.

There was a crowd here, too. At the foot of the guest stairs, one of the taciturn senior concierges stood sentry, allowing no guests to pass – while, up above, a group gathered on the first landing. Frank got closer, ducked under the arm of the concierge and loped a little up the steps. Something seemed to be drawing him on to whatever spectacle this was – not just Billy, who had gone before him, but something else, something deep inside him.

All the joy that had been building in him since breakfast was gone. He felt an emptiness creeping through him.

Mrs Moffatt was here. So was Maximilian Schank, from the Winter Holler Company. It wasn't until Frank got close that he realised there was another ambulance man, dressed in the same woollen blue, here as well – nor that a duo of other concierges had been stationed on the staircase above, directing guests to the lifts instead of the final flight of stairs.

'Billy,' he whispered, mere steps away now, 'what happened?'

Billy was unable to form a single word.

That was when Frank knew something irrecoverable had occurred. He had never known Billy Brogan speechless before.

He took another step up, vaguely heard Mrs Moffatt telling him to get away, to give the ambulance men the space they needed. But the ambulance man looked up, told Mrs Moffatt that it was all right, that there was nothing more they could do.

'He would have died straight away,' the ambulance man intoned. 'The moment he fell. Poor bugger landed badly, that's all. Such a waste. Such a crying shame.'

Frank looked past them, at the place on the stairs where a fallen body lay.

It was all angles and points. An arm was outstretched, a face buried in the carpet.

Frank couldn't see the face, but he knew already who was lying dead on the stairs.

The fallen body belonged to no other than Ansel Albrecht.

# Chapter Nineteen

A FRIDAY NIGHT AWAY FROM THE ballroom was a rare luxury for Raymond de Guise – and, as he helped Nancy out of the taxicab onto the frosted paving stones of Whitechapel Road, he felt as light as the air.

Arm in arm, the two lovers walked on – until, some time later, they looked up at the face of one of the tumbledown red brick terraces. Lights were playing in the windows. There had been times, in the past, when approaching this house filled Raymond with a sense of regret. Now, as he looked up at the restored chimney stack – once turned to rubble and dust – and the new windows, where there had once been old boards, he felt the warmth of a homecoming. It was between these narrow walls that Raymond de Guise – then the roustabout Ray Cohen – had learned his first dance steps, standing on the feet of his departed father Stanley. Stanley Cohen, the devil of the dance halls. The whole terrace seemed to echo with his memory.

The door had opened, and there stood Raymond's mother, Alma, with her apron patterned in gravy and blackberry jam.

'Ray Cohen!' she said, and then, 'The future Mrs Cohen as well. Get inside, you two, it's getting too nippy out there.'

It was 'nippy' inside the house too. Alma Cohen had inherited her frugality from her dear departed Stanley, who had refused to light a fire in the hearth until the first snow fell each year. Even now, nearly seven years after his death, his eccentric rules lived on.

'I'm going to light it, Ma,' said Raymond, as Alma showed them into the living room – where the table had been set for six, with all the best china and the silverware Stanley had brought home the Christmas after the Depression first bit, refusing to tell them all how he'd been able to afford it. 'You're not as young as you used to be. And Aunt May and Rebecca too . . .'

In a flash, Alma had whipped up a wooden spoon and rapped him over the back of the knuckles.

'You'll do no such thing. We're hardier than you lot, up there in that Buckingham Hotel, and don't forget it. You've got too coddled, Ray. I'll bet there's a servant bringing you a hot water bottle every night. Somebody checking in to put blankets on you while you sleep.'

Nancy herself couldn't help but laugh at this.

'Do you know, Alma,' she said, 'you're almost right.'

'And anyway,' Alma went on, 'my soup'll warm you up as good as any fire. Now sit – *sit*! Artie's on his way, and we've been cooking up a storm.'

The finest dinners of the Queen Mary restaurant could not compare to Friday night with the Cohens.

Somehow, nights like these had started to feel like home for Nancy too. The chicken was fat and crisp with butter and sage, and the potatoes were crisp but fluffy inside. There was nothing that made Nancy think of family, now, like a night with the Cohens.

They didn't get the chance to come here often – once a month, perhaps twice, but that only served to keep it feeling special. Alma was a fierce sort of woman – as any woman who'd brought up two boys, with a husband in and out of a prison cell, had to be – and the fact that she looked after her two aunts was even more incredible to Nancy. May – a true Cohen woman, small and squat and with fire in her belly – was the only one related to Raymond by blood, being Stanley's eldest cousin by birth; she'd met Rebecca – long and lean, with a sweep of silver hair – a generation ago, in the stalls at the Pavilion Theatre, and soon after they'd started living together, just down the road.

The other face around the table turned up late, as always he did. It used to be that Artie Cohen tumbled in late because he was playing dominoes in some public house – or else, Alma still feared, sizing up whatever railway yard he was planning on robbing next. These days, it was because he was standing guard outside the Daughters of Salvation. Tonight, he crashed in just as the chicken was being carved, and ruddy from the cold.

Rubbing his hands together with glee, he said, 'I can smell it from down the road, Ma. My belly's been crying out for this.' He'd already whipped up a piece of hot chicken when he said, 'How now, Ray. Looking smart, I see.'

'Thank you, Artie.'

'And the delightful Miss Nettleton. Still planning on marrying this one, are you?'

Nancy said, 'I'm afraid nothing's changed there, Artie.'

'And it oughtn't,' said Alma, battling her second-born son back into his chair with the threat of her carving knife. 'You could do worse than think about finding a nice lady friend yourself, Artie. Somebody to straighten you out.'

'Ma!' Artie objected, with a grin. 'I already been straightened!'

'Oh, aye?' interjected Aunt May, sharing a knowing look with Rebecca. 'We was just saying – you're spending so much time down with these Daughters of Salvation, it might be you've got a lady friend you're not telling us about.'

'You're the only girl for me, Aunt May.'

'Well, they'd better be paying you extra for all these shifts,' said Alma. 'That's all I have to say. Now, sit! Dinner is served.'

There was only one topic of conversation in the Cohen house that night, and Nancy had been preparing for it all day. She'd barely taken a mouthful before the barrage of questions began. Had she found a dress yet? Had she chosen her bridesmaids? That much, at least, was easy.

'Rosa and Ruth, who I work with at the Buckingham. I'd thought Miss Edgerton might, but—'

'Artie's Miss Edgerton?'

Artie started spluttering. A single piece of parsnip erupted from his mouth, landing in the gravy pooling on Alma's plate. She glared at him.

'And you'll be asking Monsieur de la Motte,' said Alma, rising to her toes to make an ostentatious bow, 'to be your best man, of course.'

Raymond set down his knife and fork neatly, as a gentleman should, and looked around the table, inviting silence from all.

'As a matter of fact, Georges won't be my best man on the day.'

'What?' scoffed Artie, with a wolfish grin. 'Can't take time out of his busy California schedule to be at the wedding of his apprentice?'

'Well, actually,' said Raymond, 'he'll be sitting with the rest of my colleagues, as a humble guest.'

'But—'

'Because, Artie,' Raymond pronounced, 'I'm asking you, here and now, to be my best man.'

Knives and forks clattered onto plates. Artie himself was still. His face creased in bewilderment, he reached for the tablecloth, wiped his mouth of gravy – and Alma, who ordinarily scolded him for behaviour like this, said not a thing.

'*Me?* Your ex-con of a little brother? Your ne'er-do-well laya-bout? Your—'

'Brother in arms,' said Raymond.

Nancy, who'd heard from Raymond only days before, turned to Artie and grinned.

'You've been there throughout, Artie. Thick and thin. High and low.'

'Inside and out.' Artie laughed, thinking of his old Penton-ville cell.

'I wouldn't have it any other way.'

In seconds, Artie was on his feet, sending his plate – and all its contents – sloshing across the table.

'Come here, you old rascal!' he said – and the Cohen brothers, still separated by Raymond's future wife, put their arms around each other, making a pyramid above Nancy's cringing head. 'I'll do you proud, Ray. Get you to the service on time. Sort your hair out, even, if you like!' Artie was crowing with laughter now. 'You and me, we'll have to get some time in together, plan this thing to perfection. And an old Cohen-style celebration, too, to send you off into respectability.' Artie looked him up and down. 'As if you need any more of *that*!' he guffawed.

Once the commotion had passed, and Artie had sunk back to his dinner (doing his best impression of a pig at its trough), Aunt Rebecca chipped in.

'It's just what Stanley would have wanted. The Cohens back together! I don't suppose you're thinking of moving back east after the ceremony?'

They'd have to find a place close to the Buckingham, Nancy said. That much was certain. And, though she decided not to tell them that she planned to keep on working – if the Buckingham would have her – she got the feeling that the Cohens wouldn't bat an eyelid at such a thing. Women in the Cohen family always worked. They had done for generations.

'No,' Alma had once told her, 'it's not like the starlight world you all live in. Real folks have got to graft for a living.'

'Well, we'd have loved to have you back in the old streets, Ray, but there's more to worry about in the world this year,' Alma said, as she tidied the chicken carcass away, and brought out the cake. 'I was talking to Dot – you remember Dot, Ray? – at the grocer's last week. She's one of those fawning over Mr Chamberlain. Says he's made the world a safer place. But what does she know? So Mr Hitler says he's not going to march into anyone else's country and turn it into his, does he? Well, what's a promise from a snake like that? And, even if he keeps it, he can do whatever he wants inside his borders, can't he? Six days it took him, since Mr Chamberlain's speech, to snatch the passports off people like us, all over Germany, all over Austria-that-was. Maybe he's said he won't fight the English, but he's already at war with the Jews. If we was over there, we'd have had our passports taken too. We'd not be citizens at all. Thank goodness we were born here.'

Artie, who had stood up on Cable Street two autumns before – and been beaten down for his impudence – muttered darkly, 'Don't matter where you're born at all. There's fascists right here, right now. Only difference is they don't have power.'

'Why, the king himself is one, I heard,' Aunt Rebecca chipped in. 'And the old King Edward, for certain.'

'Wasn't Miss Edgerton's father one of those standing with the Union on Cable Street that day?'

'Stepfather,' Nancy interjected. 'And hardly even that.'

'Aye,' muttered Artie, 'it's hardly Viv's fault who her mother took up with.'

*Viv?* thought Nancy, barely able to suppress her surprise. *Viv?*

But she never got a chance to ask because, in that same moment, Alma reappeared from the kitchen, carrying a mountainous cake, teetering under the weight of its own layers. Icing positively cascaded down its sides – and, picked out in blackberries around its edge, were spelled the names NANCY AND RAYMOND.

'Well, no doubt you'll have some hoity-toity French *pâtissier* making a wedding cake for that reception in that ballroom of yours. So we thought we'd seize the chance while we had it. Tuck in, everyone! This is going to get messy.'

After the cake, while Artie dragged Raymond into the little yard out the back, Alma ushered Nancy upstairs, down the narrow landing, to the bedroom at the very end. The room was dominated by the bed Alma had once shared with Stanley. Apart from it and the wardrobe, there was only one other piece of furniture: an old trunk, which sat open at the bottom of the bed, spilling out bedspreads and old blankets, Stanley's old fishing nets and tools.

'Wait there,' she said, and ferreted in the trunk's oddments until she emerged with a little black box. This she placed into Nancy's open palm, unfastening the clasp to reveal a single silver band. 'It was my mother's. Didn't leave her finger until the day she died. Must have seen death coming, because she took it off and put it on her bedside for me to find. Always thought I might give it to a granddaughter, if ever I had one. But I'd rather give it to you now, Nancy. A little piece of Cohen family history, for your very own. Well, since you're about to be one of us.'

Nancy lifted the ring from its box and laid it in the flat of her palm.

'Alma, I don't know what to say. I'll always treasure it.'

'See that you do. And, one day, if you're blessed with a girl of your own, make it hers, and her children, for evermore. You're one of the family, Nance.'

To Nancy, whose family extended to Frank alone, the world seemed suddenly so much larger. Just to hear it out loud stirred something deep within her.

'I know I'll be a "de Guise",' she said. 'But, with this ring, I'll know myself a Cohen as well.'

Alma closed her hand over the ring that still lay in Nancy's palm and added, 'Aye, but in your heart, you'll always be Nancy, just like I never forget I'm Alma Stern. Your and Raymond's souls might be entwined forever, but you don't stop being you. Takes some women a lifetime to figure that out – but you, you've got it already. I can see. Love each other. Cherish each other. And you both will. But always be yourself, my girl. And that's all the advice I'll ever give – from one woman to another.'

# Chapter Twenty

IT WAS NEARING MIDNIGHT IN the Buckingham Hotel, and Maynard Charles needed a drink.

The body of Ansel Albrecht lay in the Benefactors' Study, where in a few short days the hotel board would gather, again, to discuss the matter of Hélène Marchmont. Problems like Hélène seemed so trivial tonight. Maynard closed the door on the dead boy, turned the key in the lock, and studied the time on his watch. Soon, the final song would be played in the Grand Ballroom – and, after that, he and Maximilian Schank would have to gather Jonas Holler, Karina Kainz and all of the rest. It would be Maynard who broke the worst of all news to them, for the boy had died in *his* hotel. Nothing else would have been right.

There had been other deaths in the Buckingham, over the years. There was always some old fool who'd drunk too much, or cavorted with his mistress in one of the palatial suites, ignoring the fact that his heart was no longer the heart of a young man. Deaths like these, though, were more easily accounted for. Maynard could shrug and say, 'the world keeps turning', and diligently organise their removal so that no scandal was spread. There had been measles, once, on the second storey; three had fallen victim to it, and each one of them made to vanish from the hotel before the rumours started to take hold. He'd never felt this aching sadness about any of them – but, then, Ansel Albrecht was so young, so full of vigour and promise.

Yes, he sorely needed that drink.

He opened his office door, ready to reach for the brandy decanter, only to find that two glasses had already been poured. The first sat untouched by the Olympia Elite typewriter on his side of the desk. The other was being swirled in the hands of the middle-aged rake of a figure who lounged in the upholstered chair on the desk's opposite side, his dark Bollman trilby crumpled up on his lap.

'You choose your nights perfectly, Mr Moorcock.' Maynard sighed as, without complaint, he went to the desk and drained his brandy in one. 'You'll forgive me for being distracted this evening. We're dealing with bad news.'

Moorcock nodded vaguely. 'I'm afraid I'm about to make your evening much worse.'

Maynard slumped at his desk. He was in no mood for this tonight. He kept thinking, not only of Ansel, but of all the other young men he'd seen perish, across Flanders and France. His mind always took him back there, to those dugouts and foxholes in the ground. A whole generation of men had died there, but sometimes it seemed that those who survived had been born there too. May-nard himself recollected so very little of the golden years before.

'You look ragged, Mr Moorcock.'

'I feel it, too.'

Maynard poured them each a further two fingers of brandy.

'Then let's dispense with the small talk, this evening. I've spent my year doing all that I can. When the Bechsteins and von Hessens were here this summer, I sent you dispatches. When they dined with Lord Edgerton, I gleaned what little I could. There is always tittle-tattle, Mr Moorcock. I had a letter sent out to you just this morning, to tell you that the Duke of Coburg dined with our friend Conte Grandi from the Italian embassy.' He stopped. 'The talk is changing. I dare say it is of little value to your Office, but since the agreement in Munich last month – well, people are speaking of growth and peace. They understand the British Lion is sleeping, and it makes them happy.'

Moorcock stood, his hands turning to fists. It was quite the most remarkable sight Maynard had seen – for never before had he seen Moorcock betray an ounce of emotion, not unless it was sneering dismay.

'Mr Moorcock, if this is the demeanour of the British intelligence services this year, might I politely enquire if we are, all of us, in just a spot of . . . bother?'

Rarely, in history, had anybody made the news of impending war sound quite so understated.

'Mr Charles, you'll remember our conversation of springtime – how His Majesty is sleepwalking to disaster, and it's our appointed task to stop it. My superiors have finally formalised their conclusion that His Majesty's taking up arms against his Germanic cousins is no longer a question of *if*, but a matter of *when*. Whether we prevail in this war will depend on British pluck and perseverance, as ever it has, but you and I do not belong in a children's story of valiant soldiers and brave, loyal infantrymen. You and I know war, and let us not pretend it is anything other than brutish, nasty and hard. We must seek what advantages we can – and the principal advantage, as we see it now, is in choosing *when* and *where* the first salvos in this battle will be fought. Do you follow me, Mr Charles?'

Maynard whispered, 'You had me searching for gossip to try and waylay a war. Now you mean to *propagate* it?'

'It is not as dirty as it sounds. Mr Chamberlain, honourable man that he is, has made a grave miscalculation – and, at last, we in the intelligence community have found the courage to say so. It is as Mr Churchill has been pronouncing for too long now – by appeasing the German wolves, we make them stronger while, simultaneously, weakening ourselves. Were it to continue, we would one day find ourselves up against a Goliath we have no hope of ever slaying.' Moorcock paused for breath. 'You will recall that I told you about elements in the high German gentry who might be sympathetic to our causes. Well, we have now identified a coterie of men who believe they can make a difference. They see what we see – war is to come, and Herr Hitler must be defeated in open battle . . . or not at all.'

'Mr Moorcock, what more aid I can give you, I scarcely know.'

'This delegation of German gentry will make landfall in Britain in the first week of December. You will know them as among the von Amsberg and Wittekind lines. Families that trace their ancestries to high German nobility, and who are watching, aghast, as Herr Hitler invites ruin on their world. Outwardly, they come here for the wedding of a cousin, to take place at St Paul's. But the true purpose of this delegation is to petition the Crown to effect a change in His Majesty's government's direction – to draw a line in the sand, to tell the Führer that enough is enough, and that Britain will no longer be cowed. Mr Charles, this delegation is to take residence in the Buckingham Hotel. Their mission must succeed.'

'You fool, Moorcock.' Maynard laughed. 'Haven't you and I been spying on the guests in this hotel for years, now? You know the manner of men who frequent my hotel. British fascists, continental fascists, and worse. Find your men a country residence from which to do their business. Find them a—'

'They are not *my* men, Maynard,' Moorcock snarled. 'We know of their coming, but we do not direct it. We would rather they were sequestered in perfect solitude than in this hotel of yours – but, since this is the route they have chosen, we will turn it to our advantage. Your job is to ensure that their presence and purpose here in London is not communicated. To preserve the secrecy of this mission, until their work here is done. And if they are discovered, and worked against by elements seeking to continue Mr Chamberlain's course of action, we would know about it too.'

'And how am I to do that?'

Mr Moorcock sneered. 'By controlling the flow of information, Mr Charles. By mastering your hotel. No letter is to leave this hotel unless it has been steamed open and vetted by you. Where other guests congregate, their gossip is to be recorded and relayed to me, in intimate detail. Do I make myself clear?'

Maynard nodded.

For a time, there was silence in the office. Then, at last, Maynard said, 'Do you think there is any hope, Mr Moorcock? Great Britain is weary of war. We're still in mourning from 1918. Is there any other way?'

Moorcock straightened out his trilby and planted it squarely on his head.

'I am afraid not, Mr Charles. Count yourself fortunate that, this time, you are too old to take up a gun.'

After Moorcock was gone, Maynard poured himself another large brandy. The matter of breaking the news about Ansel Albrecht had flitted out of his mind while Moorcock prowled the office, but now it cascaded over him again. The brandy would steel him.

But first there was another job he had to do.

Reaching for the telephone on his desk, he dialled for reception and said, 'Send Mr Brogan through directly.' Then he placed the receiver back and waited for the opening of the door.

'You wanted to see me, Mr Charles?'

Maynard looked at him. Young Brogan. He had a fleeting image of Billy, and Frank Nettleton, all the younger men of the Buckingham, dressed in fatigues and lined up at barracks for their first infantry training. Did it really have to come so soon?

'Billy, I've a task for you. Consider this your last night as a concierge. From tomorrow morning, you're to take up a new role as apprentice to Mrs Farrier in the post room. Now, I can see, by the look on your face, that you consider this a demotion. My boy, it is nothing of the sort. Communication, Billy. It's the lifeblood of civilisation, and you're to be at its centre. Mrs Farrier is old. She carries her department well, but it is unfair for her to do it alone. And, Billy . . .'

'Yes, Mr Charles?'

'I shall be needing extra services of you, once you're installed in the post room. These extra services, of course, will come with extra remuneration, which I'm quite certain your family will appreciate, in the days to come.' Maynard paused. 'We have always worked so well together, you and I.'

Billy could sense, in Mr Charles, some air of unutterable sadness, but he dared not ask why.

'I'm afraid there's a task appointed to us. I had hoped we were finished. But we must return to our old trade, Mr Brogan. The trade of listening in. The trade of discovery. This terrible trade of secrets and lies.'

# Chapter Twenty-one

VIVIENNE LOOKED INTO THE ORNATE mirror in the office behind the Daughters of Salvation, and decided there was no longer any way of denying it. Her body had changed. During the first months it had been easier to conceal. Now, though, her body was giving quarter to the new life growing inside her. Her cheeks, she felt certain, were becoming more rounded. Her ankles swelled further the longer she was on her feet. And the plumpness in her belly, which was once so easy to hide beneath the dowdy gowns she'd adopted recently, was growing rounder by the day.

At least she didn't feel sick anymore. That, perhaps, had been the hardest thing to conceal. Like that time when, out browsing bridal gowns with Nancy and her fellow chambermaids, she'd felt it come upon her – and had to take herself away, sipping at water from the lavatory tap, until the feeling had passed. She was quite certain Nancy suspected something. She'd *wanted* to tell Nancy, she really had. But Nancy had other things on her mind this year. She was *allowed* to have a few months to think about herself for once, to luxuriate and enjoy the time before her wedding. Nancy had done so much for Vivienne. Troubling her now would be the worst thing Vivienne could do.

In her heart, Vivienne would have liked to have been her bridesmaid as well. Had things been different, she would have accepted in an instant. But the thought of ruining Nancy's day with all the gossip and tittle-tattle had made her demur. She only hoped that, some day soon, Nancy would understand.

At least Mrs Moffatt had been kind. It was clear why all of the chambermaids loved her so.

She was still standing there, studying herself in the mirror, when there came a tap at the door, and Warren Peel appeared, quite uninvited.

'Vivienne, you've been in here a while. Mary's started to think you're . . .' He stopped. 'Are you feeling unwell again?'

Warren had changed too. The year since they'd met had hardened his face, and though the cornfield gold of his hair was the same vibrant hue, these days Warren kept it trimmed neatly. He was even beginning to show signs of stubble. He'd come later to it than most – at nineteen years of age, he was almost as old as Vivienne – but she had often thought he was growing into a handsome man.

'Not unwell,' Vivienne said. 'I think all that's passed.' She had been looking at him in the mirror, but now she turned around. 'You're sweet to keep asking, Warren. I'm sorry. I'm not used to it. But . . . thank you.'

He came to her side – and, had anyone been there to see it, they would have seen the easy familiarity between them.

'I need to go,' she said. 'I'm sorry, Warren.'

'Don't be. Between Mary and the girls, it's plain sailing tonight. And Artie's still on the door.'

*Guarding us all. Guarding me*, thought Vivienne. *Like he always is.*

'Thank you,' she whispered, and kissed him on the cheek before she took off into the night.

*I have to tell him soon*, she thought. *It isn't right. He ought to know. They all ought to know.*

The taxicab was idling at the end of the cobbled row when Vivienne clambered in. Soon, they were coursing along the Embankment and, from there, up through the palaces of Westminster, bound for Berkeley Square.

To Vivienne, it was like passing from one world to the next – like stepping through a magic door, from the poverty of the Daughters of Salvation, to a world where what mattered most was not how you kept your belly full each night, but how priceless the diamonds were that dangled from your neckline. Only a precious few people passed from one world into the other. Vivienne supposed she was special to be one of those people – but, as she stepped through the hotel's famous revolving doors, she knew it was not to last. She'd been living on borrowed time, ever since she stopped spending her stepfather's allowance on champagne and opiates, and started spending it on the Daughters of Salvation instead. And now her days here were numbered: every day that her baby grew within her was another day closer to the end.

In the reception hall, the night managers were on shift, and Billy was nowhere to be found – which was certainly a blessing, because there was nothing he liked more than to engage her in idle chit-chat. And tonight was not for light-hearted nothings. Tonight she was to go back to Mrs Moffatt, and finally work out what she intended to do.

Mrs Moffatt was the light by which she'd steered her life, these past few weeks. Mrs Moffatt hadn't judged. She hadn't condemned. She had barely told her what to do, just sat there and listened and made tea. There had been something about Mrs Moffatt that night, as if all the world's wisdom was being channelled through her.

'There's something I learned today,' she'd said, 'something that will stay with me forever. The one thing you should never regret is doing the right thing, no matter how hard it is.'

'But what's the right thing?' Vivienne had asked.

'Well,' said Mrs Moffatt, 'that's the hardest question of all.'

Perhaps, Vivienne had thought, until Mrs Moffatt had posed her another one.

'And the father, Vivienne?'

*The father. The father. The father.*

Taking one last breath for courage, Vivienne disappeared into the housekeeping hall. There, at the door to the housekeeping lounge, Mrs Moffatt was waiting once more.

'I was nearly ready to give up on you, dear.'

Vivienne whispered, 'I've been ready to give up on myself as well. But, Mrs Moffatt, I believe I know what I must do.'

'Come on, then, dear, let's get you sorted. I've a pot of tea already brewed, and lemon tart from the kitchens. That's a treat I'm sure your baby will thank you for.' Her hand was balanced on the Housekeeping door, when she looked back and said, 'My dear, there's somebody I think you should talk to.'

She opened the door – and there, at the table where the chambermaids would, in only a few short hours, congregate for breakfast, sat Hélène Marchmont.

Vivienne froze. Perhaps she might even have beaten a retreat, if only Mrs Moffatt hadn't already taken her hand, and led her inside.

'You have every right to be cross with me, Miss Edgerton,' she said, as she rattled the teacups and saucers and arranged shortbread biscuits in a fan around each. The lemon tart that was sitting in the middle of the table was a huge, glistening affair of crystallised lemon and cream. 'I didn't mean to break your confidence. But you know the stories, just like everyone. Miss Marchmont's been where you're standing. I thought she might help.'

'Come, sit down,' said Hélène. The chairs were already waiting. 'You don't have to talk to me if you don't wish to, Miss Edgerton. But all I can say is that, if there was somebody I could have spoken to after Sidney died, somebody who'd been in my shoes ... Perhaps things wouldn't have turned out differently, but they'd have been different in my heart. I know how you're feeling now. You're feeling pent-up. You're feeling alone. You're ...'

Mrs Moffatt carved out slices of tart, an extra thick portion for Vivienne, and settled herself at the table.

'How have you been, Vivienne?'

'I'm showing too much, Mrs Moffatt. I've had all the looks, down at the Daughters. I'm yet to tell Mary Burdett. I'm yet to tell the father. But I'm ...' She shook her head. 'I listened to everything you said, and I feel better for it. I feel stronger. You keep a secret, and it hardens in you. It becomes like rock. You have to carry it around.'

Hélène knew this feeling only too well.

'Carry it for too long and *you* turn to rock,' she said. 'But, Miss Edgerton, this isn't a secret you can carry for much longer – not without a plan. Do you have a plan?'

Vivienne said, 'I'm going to keep my baby.'

The silence was perfect. A smile touched Mrs Moffatt, and she nodded her head.

'But how do I do that?' said Vivienne. 'I hardly know what lies I could tell to make this easier.'

'Perhaps that's as well,' Hélène said. 'My story's a little differ-ent from yours, Miss Edgerton. I married Sidney, without a soul knowing except his parents. We would have raised our daughter together, if he'd lived. But, when he died, I had to make lies and plans of my own. They lasted for a time – but secrets and lies have a habit of breaking free.' She folded her arms. 'I don't know how long I'll last here, Miss Edgerton. I feel the walls bearing down on me. Even when I'm out on the dance floor, even when I'm dancing with Raymond or Gene or some guest, I'm not really there. At first, I thought it was the gossip. But the truth is – it's been crashing down, since the day I discovered I was preg-nant. All my concoction of falsehoods and misdirections did was delay this moment. It . . . robbed me of any control. *That's* why my head hasn't been in the ballroom for years. *That's* why I've been spinning, spinning away from this place.'

And now, Hélène thought, this thing from Archie Adams – though she dared not say it, for she still hadn't made sense of it in her own mind. Chicago: the great unknown. It hadn't left her thoughts in weeks. Three nights ago, she'd been brave enough to sit down with Noelle and Maurice, while Sybil cavorted around them, and told them what Archie had offered. The look on their faces had destroyed her more than the tittering of a few kitchen porters and concierges ever could. The way they kept the hurt inside, and told her she should do it – that for Sybil and Hélène to live a life together, even if it meant they rarely saw the grand-daughter they doted on ever again, was the most important thing.

Some people were selfless. Others were selfish. Most of human-ity lived somewhere in between. But the Archers had given Sybil and Hélène more than anyone else in the world, and Hélène was not sure she would ever be able to repay them. If she took Sybil to Chicago, to begin a new life together as mother and daughter, it would be like telling them she wasn't even going to try.

'What I mean to say,' Hélène went on, 'is that, however high you build the walls now – some day, they're going to crash down.'

Mrs Moffatt nodded. 'And if you turn those walls into great fortifications, great castles, well, they'll crash harder still.'

There was silence in the room. From the other side of the table, Vivienne and Hélène looked at her with searching eyes. There was something in this thing she'd said, something in her faraway tone, that spoke of yet more secrets. But Mrs Moffatt wasn't sure she was ready to spill them. In her heart, she knew she ought to. These girls – *both* these girls – were crying out for understanding. She realised, now, how they'd been crying out for it all along.

And she was damned if she wasn't going to help them. Even if it meant risking everything she had.

'Girls,' she ventured, 'you're not alone.'

So she told them everything. She told them about her grand romance, how it had all been the foolishness of a young woman old enough to know better. She told them about the moment she revealed her pregnancy to her mother. She told them about the Sisters at St Maud's, and of how she'd named her baby Michael. She told them how he'd smelt in those few brief moments she got to hold him close, before he was swaddled up and whisked away. She told them about the emptiness of the weeks and months that followed; about running away, devastated in the knowledge that her family no longer knew her for who she really was – and devastated, too, by the knowledge that she had stopped loving them. She told them about the long years. The not knowing. The days when she could almost forget. The weeks, wondering who he was, where he was, *if* he still survived. The days she had longed to – and failed to – tell Jack.

And then she told them about a man named Malcolm, and how she'd set eyes upon her son for the first time in thirty-three years.

As her tale came to an end, Mrs Moffatt took in the two faces staring into hers and smiled.

'Shocked, I see. Miss Marchmont, you're not the first in this hotel to turn her life into a lie. Miss Edgerton, the road you're about to travel has been travelled by many hundreds before.'

'Mrs Moffatt,' Hélène began, 'I don't know what to say.'

'I'm quite well, dear,' Mrs Moffatt said.

And she was. She'd felt lighter, freer than she had in years. It was in part down to Archie Adams, the way he kept coming down to the Lounge when things were quiet to partake of a pot of tea and a blackberry slice; but the truth was, she hadn't known she was carrying such weight around with her. Telling Archie everything had changed her in ways she hadn't, at first, understood. There was such loneliness that came with keeping secrets. It was little wonder that she'd never found love, not since her Jack was taken so cruelly away. Secrets cocooned you. They kept others at bay.

'You've got to share it,' Mrs Moffatt finally said, 'so the secret doesn't fester. So you don't live a life full of lies. That's why I asked you here, tonight, Vivienne. It's why I asked you, too, Miss Marchmont. Now, you're both grown women. Admirable and proud and single-minded, the pair of you. My goodness, what the two of you have already achieved! What the two of you could do, if only the world was a little different. I dare say we wouldn't be talking about war at all this year, not if we had good, dependable ladies like you in charge. We'd sit around a table and thrash it out and we wouldn't have to dream of all these ways to kill each other at all.' She paused. 'But that isn't the world, and here we are. You have lives ahead of you, full, rich lives to lead. So I'm imploring you both. It won't be easy. These are roads most of us don't have to travel. They're roads peopled by shame and gossip. But we should walk those roads without fear. We should walk them, dare I say it, with pride. We are who we are, and there's no changing that. Let's not waste another second. I'm writing, tonight, to my son to invite him for Christmas dinner, right here at the Buckingham. Write your own letters, girls. Tell the people you feel you can tell. Tell friends. Tell family. Break down the secret, Miss Edgerton, before it hardens around you. Even if it's only to tell a friend, don't bottle it up and keep it inside.'

'I've been longing to tell Nancy. I had to tell her I couldn't be her bridesmaid, and I'm quite sure she thinks it's because I'm a terrible snob. But . . . I couldn't possibly tell her. She knows the father too well, and . . .' Vivienne stopped. 'I've a friend in New York, though. Miriam. She won't be surprised. She always thought me too wild. Maybe I'll write to her tonight.'

And Hélène said, 'There are people I should talk to as well, though the secret's already out for me.'

She was thinking of her mother, her aunt, her father on his sickbed. It was the last thing the Archers had said to her, after she'd broken the news: that perhaps, before she set sail, she might give them one last chance. One last chance to make amends, before the end times truly came.

Mrs Moffatt extended a hand across the table, and soon the fingers of all three ladies present were intertwined.

'We must be here for each other. We women of the Buckingham, we deserve a little fortune in our lives, do we not?'

271

# Chapter Twenty-two

TWO DAYS SINCE HE'D GONE, and to the men and women of the Winter Holler Company, it felt like an epoch had passed.

Was it really only two nights since Ansel Albrecht had been found there, at the foot of the guest stairs? Now there was no sign of him ever having been here. No stain on the carpets. No impression in the thick pile. No plaque nor monument to say that here was extinguished one of the best of them. By mid-week, the company would be back dancing in the Grand Ballroom, marching their imperious tangos as if a little piece of them hadn't been carved away. The dances had to go on.

What was it Maynard sometimes said? The world keeps turning . . .

Jonas Holler and Karina Kainz were clasping hands as they lingered at the foot of the stairs. Not a soul had seen them holding one another outside the ballroom in all the days the company had been at the Buckingham, but in the last two days Frank had seen their hands entwined wherever they walked. It was tragedy that brought it out of them – and now, as Frank followed them from the foot of the stairs and into the Grand Ballroom, he saw the way she rested against his shoulder, and wondered that two people could ever be as entwined, heart, body and soul. The good and the bad, the dark and the light, swirling all around him.

He hadn't realised how much he'd miss Ansel. He'd gone to bed last night, at the Brogan house, with the emotion of it rising up through his gorge. In the end, he'd had to cram his face into the pillow, for fear of upsetting the smaller children sleeping on the other side of the wall.

He longed for the taste of cherry brandy.

He wanted to jive with Ansel, as absurd as it sounded.

Rosa had been so kind. He was going to her later, just to drink tea and eat scones, to sit together in perfect silence. He'd feel better after that; he was certain of it. It was like Jonas and Karina: the grief of it only made the love so much more acute. But first, there was the Grand.

The Winter Holler Company were gathered on the dance floor. Ordinarily the ballroom saw no life on a Sunday afternoon – and yet, here they all were, gathered together while Maximilian Schank took to the stage. Up there, Archie Adams's grand piano was draped in a dust sheet that put Frank in mind of a funeral shroud. He had to try hard not to be thrown back to the memory of his father's funeral, a few short years ago – and this was made an even more difficult task when he saw Nancy standing there, with Raymond and the other dancers from the Buckingham troupe. They'd had to carry the show last night. Frank had seen the gravity of it in Raymond's eyes: the grit, the determination, the honour he took in putting on a good show while, all around him, the world was giving in to grief and desolation. The lords and ladies had left the Buckingham ballroom without any hint of the tragedy that had befallen the dancers only hours before, and that was a testament to Raymond's courage.

Frank only wished he had a little courage of his own.

He sat in the corner, away from the balustrade where the real dancers were gathered, and listened.

'My friends,' Schank began. 'My dear, dear friends. There is nothing I can say today that will take away the feelings that have set upon us since the tragedy of two nights past. I cannot wave a wand to dispel the heartbreak we are all feeling. Dancing does not bring back the dead. Ansel Albrecht was a young man of the greatest promise. I had known his mother many years, when she came to me and told me her son was a dancer. His father, of course, wanted a different life for him – to follow in his own footsteps, and join the police force in Vienna. But Ansel had inherited his mother's flair, her passion and love. The dreams of generations were in that boy – not just for his family, who now grieve and will grieve for evermore, but for each of us here. One day, Ansel would, I feel certain, have led this troupe. Now, instead, we must say goodbye to our friend. Mr Charles has made arrangements for his body to be repatriated to the parents who adored him. And, in the emptiness of the ever after, we must dance on, with Ansel in our hearts . . .'

There were tears on the dance floor – and, although Schank had not yet finished his eulogy, Frank heard no more. His world, too, had become occluded by tears.

Soon he felt a hand on his shoulder. A little part of him thought it must be Nancy, come to comfort him – but when Frank looked up, it was to see the round, jowly face of Mr Charles looking down at him. The hotel director was down on his haunches and said, softly, 'I think a day off might be in order, young Nettleton.'

'I'm all right, sir. I wouldn't want to let the hotel down.'

'Then take the time, Frank. This hotel needs you well.'

He was quite certain it wasn't true, but the kindness of it made Frank feel even weaker.

'Thank you, M-Mr Charles,' he stuttered, and took off for the ballroom doors, up towards the reception hall.

He was only halfway there when Nancy caught up with him. Her scent, of blackberries and childhood, enveloped him. She put an arm around him.

'Oh, Nance,' he sniffed.

'It's all right, Frank. It's all right.'

Surely Nancy was remembering, too, the days after their father passed on – and how, in all of the chaos of the funeral and their landlord looming, all they had had was each other.

'Come on,' she said. 'Let's have a nice pot of tea.'


Ruth and Rosa were already in the kitchenette when Nancy led Frank through. Rosa sat with him in the raggedy armchair while Nancy brewed the tea.

'He wouldn't have wanted you to cry, Frank.'

Rosa had said it to him before, and he knew it was true, but it did so little to quell these feelings. He had to concentrate just to get on top of them. And the more he recollected the kindness in Maynard Charles's weathered face, the more the tears threatened to come. How was it that kindness could undo you, just the same as grief?

After a little time, as the other girls in the kitchenette settled in their own corners, playing backgammon or embroidering, Rosa turned to Nancy and said, 'We have to snap him out of it, Nance. Get him out of here. Take him . . . dancing?'

It was the furthest thing from Frank's mind.

'I don't think I can dance.'

'Not now, Frankie, but . . . later this week? Next weekend? We could go back to the Starlight Lounge. You could get Billy, if he dares. Ruth'll promise to be kind to him this time, won't you? Maybe she'll even give him a dance too?'

Ruth, frowning as she leafed through one of the London newspapers, looked up and said, 'Maybe. If it'll cheer Frank up.' She paused. 'Oh Frank, I'm so sorry.'

Frank nodded. Nancy had brought him a tea tray with a cup and saucer, and half a scone sitting alongside it. She'd brought him some crystallised lemon pieces too. He popped them in his mouth, one after another.

'I've never known a business like it,' said Ruth, with a sigh.

Frank smiled wanly at her, through a mouth full of crystallised lemon.

'It doesn't make sense,' he said, 'for a person to be there one minute and gone the next.'

'The thing I don't understand,' Ruth went on, softly, 'is why your friend Ansel was there at all.' She lifted the newspaper, flicked through some of the pages, and turned it round to display a poster advertisement for the cinema on Leicester Square. In big white letters across a picture of two figures looming over a bedridden third were the words THE LADY VANISHES. 'It's like in these Hitchcock pictures – there's something that doesn't make sense about the whole thing.'

'Oh, Ruth, leave it alone,' said Rosa. 'It's bad enough without us poring over it.'

Ruth flushed crimson. 'I'm sorry, Frank, I didn't mean to—'

But Ruth's words had sparked something in Frank. He swallowed the last of his lemon pieces, lifted himself in his seat and said, 'No, Ruth, go on.'

'Well, it's just . . . Lord, you girls will call me a fusspot again, but I'm not meaning to be. I just don't understand why Ansel would have been coming down the guest stairs. We all know the Winter Hollers are in the staff suites. Suites, they call them, as if they're anything more than the rooms not good enough for guests to sleep in! So what was Ansel doing, that he took a tumble down the guest stairs? It just doesn't make sense.'

For a time, there was silence in the kitchenette. Then Rosa said, 'Ruth, you've got your head in the clouds again. You're incorrigible. Riling up my Frank like that!'

'Nancy?' Frank breathed.

Nancy had a faraway look in her eyes. She perched on the arm of Frank's chair and said, 'I wonder . . .'

'Oh, not you too!' Rosa exploded. 'Can't we talk about something else? Somebody died. It's dreadful and it's sad. It's not a blooming Hitchcock picture!'

'He wasn't dancing that night,' said Frank. 'Mr Schank makes him take time off, so his body's at its best. He was going to meet me in the studio – we were going to rehearse something, Nance, for the wedding day. He ought to have been down in the studio, waiting for me.'

'Maybe he'd gone for a rest first?' Nancy suggested.

'Up the *guest* stairs?' asked Ruth.

'When I saw him that morning, he was off to write a letter to his family. The last letter they'll ever get, I should think. There was something important he wanted to tell his father.'

'Well, oughtn't he to have been in his rooms, then?' asked Rosa, and immediately clasped her hands over her mouth. She hadn't meant to join in.

Ruth's face was starting to pale again, now that the others could see it too.

'That's all I meant. If he was up in his own rooms, he wouldn't have been coming down the guest staircase at all. He'd have been on the service stairs. Or he'd have hopped in the service lift. That's what I'd have done.'

'She's right,' breathed Frank. Then, letting his cup and saucer fall at his side, he repeated the same: 'She's right. Ansel oughtn't to have been there at all. And if he oughtn't to have been there, he oughtn't to have died.'

'The question is,' said Ruth, 'what could Ansel Albrecht have been doing up the guest stairs? Maybe he got lost?'

Frank was still. He turned on his heels, his eyes agog.

'I don't know,' he uttered, 'but maybe there's a way to find out.'

Down in the post room, Billy was bored.

He supposed it wasn't the right thing to be feeling, not with everything that had happened to poor Ansel. Billy had shed tears of his own. Not that he'd ever tell anybody, because he was more courageous than that. But Ansel had been a good friend. He'd tried so hard to make Billy see the simple rudiments of dance. And, when that hadn't worked, he'd uncorked his bottle of cherry liqueur and shown him a different way. Billy would never forget that.

It had hit Frank harder. Billy had seen them together and he'd known, from the start, the kind of friends they would become.

Inseparable, Billy had thought, if they'd been given enough time. Sometimes, people just hit it off.

Well, if Billy ever needed any other excuse to become good at dancing – and he hadn't given up on dancing with Ruth, perhaps even at Nancy's wedding – here it was. He'd learn to waltz. He'd learn to jitterbug and jive. He'd do it all in memory of Ansel Albrecht.

If only his feet would do what he asked of them . . .

But none of this, no matter how much it cartwheeled and cascaded through his mind, could separate him from the boredom of an out of hours post room. At least, as a concierge, there had always been something with which to occupy his mind. Being a concierge meant looking outwards, broadening his knowledge of the hotel, of Mayfair, of London. But being stuck in a post room, sifting letters from one pile to another, filling sacks and readdressing letters for onward delivery, according to the instructions set down in Mrs Farrier's book? He was above this. He was a social climber. And right now it felt as if he was at the bottom of a ravine.

He was quite certain that this was how Mrs Farrier wanted him to feel. The look on her face when he'd first turned up for duties was quite incredible. You would have thought him a hired killer, stealing upon her in the night.

'I've been here since the turn of the century, young man, and not once in all that time have I needed an *assistant*.'

She'd spat the word as if it was some unholy curse, but it hadn't done any good.

'Orders from Mr Charles, madam,' Billy had explained, forcing a smile.

It was that smile, he later realised, that had turned Mrs Farrier's irritation to righteous fury. There and then she'd given him the responsibility of working the weekends, taking letters and packages from the guests and organising them for the pick-up on Monday morning.

'And don't forget, the privacy of our guests is sacrosanct, Mr Brogan. Disrespect it, and the devil's at your door!'

*If only the devil* was *at the door*, thought Billy. At least then he'd have had some company. Six hours he'd been on shift in this subterranean hole, and not a soul had he seen. He'd have gladly made a cup of tea for the devil, if only he'd turned up.

There came a knock at the door.

*Better the devil you know*, thought Billy – but, when he tramped across the dusty post room floor and opened the door, it wasn't a demon he saw at all. It was only Frank.

The poor bugger had been crying again.

'Get in here, Frank,' said Billy, and draped an arm around him as he bustled him inside.

As soon as the door was slammed shut, he said, 'I'm glad you got here, Frank. I'm going out of my mind. Look, I've got a bottle of something. We can have a quick taste. Just something to raise a toast by. And maybe another to get this day finished. I shouldn't have been sent down here.'

'No,' said Frank, 'but I'm glad you are. Listen, Billy, there's something Ruth said. No, not about you!' He had seen the look on Billy's face. 'Something about Ansel. About why he was on the guest stairs, when he'd no reason to be there at all. And it made me think. That day, he couldn't dance with me, not until the evening, because he was writing a letter. A letter to his father. Wanted to tell him something important. And I thought . . .'

Billy's eyes mirrored Frank's: each of them, widening in understanding.

'It'd be here somewhere,' said Billy. 'The Royal Mail doesn't pick up on a weekend. Next pick-up isn't until tomorrow morning.'

They turned to survey the grey room. The cubbyhole was lined with filing cabinets, crammed full of all the ledgers and records Mrs Farrier had kept over the years. Shelves lined the walls above, filled with yet more boxes and files. And there, against the outer wall, were the seven sacks of letters, packages and parcels bound for the Royal Mail.

'Mrs Farrier would slaughter me,' whispered Billy, though he felt the thrill of it too. 'All that talk about privacy and honour – like she's a knight of the realm.'

'Well, she isn't h-here until m-morning, is she?'

'Frank, you're starting to stutter.'

'I'm n-nervous,' he said.

'Well.' Billy reached for the half bottle of port he had stowed away. 'Ansel himself taught us how to deal with nerves, didn't he?'

They upended each sack in turn, sifting through the letters guests had written, the cards they'd addressed to places in London, all over the British Isles, and further afield. The Buckingham Hotel, it seemed, was the nexus of the world.

'It'll be a Vienna address,' Frank had said. 'Somewhere in Vienna. I don't know where.'

'Here!' cried Billy – and, whipping one from the landslide, he began to tear it open.

Soon, his eyes were roaming over the pages – though they barely seemed to be taking it in. Frank watched as he stalled, watched as he crammed the letter back into the envelope and looked at the front:

VIENNA MANSIONS

NEW YORK CITY

UNITED STATES OF AMERICA

Billy muttered an oath beneath his breath.

'My mistake. It's not the one,' he said. 'Just something Miss Edgerton wrote, some letter to a friend. Put it on the desk, Frank. I'll have to stitch it up, send it on, or Mrs Farrier will have me for breakfast. If she thinks, for even a second, we've been rooting through these bags . . .'

'Got it,' gasped Frank. Rearing up from the pile of letters, he fell back on to the threadbare carpet. 'This is it. I know it is.'

Billy snatched the envelope, turned it around. The address on the front was JOSEF-HASSE GASSE 12, KAISEREBERSDORF, VIENNA. And the name on the front: HERR DAVID ALBRECHT. He gently returned it to Frank's hands.

'Are you sure about this?'

'We have to know, Billy. For Ansel.'

He slid his finger into the envelope and opened it up.

Out slid the letter. Crisp white pages, headed with the copper crown crest of the Buckingham Hotel. He could feel the indentations the ink pen had left on the pages. The last words Ansel Albrecht had ever written.

*Perhaps*, Frank thought, *the last he'd ever thought.*

Carefully, he unfolded the letter.

It spread out below him, three leaves of paper – all of it inscribed by a spidery hand, and all of it in a language neither Frank nor Billy could understand.

'Of course he'd have written it in his own language,' said Frank. 'Is it German?'

'Austro-Bavarian,' Billy said. Then, on seeing the way Frank looked at him, 'He isn't the first Viennese guest we've had, you know. I do pick up a thing or two along the way.' He paused. 'Just a pity I didn't pick up how to speak a word of it myself. Well?'

'We could ask Jonas,' Frank began. 'Or Maximilian Schank. Anyone from the company.'

'And have them know we stole Ansel's private letter?' Billy recoiled. 'Have that get back to Mrs Farrier? I think not, Frank.'

'Then what?' The emotion of it was making Frank's voice tremble again. '*How*, Billy? Because I've got to know what's in this letter. Who knows – maybe we're wrong. Maybe it's all just chit-chat about London rain and English breakfasts and Earl Grey tea. But if there's a chance it isn't . . .'

His face dropped sadly back to the letter as, in vain, he tried to make sense of words he would never understand.

'I know!' Billy said, flourishing upwards from the pile of parcels. 'We don't need to ask the company at all. We'll ask Mr Bauer, that refugee Mr Charles has up in the Park Suite. He's always been a kind old sort, hasn't he? Just potters about, minding his own business. He'll help, Frank. I'm sure of it. Why, he's from Vienna as well.'

Billy folded his arms, as if a victory had already been secured.

'No, Billy,' Frank whispered. 'Billy, we *can't* . . .' He scrabbled up, onto his feet, and opened the letter so that Billy, too, could peruse its pages. There, Frank traced each line – until, at last, it stopped, hovering over a single name, scored into the paper in deep, black lines.

Bauer, it said.

Herr Tobias Bauer.

Billy looked up. His eyes took in the ruin of the post room.

'We have to get out of here, Frank. We have to tidy this up.'

One after another, ignoring Frank's frozen form, he heaved the letters and packages back into the sacks from which they'd come. But Frank did nothing, only stared at the name blinking back at him from the paper.

'Why would Ansel be writing to his father about Mr Bauer, Billy?'

'I don't know.' Billy trembled. He was as white as a sheet, as cold as if he'd just seen a ghost.

'Ansel didn't fall at all, did he?' Frank whispered.

Billy was silent.

'Something else happened, didn't it?'

'I don't know, Frank,' said Billy, snapping out of it at last, forcing Frank bodily to the door and up along the corridor beyond. 'But we have to get that letter translated. We'll do it ourselves, if that's what it takes. Because, whatever happened two nights ago, one thing's for certain – the truth of it's in here, or my name's not Billy Brogan. Ansel's going to tell us it all, even if he has to do it from the grave.'

# Chapter Twenty-three

OF ALL THE LETTERS AND PACKAGES Billy Brogan and Frank Nettleton had spilled in the post room, only one remained out of place. There it lay, perched on the edge of Mrs Farrier's desk, torn open by Billy's own hand, forgotten in the confusion as they rushed out of the room.

And there it lay, until morning came.

Monday morning was always the time the Buckingham cleaners arrived. Long before the breakfast trolleys were warmed up, when all was still dark across Berkeley Square, Mr Winthrop and his army of cleaners set about their work.

The cleaners who visited the hotel basements set about their work with gusto. They knew this hotel and its secret corners as well as any concierge who darted up and down its halls. So, when one of the cleaners fumbled a key into a lock and swept on into the post room, they barely batted an eyelid as they swept around the room, lifting each item from Mrs Farrier's desk and dusting beneath it. They barely batted an eyelid at the scraps of paper and screwed-up envelopes that had tumbled out of the waste-paper basket. They thought nothing of it as they swept the ripped-open envelope hanging off the edge of the desk into the refuse sack they carried on their rickety old trolley.

They did not know, and never would, that, as they left Mrs Farrier's office, they were carrying Vivienne Edgerton's whole world.

Nor did they know that, when they pulled their rickety old trolley into the service lift, spilling some of its contents onto the lift floor, they left the envelope for Vienna Mansions, New York City, behind. Or that, some time later, when a porter named Daniel Broome stepped into the lift and stooped to pick up the letter lying there, they had changed the Buckingham Hotel forever.

Daniel Broome knew it. Being the sort of boy who bored easily, he had no compunction about opening the letter up and reading its contents. When he realised it had come from the hand of Miss Edgerton herself, the compulsion to read the whole thing was too much to bear.

Inside this letter was a secret too big to be contained. Daniel tried. When he told his fellow porter, Ralph, about it, he swore him to secrecy. It wasn't Daniel's fault that Ralph told three friends, and it wasn't Ralph's fault that those three friends told twelve others. It wasn't Daniel's *or* Ralph's fault when one of those friends, the sous-chef O'Neill who'd been romancing the chambermaid Yvette, took the news back to the chambermaids' kitchenette that evening.

As for the letter itself: by the time All Hallows' Eve came, a full week later, it had been passed from hand to hand, read from high to low.

Nobody ever knew what became of that letter. Perhaps some kindly chambermaid, seeing the injustice of it all, ripped it to shreds in her refuse sack. But by then it hardly mattered. In a hotel like the Buckingham, rumour was like disease.

Until, in a faraway Suffolk mansion, the telephone rang.

\*

Vivienne Edgerton had once been used to being summoned to Maynard Charles's office. She'd have imbibed too much in the Grand Ballroom the night before, or she'd have spat too much bile at some concierge, and a message would come: Mr Charles will see you now. Ordinarily, it was Billy who brought such messages, and so it had been today.

Now she stood outside the door to the office as Billy beat his retreat. Lifting her fingers, she took a deep breath and knocked.

She didn't need this today. There were things she needed to do. Ever since meeting Hélène Marchmont and Mrs Moffatt, she'd felt a new steel inside her. Being pregnant was not an ordeal she had to endure. She'd been thinking of it all wrong, just riding the waves of it, terrified to think about what came next. But those words Mrs Moffatt had spoken, they altered everything inside her. What she needed was control, pure and simple. She would take charge of it herself. It was, she had started to reflect, exactly what life had been preparing her for.

Then she opened the door, and everything changed.

It wasn't only Mr Charles in the office – though there he was, dressed in his starched shirt and braces, like always he was. Standing before the ornate desk was Vivienne's mother, and looming over her, Lord Edgerton.

'Close the door, Miss Edgerton.'

For a moment, she did not. She stood there, in its frame, and felt the roundness of her belly, pushing up against the house dress that could no longer truly hide it, and felt her heart hammering. No, felt *two* hearts hammering inside her. She took in their faces, one by one. So they'd sprung her a trap, she thought. How long had they known?

'Close the door, Vivienne,' Lord Edgerton intoned.

With gritted teeth, she did as she was told.

As the door clicked shut, her mother burst into a torrent of tears.

'Well,' Lord Edgerton seethed, 'it's true, then?'

'Mother, why are you—'

'Answer the question, damn it!' Lord Edgerton boomed.

Vivienne looked from one to another. Maynard had seen the expression that coloured her face before. It was the look she used to have when she staggered drunkenly out of the Grand, only to come face to face with one of the night managers, or Maynard himself. It was the look that said she was cornered.

'How do you know?' she breathed, valiantly trying to keep her composure.

Lord Edgerton had opened his mouth with some sneer, but into the fractional silence that followed Maynard said, 'I'm afraid it's been the gossip of the hotel, Miss Edgerton. I'm yet to discover where it originated. Have you, perhaps, taken someone into your confidence?'

She could not believe it of Mrs Moffatt. She could not believe it of Miss Marchmont. And yet here was all the evidence she needed, that her secret was out: her mother could not take her eyes off the plumpness of her belly.

What did it matter? Another week, another two, and she would have had to shed the secret herself.

'Why don't you sit down, Miss Edgerton?' Maynard began, in his most even tone.

By God, how Vivienne hated that tone! She'd heard it so many times. Maynard Charles, her royally appointed keeper, inviting her in here, bidding her to sit – and then explaining, in his rehearsed, calm voice, why she had to change her ways, her behaviour, her very character. At least, that was the way it had always seemed. Right now a little piece of her was telling her that he was doing the only thing that he could – anchoring the moment, tempering the excesses of Lord Edgerton's anger, gently guiding Vivienne so that she didn't throw herself off a cliff.

Something in her recoiled.

'You're all standing,' she said, 'so I'm going to stand. I'm not a child. You can't drag me in here as if I am. What happens next? I'm to be caned? I'm to be disinherited? I'm having a baby,' she snapped, and in the moment she was proud that she was not crumbling in the face of it. 'I haven't killed a man.'

'Vivienne Edgerton!' Lord Edgerton roared. 'Sit!'

'I won't speak to you,' she said – and though she started out tentatively, somewhere in those words she found her courage again. 'You've no law over me. I'm twenty-one years of age. Stepfather or not, you've no business telling me what to do. I'll speak to my mother, or not at all. Do you hear me, Bartholomew? *Do you hear?*'

*Bartholomew*. Maynard had never heard a word used quite as much like a weapon. Not *my lord*, not *Father*. *Bartholomew*. *By God*, he thought, *she's got some courage*. Something inside him respected that, though he was careful not to show it. He took a fractional step backwards, as if to indicate he would provoke the situation no further.

'Tell her, Madeleine,' Lord Edgerton uttered.

'Yes, Mother,' Vivienne began. '*Tell me.*'

'What have you done, Vivienne?' Madeleine gasped.

As always, her voice inspired a terrible ire in Vivienne: the way she'd shed her New England accent in favour of this crude imitation of the England of old. As soon as she'd married the old brute at her side, she'd wanted to forget: the States; New York; Vivienne's true father, five years in the ground. To Vivienne's ear, she sounded like a fool. Was there anything worse than a fraud?

'We've been so proud of you this year. No more dramas. No more . . . little love affairs, like you used to have. You'd cleaned yourself up, Vivienne. You nearly killed yourself with those *excesses* of yours, but you—'

'Call it what it was, Mother,' said Vivienne. 'I was a nasty little addict. Opiates. Champagne. Whatever I could get my hands on. It carried me through for a while.' She shrugged, openly, inviting further attack. 'I'm not that girl anymore.'

'But *look at you* . . .'

Vivienne folded her arms around her bump.

'It's a baby. It isn't a—'

'A baby, out of wedlock, fathered by Lord knows who!' Madeleine exclaimed. 'You'll ruin our lives. Can't you see what this will do to us?'

'Your wretch of a daughter is to be my undoing,' Lord Edgerton seethed.

Seemingly, he had forgotten his gadabout son, engaged to be married to some different heiress every season. He could drink and whore his way across the Continent, thought Vivienne, and nobody batted an eyelid. But the rules were different for women, weren't they?

'I've something important to say to you, then,' Vivienne declared – and, not for the first time, she clung on to the things Mrs Moffatt and Miss Marchmont had said of their lives. 'I'm not your undoing. I'm not going to ruin your life. This is *my* life. And I'll ruin it my own way.'

She turned on her heel, as if she might leave – but some vital piece of courage had deserted her, and when she hesitated, her mother asked, in a faded, fragile voice, 'Who is the father?'

Vivienne's hands had turned into claws.

'A better man than the one you chose to be my stepfather.'

'I'll hear no more of this!' Lord Edgerton thundered. 'You've been happy enough to take my stipend each month. You've been happy enough to live in my hotel, without paying a penny of board. You've been happy enough to sashay around town, without for a moment thinking about your future. To leech off my family estate, as if it belonged to you. Well—'

'Leeching off you?' gasped Vivienne.

'Why, yes!' Lord Edgerton fumed. 'What else do you call it? For three years, Vivienne, you have lived at the cost of my estate. But the finest hotel in London, the generous allowance you're permitted – none of it matters to you, does it? Because, time and again, you've shown what you are. There isn't an ounce of gratitude in you. You're a spoilt little rich girl, and now—'

'You fool.' Vivienne laughed, 'I haven't spent a penny you've given me on myself since two Christmases ago. Not since that moment I . . .' *Nearly died*, she was going to say, but stopped herself. 'You've no idea, have you?' She laughed, then, wild and free. Even Maynard was disturbed. 'Haven't you noticed that I haven't been in the Grand in months – not unless it's been at your insistence. Haven't you people wondered where I go each night? Off to lose myself in some other drinking hole – is that what you think? Well, nothing could be further from the truth, *Bartholomew*. Every single penny you've given me in nearly two years, I've put to work. Oh, not like *you* put money to work – with more and more investments, just to grow the size of your hoard. I've put it to good work – the work of helping people. I'm not a spoilt little rich girl, Stepfather. I'm the manageress of the Daughters of Salvation. I've helped save a thousand lives. I've put food in the bellies of a thousand hungry people. I've helped bring hundreds out of their addictions, so that they too can help others like them. The people I've seen you ride past in the street, without so much as a second look. The people you disregard because, to you, they're just ... *ants*. They're my people. And I feed them by *leeching off you*, as you so kindly put it!'

The silence in the hotel director's office grew thick. This was not the silence of simmering tension, though that was here somewhere as well. This was the silence of a world being changed. Of understandings being rewritten. Of continents shifting against one another, as Lord Edgerton struggled to understand the words Vivienne had just spat out.

His eyes revolved, to find Maynard.

'Have you known about this, Mr Charles?'

Maynard lifted his palms in silent entreaty.

'This ends, now,' Lord Edgerton began. His face still wore its perplexity, but in his core he remained in command. 'Maynard, this wretch of a stepdaughter of mine has been stealing from me on your watch, and—'

'I do not believe you can judge it theft, sir. Her allowance was freely given.'

'To spend on the essentials of a civilised life in society. Not to squander!' He revolved again, looking imperiously down his nose. 'And the way you tell me this, with such glee, as if I cannot just *snap* my fingers' – which he happily did – 'and end it. Not a penny more will come from my estate to you, and this bastard you carry.'

'Bartholomew,' Madeleine piped up, 'please . . .'

'And, what's more, your residency at this prized address is, as of this moment, revoked. Do you hear me, Vivienne?'

She let the silence linger, then gave a wan half-smile.

She could feel her baby inside her. But she didn't mean to let her stepfather's wrath disturb the unborn child a moment longer. There and then, she swore that Lord Edgerton would not colour this child's life, not as he had coloured hers.

Neither would her mother.

'You speak about this hotel as if it's been a blessing for me,' Vivienne said, cool and collected. 'You keep telling me I ought to be grateful. I used to think it too. But that's not the truth. I didn't realise it, for a time. I'd lost myself in drink and powders. But I see it clearly, now. Granting me a room at this hotel was never a gift. It was an exile.' She directed this next to her mother. 'You let him exile me, so you could have your new life, and pretend the old one never happened. I'll never be like you, Mother. My child's going to be loved.' She stopped, reaching for the door. 'And I don't need money – yours or anybody else's – to do that.'

Then she was gone. She didn't even have the anger left in her to slam the door.

Madeleine called after her. She might even have gone to the door, if she hadn't felt her husband's vice-like fingers on her arm.

'She's already lost, Madeleine,' he whispered.

Vivienne might have moved beyond anger, but there was still wrath in her stepfather. He turned it, now, on Maynard.

'You've lost your grip on this hotel, Mr Charles.'

'My lord, I implore you. Whatever she's done, Miss Edgerton is a young woman at risk and we ought to—'

'At risk?' Lord Edgerton scoffed. 'To hear her speak of it, she's queen of this little East End hovel. You've been blind, Maynard. Either that, or you've been lying to me for years.'

Maynard was silent.

'Blind,' Lord Edgerton continued, 'just like you were blind to Hélène Marchmont. These women see you for what you are. Old bachelors like you, never married, they're too easily swayed by a pretty face. Women young enough to be their granddaughters. You're losing your touch. You've turned soft. This hotel survives by rigour, Mr Charles. It doesn't survive by you acting like a grandfather – or, worse, as if you've been bewitched. You need to pull your socks up, man. You need to start cutting losses. If there's war to come, we need to be protected. I need you—'

'Rest assured, my lord, that this will be dealt with.'

'I've already dealt with it!' Lord Edgerton raged. The brutish power of his voice quelled even Maynard. 'Clean out my stepdaughter's suite. It is to have its first new guest in two days' time. It can start making some money for us, not squandering our time. By God, man! You were this hotel's crown jewel. You could have sailed her through a hurricane at sea. But now . . .'

Maynard sensed the hesitation and seized the moment.

'I'll tidy the scandal away, my lord, as I tidy every one of them.'

'Like you did Hélène Marchmont?' Lord Edgerton laughed. 'Get a hold of yourself, man. You're losing the respect of this hotel. And when that crown slips, it never sits right again. You have one week to get on top of these things. Don't forget, Mr Charles – John Hastings isn't the only member of the hotel board!'

Maynard Charles had to steady himself after Lord Edgerton strode out of the office, trailing his tearful wife with him. It wasn't that he didn't understand his future was in the board's hands. That was the way it had been since he first arrived at the Buckingham Hotel, in those fitful days after the Great War. Men of middle rank like Maynard were never truly the masters of their own destinies. The board of the Buckingham Hotel couldn't see it – they thought him a cut above – but everybody was just clinging to another rung on the ladder, trampling on the people below to save themselves being trampled from above.

His eyes gravitated to the decanter of brandy that always sat on his desk.

His fingers reached for it.

But a little voice inside him stayed his hand.

*No*, he told himself. *Not this time.* This time, he didn't need to dull the feelings. This time, he needed to sit with them, to let them wash through him, to work a way through.

A knock came at the door.

Lord Edgerton had left it ajar as he stalked away, and through the crack between door and frame there appeared first the face of Billy Brogan, and then the anxious, screwed-up face of Frank Nettleton.

'Not now, Billy,' Maynard snapped, and again the thought of the brandy came back to him.

'Sir, it's important.'

'Can't you see I'm busy?'

Frank's head had disappeared, but Billy's remained. Maynard supposed it was his fault. He'd used the boy for so many of Moorcock's little errands – eavesdropping in the Queen Mary, asking prying questions at the concierge desk, and now off to the post room – that he'd become overly familiar.

'Mr Brogan, this had better be important.'

'It is, sir.' Billy turned over his shoulder, into the corridor, and said, 'Come on, Frank. Mr Charles hasn't got all day!'

Maynard had almost lost his patience at the prevaricating that was going on in the corridor outside. His anger was beginning to give way to a kind of guilt – guilt that he hadn't known what was going on under his nose: that he hadn't understood how Vivienne was resourcing this project of hers; that he'd been steadfastly looking the other way for so long that he hadn't noticed the changes in her body. But all of those thoughts vanished when Billy dragged Frank within and, swiftly and deliberately, closed the door behind them.

'Mr Charles, when you sent me to the post room, I thought I'd just be sitting there. Slumped at the desk and listening to Mrs Farrier's stories. But then . . .'

Frank bustled forward and pressed a bundle of papers, and one ragged envelope, into Maynard's hands.

'What is this?' asked Maynard, turning the pages in his hands, even as a feeling of terrible disquiet overcame him. One of the leaves was in a Germanic language; the other was in English, though with so many amendments and crossings-out that it, too, looked like a kind of hieroglyphics.

'The first is the letter Ansel Albrecht wrote the afternoon before he was . . . found,' said Billy.

'*Killed*,' corrected Frank.

Maynard Charles looked up, his face a mask of thunder.

'What the devil are you talking about?'

'I know we shouldn't have, M-Mr Charles,' Frank began to stutter. 'It was something Ruth – she's one of the chambermaids – said that got me started. How Ansel oughtn't to have been on the guest stairs at all – so how was it he was found there, dead?' Frank had turned crimson, but he did not stop speaking. 'Then I remembered what Ansel had been doing that afternoon. He was going to write to his father. He said there was something important he had to write home with, straight away. And, well, Billy and I thought – it's the weekend, so that letter hasn't been sent yet. We'd go and find it . . .'

Maynard hung his head. 'Does Mrs Farrier know?'

'Know, sir?'

'That you two detectives have been sifting through her post bags.'

Billy interjected, 'It's what you sent me there for, Mr Charles.'

To be caught in a moral trap by Billy Brogan! The thought was unimaginable.

Maynard found his spectacles, balanced them on the bridge of his nose. Then he drew his desk lamp nearer and began to read.

'Who translated this?'

'We did, Mr Charles.'

'*You?*'

Frank nodded, feverishly. 'Billy's father has a friend, down at Billingsgate. Came over from Salzburg just after the Great War. He helped. He was only five when they left, but he had a dictionary. And . . .'

Maynard Charles heard no more, for he was lost in the letter.

Dear Papa,

Where to begin? First off, know that I am well and in good health, and that our English adventure continues to amaze. Now that the Autumn Serenade is over, we look to the Christmas season. I have written to you of the magnificence of the Serenade before, and I still carry it in my heart. Mama would have fallen in love with it, I'm sure. But you, Papa, even if you had resisted its charms, you would fall in love with what Christmas has to offer. There is to be a wedding in the ballroom. And, after that, the Midwinter Ball.

But enough of the ups and downs of ballroom life – though I know you love it so!

Something happened at the Serenade that I am yet to understand. Papa, I believe I need help, and I dare not ask Jonas and Mr Schank, for I do not want them to think I am undermining the beauty and success of this voyage. I want to dance with them forever. I would not want them to think I was causing a fuss.

As I danced during the Serenade, I looked up – and there, at the railing overlooking the dance floor, was a face I have never forgotten. Lukas Jager was staring back at me. I would recognise those eyes anywhere, Papa. The way they look upon you so kindly, hiding all that is hidden underneath. I have never forgotten, Papa, that night when I was eight and he came to dinner, and the way he fawned over Mama, while belittling all of your work. To think, that a man like that could rise to become a kommissar in the police force, while you remain a staff sergeant. To bully and belittle his way to the top . . .

I have not thought of Jager in so long. I admit, I was afraid of him when I was small, and even more afraid in this last year, with all that happened in our dear Vienna. Indeed, I fear writing too much, in case these letters are read by people with no business to read them, and I cause trouble for you, Mama and Lisette. But I am afraid, Papa, and

*I don't know what to do. For I have done some investigating of my own, just idle questions here in the Buckingham Hotel, and here Jager does not go by the name of Jager at all.*

*Here his name is Mr Tobias Bauer, and he lives in the hotel's Park Suite as a refugee from the after-effects of the Anschluss. The Anschluss! That occupation of our dear Vienna that you and your brothers in arms did so much to resist. That destruction of our home from which there is no turning back. That Anschluss which, no matter how much our friends and their families resisted, Lukas Jager was always at ease with, in a way that I remember made Mama's skin crawl.*

*I do not know the meaning of any of this. But Lukas Jager, who vanished from Vienna, is alive and well and living at the Buckingham Hotel. And I cannot help, Papa, but remember how he tried to convince you and your fellows to step aside, to let the German tanks roll into Vienna, to stop the pointless resistance of the Viennese police.*

*Lukas Jager is here, and I do not know what to do.*

*Send me word, as soon as you can. Until then, I am praying that his path and mine do not cross again.*

*Your son,*

*Ansel*

Maynard Charles set the letter down. Somewhere along the way, he had started reading it out loud.

'Who else has seen this letter?'

'Not a soul, Mr Charles. We came to you as soon as we had it.'

'We think it's accurate,' chipped in Frank. 'We checked every word, over and over.'

Maynard tried to make sense of it. He cast himself back to the spring, when he'd sat in this same office with Tobias Bauer and promised him the world. A refugee in need, he'd thought.

An old man whose world was falling apart. This letter – if it was true – changed everything. He scoured it again.

'It might be that Ansel was mistaken,' he said. 'A case of mistaken identity. It happens.'

'But . . . he's dead, sir,' Frank whispered.

Maynard nodded. Some things were absolute. Once again, he searched for more certainties in the letter.

'Why would he change his name, if he was genuine?' Billy asked. 'That's the thing we've got to cling on to, Mr Charles. Proves he's a liar, at least.'

'I have his passport,' Maynard began.

He stood, shifted aside the portrait of the Buckingham's original board that hung on the wall, and revealed the safe hidden behind it. A few twists of the lock later, he brought out a leather passport book marked with REPUBLIQUE D'AUTRICHE on its front. When he opened it up, both the picture and the name of Tobias Bauer peered back.

'It's all present and correct.'

'He wasn't mistaken, Mr Charles.'

There was such certainty in young Nettleton's voice. Maynard absorbed it and started feeling it too.

But if Ansel Albrecht wasn't mistaken, that left only one real option. There were agencies in the world who provided fraudulent passports. Forged identification papers, so that people might travel unseen. No doubt Moorcock, and everyone he worked with, had fake papers in dozens of different names. And that meant . . .

'A spy,' Maynard whispered, 'in my hotel.'

'He saw Ansel, that night in the Grand.'

All of a sudden, Maynard remembered it too. Ansel Albrecht had become separated from his partner on the dance floor. A commotion had erupted above. Not just Hélène, going to pieces, taking flight back through the stage doors; Tobias Bauer, reeling backwards, professing how magical the air of the evening was – while, at the same time, stumbling unchecked away from the dancing throng. Ansel Albrecht had been following him with his eyes. He remembered it vividly.

'What if Ansel went to confront him?' Billy began. 'A man like this Lukas Jager wouldn't want his secret to be out. What if Ansel went there to promise him he wouldn't breathe a word, but Jager couldn't—'

'Supposition,' said Maynard, though he dared not admit how close to the truth he thought Billy must be. 'All conjecture, until we know otherwise. Boys, sit down.'

There was such force in Mr Charles's words that both Billy and Frank did as they were told.

'We need to go to the police, Mr Charles.'

Maynard shook his head. 'We'll do nothing of the sort. Not until we know the facts.'

'But, Mr Charles!' Billy protested. 'It's a murder. Ansel was murdered. That fall was no accident. If we don't go to the police, we're just letting it—'

'You're not availing yourselves of the facts. You're not asking yourselves the right questions. Boys, I've asked you to perform certain tasks for me before. Fascists and Nazis in and out of this hotel, turning over the fates of millions in my dining room, plotting up and down my halls. You know the kinds of games that get played. You've listened and reported for me.' He stopped. 'So ask yourselves a question. Not *what* did Bauer – or Jager, or whatever his name is – do, but . . . *why.*'

'Well, to stop his secret coming out, sir! To preserve all his lies!'

Frank came out of his silence, picked himself up.

'That's not what Mr Charles means, Billy. He means . . . w-why is Jager here at all? Why come here with a fake passport and a fake name and take up residence in the Park Suite? It can't have been for Ansel. That w-was an accident. He can't have known the Winter Hollers would come here. So . . . why is he here?'

The three of them remained in silence, until at last, Billy said, 'We're listening to them. But they're listening to us too.'

'Billy?'

'Mr Brogan's right,' said Maynard, with a terrible solemnity. 'What I'm about to tell you must go no further than these walls. Do I make myself clear?'

Frank wasn't certain he wanted to hear at all, but Billy was already nodding.

'The Buckingham is awaiting the arrival of a delegation from Germany's old aristocracy. You may not think this worthy of note, for we've long been a home to aristocrats from across the Continent. But this delegation comes with a different aim – they seek to petition the Crown to change their course of action against Nazi Germany, to stop ceding control of Europe to them, to stand up for what's good and right. This, of course, would not suit those fascists in Berlin. They seek to keep Great Britain toothless for as long as they can – until, in the end, any chance of being resisted is gone. They are quite content with Mr Chamberlain's "peace", quite content with His Majesty sitting back and twiddling his thumbs.' He paused. 'If Jager is here at our hotel, it means he's listening too. Perhaps he's here to identify them. To eavesdrop on them, and report back to his paymasters – just as I've been reporting to mine. Perhaps, even, to change hearts and minds, to tip the balance back in favour of this damaged, fractured peace.'

The queasiness in Frank's belly started to grow. He needed the fresh air. He needed to get out.

'Kick him out, Mr Charles,' Billy declared. 'Eject him from the hotel. Tell him he's no longer wanted.'

*No*, thought Maynard. *I couldn't.*

'Murder is murder. Isn't it, Mr Charles?'

If only the world was that simple. Maynard looked at Frank, then, with something approaching envy. How he wished he was as young and naïve as that simple lad, wanting only to dance, not knowing the true measure of evil in the world, nor the real cost of a life.

'If I kick him out – if I drag the Metropolitan Police in here – I'm sending them a message. His paymasters will *know*. And . . . without evidence, what good am I doing? He has a passport. He has his papers. All we have is a letter from a poor dead boy, and a case of mistaken identity.'

'It's not a mistake though, is it, Mr Charles?'

'No, Billy, I'm afraid it is not.' Maynard reached into a drawer of his desk, scribbled a note on a piece of headed notepaper, sealed it with wax into an envelope, and pressed it into Billy's hand. 'Take this, at once, to the post room. It's to leave with the evening pick-up, and you're to be there when it happens. In the meantime, Frank, you're to get some rest. This has taken the wind from your sails, boy, and you've more work to do yet. I'm sorry, but you're both to keep this a secret. Justice will be served for Ansel – you have my word. But, in the meantime, you're to keep yourself out of trouble. Keep out of Tobias Bauer's path. If you see him about the hotel, you're not to look him in the eyes. You're to give him the widest possible berth. Do you understand?'

Frank nodded, but all of his words were gone.

'That will be all, boys.'

As Billy stood, teasing Frank up from his seat alongside him, he said, 'What are you going to do, Mr Charles?'

'I'm going to seek the counsel of people who live and breathe this world more deeply than me, Mr Brogan. I know you'll find this hard to believe – but I'm going to follow my orders.'

That night, as Billy Brogan waited in the post room for the Royal Mail vans to arrive, and Frank nestled in the chambermaids' kitchenette with Rosa, trying desperately not to think of Tobias Bauer, Vivienne stepped out of the back door at the Daughters of Salvation. With her woollen winter coat wrapped around her, she made haste for the high road.

The taxicab was waiting. She said little as she got into the back. All day long she'd worked in the offices behind the red brick chapel. For a time, the work had been enough to keep at bay the echoes of her mother and stepfather, the bitterness and bile. Now, as the day neared its end, she felt spent. The baby was turning inside her, and she had to remind herself that this was a joyous thing. Perhaps her mother didn't want her, perhaps her stepfather had finally found the excuse he wanted to be rid of her forever – but she would never be alone again.

The taxicab took her north from Whitechapel, through the grand estates around Old Street – and, at last, to the little garden oasis of St Luke's Fields, where there sat a veritable mansion behind iron railings. In the summertime, Vivienne had stood here and listened to a beautiful string quartet playing, while the owner of the house petitioned his wealthy friends to contribute to the Daughters' cause. Now she made her way along a thin, meandering path in the dark.

The deep October night had drawn in around her, and she began thinking of a warm bed, a thick eiderdown, cocoa and teacakes and a hot bath in which to soak her weary feet. The thought that it would not be at the Buckingham – that it never would be again – had not yet truly dawned on her.

She knocked on the door.

'Hello,' she said, when it finally drew back. 'You said . . .' Before she could say any more, her voice broke open, unleashing all the pent-up emotion of the day. 'You said there'd be a place for me, if ever they found out.'

The figure in the door stepped back, inviting her to the warmth within.

'There'll always be a place for you here. You know that. But, Vivienne, what's happened? Is there something wrong?'

She hadn't wanted it to be like this. She hadn't wanted to tell anybody, not until the time was right. Certainly not the man standing in front of her now. But she found her composure, tried to smile – for really, this was joyous news – and declared:

'Warren, I'm pregnant.'

November 1938

# Chapter Twenty-four

IN THE SEASIDE SKIES ABOVE RYE, the snow clouds curdled.
Winter was already here. Hélène could feel it in the air
as, disembarking from the bus outside town, she and Sybil
walked along the coastal path and saw the Marchmont manor
house looming ahead.

Hélène crouched down, fixing Sybil's hat and scarf. A little
bundle like this might not have felt the bite of the winter wind
coming up from Camber Sands, but Hélène surely did.

'I'd come down this path every morning, sweetheart,' she
whispered. 'Aunt Lucy would meet me right there at the bus stop,
two days a week. She'd have a bag of sherbet lemons.' She whispered, 'I wasn't allowed sweets. Sir Derek Marchmont thought
they were frightfully uncouth. It made me love them even more.'

This wasn't the only memory that came rushing at her as she
lifted Sybil and headed along the coastal path. Out across the
harbour, where the boats all lined up in pretty rows, the sky was
thick and white. She remembered her childhood. The summers
picnicking on Camber Sands, and the winters when the snow lay
thick and crisp inland. Happy memories, each and every one of
them. She felt a stabbing sadness at the way things had changed.

'But you've got it all too, haven't you?' she whispered – and Sybil reached out, with a mittened hand, to tweak her nose. 'Noelle and Maurice, and all your uncles and aunts. That little back bedroom, with kittens on the wallpaper! And those cakes Noelle makes – when *I* was a girl, we never had cakes such as those.'

By the time they reached the old Marchmont manor, fat flakes of snow had started to fall. One last memory rushed upon Hélène as she came through the gate into the grounds of the manor, and set Sybil down so that they might walk together, up through the bare orchard towards the house.

'I remember staying awake, every Christmas night,' she said, taking Sybil's hand and directing her to one of the bedroom windows above. 'As late as I could, right there in the window, in case I saw Father Christmas. It always snowed at Christmas back then. It looks like we'll have another white Christmas this year as well.'

The Christmas tree in the hall. Chestnuts roasting the evening before. The little tipple of sherry she'd been allowed, ever since she was six or seven years old. What a childhood it had been! They'd given her everything she could have wished for.

Until she was fully grown, and needed them more than ever.

She hadn't been meaning to come. She'd been trying to make her peace with that, telling herself, night after night, that it was *their* choice, not hers. In the end, it was Noelle who'd convinced her.

Late at night, after Sybil had been put to bed, she sat with Hélène by the fire, listening to the wireless crackle with the BBC *News*, and said, 'Once he's gone, there'd be no going backwards. Or ... if you set sail for Chicago, there's no coming home – not while he's still alive. It's your path to take, Hélène. Your heart to follow. But one more chance wouldn't diminish you. To give them one more chance – why, that can only lift you up. It would be for *you*, not *them*.'

There were unspoken things in Noelle's words too.

'Give them one more chance,' she'd said – *and perhaps we, Sybil's grandparents, will have one more chance to be a part of her lives. Perhaps you won't really have to go to Chicago at all* . . .

She had reached the door to the manor. By rights, she shouldn't have to knock, but she set Sybil down, dusted the snowflakes from the top of her head, and lifted the knocker. It was brass, and in the shape of a wolf.

'I made up stories about that wolf,' she told Sybil, though her daughter only blew a raspberry in reply. 'I used to think that, at night, he'd come alive and howl up at my bedroom window.'

She knocked.

They weren't expecting her, of course. That had been a part of the pact that she'd made for herself – so that, even as she disembarked from the train at Rye and waited for the country bus, she could still turn and flee. Now that she was here, she wondered if she ought to have done just that – but, even as that thought formed, there were footsteps on the other side of the door. Instinctively, she bowed down and lifted Sybil.

'Mama?' the little girl began.

The snow was turning to a blizzard at her back. She looked over her shoulder, through the grounds, and realised she could hardly see the trees in the orchard.

'We'll be inside soon, little one. They'll have a big fire burning in the sitting room, you can be sure of it.'

The door opened up.

\*

It was Lucy who opened the door. Hélène was thankful for that, because she hadn't been certain if Lucy would be here at all.

'Aunt Lucy,' Hélène said – but that was all.

Lucy stepped back, and when Hélène lingered with Sybil on the doorstep, she said, 'You don't need to be invited into your own home, dear,' and Hélène shepherded her daughter inside.

Hélène had been right. Somewhere, here, an enormous fire was crackling. Its heat radiated outwards, filling the reception hall with its homely smell. Sybil, who was at Hélène's feet – gazing at the ancient oak staircase that wound above – had a look as if she had walked into a different world. Something in it must have unnerved her, for as Hélène stopped and helped her out of her coat, taking off her wet hat and mittens, she tried to scrabble up into her mother's arms.

'It's all right, sweetheart,' Hélène cooed into her ear. 'This is our family.'

It didn't feel that way – not to Sybil, and not to Hélène. In the world-that-might-have-been, Sybil would have grown up thinking of this place as a second home. In the summers she'd have gambolled in the grounds, picked raspberries and apples from the orchards. She'd have been bathed in the tin bath in front of the fire, and at Christmas time she'd have laid out her mince pies on the ledge, just the same as Hélène once had.

'Aunt Lucy,' Hélène said, 'this is your great-niece, Sybil.'

Sybil beamed at the sound of her name.

Lucy reached out and touched Sybil's finger. Sybil, nervous at first, recoiled against Hélène's bosom, then, slowly, by degrees, dared to reach out and poke Lucy's fingertip.

'Well, aren't you beautiful?' said Lucy.

Sybil beamed.

'I never thought to see you here again,' Lucy said, turning her eyes to Hélène. 'And your daughter. She's . . . magnificent.'

'She is,' said Hélène – and though she wanted to add, *and she has been for three whole years*, she managed to strangle the bitterness at birth. 'Aunt Lucy, is my mother here? My father?'

She got her answer to the first straight away – for from the drawing room at the bottom of the hall another figure appeared.

The expression on Lady Marchmont's face was one of the utmost bewilderment. To Hélène, she seemed a ghost, sailing along the corridor towards her. Once upon a time, Hélène had been Sybil's age, standing on this very same spot, having tumbled in – ruddy-cheeked and cold – from playing in the snowstorm outside. All of history was here. Hélène had to centre herself, thinking of Noelle, to remember that all of that was a different age: that she was here, now, as a different woman.

'Hélène,' her mother ventured, eyes darting into every corner of the reception hall, unable to settle on any one thing, 'we weren't expecting you.'

'I know, Mother.'

'If you'd said, we could have laid on a spread. We could have . . . prepared.'

Hélène said, sadly, 'That's why I didn't send word, Mother. You shouldn't have to prepare. I don't want a spread. I don't want a fuss. I just want to . . .'

'You've come to see him.'

Hélène nodded. 'I have. Is he . . . ?'

'Still with us.' Her mother instinctively folded her arms across her breast, as if there was something she had to protect – or something she had to hide. 'He's been sleeping. Why don't we . . . ?'

She made as if to usher everyone through one of the doors, the one that led to the great sitting room where Hélène used to perform her dances, each year, for her parents to judge.

Hélène looked back through the frosted glass in the door. The whole world beyond was a chaos of white. Fat snowflakes cavorted and danced. This place would look resplendent come Christmas. She could imagine the baubles. She could imagine the lights.

But there'd be no love in this place, not unless they let love in.

There was no going back. Not now. Until there came a gap in the snowstorm, she wouldn't take Sybil out into it. So she followed Lucy through to the sitting room, and let the memories thunder through her.

Some time later, only when she was certain that Sybil had found her feet in this strange environment, Hélène followed her mother to the bottom of the stairs. Looking back, she could see Sybil on the sitting-room carpet, the fire flickering a fandango behind her, and Lucy cross-legged beside her, spreading out the pieces of an old wooden jigsaw puzzle. Hélène had been amazed to see it; she hadn't imagined, for a second, that all the books and toys of her childhood were still in the old trunk in the second sitting room.

'She'll be fine,' Marie said. 'I promise. The moment she wants you, I'll come and get you.'

It wasn't right, to be this fearful of leaving your daughter with her own relations. But nor was it right to feel so at peace, seeing Sybil play with her own old toys. A mixture of emotions like this could never be explained. It was better that she ignored it.

'Hélène, before we go up, there's something I should say.'

'Mama, I know you feel let down. I don't need to hear it – not today.'

'I'm sorry, Hélène.'

'Sorry?'

The word was almost unimaginable.

'It's my fault you're in this bind. I let my emotions get the better of me. You were always better at that than me. You take after *him* in that regard.' Together, their eyes took in the top of the stairs and the doorway on the landing, with the sleeping Sir Derek Marchmont beyond. 'I hope I haven't ruined things completely at the Buckingham. You're still dancing?'

Hélène was too weary to explain. 'I'm dancing,' she said.

'I always loved you, you know.'

*No*, thought Hélène, *I don't know any such thing.*

Nor did hearing it said out loud change anything. She looked back, at Sybil, in gales of laughter at some face Lucy was pulling, and thought: *why couldn't time stay the same? Why couldn't relationships?* Her mother had loved her once, she was certain of this much. But where the love had gone, how it had changed into something else, was a mystery she dared not indulge. She took a step on the stairs.

'Will he want to see me?'

'Oh, Hélène, of course.'

They came, together, to the top of the stairs. Soon, Marie had drawn ahead of her, as if she needed to be told the way – though this was the same hall she'd cantered down every morning as a child, desperate to see her daddy as he woke; this, the same hall along which she'd brought him his pot of tea every Sunday morning. There was a photograph framed against the wall:

a younger Hélène, sitting on Sir Derek's knee, with their old cat Smudge sleeping at their feet.

The bedroom door was ajar. Hélène could smell the mustiness as they approached. Some of it was old and familiar – the scent of her father's pipe, of tar and the peppermints he liked to suck – but there were new hints here, too. The harsh vinegar and carbolic the maid had used to scrub the surfaces. The ash from the bedroom fireplace, so rarely used when Hélène was a child.

She followed her mother inside.

There was her father: propped up in bed, buttressed on every side by pillows, his head lolling to one side.

Hélène lifted a hand to her mouth. He looked already dead.

'Derek,' her mother said gently, and went to rouse him. With a hand on his shoulder, she repeated, 'Derek, you have a guest.'

The old man opened his eyes.

Once upon a time, he had been so big. Now, though his face retained some of its jowls, he seemed to vanish into the bed sheets. Her giant, Herculean father had become a wraith. As he came back into wakefulness, he seemed like a scarecrow coming to life. Marie took his big hand and stroked his dewy forehead.

'You haven't been drinking,' she said. 'I'll bring you lemon water.' She looked up, at Hélène. 'We fill it with honey. Some days it's all he takes.'

It was only then that Sir Derek realised there was somebody else in the room.

'Hélène?' he croaked.

He picked himself up, and the first of the bed sheets sloughed off him.

'Get me from this bed, Marie. My daughter . . .'

Hélène whispered, 'You can stay there, Papa.'

316

'I won't,' Sir Derek began, some gravitas coming back to his voice. 'I won't take guests in my bed sheets. I'm a knight of the realm.'

Hélène knew not what to do. She simply stood there as Marie guided him to the rocking chair at the bedside, helped him into a navy-blue jumper.

'Lemon water,' she said. 'I'll be back shortly.'

'Bring my daughter whatever she desires,' he called after her.

Then there were only Hélène and her father in the room.

'Well,' Sir Derek said, 'pull up a chair, Hélène. Come to see your old father one last time, have you?' He gave a gap-toothed grin. 'Yes, well, I shan't keep you long, my girl – though I'm glad to look on you, once more.'

Hélène whispered, 'I had to see you, Papa.'

'Then sit!' he cried. 'Sit! It's been too long. Look at you. You've grown!'

She shook her head ruefully at this, but she sat at his side, all the same. The second rocking chair was piled up with books, on top of which sat his Bible, and she gently shifted them aside.

'They sent for you, I shouldn't wonder. Told you I was setting off, did they?'

'Papa . . .'

'Well, it's right that they did.' His voice broke. He reached for her hand. She let him take it. 'I've missed you, Hélène. I've missed you, and here you are. My beautiful girl. My only, beautiful girl . . .' He stopped. 'Tell me about yourself. Are you still dancing?'

'Always.'

'I remember you dancing, right here in this bedroom. In the drawing room downstairs. In the orchards. I remember coming

317

to see you at the Royal Albert Hall. My perfect Hélène – oh, I'm a sentimental old fool! Nothing could have been better.'

'I remember that too.'

Memories were safe. In memories, she could ignore the daughter who scampered around downstairs, and live, for a moment, in a different world. So they sat and talked about the first tea dance he'd taken her to. They talked about Christmas dinner, when Sir Derek had invited everyone from the estate, and Hélène had opened the curtains at dawn to see her first pony, Black Magic, standing on the frosted lawns. They talked about the night before the Royal Albert Hall, and how Hélène – sick with nerves – had sat with her father by the fire. They talked about everything, but it was as if time had stood still in 1933: before Sidney, before Sybil, before Hélène had sullied the family name.

A little piece of her thought she could leave it like this. Then he could die, with some pretence at happiness. Something tempted her in the idea.

'I have a gift for you,' her father said. 'My Christmas gift for my daughter. Your mother helped me, in case I don't live through December.'

'Oh, Papa . . .'

'Go,' he said, and waved a hand at the old seaman's trunk sitting at the bottom of the bed. 'It's at the very top.'

Hélène opened up the trunk and took out a parcel wrapped in paper of red and green, with stencils of little Scottie dogs sitting between Christmas trees. This she took back to her chair.

'Open it,' her father smiled.

So she did. Inside it was a book filled with portraits, the ones they had taken each year: Hélène at eight years old, with her mother and father in the photographer's gallery; Hélène aged nine, with her mother and father, down there in the orchard itself; Hélène at ten, eleven, twelve – the chronicle of her young life, and her father always at her side. She flicked to the back. Cuttings from the society pages. Reviews and write-ups of the decorations she'd received. The covers of *Vogue* and *Harper's Bazaar*: her own face, smiling back at her.

'Thank you, Papa,' she said.

Something seized her. It was the feeling of guilt rushing through her, because there was no doubt that the book of photographs had moved her. But time hadn't ended in 1933. Time had moved on. It was moving still.

'I've got a present for you too, Papa.'

She stood, smiled at him, and slipped out of the room.

When she returned, she was holding Sybil in her arms.

The old man knew not where to look. There was surprise on his face, but there was horror too. His eyes darted around; he moved as if to lift himself, but didn't have the strength.

Hélène had not meant to taunt him. She watched him shrinking in his chair and, upon realising there was nothing else he could do, simply slump and stare at her. Sybil must have sensed the change in atmosphere because, at once, she stopped wriggling in Hélène's arms. She lay her head on her mama's shoulder.

'Papa,' she said, 'I don't want to upset you. It isn't what I came for. Everything I've said is true – I wanted to see you again. I don't want you to go, without telling you I love you and without you telling it to me – and meaning it, Papa, for all that I am. All those things we've talked about. All these pictures. They're still so true. They still happened, and they're still in *here*.' She balanced Sybil in one arm and held her heart with the other. 'But so is this. So is Sybil. She's your granddaughter, and she's the most beautiful thing in the world.'

'You've come to terrorise me,' he said, quaking in his rocking chair. 'After everything you've done to this family, you've come to flaunt it. I gave you everything, Hélène. My whole world was built around it. This manor? What's this manor to me anymore? It was all for you.'

'I don't want it, Papa. I want you to look upon her, all the years you've missed – all the years I've missed, too, because of what you did – and know that there was love here, all along. There was my love, but there was Sybil's love too. Oh, Papa, it could have been fantastic. Even after poor Sidney . . . We could have made a family, right here, and hang what the world thought. She could have grown up happy and secure, with all the wonderful things I had. And, no, I don't mean the ponies, and I don't mean the ball gowns, and I don't mean this big country estate. I mean you and Mama, and Aunt Lucy, and, by God, Papa, that feeling of *home*. Sybil doesn't want for love. Her grandparents cherish her. But there could have been so much more.'

She dared not sit down, for fear of what he might do – and, besides, Sybil had sensed the tension in the room and was clinging on to her more fiercely still.

'What do you want of me, Hélène?'

She said, 'Say hello to her, at least. She's your granddaughter.'

He rolled his head back. For a moment, Hélène wondered if he was having some sort of a fit. But it was only anger – what strength he had to summon it.

'You know children aren't allowed in my bedchamber, Hélène. That was the rule when you were small. That's the rule now.'

She was silent.

*Was that it?*

*The end of the story?*

'We can do the right thing here, Papa.'

'My house, my rules, Hélène.'

She turned against him. The most surprising thing was: there were no tears. She'd shed them already. She was holding her head up high, whispering sweetnesses in Sybil's ear, as she crossed to leave the room.

'It doesn't have to be like this.'

Those words – she'd never expected them from her father. She dared to turn back around. His face was open. His eyes were on her. He seemed settled. He seemed serene.

'Papa?'

'There's still time for us to make this right, isn't there? I'm not dead yet. Your mother can summon my solicitor. We'll rewrite the will. All of this could be yours, Hélène, just like I meant for it. And this girl of yours, she's being looked after well enough, isn't she? You said it yourself – she has people who cherish her. Her grandparents. Well, let them. Let her stay where she belongs, and come home, Hélène, come back where *you* belong. All this business in London and at the Buckingham Hotel – I could make it go away. You'd be comfortable. When I'm gone, there'll be somebody needed to run the estate here. Lord knows, your mother won't cope.' He paused. 'But you could. Living here, you'd meet a new man in a moment. So many eligible young men, looking for somebody with class like you. They could overlook your past, for a life like this. You could start again. I'd be helping you do it, Hélène – even from the great beyond. Even after everything that's happened . . .'

Hélène took a moment, as the words washed over her. It was the strangest thing – for it wasn't tears that came to her, but a kind of lightness instead.

For the first time, she *knew*.

'Oh, Papa,' she said, 'you haven't heard a word. I could never, ever give Sybil up.'

She turned, left her father alone, and held on to her daughter as she reached the top of the stairs.

*But I could give up you.*

# Chapter Twenty-five

B ILLY LOOKED OUT OF THE porthole window in the tiny
garret, but he couldn't see a thing. The snow that had
been falling all night long had plastered itself across the
rooftops and windows of the Buckingham Hotel, turning it into
a palace of pure white.

Billy's quarters were small but, ever since he'd moved in here,
he'd treated them as if they were the quarters of a prince. Every
night, after his shift was finished, he swept the floor around the
bed. Every night, he polished the desk that sat in the window,
dusted the bookshelf by the door, straightened his uniform shirts
in the little wardrobe set into the wall – and made certain that
the contours of his cap were not creasing out of shape. There was
nothing that made Billy more proud than fulfilling his duties to
the Buckingham to the utmost of his abilities.

It was just a cruel twist of fate that, of late, his duties provoked
such fear.

An hour before the chambermaids awoke, when the Buckingham was populated only by night porters, Billy dropped through
the chilly hotel and slipped into the post room. The clock on the
wall told him it was not yet five o'clock; that gave him two hours

until Mrs Farrier arrived, expecting to find the place spick and span and ready for the day's deliveries.

So he set about his work.

It had been two weeks since Ansel died; two weeks since Billy had received his new instructions, and he was only just beginning to conquer the nerves of it. As he sifted through the sacks, searching out yet more letters bound for Vienna, he kept pausing to control the hammering of his heart. It wasn't as if he'd never done special tasks for Mr Charles before. He'd spent years accepting his little missions, eavesdropping on dinners in the Queen Mary. Intelligence gathering, Mr Charles called it – which always made Billy feel proud, because most people liked to tell Billy Brogan he needed to gather some intelligence of his own. This, though? This felt different. He sifted through each sack and when, at last, he found the envelope he knew would be here – addressed to Vienna, in a familiar spidery hand – he made sure that everything else was straightened up, and settled down at Mrs Farrier's desk.

It was half past five.

Sliding his finger carefully into the envelope, he teased it open. The trick with this sort of envelope was that, if you softened it, just slightly, with the tip of your tongue, the paper moistened enough that it came apart without any damage. Then he could slide the letter out.

All of these words, all of these symbols – and Billy hardly knew what a single one of them meant. It was just as well. He often thought that, if he'd known what was in these letters, he wouldn't have dared to be sitting here, in the cold dark of the hotel basement, transcribing every word.

By the light of Mrs Farrier's lantern, Billy set about his work. On one side of him: the letter to Vienna – and, at its bottom, the signature of the man who called himself Tobias Bauer. On the other: a blank page, onto which he diligently copied every letter and curlicue, every full stop and stroke of the pen.

It was quarter to seven by the time Billy, having completed his task, had sealed the envelope again, clamping it tightly between his fingers to invigorate what little of the adhesive paste was left, and made haste to Mr Charles's office. There, as every morning, Mr Charles was waiting at his desk.

'Another one, Billy?'

'It's the third this week, sir.'

He handed Mr Charles the page and waited as the elder man's eyes scoured the letter.

'Thank you, Billy. You may go.'

Billy turned on his heel, feeling the great weight lifting off him, and plodded back across the office, looking forward to another day listening to Mrs Farrier's hard luck stories and ferrying her pots of tea.

'And, Billy?' Maynard called after.

'Yes, sir?'

When Billy looked up, the hotel director was giving him the strangest look: it was a look, he thought, of simple gratitude.

'Keep up the good work, Mr Brogan. It may make all of the difference in the world.'

Some nights later, with the snow lying deep and crisp across Berkeley Square, Maynard entered the Candlelight Club and, among the sea of bobbing heads, identified Moorcock in the booth closest to the terrace doors. That weathered face, scored in lines – he could pick it out anywhere. How the man called himself a spy, Maynard did not know.

He did not go to him straight away. There were protocols to observe. Instead, he took a dry Martini at the bar, engaging passing guests in conversations of his own, then waited until the hour approached midnight and, inevitably, the guests began to depart. Only when the Candlelight Club was approaching its closing did he settle down at Moorcock's side.

'You do like to keep a fellow waiting, Mr Charles.'

'I'm observing decorum, Mr Moorcock. I'm a man who likes to do things by the book.'

As Maynard sat down, he reached inside his jacket and produced the papers that had been folded into his inside pocket. These he fanned out across the table, so that Mr Moorcock could see. Each one of them was written in Billy's hand, just as Maynard himself had instructed – but recreated, too, were the little flourishes of the pen that Lukas Jager used, his lettering depicted exactly as Brogan had seen it.

Moorcock nodded, without a word. Then, sliding the papers into the inside pocket of his own jacket, he said, 'Your man Brogan's doing a good job. But how long can he last? The last time we spoke, you seemed doubtful.'

'I don't doubt the boy's nerve,' Maynard replied. 'He's shown me, often enough, the stuff he's made of. I'd want Billy Brogan standing with me to go over the top – though heaven forfend he should ever know it – the thought alone would make his head swell. But I do fear for him, and I do worry where his loyalties lie. He's a simple boy, Mr Moorcock. He came to the hotel to make a wage for his family, down in Lambeth. He has brothers

326

and sisters he looks out for. His mother and father depend on him. He's been stealing from this hotel for years – just bits from the kitchens, raiding the larders here and there. He thinks I don't know about it – but the fact is, I've been turning a blind eye to Mr Brogan for many years. I like him, you see. And I believe I know him. It's true that he's in love with this hotel, but in the end, his family will come first. If I ask too much of him, if he fears he may get ejected from this hotel – or worse, that something terrible might happen to him, as it happened to young Ansel Albrecht – he'll retreat from this. He needs to know he's safe.'

Moorcock nodded. 'Don't fear, Mr Charles. I've been running agents half of my lifetime. I know how to look after a soul like Brogan.'

'These letters,' Charles went on. 'I can understand so little, but they don't seem to say anything particularly untoward. It's just dear old Herr Bauer prattling on about his luxurious exile. London in autumn. London, when the first snows came.'

'The man you have staying in your hotel is not so amateur as to be writing to his superiors with a neat list of all the intelligence he's gathered. I'm afraid, Mr Charles, that we have concluded our initial report into this man you accepted into your hotel – and it is most troubling indeed.' He hesitated. 'Lukas Jager began working in law enforcement in Vienna long before the assassination of Archduke Franz Ferdinand. He's been a policeman more than half his adult life. Excepting his years as a commissioned officer on the Western Front, Jager devoted himself to following in his father's footsteps, and rose through the ranks of the Gendarmerie, the Austrian police. He was good at it, too. A brute like that, diminutive as he seems, always will be. From what we've seen, it seems he took great strides in his career with the downfall of the Austrian Republic in 1934. Perhaps you can guess my inference at this.'

'You'll have to enlighten me.'

'Well, the end of the republic and the birth of the Federal State of Austria has some interesting ramifications. The historians can pore over the finer details of it, Maynard. Let us leave that to our children's children, should humanity survive that far. The short story is that, with the rise of the Austrofascists, Lukas Jager found an administration more to his liking, more in step with his own thoughts about the way the world should be.' When the silence stretched on for too long, Moorcock added, 'Jager's a nasty little fascist, Maynard. While the rest of the police force in Vienna put up a resistance to the Anschluss earlier this year, Jager welcomed it with open arms.'

'He said he came here as a refugee from the Anschluss.' Maynard sighed. 'I believed him.'

'And you, the man who knows every little thing going on in his precious hotel . . .'

Maynard felt withered by this. If it had been just one little slip, perhaps he needn't have worried. But he'd overlooked what was happening with Miss Marchmont, hadn't he? He'd turned a blind eye to Vivienne Edgerton as well. It was like Lord Edgerton had said: he was old, tired, and losing his touch.

'I'll admit I was wrong, Mr Moorcock. What more do you want me to say? I saw an old man, who needed help, in an indifferent world.'

'You made a mistake, Mr Charles – but, in doing so, you have given us an opportunity my superiors insist we exploit. But first, let me finish my story. It is best that you are fully briefed. Jager's fellows in the police force knew him for what he was. Some time before the Anschluss, he deserted them. Retired, they said – the world was not kind to old policemen like him. But the facts, as we now know them, were different. Jager had not retired, but been tempted by darker forces. We believe he made his deal before the Anschluss was even completed – to work for the intelligence services of Herr Hitler's Third Reich. To help bring about the empire Herr Hitler seeks.'

'Then he did kill Ansel,' Maynard whispered. 'Ansel knew him for who he really was, and paid the price for it.'

'Let us suppose the boy was lured to Jager's suite on some pretext. Let us suppose he went willingly, to make sense of this aberration he'd perceived. Well, he paid with his life to keep Jager's secret. Pushed down the stairs, to preserve a spy's cover. Simple tradecraft, but effective. Who would ever suspect poor, tottering Tobias Bauer?'

'I would eject him from the hotel, if I could.'

'You already know that you can't. Mr Charles, these letters he sends – they are not just the diary entries of a gossiping old man. When he recounts the comings and goings of British gentry through this hotel, when he makes notes of who he has seen dining with who, what they have said, how he has tried to engage them in idle talk, it is not just meaningless meandering. These are critical reports on the movements of British lords who can be leveraged to be faithful to Mr Chamberlain's cause – and, by doing so, let Herr Hitler do as he pleases on the Continent. These are documents providing clues as to how influential British peers might be pressured into saying the right thing into the right ear – all so that His Majesty keeps letting Nazi Germany conquer whichever poor country they desire.

'Take the last batch of letters. In the final one, Herr Bauer was at pains to explain to his "dear cousin Emma" about Miss Vivienne Edgerton's disgrace – a pregnancy, out of wedlock, and hidden from her poor mother! It might seem tittle-tattle, but it is anything but. Rest assured that men in Berlin are, even now, devising ways to use this kind of information to sway the heart and mind of Vivienne's stepfather. All a department like mine needs is a little scrap of information to exploit. You would be surprised how much *control* a little piece of information can provide.'

Maynard thought: *I really wouldn't. It wasn't long ago that you, Mr Moorcock, held one of those pieces of information over me. I danced and sang for you and your Office, all to keep it a secret.*

At least, now, he was here of his own free will. There was power in that.

'He's not the only one in London,' Moorcock went on. 'This city is nothing if not a home for rats.'

'Why keep them here at all? Why not round them up and be done with it?'

'Because, Mr Charles, they are better off where we can see them. You know how serious things have become. This delegation coming to London to petition the Crown cannot be compromised. Herr Jager's little scheme puts us in danger, but it presents us with a possibility as well.'

'If Bauer reports on them to Berlin, the Nazis might understand what they're here for.'

'Yes,' said Moorcock, 'but *his* reports won't be reaching Berlin.'

'You mean for me to destroy his letters?'

Moorcock laughed and shook his head.

'You are not that naïve, Mr Charles. If Bauer suddenly stopped writing, what kind of a message might that send? No, these shadow wars of ours go a little deeper than that.' He paused. 'Mr Charles, here's what must happen. Your Mr Brogan must lift each letter "Bauer" writes from the hotel post room. Instead of opening and transcribing their contents before sending the original on, I would have him deliver each letter, after midnight, to this address.' Mr Moorcock took out a notebook and pencil and scrawled down the address of a gentlemen's club overlooking Green Park. 'Before dawn, he will return to the club and receive a letter in kind, which he will then deposit in the post room for onward delivery to this Vienna address, and Herr Bauer's cousin, Emma – though, of course, no such person exists.'

Maynard Charles said, 'I understand.'

'Do you?'

'The letters Billy takes back to the post room – they won't be the letters Bauer wrote. They're ones you devise, to take their place.'

Moorcock smiled. 'We have men whose lives are built on this kind of work. The dark arts, they call it. Experts in lettering and imitation. Bauer's stream of reports mustn't be interrupted, lest they know his cover is blown. It's important that he keeps writing. But it's equally important that his reports reveal nothing we don't ourselves control. We would tease out a sentence here and there, replace them with sentences of our own. The flow of information, my good man. *That* is how wars are won.'

Moorcock stood, fastened the buttons on his overcoat, and finished his drink.

'You could have been one of us, Mr Charles. Welcome to the world of counter-espionage. The real looking-glass war.'

331

After he had gone, Maynard began to feel the dirt of it. He felt the weight of telling Billy Brogan too. If he could have done it himself, he would gladly have stepped into those shoes, gladly have spared the young man his fate. But a hotel director was always noticeable; Billy would go better unseen.

Eager for the fresh, clean air, Maynard demanded the keys to the Candlelight Terrace from Diego, who was finishing tidying up at the bar, and slipped out into the balcony gardens. The shrubbery, as naked and stark as the winter, shielded him from the worst of the wind, but there was no denying the cold of a November night. He came to the railing that ran around the terrace and looked down, through curling ripples of snow, to the square beneath him. What a beautiful thing winter was. The snow captured the lights of the stars and made it seem as if it was almost day on Berkeley Square.

He fancied he could see Moorcock, turning his collar up as he vanished back to the night. Such a diminutive man, to be directing a game like this. Maynard watched him as he skirted the edge of the square, as the flare of a tiny cigarillo appeared at his lips. But then he blinked – and, just like the ghost that he was, Moorcock was gone.

# Chapter Twenty-six

THE SLEEPER TRAIN HAD REACHED the chalky expanses of the Chiltern Hills, but in the cramped compartment, Artie Cohen was not interested in sleeping. Two hours ago, they'd left behind a London cosying up beneath a fairytale covering of snow, and in the bunk beneath him, Raymond was studiously trying to get some sleep. But not his brother. Artie sat, with his legs dangling over the edge of the bunk, and his flask of hot rum and sugar in one hand. Every now and again, he rubbed at the porthole windows with his cuff, clearing away the condensation so he could see the crystalline snowscape outside. The train kept stopping, grinding forward for another few miles and then stopping again – no doubt as the brave guards got out to clear the track of a particularly troublesome drift of snow – but even this was to Artie's liking. He began to sing:

'*Heaven, I'm in heaven! And my heart beats so that I can hardly speeeee-aaaaaa-kkk!*'

A hand shot out of the bottom bunk, grabbed Artie by the shin, and pulled him so that he toppled to the ground.

'Ow!' Artie roared, staggering to keep himself upright. 'What was that for?'

'You were murdering one of my favourite songs.'

Raymond emerged from the bottom bunk, rubbing his weary eyes.

'You're really not going to let me sleep, are you?'

'Ray, I told you before – this isn't a sleepy little trip we're going on. This is an adventure. This is for old times! This is . . . my wedding present to you!'

Raymond looked around, taking in the entirety of the cramped compartment in a fraction of a second. Then he rolled his eyes at Artie.

'Have a drink with me, brother.' Artie thrust the flask towards Raymond's hands. 'Just one night, you and me. Blackpool, Ray!'

Raymond considered the flask with a sense of dissatisfaction.

'I know it's not Moët, but it'll be fun. Ray Cohen, you don't fool me. You have all your fancy airs, all your graces, your dashing new name – but you still use the same water closet as the rest of us. You still get dandruff in that beautiful black hair o' yours. And you still—'

Raymond snatched the flask and took a drink. 'Yes, I heard you, Artie.'

'Then that's settled,' Artie grinned. 'The Cohen boys are going on a voyage!'

Outside, fat flakes of snow drifted peacefully down.

By midnight, they were grinding their way through the Midlands. By the small hours, they were sitting in a railway siding somewhere north of Manchester while the coal tender was decoupled and a full one loaded. Outside, the serenity of the snow was in stark contrast to the roars of laughter and stories being told inside the carriage. Stories of their first nights, following their father into the dance halls (and realising what a man about town he was when their mother wasn't looking). Stories of their scrapes with the Marlowe boys from the other side of Stepney Green. Stories about Mara, the girl they'd both chased – back when they were just little kids. Every story, full of joy. They did not touch on the sad times tonight: Artie in Pentonville, while Ray cantered across the Continent with Georges de la Motte. In the little sleeping compartment, they existed in their own little bubble in time.

'It's good to see you up and on your feet, Artie,' said Ray, as the train took off again, the looming outline of the Peak District – a horizon of glistening white – somewhere off to the east. 'I've not known you as happy in years.'

*It was purpose that brought it out of him*, thought Raymond.

The Daughters of Salvation wasn't just saving the needy and destitute of Whitechapel; it had saved Artie Cohen as well.

'Aye, well, it's good to have something to do,' said Artie, as if he would rather talk about anything else.

'This business with Vivienne . . .'

Artie raised his eyebrows. 'What of it?'

Raymond shrugged. The snow moved hypnotically against the windows.

'Things will change, I suppose. Nancy's upset that Vivienne didn't confide in her. They used to be so close.'

It had taken Raymond some time to wheedle out of Nancy why she was feeling so sore, some nights ago. They'd stepped out together, for dinner on the Strand – and, walking home, through snowbound London, he'd asked her what was wrong. Nancy wasn't used to not being trusted. She felt it like a bruised heart.

'You know Viv.' Artie shrugged. 'A law to herself, that one. Does what she wants when she wants it, or not at all.' He paused. 'I think she thought your Nance deserved a little time just for herself. Viv's dumped enough problems on her over the years. Maybe she thought it wasn't right to bring another . . .' Artie yawned. 'But we must only be a few hours from Blackpool. We're really going to need to get some shut-eye. I can't stay up, jawing with you all night.'

Raymond didn't have an answer to that. He looked at Artie with an inscrutable expression, was about to remind him whose idea this sleeper carriage tipple had been . . .

But Artie Cohen had already toppled backwards, into the bed.

He was already fast asleep.

Blackpool at dawn: the frigid air coming in from the sea, the sound of hungry seagulls wheeling overhead. Raymond and Artie had staggered from the sleeper carriage with their heads betraying the first savagery of the hangovers to come, and as they reeled out of the station, Raymond felt a roiling in his belly. How Artie was still standing upright, he did not know.

'That's too much champagne and caviar for you, that is.' Artie clapped him on the back as they dragged their suitcases through the station door. 'If you'd started on grog like me, you'd be better prepared.'

'I'm never drinking again,' moaned Raymond.

'Only a nice glass of Moët,' Artie returned.

This early in the morning, the North Pier was quiet. Only a few old men braved the winter chill to potter with their dogs, up and down the promenade. Along the Golden Mile, the attractions that drew in day-trippers all summer long stood as silent sentries against the winter. The Blackpool Tower, as imposing as the Tour Eiffel after which it was modelled, was a lattice of ice, reaching into a sky still pregnant with the promise of more to come. The fairground attractions wore crowns of white. Great drifts of snow had grown up around the carousels. And there, sitting on the lee-ward side of the tower, were the rooftops of the Winter Gardens themselves.

'There you have it, Ray. We'll be dancing there tonight. Told you I'd show you a good time!'

Raymond had been here a few times before, with Georges. He remembered walking into the Empress Ballroom for the first time, his eyes drawn up to the barrel-vaulted ceiling with all its delicately patterned panels, the twelve glass chandeliers that spilled glittering light all over the dance floor below. It had been the first time Raymond danced on a sprung floor, the first time he felt the sensation of soaring as he waltzed. They'd replaced the floor in the ten years since he'd last been here. Ten thousand pieces of mahogany and walnut had been intricately interleaved; a new stage had been built, a new Wurlitzer organ hoisted into its place.

He was so caught up in his memory that he didn't see, until it was nearly too late, that Artie had doubled over beside one of the drifts of snow.

'That rum's catching up with me, Ray. Dirty stuff. You should never have made me drink it.'

Raymond laughed. 'We'll find a hotel. There's a place Georges and I once stayed, overlooking the seafront somewhere north of here. A beautiful boutique little place – you'd think it a little corner of the Buckingham itself, uprooted and brought here.'

Artie craned around, looking up at him with a sickly grimace. Against the stark white of the snow, his face looked a lurid shade of green.

'You won't catch me in one of your fancy gaffs, Ray. No,' he grinned, 'this isn't the "de Guise" show. This is the Cohen boys, on the weekend of their lifetimes. We're staying some place that's right for the Cohens, not the de Guises. I already booked us a nice little spot.'

'It's a dosshouse.'

The Yeoman's Hostelry called itself a hotel but, by the look of its frontage, it was little more than a backstreet hovel, with walls as flimsy as any beach shack on the seafront, and gates across its windows.

'One of our regulars told me about it, down at the Daughters of Salvation. He used to live up here, before he made his way south. Looking for gold, like the rest of them. But the only gold he found was in his ale.'

'And you got us rooms.'

The door had fallen open under Artie's touch, revealing a reception hall as narrow as the galley kitchen in some cramped little terrace, and behind it not a soul to be seen.

Artie marched over and, by the pallid light spilling in through the snow-caked windows, rang a bell.

'Correction!' Artie announced. 'I got us *a* room.'

Raymond just glared at him.

'One room, Ray. Well, I'm not made of money. Times are hard, don't you know? And, besides, we Cohen boys don't need two rooms, do we? Now, Raymond de Guise – he'd need a whole bloody *suite*. But Ray Cohen that was, all he needs is a rag for a blanket and a place to lay his head. Am I right, or am I wrong?'

Raymond thought about it.

He thought about it again.

'You're right,' he said, as a sallow-faced man appeared from a back door and started running a long black fingernail through the guest register. 'Because right now, Artie, I'd sleep wherever I laid my head. I'd sleep out there, in the snow, if I just . . .'

The sallow-faced man, having taken Artie's name, was holding a key in his grubby hand. Artie snatched it.

'Then let's get you sorted. This trip of ours, it's only just beginning.'

A hotel like the Yeoman's did not have a restaurant, nor a bistro, nor even a little canteen – but the man at the desk, who eventually introduced himself as Fox, did have a clapped-out toaster in the office out the back, and agreed to make them a breakfast of toast and honey for only a modest fee. Raymond didn't care; he was just glad of the ballast to put right his belly. Once he'd eaten, he fell asleep almost as soon as his head hit the pillow.

It was, even Artie reflected, just as well – for the room was even dourer than he'd imagined. So small that its two single beds might as well have been an intimate double, it had a smell of damp that brought back Artie's own vagrant days. Around the windows, black mould climbed the walls – and, at the skirting, the scat of the mice Artie could hear in the walls lay in thick clumps and trails.

Artie slept too. It was mid-afternoon by the time they awoke, to sore heads and sorer moods, and went out, again, into the snow. By now, Blackpool was a little more alive. Lights glowed in its shopfronts and houses, steam fogged the windows of the cafés they passed, and here and there motorcars ground their way across roads turned to tablets of ice. The roller coasters that soared over the promenade at the Pleasure Beach were like interlocking spirals of ice, magnificent structures bewitched by an ice queen straight out of Hans Christian Andersen. The new Fun House and Grand National rides had only been closed since the summer, but to look at them now was to think they'd been sleeping for a hundred enchanted years.

Stopping into the first café they found, Artie ordered up a double serving of steak and eggs, but the thought of it turned Raymond's stomach – so he sustained himself with more hot buttered toast. Piece by piece, he began to know the shape of himself again.

'You want to get some ballast in your belly. You can't dance on toast.'

'I'm not sure I feel like dancing, Artie.'

'Nonsense! Come to the Empress Ballroom and not give her a little tango? You're off your rocker!'

As Raymond nibbled meekly at the toast, Artie snatched a newspaper from a neighbouring table and began to leaf through it.

'Look here,' he said, and turned the newspaper around.

It was a copy of the *Manchester Guardian*, and across its front page the headlines screamed out:

GERMANY'S DAY OF WRECKING AND LOOTING

GANGS UNHAMPERED BY POLICE

SYNAGOGUES BURNT DOWN IN MAJOR CITIES

Raymond's head was pounding, but something in this steadied his eyes. He began to read. Soon, the words were flying past: a young German diplomat, assassinated on the streets of Paris; violent reprisals echoing across the whole of the Third Reich.

'And here.' Artie had taken the innards of the newspaper out and was himself perusing another article. "Homes wanted, for child refugees". Poor little mites,' he muttered. 'The bastards burn down their houses, smash up their shops, beat up their mas and pas, and then rout them out of the country. They'll roll up here, without a word of English – and be lucky not to find the same sods right here, trying to drive them out.'

Raymond felt a flash of guilt. Artie had stood on the barricades at Cable Street two years ago, when the British Union of Fascists had marched through. He'd been brutalised for it, too – left in a gutter, his arm broken in two places, teeth chipped . . . and pride intact.

Raymond watched as he folded up the newspaper, shoved it into his back pocket, and slurped up the rest of his tea that had sloshed into its saucer.

'I don't know about you, Ray, but that's sorted me out. I feel right as rain. I could visit an alehouse again now.'

Raymond – who still felt in the foothills of his own hangover – nodded weakly.

There were alehouses aplenty in the backstreets of Blackpool. The first they gravitated towards was filled with old men and their dominoes – Artie won a handful of copper coins, while Raymond lost so badly he had to stand everyone a drink – and, in the second and the third, were such roustabouts that, although Artie felt quite at home, Raymond wondered if he'd make it back to the Buckingham and married life at all. It wasn't until the fourth taproom, where only a few scattered souls were drinking their way merrily through the winter, that Raymond started to come out of his hung-over fugue.

'I told you! It's like our old man used to say – the only good cure is a hair of the dog that bit you.'

'This dog's particularly . . . yeasty,' said Raymond, as he put his new tankard to his lips.

Artie shook his head. 'I'd ask 'em for a magnum of Veuve Clicquot, but somehow I think we might get laughed out of the place.'

'By the way, I think I've found us a place to live,' Raymond told his brother. 'An old dancing friend put me on to it. A little corner of Maida Vale, overlooking the canal.'

'Oh, fancy! You told Nance, have you?'

'Not yet. I thought it might be a surprise. I'd take her there and cut a ribbon and carry her over the threshold . . .'

Artie rolled his eyes. 'What have I told you about all these grand romantic gestures you think you have to make? Ray Cohen, you sanctimonious old sod! She's marrying you for *you*, not for all your airs and graces. I mean, there's you, in your fancy ballroom, courting duchesses and princesses, and you don't know a bloody thing about *love*.'

'This, coming from the man who hasn't been in love in his life!'

Artie grabbed Raymond's pint, deliberately put it to his lips and downed the whole lot.

'What was that for?'

'Because you're being a lordly lackwit again, and I can't stand it. Look, we didn't come here to talk about love. We came because it's us – me and you, Ray, the Cohen boys. One last blowout before you're off to holy matrimony. Let's have a bit of fun!'

Raymond smiled. There was a sozzled look in Artie's eyes, and – to be perfectly honest – he was grateful not to have had to finish that last ale.

'Come on, you old rascal.'

Artie took him fiercely by the arm, wrenched him upwards and out of the taproom, kept hauling him through the streets, until Raymond had to run to keep up.

'There!' cried Artie. 'It's time. I hear music, don't you? I hear song. So let's get ourselves in there, Ray, and have at it. We're going to make it a night to remember. And . . . you and me, we're going to dance.'

Raymond looked up. Above them both, picked out in silver lettering that reflected the starlight captured in the snow, were the words WINTER GARDENS.

In the Empress Ballroom, everything had changed, but the feeling was exactly the same.

If it was the warmth of the place that hit Artie, drawing him forward like a moth to a flame, it was the *scent* that brought Raymond back to his senses. The heat of the bodies out on the ballroom floor was incandescent, and in the air the smells of rosewood and varnish took Raymond back in time. Together, the brothers stood in the great arch of the entrance, listening to the orchestra working up a tango, and just gazed at the dancers turning the ballroom floor into a riot of passion and motion.

Raymond gazed up. The ballroom was garlanded by tiers of balconies, in which groups of old friends gathered to watch the spectacle below. He remembered being up there himself, watching Georges de la Motte compete on the floor below. Further

343

up, the ballroom's twelve chandeliers lit up the vaulted ceiling in radiant array. *They're like a constellation of stars*, thought Raymond. They spilled their enchanted light, turning the mundane to the magnificent, the good to the great.

While Raymond took in the splendour, feeling the music pulsing in him, Artie's eyes were scouring the ballroom for an altogether different reason.

'There isn't a bar,' he finally announced.

'There's a lounge bar,' said Raymond. 'But Artie, you said we were going to dance!'

Artie beamed. 'I did indeed . . .'

Until that night, Raymond had not understood the charm of a man like his brother. Ruddy-faced from the snow, wet and bedraggled as he was, it took Artie mere minutes before he'd inveigled his way into conversation with a group of ladies who'd come to the ballroom for their cousin's birthday. Bringing them back to where Raymond was standing, still admiring the spectacle of the chandeliers above, he introduced the two eldest as, 'Hilary and Rita, Ray. Hilary's daughter's thirty years old today. Quite an occasion. Rita here's her daughter too.'

'Sister!' Rita, tall and with braided black hair, cried out, with a smile she found hard to suppress.

'Sister?' Artie gasped. 'But you must be barely twenty years old.' He leaned in close to Raymond and whispered, 'You've got the looks, Ray, but I've *always* had the charm.' Then he lifted himself again, as if standing to attention. 'Be gentle with Raymond, Hilary. He doesn't like to dance. Grew up with two left feet, you see. Can't hold a candle to his brother. But, well, he's getting married next month – so he deserves a good night.'

'Congratulations, young man,' Hilary said, waddling over to Raymond's side and taking his hand. 'But you'll have to learn a dance or two, if only to impress this lucky girl on her wedding day.'

'Oh,' said Raymond, 'I think I can manage.'

Artie was already leading black-haired Rita onto the dance floor, winking at Raymond over his shoulder.

'Shall we?' Raymond began.

'I should think my old man, Gus over there, will have a fit to see me dancing with a handsome young man like you. It's a good job you can't dance, son. He's likely to explode if he thinks someone's a better dancer than him!'

As they wended their way onto the dance floor, Raymond caught sight of Artie already driving his tango across the ballroom, and smiled inwardly. If there was one thing he'd learned in the Grand, it was that you had to give the guests what they were expecting. Down there it was enchantment. It was being whisked away. It was the impression that they, too, were stars of the ballroom. Well, up here, he supposed it was going to be different. *Give her what she's expecting*, he told himself.

How was it Billy Brogan danced again? The stumbles and the falls, the missteps and sideways trot? *Yes*, Raymond thought, *I could just about manage that . . .*

They danced with Hilary and Rita. They danced with another pair of sisters, out for a good night. Artie danced with an overly amorous older lady, who was happy to be swept into his arms but could hardly understand why he didn't want a drink afterwards, and Raymond danced with two old dears who came to the Empress for the atmosphere and were nervous to take to the floor at all.

It was strange how time was dilated in a place like the Empress Ballroom. Memories popped into the air all around him as he turned and tangoed and waltzed, and soon Raymond de Guise had forgotten all about the roiling in his stomach that had been plaguing him all day. Soon, as the midnight hour approached, he and Artie were picking their way to the lounge bar, where they took two flagons of ale to a table in the corner.

'Well, Ray, what do you make of that? I told you you'd have a night to remember. One last time, before your happy ever after!'

They had been sitting there for some time, the ballroom emptying and all its dancers heading out through the bar, when one of the stewards approached them from behind.

'Come on, gentlemen,' the old man said. 'It's midnight now.'

Artie whirled around. 'Don't you know who this is?' he slurred, with an arm around his brother.

'I'm afraid I do not.'

'Only the greatest, the most celebrated, the champion . . .'

As Artie's words turned into a stream of unintelligible noises, the elder man shook his head sadly.

'You've had your fun, lads. Now, on your way. We've got to get this place shuttered up. You'll be tucked up in a warm bed, and I'll still be sweeping these floors.'

Muttering oaths, Artie stood and, smashing his arms back into the sleeves of his overcoat, tramped away. Muttering apologies, Raymond followed.

'Anywhere we can get a drink in town?' Artie called back.

The elder steward nodded. 'Plenty, I should think. But you boys look like you're old enough to know better.'

Now that the night was spent, the Cohen brothers tramped together, back into the snow. The other revellers fanned out around them as they pulled their collars high. Winters were cold in London, but none as bitter as this northern chill.

'Things are going to change, aren't they, Artie?' Raymond slurred.

'Aye, well, they will, if you go and get married. That's in the nature of it.'

'I don't just mean that. I mean the Buckingham. I mean . . . Hélène. Archie's found her an opportunity, a new life in Chicago. She'll take it. She'll have to. And then . . . it's a new generation in the ballroom. I'll be the oldest one by years.'

'You can feel your dotage coming, can you, Ray?'

'And John Hastings and war, and that poor boy from the Winter Hollers. It's all moving too quickly. I can feel the world groaning with the weight of it. And this thing with Vivienne. That girl! Well, at least she hasn't had to hide it, not like Hélène. When I think of what she had to do, of why she had to do it . . .'

Artie grunted. 'You're drunk, Ray.'

By now they were back on the seafront promenade. Raymond looked up.

'Life's like one of those,' he said, gesturing at the roller coasters that arced overhead. 'It just goes round and round and round, and if you don't cling on, you get thrown off. Hélène clung on as long as she could. And me and you, Artie . . .'

'We're still riding it, Ray!' he roared. 'But you – one more drink, and you'd go straight over the edge.'

'It's like Vivienne's life. Such a whirlwind. Well, it always was. Back before you knew her – the terror of the Buckingham halls! And now, even though she's straightened her ways, even for all the good she's doing, she's still a tornado ripping through life. Well, good for her, I say. Why the devil not? You've got to take your chances. And Vivienne, at least she *lives* life.' He laughed. 'She's landed on her feet again, of course. Living with the Peels, Nancy says. Got herself a new family in double-quick time. They'll see her right. Warren Peel's had his dark times, but Nancy says he's a reformed man. At least they won't go wanting. Vivienne can cast off the shackles of the Edgertons and turn into a Peel.'

It was some moments later that Raymond realised he was marching alone. He turned over his shoulder, only to see Artie standing some distance behind, his hands firmly planted on his hips, a look like a blizzard plastered across his face. The rippling veil of snow separated them, but Raymond could feel his fury from here.

'Artie?'

'You think you know it all, don't you, Ray? You got life all figured out.'

'Artie, what did I say?'

Artie burst forward. For a fleeting instant, Raymond thought he was about to throw a punch – he'd been on the receiving end of one of Artie's right hooks more than once in his life – but instead he just marched past, knocking Raymond off kilter as he came.

'Artie, wait up!'

Raymond reached out for his shoulder, spun him around.

'Just because you're lord of the manor, it doesn't mean you know what's going on in the world,' said Artie. 'Viv might have gone to stay with Warren Peel, you stuck-up toff, but she isn't in love with him. She's gone there because she needs a roof over her head. No, Ray, you got it all wrong. There's no way our Viv's going to marry little Warren Peel. I'd hazard Warren would love it, but he's not for her.'

'Why ever not?' gasped Raymond. 'Artie, you're making no sense. They'd be good for each other, wouldn't they? And if she's having his child—'

'She's not having his child, you blind old sod!'

Raymond was still. He thought he saw a look like jubilation flashing across Artie's face.

'She's having mine!'

December 1938

# Chapter Twenty-seven

IN HER QUARTERS HIGH ABOVE the suites of the Buckingham, Nancy awoke to the creaking of pipes.

These were the sounds of the hotel waking up, slowly coming back to life after its hours of slumber. She lay there a moment longer, until she heard the chatter of the other chambermaids through the walls – and then, rolling over in the twilit room, she looked at the calendar on the wall. December had dawned, so she reached up and took the pencil she kept at her bedside to mark an 'X' against the 1st. Then she looked down.

Only nine more nights separated her from married life.

She stared at the date, and allowed herself to feel a thrill of wonder. The girls said she was a stick in the mud, that she wasn't excited enough – but they were wrong. Nine days until she wore Raymond's wedding ring and counted herself his wife. She could not wait.

Her eyes took in the wardrobe on the other side of her room. When she opened it up, it stood barren – with only her chambermaid uniforms hanging there. If there was anything that prickled her about the wedding day, it was only this: with nine days to go, there was still no dress. She had resolved to solve this particular problem today, and by mid-afternoon she would be back at Regency Bridal. Without Ruth and Rosa to pour their own thoughts and dreams at her, she felt certain she would find the one. No matter what, she was coming home with a dress tonight.

Nancy was late coming out of her room, so it wasn't until breakfast was already being dished up that she approached the housekeeping lounge. Today, Mrs Moffatt seemed in better cheer than she had all year long; perhaps, the girls said, it was because of those letters she kept carrying around with her. Or perhaps, Rosa had cheekily suggested, it was because of Archie Adams – who had, on more than one occasion now, delivered flowers to the housekeeping lounge.

'See, Ruth,' Rosa had laughed, 'you can fall in love at almost any age. You're not an old maid yet!'

'Girls!' Mrs Moffatt announced, once the crumpets were being passed around. 'It's nice to see you all here, bright and early. And at such an auspicious time!' At this, Rosa elbowed Nancy in the side, grinning broadly – but Mrs Moffatt demurred. 'I was speaking of Christmas, girls, not Miss Nettleton's coming nuptials. Though what a day that will be as well.'

The girls cheered – and Nancy, who was blushing too much this month, purpled further.

'Come on. You old hands know what I'm speaking about. You new girls are about to see something magnificent.'

Mrs Moffatt led them, in procession, down the housekeeping hall, and at last into the pre-dawn of the reception hall, where the black and white chequers were speckled with a trail of green foliage and the art deco obelisk had been taken away for winter storage.

Now, in its place, five workmen balanced on ladders, with ropes in hand, as together they heaved a towering Norwegian fir into place. Braced in position by the men up their ladders, the tree stood resplendent, filling the reception hall with the scent of a winter forest.

It was still dark in Berkeley Square and, in the reception hall, the only light that illuminated the tree came from the little lamps at the check-in desks. But when the first guests emerged for breakfast, they would not see a naked fir tree casting its shadow over the hall.

'We have one hour, girls,' said Mrs Moffatt. 'One hour, in which to capture the magic of Christmas!'

She stepped aside. Behind her, Frank Nettleton was approaching, bearing the big chest of Christmas decorations out from the basement store cupboards. One of the porters' trolleys held the main trunk and, on top of that, were all the other boxes and crates that hadn't seen the light since last Twelfth Night. Frank, who couldn't stop smiling – *it's good to see him smile*, thought Nancy – opened it up, revealing a pirate's treasure of glittering baubles, garlands and stars.

'Let's get started, girls,' Mrs Moffatt announced. 'Let your hearts sing!'

As Rosa, Ruth, and all the rest of the housekeeping staff descended on the trolley, Frank reached out for the smallest of all the boxes, a parcel of yellow crêpe paper wrapped in a length of silver ribbon. This he clutched close to his heart as he urged Nancy to join him underneath the archway leading down to the Grand.

'Nancy, it's for you.'

She took it, with a bewildered expression.

'I know it isn't normal,' said Frank. 'I know gifts should be for your wedding day. But I heard you were going back to Regency Bridal today and I thought, if I don't show it now, I never will. Open it, Nance.'

The girls were already organising the baubles and stars into piles of different colours. The workmen, meanwhile, were shifting their ladders, bracing a single one in place so that they could help the girls reach the uppermost branches.

All of the colour exploding behind him couldn't tempt Frank to look away from the parcel he'd just given Nancy. He watched, eagerly, as she pulled on the ribbon, allowing the paper to unfurl and reveal a little spotted box within. When she opened its lid, it revealed a dress made of decades-old silk, worn in places, still shimmering in others. She allowed it to fall down, held it up against herself as its wrapping clean fell away.

'I remembered I had the silk from Ma's wedding dress. All those years, we used it to line my old toy box. And I had that box over at the Brogans'. Well, Mrs Moffatt helped. She sent me to the hotel seamstresses, and they did their best. I know it ain't perfect, Nance, and I know it's late. I've been lost, after what happened to Ansel, and . . .'

Nancy could still smell the old toy box on the fabric. She lifted it to her nose. It smelled of home.

'It's like the one she wore,' she whispered, remembering the wedding portrait she still kept in her drawer upstairs.

'Not perfect. I showed them a picture. There wasn't enough left to make it as it should be. But Ma's in it, isn't she?'

'She is.'

'I should think she'd like that, Nance.'

Nancy put her arms around her brother and held on to him. Then, together, their eyes turned to the tree, as the glitter and colour spread up its branches, bringing every bough to life.

Arms around each other, they gravitated closer to the tree.

'Just like *we* used to do, isn't it?'

Nancy gazed up and ever upwards. 'We never had a tree quite this big, Frank.'

'Still reckon I can climb up and put the angel on top though!'

'Go on then, Frank!' Rosa chipped in.

She was holding, in both of her hands, an enormous angel made of satin and lace, her face embroidered with silk and gold thread. Marching forward, she placed it delicately in Frank's hands.

'Shall I, Nance?'

'Go on, Frank!' Rosa cheered.

The workmen at the ladder stepped aside, inviting Frank aboard – but, although he cantered up the first steps, after that he needed it no longer. Halfway up the ladder, and having first tested its balance and strength, he took to the tree itself, shimmying up between the branches with all the talent and skill of a boy who'd grown up in the country.

At the top, Frank balanced himself with his legs wrapped around the trunk, reached up – and delicately slipped the angel over the tree's highest point. Then he turned around, opening his arms wide as if he was some circus acrobat – Rosa cheered, while Ruth's eyes flitted admiringly between them both – and opened his mouth in an uncontrollable smile.

Frank Nettleton: the king of the world!

Christmas had come to the Buckingham Hotel.

Throughout the day, there was not a guest who didn't stop and stare in awe at the traditional Norwegian fir in the reception hall. During the midnight hours, decorations had appeared across each restaurant and hall as well. Wreaths of mistletoe and holly materialised on every door of every suite. In the Queen Mary restaurant, the menu had become their traditional Yuletide fare of pheasant and venison, roast chestnut and sage; sprigs of plump red berries adorned every table.

But as the hotel buzzed with preparation for the festive season and the forthcoming wedding, the worries of one member of the Buckingham Hotel blinded them to the beauty of the coming Christmas.

The middle of the afternoon, the skies once again paling towards darkness, and Billy waited by the check-in desks, with Maynard Charles at his side. A long morning listening to Mrs Farrier's tales of Christmases past had dulled his senses, so that, when he emerged to take in the new magnificence in the reception hall, it took him a long time to readjust. Now he waited in solemn silence, the reception hall bustling around him, Maynard Charles's voice tolling in his ear.

'Here they come. Keep your eyes on them. They'll dine in the Queen Mary tonight, and tomorrow be about their business. We've seated Herr Bauer on the other side of the restaurant, but he'll have his eye on them throughout. There'll be a missive tonight, Billy. You'll know what to do.'

Billy watched as the revolving brass doors turned, disgorging a tall lion of a man, with hair the colour of a cornfield and a prominent jaw that made him seem like a hero from one of the ha'penny children's stories Billy used to read.

'Reichsgraf von Amsberg,' Maynard whispered, watching the burly man, dressed in a suit of dark green, with a gnarled oak cane in one hand and his gentleman's umbrella in the other. 'Moorcock says his line goes back to the Holy Roman Empire, though there's some would dispute it. Fell out of favour in 1919, by all accounts – like so many did.'

Billy tracked him with his eyes, as the day manager received him at the check-in desk, and stopped studying him only when the revolving doors turned again, revealing a man of much swarthier complexion, with hair as black as pitch and tight coils of beard. This man, smaller and portlier than the lion who'd first stepped through, resembled nothing more than a big, black bear – and one, by the look of him, who had just come out of hibernation, for there were dark rings of exhaustion around both of his eyes.

'Reichsritter Wittekind,' Maynard explained, 'though he can't go by that name any longer – traces his ancestry back to the last free knights. According to Moorcock, he holds to much the same dogma as his ancestors did – vassalage to no more powerful noble. With a heart like that, it's little wonder he hasn't bent the knee to Herr Hitler. Billy,' Maynard went on, more softly now, 'you have a heart like that as well. You know that, don't you?'

Billy whispered, 'Mr Charles?'

'I've asked you to do some underhanded things in this hotel, Mr Brogan. Never without good reason. Never without hope that, in our own small way, we're helping to forge a better world. I've asked you to sneak and spy for me often – but never in a moment of greater import than this.' Billy felt Maynard's hand resting in the small of his back. Such a strange thing; he was quite certain Mr Charles had never deigned to touch him before – not even to shake his hand. 'There'll be letters from von Amsberg and Wittekind too. I'd wager my soul on it. When they come, deliver them as you would Herr Bauer's. And, Billy, look over your shoulder at all times. Do I make myself clear?'

'You do, Mr Charles.'

'Then it's settled. Another day, another two, and we might be seeing the back of Herr Bauer, Billy. Let us hope it is so.'

That night, Billy circled the Queen Mary restaurant twice, keeping his eyes on the two German nobles dining with a third gentleman, and on Tobias Bauer, in a secluded corner of the restaurant, pretending to peruse the evening newspaper. Not once did he venture within. For a time, he retired to his quarters, meaning to rest – but sleep did not come and, when he closed his eyes, all that he saw was Ansel Albrecht, lying at the bottom of the guest stairs. He did not realise that the image had been imprinted on him so vividly.

Unable to sit still, he prowled up and down, stopping intermittently to look out upon the serene beauty of Berkeley Square. When even this did not still his mind, he decided that he ought to go and find Frank – until he remembered that he was bound to be in the chambermaids' kitchenette, cosied up with Rosa and a pot of hot cocoa. Billy would have liked to have gone there too. Perhaps he would have taken himself there straight away, if only the idea of Rosa bullying Ruth into sitting beside him hadn't weighed on him so heavily. Nancy had been right, that night in the Starlight Lounge: you couldn't cajole it into happening; Ruth had to *want* it.

The wedding was mere days away now. Billy had his invitation propped up on the desk by the window. He'd given up on the idea of dancing at the reception. The dream, he supposed, had died with Ansel. Frank hadn't wanted to rehearse much after that either. But perhaps if Billy were to put in a little time on his own, that might ease things along? There were worse ways, he decided, to rid his body of the jitters he was feeling right now. With a bit of lubrication – and he had a half bottle of cherry liqueur that Diego from the Candlelight Club had ferreted away for him – he might just be able to jitterbug the jitters away.

But when he stole down to the little studio behind the Grand, it was to discover that the room was already occupied. To the music of the tinny gramophone in the corner, Raymond de Guise was turning Nancy in a classical waltz.

Nancy stumbled out of hold the moment she saw Billy come clattering in. Billy, who stood there with the bottle of liqueur clutched in his fist, began to retreat almost at once. Even when Nancy called after him, he stuttered an apology and stepped backwards, through the closing door.

When Nancy's focus remained on the closing door, Raymond said, 'There's been something troubling him for days.'

The record was not over yet, so Raymond swept her back onto the studio floor, taking her through the motions one more time. When Nancy danced, she always held something back. Raymond was quite certain it wasn't the old injury to her leg; rather, it was the way she thought about her leg, the little idea that had taken root in her that she had to focus on it, to make up for it. Only by dancing could thoughts like that be forgotten.

And so they danced.

Raymond had something a little more devilish planned for their wedding as well.

'The Grand Ballroom has never seen a jitterbug, Nancy. It's never seen a jive. Why, they'd nearly faint if they saw it, all those stuffed-up ladies and lords. But on our wedding day . . .'

Secretly, he thought it might help Nancy as well; a dance like the jitterbug didn't care whether one leg was weaker than the other, nor even whether you knew its movements or had studied its lines. All it cared about was that you loved it.

'Raymond,' she said at last, 'there's something I want to show you.'

She did not take him by the hand, for there was still decorum to consider, but he followed her all the same, all the way to the service lift and up, up, up to the chambermaids' corridor high above. There, past the kitchenette where the girls were idling away their evening and Frank was being roundly beaten at backgammon by Rosa, Nancy took Raymond into her room and opened up her wardrobe. There hung the dress which Frank's seamstress friend had brought back to life.

'What do you think?'

Raymond fingered the new gown, picturing her in it.

'It's bad luck to see the dress before—'

'Oh, hang traditions!' Nancy exclaimed. 'We've been hanging traditions all along, you and me.' She paused. 'Frank had it made for me. It's the silk my mother wore on my parents' wedding day. And . . .' She sighed. She smiled. 'I have everything I need, now. I have you, and I have Frank, and I'm going to have my parents with me as well. That's everything. The whole world.'

Raymond's fingers were still caressing the fabric. In a bridal boutique they might have called it a ruin; they might have called it patchwork. But Raymond fancied he could feel, in its touch and weave, the real love of its creation. She would look beautiful in it. He told her so.

'I hope so,' said Nancy, softly. 'But I'll feel loved, and that's what matters. That's my family – just the two of us, everything I need.'

Raymond paused. He could hear laughter radiating out from the chambermaids' kitchenette.

'Well, not *just* the two of us,' he ventured. 'Our trip to Lancashire yielded more secrets than one. You see, Nancy, there's something else I haven't been telling you. Something I was sworn to keep to myself. But . . . well, you're to be my wife – and this isn't the sort of secret I could ever keep for long. Nancy, your family's about to get bigger.'

'Raymond?'

'It seems I'm not the only Cohen boy who's fallen in love. And it seems I'm not the only Cohen boy whose life is about to change beyond all recognition.' He paused, watched the look of confusion ghosting across her face. 'There's a reason Vivienne didn't confide in you about her pregnancy. It's my brother, Nancy. Artie and Vivienne are in love. He's the father of her child.'

Midnight on Berkeley Square. In the middle of the snowy expanse, a lone fox startled, its eyes catching the glow of the street lamps as it watched the straggler hurry past.

Billy Brogan had wrapped up against the cold, drawn the collar of his overcoat high, and barrelled out of the tradesman's entrance, off into the night. Tonight, cringing into the strafing snow, he was grateful for the scarf that hid half of his face. His heart was beating in wild percussion, his breath pluming raggedly. This was his thirteenth night making this odyssey for Mr Charles and the mysterious Mr Moorcock, but it never got any easier. Billy had often thought he'd make a diligent soldier, but he made a lousy spy.

The Merchant Colonial Club was on the other side of Piccadilly, with its windows looking down upon the open white landscape of Green Park. This late at night there were few patrons braving the bitter cold, but as Billy passed under the colonnades outside the Ritz Hotel, he caught the eye of the long-suffering doorman, and some flicker of solidarity passed between them. Then he was off, past the jaws of the sleeping Underground, along the edge of the park, and to the little black door where the lights still shone.

The doorman knew Billy, so stood back promptly when he arrived. At the desk, he asked for Christophe – a short, balding man with enough hair sprouting out of his ears to make up for the hair he lacked up on top – and, when he waddled out to greet him, Billy reached into his overcoat, produced a single yellow envelope and handed it over. Then, with his heart beating wildly, he returned to the night.

Something in him called out for home, so instead of return-ing to the Buckingham, he made for the river, the only soul in the streets around the abbey at Westminster, and crossed by the Lambeth Bridge. From there he hurried back into the old ter-races of home, and slipped through the door at 62 Albert Yard. It was only here, breathing in the familiar scents of home, that his heart stopped pounding.

He shouldn't be afraid. He was Billy Brogan. He was made of strong stuff.

Frank had the old bedroom, and would be up there now, no doubt dreaming about dancing at the wedding reception on Saturday night – and Billy did not begrudge him that; after Ansel, everyone deserved a little happiness this Christmas. But somehow he could not keep hold of any of his own. His thoughts strayed to Ruth. Dancing hadn't swayed her. Well, Billy just didn't have the knack – he could admit that to himself, at last. But maybe boldness and derring-do – maybe that was the thing. Maybe, if she knew what he was doing for King and country, she might give him a chance to prove himself then.

He pulled up a blanket, lay down on the sofa by the dying fire, and closed his eyes – but, when sleep came at all, he was quickly wrenched out of it. In his dreams, he was that fox out on Berkeley Square: desperate for survival, hunted from all corners.

Mere hours had passed before he returned to the barren Lambeth streets, back through the palaces of Westminster, through the monochrome dells of Green Park and to the doors of the Merchant Colonial Club.

The doorman, a dour Scot in his early sixties, allowed Billy to slip in without any fuss. Moments later, after Billy had received the envelope back from the understated fellow at the desk, the doorman let him back out. It had all happened inside a moment, and not one person had spoken a word.

There were still lights in the face of the Buckingham as Billy slipped in along Michaelmas Mews. Here and there, lanterns illuminated windows encrusted with frost, and from the reception hall, he could see the glittering baubles in the Norwegian fir. Billy paused, once, to look up at the tree. In any other year, it would have filled his heart with wonder. If only there was a way to bring that enchantment back tonight . . .

Alone, he slipped into the hotel basement. Alone, he fumbled a key into the lock of the post room. Alone, he slid the letter from the Merchant Colonial Club into the sack that the Royal Mail would pick up after dawn.

Then, alone once more, he slipped back out of the post room and hurried up the hall – his subterfuge finished, for another few nights.

But Billy was not as alone as he thought as he reached the basement stairs and, taking them three at a time, returned to the concierge desks.

A second set of eyes was watching him from the bottom of the guest stairs. A second set of eyes whose owner would soon step out of the shadows and shuffle off to the Queen Mary restaurant, where he would sit perusing the morning papers, taking account of each guest who arrived, making the detailed mental notes on which his trade relied.

At the bottom of the guest stairs, the man the Buckingham Hotel knew as Tobias Bauer waited and watched, and bided his time.

# Chapter Twenty-eight

BY THE END OF THE WEEK, the snowfall had gentled across
London and, street by street, the sleeping city was coming back to life.

At the Daughters of Salvation, Nancy Nettleton watched the
first of the evening stragglers arriving at the back courtyard gate
and noted the look of expectation in their eyes. Soon, Mary Burdett would be opening the portcullis; her girls were already lining up at the stove top, ready to dish out the hot broth they'd
been cooking that afternoon. Nancy had already warmed herself
with a bowl, and a heel of yesterday's bread. Simple fare, but as
good as any she and Raymond had dined on in London's most
fashionable restaurants.

It was exactly the thing that she needed this Friday night, the
eve of her wedding.

From inside the chapel, she heard Artie Cohen's voice exploding in a riot of laughter. He'd taken to playing cards with some
of the destitutes – gambling was strictly forbidden, except with
twigs and matchsticks – and it seemed, now, that he was devas-
tating his opponents. Nancy drifted through. In the reception
hall, with an upturned crate as a table, Artie was launching an

attack on the matchsticks of his companions, sweeping them all up with a valedictory guffaw.

'All mine!' he roared. 'Boys, it was always written in the stars that I'd win tonight. My brother's getting married tomorrow, don't you know? I'm the best man. So it stands to reason, the gods would smile on me.'

Artie stood up, cramming matchsticks and lengths of twig into his pocket and said, 'I'm off then, boys. You've got Warren standing on the door tonight. Play gentle with him. And if any unsavoury types show up – more unsavoury than you lot, o' course! – give him a helping hand, won't you?'

Artie swivelled on his heel – he might not have been Raymond, and he hardly cared for it at all, but he too was a formidable dancer. He was about to exit the hall when his eyes landed on Nancy. For a moment, they held each other's gaze. Some piece of knowledge passed between them – and then, with another of his wolfish grins, he was gone.

Nancy found Vivienne in the back room. There she sat, running a finger along the latest page of the ledger books, adding up figures in her head as she went. Nancy watched her for a moment, the way she mouthed each number in turn, before she said, 'Miss Edgerton.'

Vivienne looked up. 'It's been an age since you called me that, Nancy.'

'Vivienne, I haven't seen you in days. Not properly in weeks. And—'

In a moment, Vivienne was on her feet, whisking past Nancy to close the office door. It was only clapboard, but at least it was some privacy.

'I know you know, Nancy,' she said. 'It's Artie. He couldn't keep his mouth shut, could he? I knew it – as soon as he said he was off with Raymond, I knew he'd tell it all.'

There was frenzy in Vivienne's voice, but with these last words she calmed. She had seen the look on Nancy's face.

'Vivienne, you're going to be my sister.'

Vivienne hissed, 'He hasn't asked me to marry him yet. Artie Cohen thinks *I* should be the one to ask *him*. I've you to thank for that, he says. Says *you* were going to pop the question to Raymond yourself, if he hadn't got there first.'

Nancy laughed. 'I was!'

'The world's gone topsy-turvy. It's all this talk of war and . . .' She took a deep breath. 'I'm scared, Nancy. I'm happy and I'm scared. It's the most infuriating thing. The Peels are happy for me to stay for a time. Warren's father rather likes the idea that he's baiting my stepfather with it. It seems they've run into each other, here and there, across the years. But . . .' She led Nancy back to the desk, where they both sat down. Nancy began to pour from a hot teapot, adding copious amounts of milk from a jug on a tray. 'Can it be fair, to bring a child into this world? Not knowing what's to come, Nancy, and not knowing—'

'Shhhh,' Nancy said. 'They'll be loved. That's all that matters.'

'Yes,' said Vivienne. 'Loved.'

There was a question Nancy hadn't dared to ask, but now she found the courage.

'Do you love him, Vivienne? Artie?'

There was a long pause and, in it, it seemed to Nancy that Vivienne was doing nothing other than taking an inventory of her life.

'I do,' she said, and there must have been something amusing about the idea, because she started to laugh. 'I completely and utterly do. He's different, Nancy. Different to how he acts out here – roustabout Artie Cohen, dirt under his fingernails, always with his eyes darting around, as if he might scurry off any moment. When I think of all those men I' – she blushed – 'indulged, back at the Buckingham. I thought I was meant for that sort of man. It took Artie to make me see the world isn't like that. I was born into one world. It doesn't mean I have to stay in it. Love can get me out.'

'I don't think it's love that got you out of that world, Vivienne. I think it was *you*, plain and simple. If you don't mind me saying it, that world was killing you. Oh, I don't just mean the powders and the champagne and the cocktails. I mean the money of it. The expectations. And the isolation too. When I think of what it was like for you . . .' She paused. 'How did it all happen?'

Vivienne shrugged. 'A late night,' she said. 'Too many late nights here, Artie escorting me to my taxicab like he was some wandering knight errant. I think he liked to play that role. Somewhere along the way, things *changed*. It's never been like that before, Nancy. Before it was always so fast and useless. Things that happen so swiftly die the same way. With Artie it was different.'

'And when you told him about the baby . . . ?'

'Out there,' she said, indicating the frosted window and the cobbled row beyond, 'that night after I left the hotel. I hadn't known how to tell him until then. Every night, I kept holding it in – and Artie, he knew something was wrong, he knew I was hiding something. I think he thought I was done with him. Spoilt Vivienne Edgerton could never take up with a man like Artie Cohen – that's what was going through his head. But when

I told him, why, it was like the whole world made sense. Artie saw that too.'

'When I heard you'd gone to the Peels, I thought it must be Warren. We all did.'

Vivienne shook her head. 'It's Artie. For now and evermore. I just need to find a way to make it happen. But we found a way to make *this*, didn't we?' She opened her arms, taking in the entirety of the Daughters of Salvation itself. 'So a little thing like this ... well, it ought to be a trifle. It's just that, sometimes, the smallest things are the most difficult to make happen. My mother wrote to me, not three days ago. She said she was sorry. That she'd help me. She knew people who could find a home for my baby and ...' Vivienne's mind had strayed to Hélène Marchmont, and then to Mrs Moffatt; all of their history seemed to course through her tonight. She shook her head defiantly. 'It's my life to wreck my own way. That's what my stepfather used to tell me, every time I'd brought shame on him at the Buckingham. Well, here's how I'll wreck it, Nancy. With my baby and Artie Cohen and, well, as much love as the three of us can muster – however long we've all got left.' She paused. 'I'm sorry about your wedding, Nancy. I would have loved to have seen it.'

'You still can.'

Vivienne shook her head. 'And risk ruining your day? Vivienne Edgerton causing another scene in the Grand? No, Nancy, this day's for you.' She paused. 'There's something else I'd like to give you.' She reached into the desk and drew from it a small envelope, which she placed delicately in Nancy's hand. 'I've been saving, little by little, each month. Just what little I could keep, and not let the Daughters down. I'm afraid it isn't much. But I should like you and Raymond to have it – for a trip, Nancy, a honeymoon in the New Year. Back north, perhaps, so Raymond can see some more of your home county.' She smiled. 'The way I understand it, Artie had him drinking so much he might not remember very much from his last voyage north.'

'Oh, Vivienne,' she said. 'Thank you.'

She meant it from the bottom of her heart.

She was almost at the door when, fearing the chance would not come again, she looked back and said, 'Why didn't you tell me, Vivienne?'

And Vivienne, who had already returned to the ledgers, looked up and said, 'I wanted to. Ever since that moment you asked me to be bridesmaid, I knew that I should. But this is your year, Nancy Nettleton. Your wedding. Your romance. My recklessness has upended your life on more than one occasion already. I wanted you to—'

'This is *our* year,' said Nancy. 'Whatever happens next year, whatever the world throws at us, we'll always have this.' She stopped. 'You're coming to my wedding, Vivienne. If not as my bridesmaid, you're coming as my friend, and that's an order.'

The calendar chart on the wall had but one empty square left. In the pre-dawn darkness, Nancy lifted her hand to cross it out.

Her wedding day had arrived.

She was still lying there, bleary-eyed and listening to the creaking of the pipes, when too many hands grappling at her bedroom door forced it open, and in the portal of light, Rosa, Ruth, and all the other chambermaids came tumbling over one another to get in.

'Nancy!' Rosa thrilled, taking her by the arm and hoisting her aloft. 'Nancy, you can't go lying around – it's here! Stand back, girls – stand back! Nancy needs some room. This is her big day. She's got to get ready. There's hair and there's make-up, there's that dress of hers to get ready as well, there's breakfast to be had, and nails to be polished, and, I should think, a nice drop of champagne to be drunk – we've still got that bottle, haven't we, Ruth? Nobody's been at it yet, have they? Good! Well, Nancy, here we are, the biggest day in your life!'

Nancy found her feet at last, and felt the girls' excitement bubbling out towards her. Then she looked up, beyond the gaggle of excitable faces and nightdresses, and saw that another face had just joined them in the door. Big and happy, framed in its familiar mop of tight white curls, Mrs Moffatt's smile was as broad as Nancy had ever seen it – even on those occasions when Archie Adams arrived at the housekeeping lounge, looking to share a nice pot of tea.

'Girls, girls, girls, it's *Nancy's* day. *Nancy's* the one who'll be Mrs de Guise by this evening, not any of you. Now, those of you who are going to the service, get into that kitchenette and let's get this day started. Those of you not lucky enough to be watching our Miss Nettleton take her vows, there's a housekeeping lounge waiting for you.'

Half of the girls groaned and, contorting their faces into pantomimes of disappointment, slumped their shoulders as they tramped out of the room.

'There's still the reception for you girls!' Mrs Moffatt called. 'A treat like this is coming round only once in a lifetime, but there are suites that need sorting first!'

Nancy heard a chorus of, 'Yes, Mrs Moffatt!' as the other girls floated away. Then Mrs Moffatt turned to her and, with a cheery wink, said, 'The Buckingham waits for none of us – except for you, dear Nancy. And except for me.'

Still clinging to Nancy's hand, Rosa said, 'Mrs Moffatt?'

'Girls, it isn't often one of my own ties the knot.' She turned to Nancy herself. 'The girls can cope on their own today, Nancy. Me, I'd rather be with you. And there's somebody else who wants to see you too.'

Mrs Moffatt stepped aside and into the doorway came Vivienne Edgerton. The tan house dress she was wearing was loose fitting, but not loose enough to hide the child she was carrying. Rosa's eyes goggled. Nancy just beamed.

'You came,' she breathed.

'I can hear the corks popping already,' said Mrs Moffatt. 'Nancy, your breakfast awaits!'

Three miles away, in a different world, hands grappled Raymond de Guise by the shoulders and shook him back into wakefulness.

'Out of bed, you lazy dog!' Artie Cohen crowed. 'Ma's cooking up a storm. Kippers and eggs.'

Raymond's eyes snapped open. There was his brother's face, up close and leering into his.

'What time is it?' he gasped, heart beating wildly.

'We'll get you to the town hall on time.' Artie laughed. 'Don't you worry about that. But we got to tidy you up first. You look like you just got out of bed.'

Raymond, still tangled in his sheets, said, 'Artie, I feel strange. I feel shivery. It's tingling up and down me. Like someone's walking over my grave . . .'

'That's nerves.' Artie had crossed to the bedroom window, where he tore the curtains open and revealed the wonderland of white outside. 'Have you never felt nervous before, Ray?'

Raymond picked himself up. 'Not in a long time.'

'Aye, well, this isn't just any old dance you're embarking on today, old boy. This is the dance of life.'

Artie was chuckling to himself as he ripped open the wardrobe, revealing the tailored slate-grey morning suit in which his brother was going to be married. He reached within, lifted out the top hat from its box, and perched it delicately on his own head. Then he considered himself in the mirror.

'You're dancing the dance of life yourself, Artie,' Raymond said, rising behind him to snatch back the hat. 'How many months till you become a father? Four, now? Three?'

Artie grunted. 'You keep that to yourself, Ray Cohen. You know I haven't told her downstairs.'

'There's no hiding it, Artie.'

'Yeah, well, one more day, old boy. I wouldn't want to upend your big day. O' course, if I were to let it slip, your day would soon be forgotten about, so the fact is you ought to be thanking me for my generosity.' He grinned, wolfishly. 'Viv and I can celebrate another day!'

There came a knocking at the door and, without waiting for a reply, Alma Cohen pushed on through.

'Gregor's dropped you the car round, Artie. Nice, big, black shiny thing it is.'

Raymond froze. After a moment, with Artie flushing a guilty shade of red, he bustled past his mother, strode into the next bedroom along and, opening the window onto the snowdrifts in the street below, saw a gleaming black Rolls-Royce limousine sitting there, bedecked with a garish, ridiculous rainbow of ribbons.

Artie had joined him at the window. 'Isn't she a beauty?'

'We were getting taxicabs, Artie.'

'Not on your life, old son. Look, you designated me best man, so trust me – I know what's best. And what's more, I'm driving you myself!' He paused. 'It isn't costing me a penny. My pal Gregor borrowed it for the morning, that's all.'

'*Borrowed* it?' Raymond asked, emphasising the word meaningfully. 'Like you used to *borrow* railway sleepers from the sidings?'

'*Borrowed* it, Ray. Isn't she a beauty? She'll get us there in style, you'll see.'

Raymond already had a sinking feeling in his stomach.

The feeling didn't leave him all breakfast. It didn't help that the kippers were so salty and smoky that, as the family piled into the car and Artie choked the starter to bring the engine to life, he already felt ready to retch. *Nerves*. He'd never felt nervous before, not since his first days stepping out onto a ballroom floor. Now, his stomach was revolting against itself. He sat in the front passenger seat, his feet dancing a fandango quite of their own volition, and tried to still himself.

'Oh, Ray!' his mother cackled from the back seat, where she was sandwiched between Aunts May and Rebecca. 'There's nothing to it. Your father didn't cause even half of the fuss on *his* wedding day. Of course, he'd had a bit of practice. Jilted his first lover at the altar, as you'll remember, when he was but twenty years of age. Who knows – maybe that took the edge off for him. He knew he could always do it again!'

Shrieks of laughter filled the back seat.

'Our Ray's not nearly half as much a devil as Pa was,' said Artie. The car spluttered in protest as he guided it out onto the road. 'Look, just stand up, say the right lines, and you're done. Job's finished. Then you can get back to doing what you do best. You can dance.'

Raymond heard the bells tolling out eleven o'clock: Christ Church, up in Spitalfields, pealing in chorus with St George in the East. In one hour, he'd be standing there, turning over his shoulder to watch Nancy approaching down the aisle. He tried to keep his focus on that. The very idea of Nancy could still his quaking heart.

'Ray, you've spilled porridge all down your waistcoat.'

Raymond looked downwards, horrified – only to be caught off guard again by yet more shrieks of laughter.

'The oldest jokes are always the best!' cried Artie. They'd reached the basin at Shadwell and were preparing to follow the river west. 'You've been falling for that one since we were knee-high to a . . .'

It was then that the engine started to die.

At the reception desks, Frank – dressed in a navy-blue suit whose cuffs were just a *little* too long for him – was stuttering so rapidly that it was like artillery fire.

'B-Billy!' he stammered. 'I j-just can't get it out!'

The paper hanging in his hands was the speech he'd been diligently preparing for months. By rights, he ought to know it off by heart – but, for some reason, at the last moment, all words had failed him.

He'd stayed here at the Buckingham, bunked up with Billy, last night.

'I heard you muttering this thing in your sleep, Frank! Just going over and over it. You had it down word perfect.'

'Yes, B-Billy, b-but I'm not going to be asleep, am I? And there are g-going to be h-hundreds of faces staring at me.'

'Frank!' Billy snatched the paper off him. 'You've been boss-ing me around all year. "Let the music flow through you, Billy,"' he said, in the worst affected Lancastrian accent Frank had ever heard. '"You just got to *feel* it. The dancing will come! Stop thinking, Billy!" Ha, well, it's time you took your own advice. Just stop . . . overthinking. Look, if you mess it up, I'll jump in and help you – how does that sound?'

Actually, it sounded very good. Almost immediately, it calmed Frank's heart.

'Hey, Mr Charles!' Billy called out.

The hotel director had appeared through the revolving brass doors, dusted in a fine sprinkling of December snow. On hearing his name, he marched over to Billy and Frank with a look like thunder.

'Might I remind you,' he whispered, 'that, although this is a great day in the life of our good friends, the business of this hotel goes on unabated. So address me, please, with the respect that our hotel benefactors expect.' Then, his piece said, he softened. 'What is it, Mr Brogan?'

'Frank here's looking for some tips with his speech. He's nervous as a dog, Mr Charles.'

Maynard adjusted his spectacles and, taking the ragged piece of paper from Billy's hand, took in everything that was written there.

'It's an excellent speech, young man. Simple and from the heart – much the same as your good self.' He folded it and pressed it back into Frank's hands. 'But I'm afraid, young man, that you'll have to worry about this in a little while. This show is about to get started.'

Placing a fatherly arm around both Billy's and Frank's shoulders, he ushered them past the Norwegian fir so that they could look, through the frosted windows, out onto the square beyond.

A horse and carriage was just coursing into view.

In the chambermaids' kitchenette, Nancy watched in a small hand mirror as Rosa ran her fingers through her hair, fixing one curl after another, sliding in pins and twists of white ribbon, until at last she stood back and smiled.

'Hélène Marchmont never looked half as stunning as this, Nance,' said Rosa.

Ruth – who'd been watching from behind, ready to help Nancy into her dress – added, 'I hate to admit it, but Rosa's done you proud.'

A champagne cork popped.

'Teacakes and toast, hot buttered scones and champagne!' Mrs Moffatt announced.

In the kitchenette, the gaggle of girls cheered. Soon they were raising glasses.

'The first toast of many,' sang Mrs Moffatt. 'To Nancy Nettleton – soon to be Nancy de Guise!'

'Now for the dress,' grinned Rosa.

She was already holding it up against Nancy, and Nancy fancied she could feel, in its silken touch, the way her mother used to hold her tight. She felt a tear come to her eye, but battled it down. This was not a day for sadness. This was a day for celebration. Her parents would be celebrating with her too.

At that moment, footsteps floundered into the kitchenette – and, when the girls turned as one, they discovered Frank standing there.

Frank's eyes were on his sister. 'You look just like Ma, Nance.'

'Off with you, Frank!' Rosa continued. 'Honestly, have you no sense of—'

'Had to come,' Frank panted. 'Came as fast as I could. Horse and carriage is here. Just turned up on Berkeley Square.'

'Horse and carriage?' breathed Nancy. 'But Frank, we're getting a taxicab.'

Frank shook his head. 'Seems not, Nance. He's sitting out there right now, two bright white stallions knee deep in the snow. Says Raymond reserved him all the way back in September. Says it's been in his calendar for months.'

All around the kitchenette, the girls – even Mrs Moffatt – broke into spontaneous applause.

'I'll bet Raymond's not getting there in nearly as much style.'

The fact was, Raymond wasn't getting anywhere at all.

The Rolls-Royce limousine had stuttered to a halt somewhere on the Wapping Wall, where the warehouses crowded the river. Between a gap in the buildings, Raymond – who stood with his face screwed up, the bonnet open and the engine exposed to the air – could see the snow swirling over the river and, on the opposite bank, the Prospect of Whitby public house, shrouded in ice. In the driver's seat, Artie kept heaving on the starter.

'What do you see, Ray?'

*Nothing*, thought Raymond. *Nothing at all.*

'I'm a dancer, not a mechanic!' he called. He'd taken off his jacket and rolled up his sleeves, but there was oil on his fingers from where he'd opened her up and, somehow, he'd already smeared it across his face. 'Artie, we're meant to be there already.'

'All right, all right, keep your hair on, old boy. I suppose I'll have to have a look myself.'

Soon, both Cohen boys were standing in the strafing snow, staring at the engine's innards.

'This wouldn't have happened if we'd got a taxicab like I wanted.'

'It's just a bit of an adventure, Ray. Not everything in the world runs like your Buckingham Hotel. Sometimes things go wrong. You just got to . . .'

Artie had reached his hand into the engine, and now he recoiled, sucking on burned fingers.

'She's overheated,' he said. 'That's what it is.'

Raymond turned a pirouette, taking in the frozen city.

'It's the dead of December.'

'Car doesn't know that, does it? Can't blame a chunk of machinery for the cold. She'll just have to cool down . . .'

'You don't know that.'

'Look, Ray, you might know more about chassés and glides and shimmies and *tours en* bloody *l'air*, but you don't know a thing about cars. Just leave this to someone who does. I'm your best man, aren't I? Am I really going to let you down?'

'Artie, you're insufferable!' Raymond cried. 'The only thing you actually know about cars is how to steal one!'

Artie scowled. 'It's going to be like that, is it?' He would have stalked off, there and then, if only there was anywhere to stalk to. 'Look, if we're a little late, what's it going to matter? It'll be something to remember.'

Raymond gasped. 'I wasn't aware I'd need a complete and utter disaster to *remember* my wedding day.' He paused. 'Look, imagine, for just one second, that this was happening to you.'

'It *is* happening to me. I'm here, aren't I?'

'Imagine it was you marrying Vivienne today and—'

Artie snorted. 'I won't be getting to *my* wedding in a Rolls, Ray, you can wager your life savings on it.'

'Neither would I,' Raymond roared, 'if you hadn't found one!'

'There's the spirit!' laughed Artie. 'Now you're getting into the swing of things. A bit of a laugh, Ray, that's all this is. We'll be out of here in—'

'Vivienne wouldn't let you hear the end of it.'

'Our Viv wouldn't care.'

'Artie, you think you know Vivienne, but you only know the thin end of it. You've got a world of chaos coming your way, with a girl like her. You don't know it yet, but you can't handle her. Not the Vivienne I know.'

Artie snapped, 'It's you who doesn't see it, Ray. It's *you* who can't handle someone as fiery and truthful and honest as Nancy Nettleton. All of these big romantic gestures you do – it doesn't mean nothing to a girl like Nancy. All of your grand gestures and postures, like life's one of your dances, with all of its drama and its big fancy show. Yeah, Ray, it's *you* who doesn't know what he's getting into. Married life isn't going to be like it is in the Grand, you old . . .'

While he'd been ranting, Artie had reached through the door of the limousine, hammering his fist over and again at the starter button on the dashboard. The feeble protests of the engine had continued unabated, but now – as if to imitate old Alma Cohen, who had spent too many years of her life marching into a room and roaring to stop some argument between her sons – it burst into glorious life.

Artie and Raymond looked at one another. It took less than a second for the fury to bleed from each of their faces. Slamming the engine cover shut, Raymond slipped back into the passenger seat and grunted, 'On your way, Artie. Nancy'll be getting there first. Maybe we've got a hope, though, if all this snow slows down the horse and carriage—'

'Horse and carriage?' hooted Artie. 'There you are, Ray, with another one of your romantic gestures! Horse and carriage, Ma! Can you believe it?'

In the back seat, the three Cohen women had set up a hullabaloo.

'Just drive, Artie.'

The limousine jumped forward, gliding out across the ice-encapsulated road.

'We'll get you there, Ray. We're on our way now, I promise.' He paused. 'Friends?'

'Friends,' Ray said.

'That's you and me, Ray. Just a couple of East End chancers, on our way to better things. Look, if there really is a war coming, it's better we're both in love, isn't it? And . . .' Artie could barely say the next words. They seemed to wither and die on his tongue. 'I love you, big brother,' he eventually grunted.

Nor could Raymond look him in the eye when he said, 'Yeah, Artie, I love you too.'

Up above them, the snow-capped turrets of the Tower of London hurtled by.

Marylebone Town Hall sat like it too was a bride, wearing a deep veil of snow.

When the limousine guttered to a halt, Raymond rubbed the condensation from the window with his sleeve and saw the guests already milling outside. That gave him some hope. There was still a chance he wasn't too late. Yet, as he emerged onto the hard-packed ground, where the trails of all their manifold guests had left indentations in the snow, he heard the bells pealing from St Mary's and knew that the hour had already come. Before the engine was dead, he was floundering to the white marble steps, up the stairs between the hall's great pillars, and towards the great open doors. Flurries of snow followed him as he went.

On the steps, familiar faces abounded. That they were not yet sitting had to mean something. He saw Billy Brogan and Maynard Charles. He saw Gene Sheldon and Mathilde Bourchier. Just inside the doorway, Mrs Moffatt stood alongside Archie Adams – and there, beside them, Hélène Marchmont stood in the shadow of a gentleman who radiated the elegance and grace of some elder statesman of dance. Even from behind, Raymond recognised his thick grey hair, styled like some baron from an earlier, gilded age.

'Raymond de Guise,' intoned Georges de la Motte, in his rich, bass voice, 'did I teach you nothing about making an entrance?'

Raymond staggered to a halt. 'She isn't here yet?'

'Raymond, by tradition, the groom arrives first.'

'Then I made it!'

Georges gazed upon his former protégé with an expression of astonishment.

As Raymond straightened himself, Hélène rushing to tidy the creases in his shirt and morning jacket, he heard Artie calling for him somewhere behind. When he looked back through the open doors, he could see that his mother had slipped on the ice and was being hoisted back to her feet by Aunts May and Rebecca – but, before they climbed the town hall steps, there came another sound: the striking of hooves on the road outside.

It was the signal everybody needed. Soon, all the milling guests were flocking past Raymond, along the corridor and into a hall panelled in oak, where chairs were arrayed around a simple table adorned with flowers, and the ceiling tiles decorated in bas-relief.

Bustling their mother and aunts past, Artie grabbed Raymond by the arm.

'I told you we'd get you here, you old blackguard.'

'You've got the rings, Artie?'

Artie began to pat each of his pockets, his face etched in a pantomime of panic.

'I've got them, Ray,' he finally said, laughing, shaking his head in disbelief. 'When are you going to learn to trust old Artie?'

Together, they hurried into the hall. At the table in front, the solemn-faced registrar was waiting.

As they crossed the room, one other figure caught Raymond's eye. There was Vivienne Edgerton, sitting alone at the end of one row, her folded hands barely enough to conceal the secret she'd been carrying so long. They were whispering about her in the rows behind. Some of them were staring fixedly – but Vivienne herself sat with her head held high, refusing to be cowed.

Artie lifted his brows. 'Hullo there, Viv,' he said, grinning as they passed.

Vivienne flushed a deep scarlet, but after that she could not conceal her cheer; in the corner of his eye, Raymond saw her smirking. What kind of a wonder was this: whispers were flurrying in every corner of the hall, meaning to do her down, but all it took was the flash of a smile from Artie to put her world to rights.

They had hardly reached the head of the hall and made their introductions to the registrar when Raymond heard the footsteps somewhere behind him: the clicking of heels on the marble floor outside. Soon, an expectant hush had settled over the oaken hall. Soon, he could hear the other guests cooing, the ripple of whispers and, here and there, a smattering of eager applause.

'You may as well look,' whispered Artie, out of the side of his mouth. 'You'll see her soon enough.'

So he did.

The doors at the bottom of the hall had opened, and through them appeared Rosa and Ruth, each in the eggshell-blue dresses they'd bought. As they approached, the door behind them opened again – and there, in its frame, stood Nancy and Frank, their arms intertwined, locked closely together as they began the approach.

The whole hall was on their feet now, but through the sea of people, Raymond met Nancy's eyes.

The dress she was wearing.

The chain that glittered around her neck.

The way the chambermaids had fixed her hair, so that there was nowhere to hide from the simple, faultless beauty of her eyes.

Nancy Nettleton.

In mere moments, she was going to be his wife – and Raymond de Guise, who had waltzed with princesses, who had foxtrotted across the Continent in the company of lords, who had been courted, at home and away, as a star for the ages, had never been happier in all of his life.

'Ladies and gentlemen!' announced Archie Adams, up on stage with the rest of the orchestra. 'May I introduce – Mr and Mrs Raymond de Guise!'

The stage doors opened – and there, framed between them, stood Raymond and Nancy, man and wife.

'Shall we?' Raymond whispered.

Nancy looked at him and squeezed tight on his hand.

'Let's,' she whispered in return.

'Watch me for the changes,' said Raymond. 'And have fun, *Mrs de Guise!*'

The band struck up.

It was a slow number – at first. One of Archie's old-time waltzes, it began luxuriously, and Nancy and Raymond sailed into it with the elegance of the old world. Somewhere in the heart of the dance floor, Raymond lifted Nancy for the first time and, holding her poise, she allowed herself to be whirled around, so that she could see – rushing by in fits of colour – all the guests who'd come to her wedding, and the others who were joining them for the reception. The rest of the chambermaids, wearing the gowns they'd saved for all year, were crowding at the balustrade, overwhelmed to see the Grand Ballroom come to life for the very first time. Raymond's family were cheering, as loud and uncouth as they liked, for their new family member – and there stood Vivienne between them, Artie on one side and Alma on the other. Nancy caught only a fleeting sight of her, but seeing the expression on her face lifted her heart – for it seemed like Vivienne Edgerton truly *belonged*. If they were still whispering about her here – and surely they were, because gossip and rumour did not end, not even for a wedding – they would go unheard. Everywhere was love.

The moment Nancy's feet touched the ballroom floor, the band changed number. On the edge of the dance floor, where Rosa stood with Ruth, faces screwed up in consternation. No one had ever heard Archie Adams play a number quite like this.

Rosa recognised it straight away. It was the Benny Goodman hit, 'Peckin''. Hardly a year old, already it felt like a standard.

She'd danced to it a hundred times with Frank, up in the kitchenette with the gramophone turning, or out on a Saturday night. But to hear it in the rarefied grandeur of the Grand Ballroom was to hear it as it had never been before. And to see Raymond and Nancy de Guise turning it around each other, freewheeling with skips and hops, coming together and apart again, was something more magical still. Soon, she could feel its rhythm rippling around the room.

The song reached its climax. It swelled and swelled again . . .

The doors at the back of the dance floor opened up, and out streamed Hélène Marchmont, in the arms of Georges de la Motte; Jonas Holler whirling with Karina Kainz; all of the dancers of both companies, launching into wild, ecstatic jives of their own.

And, last of all, Rosa's own Frank Nettleton, soaring into view with Mathilde Bourchier in his arms.

Rosa thrilled. Frank looked resplendent in a suit of navy blue, with his hair coiffured in a way that made him seem like Raymond de Guise in miniature. Mathilde might have stood three inches taller than him – and she in a gown that drew every eye, of silver satin and golden brocade – but there was something in the way Frank moved that sent yet more waves of joy around the ballroom. He was the heart of the storm, turning like a dervish around Mathilde, hopping and weaving and kicking, describing such beautiful arcs that, when Georges de la Motte sailed by, he gazed on the boy with a look as if he was giving a blessing.

Even Maynard Charles, who stood with his hands folded in the small of his back at the head of the balustrade, seemed to approve.

'Your young man has spirit,' he said simply, as he lifted himself and walked past.

388

'He does, doesn't he, Ruthie? My Frank? Maybe Mr Charles really might give him his chance this time.'

From the dance floor, Frank had caught her eye. She thought she had never seen him so alive.

Ruth's eyes were on Mathilde.

'Don't you get jealous, Rosa?'

'Jealous? Me?'

'Why, of Frank and that beautiful girl. She's younger than we are, Rosa, and she's so . . . beautiful.'

'Oh, Ruth, you'd think *you* were jealous of *Frank*!'

Before Ruth could answer, the Archie Adams Orchestra brought the number to its triumphant close. Archie stood, opening his arms to the whole hallowed hall, and cried out, 'Ladies and gentlemen, at your leisure!'

It was the cue everyone was waiting for. In moments, guests were flocking down for perhaps their only chance of dancing in the famous Grand. Alma was wrestling some poor unsuspecting footman onto the dance floor. Chambermaids were tumbling over each other to grab the hands of the best-looking porters and concierges. Alone among them all, only Mrs Moffatt seemed to be showing any decorum. Ruth had never seen her look quite as elegant before. Without her apron, and with her hair pinned up, Mrs Moffatt looked ten years younger than she ever had.

On the dance floor, Frank and Mathilde had come apart – and, as Mathilde was swept into the arms of some other suitor, Frank whirled Rosa around on the spot. In moments, the orchestra had struck up a new number: another wild, energetic jitterbug. Ruth gazed on – first at Raymond and Nancy, the centre of it all, and then at Frank and Rosa, who were making miniature whirlwinds of their own. Rosa was right, she reckoned. She

389

*was* jealous. She'd been resisting the feeling all year. But, as she gazed on them now, some other piece of the puzzle was becoming clear to her. It wasn't that she wanted Raymond for her own. It wasn't that she dreamed of cuddling up with Frank. It wasn't even that she wanted the same sense of union and belonging that Nancy and Rosa had found – though, to be sure, that was a part of it as well. She smiled, softly, to herself. She wanted what they had, that was true. But she wanted something different as well . . .

She was pulled from these thoughts by a tapping on her shoulder, and a familiar voice that said, 'Hullo, Ruth.'

There was Billy. She had to admit that he was looking handsome. He was wearing a black evening jacket and maroon waistcoat, and at his neck a cravat of the type she'd seen continentals wear. He'd slicked back his hair with pomade and, if you squinted properly, there was even something *debonair* about how he looked today.

He was nervous as well. That was something she hadn't seen before.

'Billy,' she ventured, 'I haven't seen you in weeks.'

'I've been moved to the post room.' He shrugged. 'Important business, for Mr Charles. Well, we've all got to make sacrifices for the good of the hotel, haven't we? And . . .' He stopped. 'Sorry, Ruth, enough hotel talk! We're here for a wedding. And . . . you're not dancing. So I wondered – would you dance with me? Now, look, I know what you're thinking. Billy Brogan can't dance! But I've been practising and I'm getting better and maybe, just maybe—'

'I'll dance with you.'

Billy had blathered on for another ten seconds before he registered what she'd said, blinked and asked, 'Really?'

'Come on,' Ruth said, 'before I change my mind.'

Down on the dance floor, Billy tried to let the music flow through him, just like Frank had said. He turned to the music, he kicked and he hopped – and when, half a song in, he began to sense that people were dancing *away* from him, as if fearful they might be caught in the fallout from some disastrous move, he retreated inside himself, counting out loud. *One, two . . . three, four . . . One, two . . . three, four . . .* Something must have been wrong, because even counting wasn't working. Soon, he had abandoned that as well, and just let it happen instead. The most amazing thing was: Ruth even let him.

'Well,' said Billy, when the orchestra was getting ready for another number, 'maybe we should . . .'

Ruth grinned. 'A glass of champagne?'

'That sounds like just the ticket.'

Back at the balustrade, they watched the others cavort. Slowly, inch by inch, Billy danced his fingers along the rail, until they touched hers.

Ruth let them linger there for a time, before withdrawing her hand.

'I'm sorry, Billy,' she said, barely loud enough to hear.

'It's all right,' said Billy. 'It really is. I've known it all year, Ruth. In here – in my heart. It's not anyone's fault who they fall for, is it? Them out there, they're the lucky ones – they fell in love with each other, right here in the hotel. It isn't like that for everyone. Sometimes, you don't know who you're going to fall for, until it hits you in the face, and . . . You're special, Ruth. You act like you ain't, but I reckon you are. It's your choice who you fall for – if you fall for anyone at all! And I hope you do, because—'

'Shhh, Billy.'

He looked at her, and she was smiling.

'Thank you,' she whispered.

'We can be friends, can't we? We can have a laugh together? This year, Ruth, it's—'

'Nearly over,' said Ruth.

*Yes*, thought Billy, *but the rest of it isn't.*

The sneaking and the spying. The shadow men, trying desperately to waylay and propagate wars. The tasks Mr Charles asked of him, which seemed to be growing darker by the day. In the middle of all that, he needed some light. If it wasn't to be love, it could at least be friendship.

'I need to laugh,' he said. 'Who knows what next year's going to bring? 1939, a mystery waiting to be solved! Until then, Ruth, it'd be nice to have a friend. It'd be nice to laugh.'

Ruth nodded. In the confusion of her heart, that was what she needed too.

'Well, if it's a laugh you need, then perhaps,' she dared to say, 'we ought to get dancing again?'

Billy Brogan smirked.

After the dancing: the dinner.

The staff in the Queen Mary restaurant, though under strict instructions not to neglect their duties to the hotel, had worked tirelessly to provide the de Guise wedding with the most delectable dinner with which a newly-wed couple had ever treated their guests. And so it was that, around the great dining tables set up in the Grand, Raymond and Nancy de Guise began their married life by breaking the crust of a Lancashire hotpot and toasting their guests.

Hélène Marchmont counted herself fortunate to have been seated beside Louis Kildare. It was, she supposed, a generosity on Raymond's part to sit her with her very best friend. There was something about being here in the Grand, and not having to indulge anybody by stepping into their embrace, that pleased her. Perhaps the feeling would not last long, but today she felt freer than she had in weeks.

The toasts were about to begin. At the head table, Artie Cohen – who looked like a scurrilous imitation of his brother – was getting to his feet, unfurling a scrappy-looking leaf of paper and sizing up his audience.

Louis leaned close and said, 'There's a man who looks like he holds some secrets. What do you think he has up his sleeve, Hélène?'

Hélène whispered, 'Nothing like the secret *we* kept, Louis, I'm sure of it.'

And Louis laughed. 'Raymond has skeletons in his wardrobe. I'm sure of it.' He paused, the laughter draining from his voice. 'Hélène, we haven't talked in so long. What Archie found for you, in Chicago . . .'

At the head table, Artie Cohen had lifted his champagne flute and, taking a little silver spoon, began tinkling out a melody on its rim. Table by table, an expectant silence spread across the Grand Ballroom.

'Later, Louis,' Hélène whispered – and, before she could say any more, Artie had begun.

'Ladies and gentlemen, that was a *show*.'

Artie clapped his hands. At his side, Raymond – his hand clutching Nancy's under the table – seemed to tense. The fact that his brother had no prepared notes in his hand was making his stomach sink.

'Most of you don't know me, but my name is Arthur Cohen, and I have had the honour and responsibility of being your man Raymond's little brother ever since I was born. Yes, ladies and gents, when your dashing, debonair lead dancer was but a squalling little pup, there was I, right at his side. Raymond's two years older than me, but even when we were little I still had a wiser head on my shoulders than your Ray would ever develop. Yes, if it wasn't for me, Raymond might never have made it through those early years. He might never have become the man we see before us today – the man who, at long, long, *long* last, has had his feet brought back to ground by the love of our dear Nancy Nettleton. Because, you see, though you know him as Raymond de Guise, the darling of the ballroom, the truth is that our story begins in much less salubrious surroundings. Ladies and gentlemen, let me take you back to the beginning. . .'

*So this is how it's going to be*, thought Hélène – and, as Artie Cohen rambled on, in a style fit more for a hearth or the back room of some East End taproom than the luxurious setting in which they now gathered, he matched her expectations word for word.

There had been a time, only a few short years ago, when the truth of Raymond's upbringing had been a closely guarded secret at the Buckingham. The arrival of Nancy Nettleton had put paid to all that; as soon as she had entered his life, his secrets had started to disintegrate. Now, there were few in the hotel who didn't know the story of how Ray Cohen had escaped the impoverishment of his childhood, rising up through the dance halls and competitions, into the tutelage of Georges de la Motte, and greater glories beyond. But to hear it told with such passion and drama – and not to mention the brotherly jibes that kept flying – was to hear it as if for the first time.

'Of course,' Artie said, getting ready to raise his glass, 'we all thought he was lost. Lost to ballrooms and palaces. Lost to places as grand as this one we're standing in right now. Lost, if I may say so, in his own dreams. Good luck to him, we thought. Maybe we'd catch sight of him one day, our dear, darling Ray, on the billboards in Piccadilly Circus. But then along came Nancy Nettleton. A force of nature, ladies and gentlemen. A force of goodness. An angel, in a chambermaids' apron, who took one look at our Ray and decided she was going to save him from himself.'

Artie turned from Raymond, who had been weathering the storm with good cheer, and faced Nancy. For the first time, though the twinkle remained in his eyes, he was hushed and serious.

'Nancy, we couldn't ask for a finer girl to join our family – and, though we won't share the same name, we'll forever count you a Cohen at heart. You have come into our lives and shown us that there is goodness everywhere in the world, if only you care to find it – in gilded palaces like this, or the down-and-out corners where the Daughters of Salvation do all their work. But, more than anything, you've brought out the very best in my brother. You're kind and gentle – and a little bossy, if I'm honest, every now and then. And that's what my brother needs. You complement each other more beautifully than two ballroom dancers ever did. There isn't anything more important than being with the people you love' – here, if Hélène was not mistaken, Artie's eyes flashed to Vivienne Edgerton – 'and especially in times like the ones we're living through right now. Nancy, we love you for it, and we always will.'

Now that he'd said what he needed to say, the devil came back to Artie Cohen. He thrust his glass high, sloshing champagne over his own head, and cried out, 'To Mr and Mrs Raymond de Guise!'

All around the ballroom, the cheers rose high.

As Artie sat down and, at the other end of the table, Frank nervously rose, the hubbub of quiet conversation could be heard rippling around. Catching Louis's eye, Hélène said, 'It's what everybody needs, isn't it? What Artie said – family comes first.'

'It's their loss, Hélène,' Louis whispered. 'You gave them every chance.'

Hélène said, 'I didn't mean them. I mean *me*. What am I doing, Louis? Why is there even a choice? I can't live my days like this. She's growing up so fast. I should be there for her. I should be there *with* her.'

She tried not to focus on it, because Frank was getting ready to speak, but you did not get to choose when moments of such clarity descended on you. Suddenly, she *knew*.

'I can't last here, Louis. It's *right* that I shouldn't. I've been clinging on to it. Just wanting things to go back to how they were. But . . . how they were isn't how they *should* have been. I have that choice now. I can go to Chicago and . . . '

Frank stuttered out his first words and, around the Grand Ballroom, silence returned.

'W-wow,' he said. 'One moment dreaming of d-dancing in here . . . and the next, not only d-dancing, but giving a speech as well. Where to begin . . . ?'

Frank might not have been the natural raconteur that Artie was, but he'd prepared so diligently that it hardly mattered. The notes were in his hand, but they were imprinted upon his heart as well.

He began to speak of his childhood: how Nancy had cooked and cleaned for him; how she'd taken him to school and read to him afterwards; how it was Nancy who'd made sure he could cope after their father's death; Nancy who had blazed the trail that he followed down to London.

Hélène heard the tapping of footsteps behind her, and was startled to feel a hand gently touching her shoulder. When she craned around, Mr Arkwright, the day manager on the check-in desks, was behind her.

He bent low and whispered into her ear, 'Telegram, Miss Marchmont. Delivered to the desk. I'm afraid it's urgent.'

'You're my world, Nancy,' Frank was saying, 'but if I have to share you with Raymond, well, I couldn't think of anyone I'd rather share you with. Mr de Guise, may you treasure Nancy, as I know you will, for all of your years. May I live by the example you set together. And may we all live many years of happiness together – one family, from now and evermore – whatever the world throws in our way.'

'Can it wait?' asked Hélène, in a hushed whisper.

'I'm afraid not, Miss Marchmont.'

Hélène looked at Louis, whose face was creasing in concern, and, with as little fuss as possible, followed Mr Arkwright out of the Grand.

In the reception hall, where the business of the Buckingham Hotel went on unabated, a party of Swiss financiers were checking in. Hélène slipped past them and reached the desk. Tobias

Bauer was waiting in line, but she sashayed past him and took the telegram from behind the desk.

'A messenger from the Royal Mail office arrived not ten minutes ago, Miss Marchmont.'

The paper was folded in her hands. She fancied she already knew who had sent it. Her parents had never been fond of using the telephone; they held with the older, more trustworthy ways.

She opened it up.

HÉLÈNE. YOUR FATHER HAS PASSED. DARLING, PLEASE BE IN TOUCH. LAST WILL AND TESTAMENT TO BE READ AT LAWTON & LAWTON, FRIDAY 16TH DECEMBER. WITH LOVE, AUNT LUCY.

Hélène must have stood there, lingering over the telegram for too long, because soon a voice said, 'Is everything all right, Miss Marchmont? My poor girl, you look like you've seen a ghost.'

When she looked up, Bauer was standing there with an expression of such gentlemanly concern on his face that it almost thawed her. Then she said, 'Quite all right, Herr Bauer,' and began to drift back towards the Grand Ballroom.

When she got to the door, she saw that the guests had shifted. Many of them were still seated, but others had stood, and all were holding their champagne glasses aloft. Raymond and Nancy, still hand in hand, had left the head table and now stood together at a table near the dance floor's edge, where a three-tier wedding cake, cloaked in white fondant with swirls etched delicately into it to give the appearance of the finest lace, was waiting to be cut. Mrs Moffatt had been the one to hand them the knife (at Nancy's request, she had been the one to bake the cake itself, though the decoration had been left to an artist from a Regent Street boutique), and now she was hurrying back to a seat beside Archie Adams.

Hélène looked over it all. The guests held their breath while, as one, Nancy and Raymond brought the knife down, carving a thin slice. And it hit Hélène, then, as she saw the smile that lit up Nancy's face, how simple things could be, if you stepped back from the splendour, if you closed yourself off from the clamour of voices, if you knew what your heart had been telling you all along.

There wasn't much you needed in life. There was the air that you breathed. There was the food that you ate. And, to give everything meaning, there was the love that you felt.

It didn't have to be the love of a husband, nor lover.

It could be the love of the girl who called you 'Mama' and clung on so tight every time you had to leave.

It wasn't so hard, when it came down to it. The truth was, it had been staring her in the face all along. Perhaps all she'd needed was for the story of her old family to truly end, before she could start forging the story of the new: just Hélène, Sybil, and the city of Chicago.

The Archers would be heartbroken, and this would forever cause her pain. But she'd make love replace that regret. Sybil would feel that love, and that would make everything worthwhile.

In the ballroom, Archie had left Mrs Moffatt behind and wended his way to his piano. So had Georges de la Motte. Together, they were weaving a song. Georges had a rich, baritone voice. It rose up and filled the vaulted ceiling above.

On a night like this, wonders could happen.

She felt as light as the air.

# Chapter Twenty-nine

MRS MOFFATT AWOKE TO THE taste of the sherry from the night before and an anticipation more wild than she'd ever had as a little girl.

It was Christmas Day, and she was about to receive the very best gift of her life.

Christmas morning, however, was just another morning at the Buckingham Hotel. The housekeeping lounge might have been bedecked in streamers – and breakfast might have been a little sweeter than usual, with big slabs of fruit cake sitting in the centre of the table – but the hotel's guests still required their bedlinen to be changed, still demanded their floors to be swept, would still file complaints with the hotel management if their doorknobs and curtain rails were not polished to perfection. A good number of the chambermaids had been permitted the day off to visit family and friends, but many more would have to toil the morning away.

'But it will be worth it,' said Mrs Moffatt. 'Everything you girls have heard about the Grand Ballroom is going to *pale* compared to our own Christmas ball this afternoon.'

Rosa leaned across the table to some of the new girls and said, 'Mr Charles normally sends down champagne. And there'll be little pastry cups from the Queen Mary. And dancing, right here in the housekeeping lounge!'

'But first,' Mrs Moffatt continued, 'we've work to do. Happy Christmas, girls!'

And as she watched them file away, Mrs Moffatt smiled to herself. The girls might have spent that morning in anticipation, but she knew no amount of work was enough to distract her from thoughts of what was coming.

Some hours later, when Christmas afternoon was already paling towards Christmas night and Rosa, Ruth and all the other chambermaids were welcoming various concierges, porters and pages into the housekeeping lounge for singing and dancing, Mrs Moffatt stood by the tradesman's entrance on Michaelmas Mews, wrapped in her thick woollen winter coat. The snow had cloaked Berkeley Square for long weeks already, and in the mews it grew in great palaces of ice against the neighbouring town house walls. Mrs Moffatt felt the bite of the wind.

She waited, and she waited, and she waited some more.

Half an hour passed. Then an hour. She reached into her coat pocket and drew out the last letter he'd sent.

*Dear Emmeline,*

*I am back from our training in the Highlands of Scotland, and have received your invitation. Please don't think ill of me for a tardy reply! I'd be delighted to accept. I still know so little of London, and all that you have said about your hotel fills me with thoughts of how I imagined England would be when I was a boy: the palaces, the spires, the guards on parade! I will be there, with all the pleasure in the world.*

*Your son,*

*Malcolm*

But he wasn't here. Mrs Moffatt had sent him directions. She'd sent him her love. She'd written to him, often, across the autumn and winter months – and he'd written back too, with tales of his escapades on the base and little snippets of his life back home. Every letter was a fraction of a step closer towards knowing who this man – her son – really was. But to see him again, to invite him into the world she'd made for herself after she gave him away, would have been such a great stride.

And he wasn't here.

She turned away from the tradesman's entrance, her thoughts returning to the warmth of the housekeeping lounge and perhaps a glass of sherry – something to take away the sting of the evening – and there she saw Archie Adams, standing on the other side of the storeroom doors.

'He didn't come, Archie.' Mrs Moffatt trembled. 'I'm an old fool.'

And she started tearing at the letter in her hands – then stood back, aghast, at what she had done.

'I'm sure there's a reason,' she said, moving towards Archie. 'He must have been waylaid. Or perhaps there's a military reason. Something he can't say . . .'

'Come with me, Emmeline.'

She let him guide the way. Soon, they had passed the housekeeping lounge, with the sounds of such raucous fun and laughter emanating from within; then, they were standing on the outskirts of the reception hall, the air filled with the botanic scent of the towering Norwegian fir. Across the black and white tiles, guests still flowed. The early evening hubbub had already begun in the Queen Mary restaurant. Billy was still standing by the check-in desks, looking strangely solemn for Christmas Day.

And there – as if he'd just stepped through the revolving brass doors, still dusting the snow off his big, broad shoulders – stood Emmeline Moffatt's son, Malcolm Brody.

Archie felt the change in Mrs Moffatt's body.

'He hadn't forgotten,' he whispered. 'He's just . . . an Australian. He doesn't quite understand English pomp and circumstance. He just brazened through the main entrance, as if he belonged here.'

'And he does,' Mrs Moffatt said.

She marched across the reception hall to join him. When at last he saw her, Mrs Moffatt didn't hold back. She opened up her arms and wrapped herself around him.

Well, it was Christmas, after all.

On the other side of London, the Cohens had forgone the traditional turkey or goose. Now that their eldest hen had stopped producing eggs in the coop out the back, she was sitting, pride of place, in the heart of the dining table. At the table, Aunts May and Rebecca had set about dishing out the vegetables. Cabbages and carrots and chestnuts roasted on the fire, while Artie grinned as he slashed the carving knife around in the air, making a ridiculous show of himself – so that Alma, when she came in carrying the gravy jug in one hand and the butter dish in the other, had to say, 'He's only showing off, dear. You know how he is.'

'Oh, I do.' Vivienne smiled, and Artie sliced into the bird.

It was only the second time she'd visited the Cohen house, though it felt as if she'd been coming here for years. From the peril of two Christmases ago, to the joy and wonder of this: the family ranged around her *wanted* her to be here; they hadn't left her to rot in a suite at the Buckingham Hotel, hadn't summoned her to their estate out of some misplaced sense of obligation, were not *suffering* her presence, but basking in it instead. As Alma put the gravy jug down, she gazed again at the roundness of Vivienne's belly and said, 'Our first grandchild. Next year, there'll be little feet running around this table. Are you ready, Artie?'

'I've been ready my whole life.'

Alma rather doubted that; responsibility and trustworthiness, dependability and duty had never been words she associated with her younger son. And yet, as she looked at him now, another thought occurred to her: that Artie, much more so than Raymond, knew the meaning of family. He'd been in his fair share of scrapes over the years, he'd made mistakes and paid for them – but he'd never strayed far from the family home, and every single time he'd got into trouble had been because he was trying to do something for the Cohens. No, Alma realised, Artie had sometimes lacked the sense to think things through, but he'd never lacked the heart to care for his family.

She was pooling gravy on Vivienne's plate when she heard a knock at the door.

'I'll get that!' roared Artie, who had finally stripped every fleck of flesh from the chicken carcass and was removing the skeleton, ready for tomorrow's soup.

But it was Vivienne who was on her feet.

'Please,' she said, 'allow me.'

Before anyone could argue, she was in the hall and at the front door. When she opened it up, it was to see a whirlwind of snowy white flakes waltzing along the terrace – and there, framed in the doorway, Nancy and Raymond. From somewhere further down the row, there came the sounds of carollers out on their evening jaunt.

404

'Vivienne,' Nancy gasped, and she stepped within, dusting the hallway with snow. 'You look—'

'Ready to burst,' said Vivienne. There were still three months before her baby would come into the world, but already it seemed interminable. 'I feel strong, Nancy. But . . .' She cupped her hand around her belly. 'Come on, come inside. Alma's already serving dinner.'

She caught the creased-up look on Raymond's face, as if he couldn't quite believe what he was seeing: Miss Edgerton, once the ruin of the Buckingham Hotel, here in his childhood home. Too many worlds were colliding in this moment; it nearly took his breath away.

Vivienne laughed. 'I feel exactly the same! Raymond de Guise, the debonair, elegant statesman of the ballroom – and here's his childhood home! We're just the same, you and I – two fish out of water.'

Alma was waiting to wrestle Nancy out of her overcoat. Then, after a dozen embraces and yet more talk about the baby to come, it was almost time for Christmas dinner to be served.

'But you wait there, you greedy lot,' Alma began. 'We're not all here yet.'

Nancy and Raymond flickered their eyes around the table, taking in each member of the family. It was not a big table, already crowded by the seven adults crammed in around it – but, at its head, at Alma's right-hand side, another place had been laid.

Alma bustled to the bottom of the stairs.

'You can come down now, dear!' she called out.

Then, when there was no reply, she dusted her hands on her apron and heaved herself up the stairs.

'So, you all set, then?' asked Artie, grinning, in his mother's absence. He was already gnawing on a chicken leg, though his aunts looked disapprovingly on. 'Off on honeymoon by New Year?'

'We're to go to Lancashire,' said Nancy, 'and see the old sights. All thanks to you, Vivienne.'

Vivienne nodded, a smile in the corner of her lips.

'The Winter Hollers have taken themselves up there for New Year,' Raymond said, 'dancing at the Empress. We'll see them too. And then . . .'

He reached into his jacket pocket and produced a set of jangling silver keys. On these, Artie's eyes lit up.

'You got it, then? It's yours?'

'Number 18 Blomfield Road, Maida Vale. I'll pick up the keys after Christmas.'

Artie whistled discordantly through his chipped teeth. 'Somehow knew you wouldn't be coming back out east, Ray.'

'But I'll be here, whenever I can,' Nancy said. 'It's decided. I'm not leaving the Buckingham, and I'm not leaving the Daughters of Salvation either.' She paused. 'That is all right, isn't it, Miss Edgerton?'

'Vivienne,' she said. She liked it when they called her *Vivienne,* or when Artie called her *Viv.* 'Not Miss Edgerton, not anymore. Actually, Nancy, Raymond, there's something you ought to know. You see' – she blushed – 'I'm not going to be Miss Edgerton much longer.' She paused, lifted herself in her seat. 'I'm going to be Mrs Cohen.'

Raymond, too, raised himself up. He reached out for Nancy's hand, only to find she was already clasping Vivienne's.

'We don't know when,' Vivienne said. 'Perhaps not until after the baby. But I'm done with people looking down on me. This is what I'm doing. And, Nancy, you'll always be welcome at the Daughters of Salvation. *Always*. Whether you have children or not, whether you're with the Buckingham or not – that place is yours as much as it's mine.' She paused. 'It's going to work. Even without my stepfather's stipend, we've worked it through. Mr Peel's still supporting us, and there are friends of his, other benefactors, who want to help too. When we can, there'll be new premises and . . .' She stopped. 'Artie and I are going to find a place, aren't we, Artie?'

Artie nodded. 'We are.'

'We'll move there as soon as we can, and we'll grow the Daughters – and I'll be a mother, the best mother I can, a better mother, I'm sure, than my own ever was. And—'

Nancy was still clasping her hand. 'Vivienne, you *will*.'

'Moving out of the family home, Artie?' Raymond beamed. 'Why, it's almost as if you're . . . growing up at last!'

Artie whipped his head around. 'Less of that tongue, de Guise.'

'Why not just stay here though, Artie? Ma would love to keep you around.'

'Oh, she's got her hands full,' Artie said. 'And me and Viv, we need our own—'

'Hands full?' asked Raymond. 'What the devil with?'

There was the sound of a creaking floorboard, of footsteps on the stairs.

'Take a look for yourself, Ray,' said Artie, dishing out roast potatoes onto each plate. 'This family just keeps on growing.'

Raymond and Nancy turned. There, in the hall doorway, at the bottom of the staircase, Alma was standing with a little girl with dark hair and a dark complexion. As tall as Alma's shoulder, she might have been nine or ten years old. She had little black eyes and plump cheeks, which might have dimpled had she smiled. Only, the nervousness that was written on her was all too clear.

'Raymond,' Alma began, 'Nancy, I'd like you to meet Leah Elkamm.'

Raymond had no words. Nor, for a moment, did Nancy. Finally, through the bewilderment, she stood and went to the girl's side, crouching to take her hand.

'I'm pleased to meet you, Leah,' she said, her voice rising with the quality of a question.

'Take a seat, Leah, dear,' said Alma, and together they came back to the table.

'Well, you'll remember, Ray,' said Artie, dolloping great splodges of bread sauce, thick with onion and clove, onto each plate. 'We was in that café in Blackpool. You know – you had that stink of a hangover, on account of not stopping drinking for even a second on the sleeper train up.'

Nancy raised her eyebrows.

'There was that newspaper, Ray. Homes wanted, for child refugees. After that nastiness in November. All these poor mites, without a place to go to. All those mothers and fathers, getting shot of their young 'uns, if only to give 'em a chance. Well, I brought that paper back with me. Showed it to Viv, and all the rest. Turns out there's thousands like young Leah here. They're bringing them in from Berlin, Bavaria, anywhere the Nazis are rounding people like us up and casting 'em out. Some viscount or other dreamed the scheme up. Bring the kiddies here, find 'em decent homes for as long as it lasts.' He looked up. 'We're going to see Leah here right, see. It ain't much, not considering what those monsters are brewing over there, but every little counts.

They say we're not at war yet, but we are. It's the war of being kind against being cruel.'

Artie might have said more, then – but hunger had got the better of him, and he had already stoppered his mouth with a whole roast parsnip.

'The family's getting bigger, then,' said Nancy, if only to break the silence. She took them all in, and thought: what a wonder family really was.

'So, who are we toasting to?' Alma grinned, raising her glass. 'My new daughter Nancy, or my daughter-to-be, Vivienne? My grandchild, cooking in there, or our borrowed daughter from far away, Leah?'

Smiles were ricocheting around the table. There was nothing better than smiles like these.

'Oh, hang it!' Alma cheered. 'To all of us, each and every one!'

Night had already cast its cloak over Berkeley Square. Christmas night – and, through the revolving doors of the Buckingham Hotel, there came the sound of carollers working their way around the opulent town houses.

But in the housekeeping lounge, there was music of an altogether different sort.

Louis Kildare, Gus Black and Harry Dudgeon of the Archie Adams Orchestra had set up in the corner. Gus had the voice of an angel, and in the confines of the housekeeping lounge they were making a riotous din. When Billy stepped through the doors and saw the tables all pushed to one side, Frank and Rosa jiving in the spot where the chambermaids ordinarily took breakfast, it brought such a smile to his face that the pent-up tension of the last weeks slipped off him. Perhaps, he thought – as he found a drink and made a silent toast to Ansel Albrecht – this was what Frank had always meant when he spoke about *letting the music flow through you.*

'Billy!' Rosa called out, spying him from the makeshift dance floor. 'Come and join in!'

'I can't stay, Rosa. I'm still on shift. Triple pay Christmas night!'

'One dance, Billy. It's Christmas!'

Billy flashed his eyes around, looking for a partner – and there was Ruth, chinwagging with two of the other chambermaids on the other side of the room. Billy waved Rosa away – she needed very little persuasion to dive back into her dancing with Frank – and hurried to join the girls.

'You won't believe what I've just seen,' he began, finding his brashness once again. 'I was in the Queen Mary and . . .'

It was hard to credit it. Old Tobias Bauer had been there, of course. Christmas dinner for one, all the trimmings – and the waiter and maître d' fawning around him, just the same as they'd done all year: Herr Bauer, their resident refugee, the most congenial of gentlemen. The sight had made Billy's skin crawl, as it did every time their paths crossed ways. This time, however, his eyes had been drawn to something else.

'Right there, in the middle of the Queen Mary – Mrs Moffatt herself! With Archie Adams and a guest for the day. Dressed up, she was, like you've never seen her before! And Archie – well, he looked like he does up on stage, I suppose, in that white evening suit of his, but . . .'

The girls shared a knowing look and, one after another, sighed deeply, as if they themselves had witnessed some beautiful act of love.

'I *knew* there was a reason she wasn't down here with the rest of us,' Rosa called over.

'Haven't we been saying it all year?' Ruth smiled. 'All those times Mr Adams came down here for a cream tea.'

'The next big wedding in the Grand!' Rosa laughed as she continued to dance. 'If it can happen for Mrs Moffatt, it could happen to any of us. Even you, Ruthie!'

Ruth had been enjoying the idea of Mrs Moffatt and Archie Adams walking down the aisle, but now her face darkened.

'Billy,' she said, 'maybe we can get a drink?'

'*Me?*' Billy said, reeling back.

'Well, you're about the only one who *doesn't* talk about me getting a nice young man these days.' She stopped. 'A walk. We could go for a walk?'

Ruth was already marching away. When Billy faltered to follow, Rosa flared her eyes at him – 'On with it, Billy, you big oaf! That's the best luck you've had all year!' – and he felt himself compelled to follow.

Soon, he and Ruth were wandering together around the edges of Berkeley Square. The moon had appeared, fleetingly, through banks of cloud, casting its spectral light over the rolling whiteness of Mayfair. Everywhere, the world glittered.

Billy, who had had the foresight to bring his coat with him but had long since offered it to Ruth, shivered as they passed the carollers on the corner.

*God rest ye merry gentlemen*
*Let nothing you dismay*
*Remember Christ our Saviour*
*Was born upon this day*

Together, they stopped and listened. Words like these warmed the heart on evenings like these, when all around was the unending cold. Billy felt Ruth inching closer to him, wondered for a moment if perhaps her hand might creep across and snake into his. Perhaps his own thoughts turned that way too – there was something about a Christmas night that dispelled all the rejections of the year gone by – but, as soon as he dared himself to dream of it, Ruth spluttered out, 'Billy, I'm sorry.'

'Sorry, Ruth? What for?'

The carol was reaching its zenith, the singers filled with passion, as together Billy and Ruth wandered on, their footfalls silent in the snow.

'Billy, we're friends, aren't we?'

*Friends*, thought Billy, with that familiar plunging feeling inside.

'Of course we are!' he declared, breezily. 'Always will be, if you'll have me.'

'Billy, I know I've treated you badly. I know I've been rude. I know I've been – dismissive, Rosa would say, and Lord, she won't shut up about it, not if you get her started. But the thing is – I know I've been hard on you. And I'm sorry.'

They had wandered a little further when Billy said, 'You don't have to be. Nobody has to like people they don't, do they? That's just my rotten luck. But it's not your fault, Ruth. We don't choose who we fall in love with. Love chooses us.'

'It's not just that, Billy. It's . . . I haven't been honest.'

Billy stopped. That sinking feeling he had, it was beginning to merge with all of the other sinking feelings he'd had since Ansel Albrecht. He looked around himself. It was only a short march through the dark here, down through the town houses and across the broad thoroughfare at Piccadilly, to the Merchant Colonial Club. The tension of those lonely trudges through the snow was like a heavy stone in the pit of his belly.

'Ruth?'

'Oh, Billy,' she said – and it seemed to him, then, that she was wrestling with herself. 'They've been asking me all year why I won't give you a chance. Why I won't give *any* boy a chance. Telling me I'll end up an old maid – and don't I want to feel like they do? I keep looking at them, at Rosa and Frank, and Nancy and Raymond, and thinking – yes, I do want *that*. I want that feeling they have. I'm jealous of it. I am! I can't deny that. And then I was looking at them dance, on the day Nancy got married. Frank was with Rosa, and the two of them, they looked divine. Like they were made for each other. I wanted to be one of them. I wanted to be . . . Frank.'

Billy was silent, as if she might say more, but when there was only the silence and the snowfall, he said, 'Ruth, we all want to feel it. When it happens, it happens. I don't know if—'

'No, Billy, you don't understand. I was watching them dance and feeling that envy I've been feeling all year. And I realised – it wasn't Rosa I was jealous of, it was Frank. I would have given anything to be down there, and Rosa with her arms around me, leading me in that dance.'

Billy said, 'Oh,' and for a time that was all.

'I think I've always known. Somewhere inside me. It's like that night we went to the Starlight Lounge. All you wanted to do was dance – and all I wanted to do was sit at my table with that girl, Martha. I didn't stop thinking about her all night, Billy. I thought I was jealous of her. She was so beautiful. She knew her own mind. I thought it was that I wanted to be beautiful too.

But, no, it was . . . the other thing.' She stopped. 'I've heard about people like me. Something wrong in the head and—'

Billy closed the gap between them, dared to put his hands on her shoulders.

'Oh, Ruth, you're not *wrong*.'

'I fall in love with girls, Billy. How can that not be . . . ?'

Together, they turned to the face of the Buckingham.

'I think it's like I said,' whispered Billy. 'We don't choose who we fall in love with. Love chooses us.'

It wasn't until he'd spoken that he realised his arm was around her, and it wasn't until some moments later that it occurred to him that she hadn't even recoiled. She was leaning into him, as if she needed him to be there – not, perhaps, in the way he'd once dreamed, but in the way that she needed it, and this was the most wonderful feeling ever. Suddenly, all of the horror he'd felt in the past few months was being washed away.

'I think I could dance with you now, Billy.' She laughed. 'You're a good friend.'

'Oh, Ruth, you've seen me dance. I've tried and I've tried, but I'm not getting any better.'

'I don't think that matters, does it?'

Perhaps it didn't. Slowly, arm in arm, they wended their way back across the picture-postcard expanse of Berkeley Square, in through the tradesman's entrance and towards the housekeeping lounge. *Another fifteen minutes wouldn't hurt*, thought Billy. Nobody would come and chastise him – not on Christmas night. And, besides, one dance with Ruth – whoever she loved – would be a perfect Christmas gift. He deserved that, after everything he'd done for Mr Charles this year.

He was about to slip past the reception hall with Ruth, when a voice halloed him from the shadow of the glittering Norwegian fir – and, when he turned over his shoulder, he saw Tobias Bauer, just emerged from the Queen Mary restaurant.

*Not Bauer*, he told himself.

*Lukas Jager*.

'Mr Brogan!' the old man was calling, in his best imitation of frailty and old age. 'I say, Mr Brogan, might I beg your help?'

Billy's heart sank. There was always a ghost at every feast.

Ruth was still hanging from his hand.

'I'll be quick,' he said. 'As quick as I can.'

'Poor old Mr Bauer,' she said, softly. 'It must be hard to be alone, and so far from home, on Christmas night.'

Billy watched as she made haste back to the housekeeping lounge. Only then, bracing himself and breathing deeply, did he turn to face Bauer. In the meantime, the old man had started hobbling across the floor, holding his cane with its carved otter head as if he might tumble at any moment. Not for the first time, Billy wondered how much of it was an act; whether old Lukas Jager might, at any moment, pick himself up, wield that cane like a baton, and come out fighting. There had to be some strength in him, after what he'd done to poor Ansel. Dancing made a man strong. Ansel wouldn't have given up easily.

Billy steeled himself as he said, 'How might I help, sir?'

The old man reached out to touch Billy's hand with his papery, trembling own.

'I wonder if you might . . .' He faltered. 'Dear me, Mr Brogan, I find myself quite short of breath! Too much figgy pudding, I do believe. It's playing with my heart.' He paused, found his composure, went on. 'I have a letter I forgot to send. A little message of Yuletide goodwill, to my sister and her family. I wondered if you might—'

'I'm afraid the hotel post room isn't open on Christmas Day, sir. But if you were to bring it to the desk tomorrow, we'll be sure it reaches the first collection when the post room wakes up.'

'Wakes up? My dear boy, what a turn of phrase you have! The post room, hibernating away – so droll! No, no, I'd feel much better – I really would – if I knew it was all taken care of. It's been preying on my mind. It shouldn't take two moments. It's on my writing desk, just upstairs.'

Billy felt coiled. In the housekeeping lounge, Ruth would be waiting. He would have liked to have danced with her, if only as friends. But here stood Tobias Bauer, and in his eyes all the seeming innocence of old age.

*All the* cunning, Billy reminded himself.

Yet somehow he was standing in the guest lift with Bauer, talking about the Christmas turkey and the chestnut stuffing the Queen Mary made each year. Soon after that, he was following Bauer – at the old man's snail's pace – along the plush crimson carpets of the Buckingham's uppermost storey, wondering again what this letter could possibly contain, what secret pieces of information the old man had picked up in the restaurant that were so vital he had to commit them immediately to paper. What interest did Berlin have in the mystery of who Mrs Moffatt was dining with? What possible purpose was there in Mr Hitler collecting intelligence over what Archie had eaten for dessert, whether the Queen Mary's cranberries were too tart this year, whether Mr Charles had dined alone or with some member of the hotel board?

'I shan't be a moment,' Bauer began, as he led Billy around a corner and to the secluded door of the Park Suite.

'I'll wait here,' Billy said.

His mind was on the housekeeping lounge. His mind was on the ticking clock. His thoughts were on Ruth, and how wounded she might feel if, having just listened to her most intimate secret out on the square, he didn't follow her down.

And perhaps it was because his mind was lost in thought that he barely even registered it as odd when Bauer said, 'Oh no, no, young man, you should come in, please, it's here somewhere. I do appreciate this, Billy. It saves an old man trotting up and down on Christmas night. I'm not a young man like you. I expect you have big things planned! I'm almost ready for bed.'

So Billy followed him in.

The Park Suite was simple and stark, unadorned with the fineries of the other Buckingham suites. Bauer left Billy at the door and hobbled over to the writing desk Mr Charles had had installed by the bedside. From the collection of newspapers and journals on top, he produced a single envelope, with the address already written on the front.

'Here we are, Mr Brogan. Come, take it.'

Billy took three strides deeper into the Park Suite, and reached out to pluck the letter from Bauer's hand.

'Letters are most important, aren't they, young man? They're the heralds we send out into the world.'

Billy looked down. In his hands, Bauer's letter was hanging.

The name on the front: BILLY BROGAN.

He looked, quizzically, back at the old man – and he perceived in him some difference of bearing, some new sense of elegance and poise. The old man's shoulders were slightly less hunched, the creases around his eyes somehow smoothed away. And the cane in his hand – he was not leaning upon it. It was, Billy saw now, little more than a prop.

Or, perhaps, a weapon.

'You may open it, Billy. It is for you, after all.'

The voice was different too. Gone was its lightness, the uncertain warble from the back of the throat. Here was a simple, honeyed voice that oozed with confidence, that expected – no, *demanded* – to be obeyed.

Billy slipped a finger into the envelope, tore it open, lifted out the page within. On it were written only six stark words, inscribed in bold strokes of ink.

I CAN SEE YOU, MR BROGAN

Billy staggered back. His hand was already reaching out for the door but, in a second, Bauer – no, *Jager* – had reached out with his cane and, hooking it around Billy's shin, toppled him to the floor. As he fell, the letter slipped out of his hands.

Billy scrabbled backwards.

He had to pretend.

He had to be everything Lukas Jager was, if he was going to get out of this room alive.

'What's going on, Mr Bauer?'

'Oh, you've no need to call me that anymore, Brogan. You may call me by my true name, if you should like.'

'Lukas Jager.'

'Very clever, my young friend. Of course, it is not only you, is it? A bog-brained boy from the Emerald Isle doesn't have the wherewithal to conduct something like this of his own accord, does he? So you've had paymasters along the way. Maynard Charles, no doubt, and whoever the spooks are running him.'

'No,' said Billy, still lying prone on the floor with Jager's aged, evil eyes staring down into him. 'Just me, Mr Jager. For my friend Ansel. He's the one who told me who you really are.'

Where the words came from, he was not sure. It was instinct, pure and simple. Because, if he wasn't to get out of this room alive – if he really was to join Ansel in the Great Beyond – then he would do it with his head held high. He wouldn't do it begging for his life, giving up the people who mattered to him just for the privilege of a few more moments of life. His family were flashing through his eyes: his mother and father; Patrick and Roisin, and all the rest of the Brogan brood. Little Gracie May, who liked to tease him so mercilessly. He wouldn't let any of them down, not by wasting his last breath begging to a man like Lukas Jager. Not by selling the Buckingham down the river.

'A hero, then.' Jager smirked. That smile changed the whole shape of the old man's face; now he looked pinched and weaselly, twenty years younger, more cunning by far. 'Fancy yourself a hero for the ages, do you, boy? Well, more fool you. I've known about your little scheme for months. Do you think men like me get the wool pulled over our eyes by little boys? What an elegant scheme! To take each letter I wrote and make forgeries of them, eliding things of import, adding little tricks of your own. Counter-subterfuge. Misinformation. The shadow wars. Well, I was leaving breadcrumbs from the start, boy. Special words slipped in, here and there, to identify if my letters were being tampered with. Little turns of phrase that, altered by even a fraction, would alert my associates that my missives were being molested along the way. It took me a little longer to work out that it was you,

Brogan. I'll give you that.' He sneered once again. 'I almost feel sorry for you, boy. You've been used, and you don't even know it. I'll bet they called you a hero, did they? Told you about the great service you were doing for King and country? Well, you imbecile, he's not even *your* king, is he? You Irishmen swear no loyalty to King George.'

'It's not about King and country. It's about what's right.'

'Well, Brogan, let's talk about right. Is what they've asked of you right? Don't you see how these men you work for want to start a war, when what they really ought to be doing is seeking to strengthen the peace? There are many of us trying to make this peace last. Good Englishmen, too. Why do you think I'm stationed in this hotel? The knowledge I've fed back to my associates, about the lords and dukes of England who want the same thing as we do – *peace* – has been invaluable . . .'

Billy was silent, though Jager thundered on. Because there was something in here, something lost between the words he was saying, that meant everything to Billy, that meant that, perhaps, everything he'd been doing this year was not wasted after all – that, perhaps, at the end of it all, even if he died right here on the hotel floor, he'd made a difference in the world.

Jager did not know about the visit of Reichsgraf von Amsberg and Reichsritter Wittekind. He didn't know of their purpose in coming to London. He hadn't reported back on the delegation sent to petition the king. There was hope in that. Buried, perhaps, but hope nevertheless.

'You fool!' Billy screamed. The sudden vitriol caught Jager quite by surprise, and Billy took the chance to scramble to his feet, staggering back from the elder man's outstretched cane. 'You don't want *peace*. Your kind never do. You want – dominion! You only want the peace that comes when good people roll over, when good people don't fight back, when good people give up and let men like you stomp all over them. You don't care about *peace*. You only care about power.'

'I won't be lectured by you, Brogan!'

Jager took a stride forward – but Billy saw, in the way that he moved, that not *all* of the frailties of old age had been an act. He was still stiff. Jager might have been a police officer once, but even police officers got old, with wearied legs and worn-out joints. Billy reached back, clawing for the door.

'You'll go the same way David Albrecht's boy went, that interfering little *schwein*. Of course, the terrible thing was that it wasn't Albrecht's fault.' Jager shook his head ruefully. 'I'm sorry, Brogan. I don't like this any more than you.'

He leaped forward, but in the same moment, Billy's hand had landed on the door and he wrenched it open, tumbling backwards into the hall. Flailing against the walls, somehow he managed to keep upright. Another three strides and he was round the corner. Another three and he was hurtling down the hall, Jager somewhere behind. Billy would have screamed for help, if only he'd had the breath. Instead, he clawed past the Continental Suite, past the Atlantic, heaving the double doors at the end of the corridor apart and throwing himself at the top of the staircase down which Ansel Albrecht had plunged.

He heard a bell ringing somewhere behind him.

At the head of the great palatial landing, the guest lift was opening up.

'Billy?'

That voice – it was the only one that could have stayed him. He looked back, saw Lukas Jager bearing down on the double doors through which he'd just tumbled, saw the guest lift hanging open. There, in its golden cage, stood Ruth. There was no lift attendant tonight – no doubt he was down in the housekeeping lounge, dancing with some chambermaid – so, as the doors rolled back, Ruth stood alone.

'Ruth!' he screamed. 'No, get back down! Go!'

Jager crashed through the doors, reeling onto the landing. The girl in the lift doors must have given him pause, because he stopped dead. Billy could see the ice in his eyes as he took stock of this new situation.

Something lifted Billy out of his stupor. He ripped himself from the top of the stairs, threw himself directly across Jager's path, drove Ruth bodily back into the lift and reached back to haul shut the gate.

'Sorry, Ruth,' he stammered. 'I'm sorry!'

With one fist, he held the golden mesh shut; with another, he pounded the button marked 'ground floor'.

Lukas Jager appeared at the gate, his face criss-crossed by a golden lattice. He too was reaching out, as if he might stop the lift from moving by brute strength alone. But his fingers failed him. Billy was holding Ruth fast as the lift began to grind its way down.

'Billy,' she gasped, 'what's going on?'

'It's Bauer. He's not who you think he is.'

'I saw you follow him into the lift. When you didn't come back, I wondered where you'd . . .'

The floors were passing too slowly. They came to the sixth. The fifth. Each time, Billy prayed that no guest was waiting. Each time, he prayed that Jager hadn't got there first. No doubt he was hoisting himself down the stairs, even now.

'I don't understand, Billy. Mr Bauer, why was he—'

'His name isn't Bauer, Ruth.'

The fourth floor ground past.

The third sailed by.

'His name's Jager. Ruth, he's the one who killed Ansel Albrecht.'

'Killed, Billy? But . . . ?'

Here came the second floor. Here came the first.

'We have to get to Mr Charles,' Billy gasped.

They hit the ground floor. The doors clicked open. Even as they stepped into the reception hall, Billy fancied he could hear footsteps pounding down the guest stairs, just around the corner. He took Ruth by the hand, screamed 'Come!' – and, even though the air was filled with the carolling out on the square, even though they could hear the humming and drumming rising up from the housekeeping lounge directly below, the terror did not leave him. One of the concierges halloed him from the other side of the hall, but Billy did not hear. He was dragging Ruth with him, and he was running for his life.

Christmas Day was but another day in the calendar for a hotel director as steadfast and dedicated as Maynard Charles. In his office, he sat behind his great mahogany desk, a crystal glass of brandy in hand, and heaved a great sigh. On the other side of the table, Archie Adams nodded sadly.

'I'm sorry to drag you away from dinner, Archie. Truly, I am.'

Until moments ago, Archie had been sitting in the rarefied surroundings of the Queen Mary restaurant, savouring his figgy pudding. Maynard had been there too. It was only after he had dined, talking variously with the guests and those among the hotel's staff fortunate enough to be invited to the restaurant this

Christmas, that he had tapped Archie on the shoulder and asked him to accompany him here.

'It came by the last post, two days gone. I've been mulling it over ever since,' he said, turning an opened envelope in his hands. 'I understand why you did this, Archie. I only wish that, perhaps, I might have known.'

Though he proffered up the letter, Archie needed to read no further than the first sentence to know what this was. His eyes roamed down, alighting on the signature of Miss Hélène Marchmont.

'A resignation letter,' Archie breathed.

'She has accepted her place at the Court in Chicago. She's to leave in the New Year. A troupe of dancers to her own. She'll dance with them for a few further seasons, and grow to be their company director. A woman like Hélène will go far, in a place like that. And to escape England now, to be as far from the Continent as the world can take her – well, who could begrudge something like this?' He paused. 'I wish you'd told me, Archie. I wanted to find a way . . .'

Archie Adams felt the weight of it, then.

'I showed her a door, Maynard. I didn't push her through it. Hélène's finished here. You've known this all year.'

'And yet . . .'

The office door crashed open. In a whirlwind of arms and legs, Billy Brogan appeared with one of the chambermaids, Ruth Attercliffe, at his side.

'Brogan,' Maynard Charles began, 'what the devil—'

'It's Bauer!' Billy panted, gulping at the air. 'He knows, Mr Charles.'

In a moment, Maynard was on his feet.

'He tried to kill Billy!' Ruth cried.

The look on Archie's face was one of pure shock, but Maynard was already on his feet, donning his dinner jacket once more.

'Billy,' he said, in the paternal tone of an officer who cares deeply for his young wards, 'where is he now?'

'I don't know, sir. He took me to his suite. Said he had a letter. He knows what we were doing, Mr Charles. He *knows*. But . . . he didn't know about the delegation. About von Amsberg and Wittekind. We steered him away from it. Even though he knew, we . . .'

Maynard had curled his arm around Billy's shoulder, and now he turned him around, returned him to the office door.

'Mr Adams, perhaps you might sit for a moment with young Miss Attercliffe. She may, of course, partake of my brandy, should she wish to – and I would suggest that she should. Miss Attercliffe, I'm going to sort this out now. Stay here, and don't step out of this door.'

Billy was still taking deep gulps of air as Mr Charles shepherded him down the corridor, towards the reception hall.

'Who else saw, Mr Brogan?' Maynard whispered.

'Only Ruth, sir. The rest are at the festivities.'

'Then let us keep it that way.'

They had reached the chequered hall, but they were not alone. Lukas Jager – once again with his cane in his hand, hobbling as if he was frail old Tobias Bauer – was already halfway across the reception area, heading into the sparkling shadow of the Norwegian fir.

'Herr Bauer,' Maynard Charles intoned.

The old man turned. He seemed to be trembling. The quakes moved up and down his body.

'Mr Charles.' He shuddered. 'There he is, that young man at your side. The most heinous of accusations, Mr Charles, the sort you wouldn't believe. I can't . . . I won't stay here a moment longer!'

Maynard glared. 'Perhaps you'd step into my office, Herr Bauer, and we could discuss this – as two civilised men. It is,' he said, without a hint of emotion, 'Christmas Day.'

'And a Christmas Day far from home,' Bauer trembled, 'without friend or family in a thousand miles – and this boy here, accusing me of the most heinous things. And, to cap it all off, his hand in my letters, Mr Charles – my personal correspondence! I've never been treated like this, not in all my years. I fled my home because of persecution. I thought it was safe here. His Majesty has no secret police – no, but you have liars and sneaks all the same!' He paused. 'Your board will hear of this outrage, Mr Charles. A flagrant abuse of my privacy. Lies and blackmail to boot!'

Other faces were watching the old man now, but Maynard remained impassive. Billy could feel his arm still around his shoulder, but no longer was it comforting; it was pinioning him there, refusing to let him move.

'Hush now, Billy,' he whispered.

'But he'll get away, Mr Charles. He killed Ansel.'

'Herr Bauer!' Maynard Charles called out at last. 'You're forgetting. We hold your passport on these premises. It remains secure, in my office safe. Come, and I'll fetch it for you. You will need your passport, won't you, Herr *Bauer*?'

The old man had stalled before the revolving brass doors. And it occurred to Billy, then, that this ruse – this act he'd inhabited for so long – was fraying apart at the edges. No hotel guest fled in the night, not without taking his suitcase and valise with him. No real guest abandoned their passport to the hotel safe.

The man who called himself Tobias Bauer ceased hunching over. He lifted his shoulders, let his cane dangle at his side, turned round with the look, not of Tobias Bauer, but of Lukas Jager, former officer in the Viennese police.

'I think you know I will not, Mr Charles,' he said – and then, with his eyes still on them, he stepped backwards into the revolving door, wheeled on the spot, and stepped out into the veil of curling snow.

Maynard bouldered after him. By the time he reached the bottom of the steps, Jager was already sliding into the back of a waiting taxicab, wheeling away through the snow.

Out there, the carollers still filled Berkeley Square with song.

Billy appeared at Maynard's side.

'Mr Charles,' he whispered, 'he's gone.'

'Yes, Billy.'

'But he won't ever face justice, will he? For what he did to Ansel.'

Maynard was quiet for a long time. He stood there until the chill of night had started to work its way into his bones.

'Now, Billy, listen to me,' he said at last. 'There are different justices in this life. Herr Jager might not find himself locked in a cell by the Metropolitan Police, but there will be justice yet. There always is, for men like him. A murderer and a spy, Billy. The world catches up with men like that. They fall foul of history, one way or another.'

Billy wasn't sure he understood what Mr Charles meant, but found himself nodding all the same.

'He doesn't know what happened here, though, does he? So there's still a hope. Maybe Reichsgraf von Amsberg made his case. Maybe Reichritter Wittekind changed hearts and minds.' He stopped. 'There might still be peace, mightn't there, Mr Charles?'

'Perhaps not peace,' said Mr Charles, 'but we've every chance of prevailing, in whatever's to come. It may seem small, Billy Brogan, what we did in this hotel – but the story of the world is built from a thousand little things. There are few heroes, like there are in myths. I learned that in the last war. But there are little heroes everywhere, if you know where to look.'

'And little villains,' Billy realised. 'There'll be men like Jager all over London, won't there?'

'I should think so.' Maynard paused. 'I've one more task for you, Mr Brogan, if you're willing.'

'Sir?'

'We'll need to send word of this to my Mr Moorcock, by the Merchant Colonial. I'm sorry, Billy. It might be Christmas Day, but the war keeps coming.'

Billy said, 'Of course. But . . . Mr Charles?'

The hotel director arched an eyebrow, as if inviting him to go on.

'I think I should like a quiet spring, Mr Charles. This shadow game – I thought I could play it with you, but it's not for me. See, I've been afraid. And – I should think I'd rather be a soldier than a spy.'

With his arm still around the young man's shoulders, Mr Charles turned Billy around and began to guide him back through the hotel doors. As they crossed the reception hall, their footfalls rang heavily.

A look of deep and grave sadness had manifested upon Maynard Charles's face. He battled to keep it at bay, lest Billy understand the foreboding he was feeling.

'Try not to wish for such things, Billy,' he softly said. 'For they may be coming sooner than any of us should like. But tonight it's Christmas. There are still four hours on the clock. There is still cake to be eaten and mince pies on which we must gorge. And, if it's to be the last before war comes back to this world, well, let us make the most of it. Let me make a toast to you. Billy Brogan – the unsung hero of Christmas night.'

# Chapter Thirty

T HERE WAS AN EYE IN the middle of every storm – and,
for Maynard Charles, Boxing Day had been it. It was
traditionally the day when the hotel director retired
to his own suite, left the day-to-day running of the hotel to his
managers, and took stock of the successes of the year. This year,
he'd been grateful for the perfect oasis of peace and quiet. A
room service trolley left outside his door had all the provisions
he needed for the day and, after he'd collected that, he was able
to luxuriate in the time spent alone. It was the restorative he
needed.

Now, in the middle of a new day, he stepped out of the guest lift
and walked across the reception hall – where, by Twelfth Night,
a team of workmen would be rigging up a scaffold to strip the
Norwegian fir naked and chop it up for the hotel's boilers. Billy
halloed him from the concierge desk – the poor boy's duties in
the post room were over now – but Maynard paid him no mind
as he crossed the hall, following the corridor beyond the check-
in desks to the doors of the Queen Mary.

Between services, the restaurant floor was still – but there,
around a table in its heart, sat the six representatives of the hotel
board. At the head of the table loomed Lord Edgerton, John

Hastings at his left-hand side and Uriah Bell at his right. The other members – Merriweather, Fletcher and Lloyd – sat on either side of them, leaving half of the great table empty, with only one seat, at which Maynard was expected to sit. He lingered, for a moment, in the doorway, just to take stock. Though he could hear the clattering of the chefs and sous-chefs through the kitchen walls, working towards the dinner service beginning in two hours' time, every door but the one he had just stepped through was sealed.

So, it seemed to him now, was his fate.

'Mr Charles,' John Hastings began, in a careful tone of voice that made Maynard feel certain he, too, was anxious about the day's proceedings. As he spoke, his eyes kept scouring his fellow board members, silently gauging the reaction of each. 'I'm glad you could join us.'

Maynard sank into the seat with his palms upturned and wide and said, 'Gentlemen, I have nowhere else to be.'

'You know, of course, why you're here.'

He supposed that he did. Jager's flight from the hotel had replayed, over and again, in his mind across Christmas night. Long into Boxing Day he'd dwelt upon Billy Brogan's lucky escape, all of the various tortures he'd had to put that boy through. There were things even a learned hotel director failed to see coming.

But he knew what was coming next. He'd known it since Jager's last words: '*Your board will hear of this outrage, Mr Charles. A flagrant abuse of my privacy. Lies and blackmail to boot!*' The looks on the members of the hotel board were lofty and imperious. Lord Edgerton had the look of the executioner sharpening his axe, but Maynard remained impassive. He was a hotel director. He *understood*.

'Mr Charles, it has been alleged to this board that, within the confines of this hotel, you have, for some months, persisted in a private business of your own – namely, that you have systematically tampered with and scoured the private correspondence of the guests of the hotel, seeking information with which you might blackmail them. Ergo, that you have spent hotel resources – to wit, your time and energies – pursuing personal gain at the detriment of the reputation of this hotel.'

Maynard Charles remembered the age-old advice that Walter Knave, the director who'd shepherded the Buckingham through the years of the Great War, once bestowed upon him: in times of great stress, take a moment, take a breath, and do precisely nothing at all.

At last, he said, 'Gentlemen, might I ask from where the accusation arises?'

'You know damn well, man!' Uriah Bell's fist flew up and pounded the surface of the table, so that the teacups in front of each board member rattled. Fletcher and Lloyd, the two lesser board members, recoiled from both the elder man's fury and, evidently, the stench of his breath. 'It's here in writing,' he fumed, flinging a letter into the middle of the table. 'Formal notification to us all of this scheme you were perpetrating. By God, man, you invited the man in. A refugee, by God! A man the world has spat on and spat out, and he washes up here, and you, *spy* on him! Accuse him of treacheries and—'

'There is another charge attached to this, Maynard,' intoned Lord Edgerton. 'Namely, that in perpetrating this scheme of yours – and Herr Bauer makes it quite clear in his letter that he believes this is far from the first time you've done this to a guest – you have corrupted other members of this hotel's staff.

Principally, Mr William Brogan – our page, turned concierge. Bauer represents to us that you purposely moved him to the post room so that he might systematically open the man's letters. That you had Brogan following his every move in this hotel, seeking some . . . advantage.'

Maynard's heart had been still, but at the mention of Billy it had skipped a beat.

'Now, listen here, gentlemen. Billy Brogan is—'

'Not in this room right now, Maynard. It is you who's been asked to explain these actions.' Lord Edgerton stood. 'There is proof, Mr Charles. I spoke, yesterday evening, with Mrs Farrier. It has been her suspicion, for some time, that young Mr Brogan was stealing from the hotel mail. It first came to her attention, you see, in the unfortunate matter of my stepdaughter, and how all her sordid business was laid bare to this hotel.' Lord Edgerton's voice had risen to a crisp ferocity, and his eyes homed in on Maynard now.

*So this is what this is*, thought Maynard – *not only concern for the reputation of the Buckingham Hotel, but an act of vengeance for which he's been searching for months.*

'A letter torn open that found its way around this hotel, and all of this happening but moments after you insert Master Brogan into the post room. A coincidence, Maynard? Evidently Mrs Farrier thought not. She's had her eagle eye on Brogan—'

'I'll stop you there, my lord.' Maynard had betrayed his own first rule, because there was too much emotion frothing up in his voice. He, too, rose to his feet – even while John Hastings, wearing the most pained expression Maynard had ever seen, implored him not to. 'Brogan acted on my instructions, and my instructions alone. The boy did not know what he was doing. He's slavishly loyal to this hotel.'

'A loyalty you have abused. Do you deny anything we have put to you, Maynard?'

He was trapped, then; pinioned by his own decisions. Maynard looked at each of the board members in turn. Lord Edgerton glowered down. Lloyd and Fletcher dared not return his gaze. Uriah Bell was purpling with fury; Peter Merriweather as disconsolate as a newly widowed woman; John Hastings, all at sea, as if the things he'd been hearing were too disappointing to imagine.

Maynard returned his gaze to Lord Edgerton. Hastings's disappointment was the only look in this room that truly pained him, but perhaps he could deal with that later.

'Gentlemen, I deny that I have ever attempted to blackmail a single one of my guests. For the rest – I do not deny a thing.' He heard Hastings sigh, but ignored it and ploughed on, 'Gentlemen, most of us here remember the Great War. Some of us fought there. All of us lost people we loved. We remember the ruin of that generation. The echoes of it live in us today, whether we were born high or low. So perhaps you might understand why, when an opportunity arose to help waylay the ruin of another generation – of boys like Billy Brogan or Frank Nettleton, men like our own Raymond de Guise – I seized it with both hands.'

'Might I interject?' John Hastings began. 'Maynard, my good man, my *best* man, be careful what you say.'

'No,' said Lord Edgerton, with a finality that shook each one of them on the restaurant floor. 'Speak freely, Maynard. Please do. I would know how you have abused the trust we put in you to run this hotel.'

'I have been doing what my conscience told me I must, gentlemen. The Buckingham Hotel is a second home for aristocrats from every English shire, and from the Continent's many countries. Men like this will always survive the war to come, but countless millions will not. These whispers of war, the fires that are being stoked upon the Continent, they have turned our hotel into a place for the world's power brokers to congregate and have conversations that will affect the lives of generations. And I am not the only one who knows this. Foreign elements know it too. His Majesty's enemies, all around us. Tobias Bauer was one of these, gentlemen. Not an aged exile, but a saboteur in the pay of Herr Hitler's government, who sought to learn secrets from the guests at this hotel. His real name is Lukas Jager. When the opportunity arose to play him at his own game, sirs, I took it – because my head and heart were in alignment. Because it was the right thing to do. Because if, in some small way, I could help prepare us for the future, I knew I had to do it. I am not claiming heroism, gentlemen. I cannot change the tragedy about to befall us – but perhaps all it takes is the small acts of a few good men to tip the balance.'

'The man's a lunatic,' Bell declared, turning to his fellow senior board members. 'You see it, don't you, Bartholomew? John? Peter? We trusted him with the reputation of this hotel and he's squandered it, trying to play God.' Bell looked back at Maynard. 'I know you suffered, Maynard. I know what that war did to you. But to risk the hotel, to ruin its reputation, all for a game of spies? Maynard, you've lost your marbles! *Reputation, reputation, reputation!* That's what you ought to have been thinking about – not about . . . changing history!'

'Now, now, gentlemen!' exclaimed John Hastings, rising to his own feet and turning out his palms, as if to invite calmness back to the table. 'Mr Charles has been this hotel's champion for nearly twenty years. Think of the triumphs he's won for this

435

hotel. This is the man who sailed your ship through the Great Depression. The man who preserved its reputation, even during the Abdication Crisis. He deserves to be heard – and I, for one, would hear every word that Mr Charles has to say.'

Maynard's eyes had landed on John Hastings. He nodded, sadly, as if in thanks – and made a silent entreaty for the great American to sit back down. This, Hastings did.

Lord Edgerton's eyes arced around the table, taking everybody in.

'Your prevarications cannot change the bare facts of the matter, Mr Hastings . . .' He paused. 'It seems to me, Maynard, that, after many years of salvaging the various petty scandals of this hotel, you have put yourself at the heart of the greatest scandal we have ever faced. A hotel director must be above reproach. Instead, you have turned this great establishment into a sickbed of secrecy and sedition. No matter what your political leanings – and we are none of us politicians in this room—'

'I beg to differ, sir,' said Maynard.

Lord Edgerton's eyes narrowed. For a moment, as each man stared at the other across the dining table, it was as if there were only the two of them in the room. Maynard held his gaze.

'Would you care to expound on that point, Maynard?'

Maynard Charles thought: *we are, all of us, politicians at heart. And there you stand, Lord Edgerton, lauded member of the British Union of Fascists. A Blackshirt, through and through. Eager to appease Herr Hitler, just like the rest of them, while he grows stronger and stronger again. You might not have marched on Cable Street, seeking to drive Jewish Londoners out of their homes as they did in Vienna and Berlin – but your blood runs just as cold.*

Of all of this, not a word was spoken – but Maynard fancied he was communicating everything with barely a flicker of his eyes.

'We are nothing without our principles.' Hastings sighed. 'Mr Charles has been guided by them throughout. Gentlemen, we owe him our clemency.'

Lord Edgerton's face made it clear he had never heard anything as preposterous in his life. All eyes in the room wheeled, first at John Hastings, and – once they had found him in want of any sense – back to Maynard.

The rest of the room was sneering along with Lord Edgerton. Even those young pups, Fletcher and Lloyd, were at it too; something in Lord Edgerton had emboldened them both.

'A principle is a very fine thing. A profit is even better. Maynard, you put this hotel's reputation at risk – and this, as you are only too aware, imperils its profits. Principles do not take precedence over profitability, my man. And so our problem is simple. There is no greater scandal than a hotel director systematically abusing the privacy and sanctity of his guests, no matter what their political creed. Had Napoleon Bonaparte asked for a suite in this hotel, he would have been given it – and afforded the same duty of care as anyone else. Had the Whitechapel Ripper taken a room, it would not have given us the right to police his private correspondence for our own gain. Now, Maynard, as you know – there are scandals that can be contained. A petty thief among the concierges, an overly amorous hotel dancer, even a boy pushed down the stairs – all of these things can be managed away, brushed under the carpet. But something of this magnitude cannot be controlled so easily.'

'*Reputation, reputation, reputation!*' Uriah Bell lamented.

'Cannot be controlled?' Maynard ventured. 'Why, of course it can – all you need is a little imagination—'

'We've had quite enough of your imagination, Maynard.'

'My lord, of all the men in this room, it is I who recognise the true importance of this hotel. Not just to bank ledgers and balance sheets, but to the twelve hundred people who work here, and the many thousands more whose homes and lives depend upon the wages they earn. This has been my life's purpose since I came back from the Great War. For twenty years, I have tidied away the scandals that might disrupt the smooth running of this hotel. Gentlemen, there are yet secrets within these halls that none of you will ever know – secrets that I have hidden away, for the betterment of the establishment. Sirs, I believe I have acted in good conscience, and according to the tenets of what is just and right. But I also acknowledge that the exposure of this, without proper handling, will have a detrimental effect on the Buckingham's reputation – an erosion of trust and faith that this establishment can hardly afford. That is why, gentlemen, I have come here today to tender my resignation as hotel director.'

Maynard was on his feet, even before the board members had acknowledged what he had said.

Opening his jacket, he reached into an inside pocket. There lay three envelopes, each sealed in wax of a different hue. For a moment, he deliberated each. Then, choosing one of the three letters, he produced it and placed it gently on the table.

'You'll find my formal notice here. My severance has, of course, long ago been codified in writing. I trust there will not be the need for the ordinary wrangling that goes along with these things. Gentlemen,' he said, primly and properly, 'I wish you all the very best in what's to come.'

Not a word was whispered in the entirety of the Queen Mary as Maynard Charles turned on his heel and marched away.

Frank Nettleton and Billy Brogan were crouching, together, at the doors of the Queen Mary when they heard his footsteps approach. Scrambling backwards – just in time to avoid being knocked over by the swinging doors – they watched as Maynard ambled out across the reception hall, past the glittering halos of light still being cast from the Norwegian fir, and down the corridor into his office.

Once he was inside, Maynard took a small paraffin lantern from the corner, ignited a thin blue flame and proceeded to tear thin shreds off the remaining two letters in his jacket pocket, letting each disintegrate into ash. He'd sat, late into the night, inscribing each of those letters. It was only when he was in the restaurant with them that he'd known which one was right to serve. They need never know what he'd written in the others.

The third letter was nearly gone when a knock came at the door. Maynard Charles knew that knock anywhere.

'Come in, Emmeline,' he called – and, when the door was pushed ajar, Mrs Moffatt stepped into the office.

'Maynard?'

'It's done, Emmeline. I wrote three of these yesterday evening. I did not know what they knew, and I wanted to be ready. So I wrote three letters, from which I might, at the last moment, choose.' The last ribbon was gone. Maynard dusted his hands of ash and turned to pour a brandy. 'As it turns out, they need never know the real reason I first started working for Moorcock and his agency. They need never know about Aubrey, about the

Park Suite, nor how Moorcock sought to leverage the love of my life against me. To them, I have died on the sword of my principles. That is a fitting end. And I do believe that, by the actions I explained in that letter, I may have saved young Mr Brogan his livelihood.'

'Oh, Maynard.'

'The poor boy may not have long before he's wearing an infantry uniform. He might, at least, have the job he loves until then. His family will be in need of every penny.'

'You shouldn't be going anywhere, Maynard. They should have arrested Lukas Jager. They should have—'

'Oh no, Emmeline. The board would never comply. A murder at this hotel would have been so messy. Better, perhaps, that it did not happen at all.'

'Then Lukas Jager is free to continue his—'

Maynard drained his glass.

'We all live to fight another day, dear Emmeline.' He stopped, considered her carefully. 'Emmeline, I am aware that, with all that's been happening in this hotel this year, I have neglected our friendship. That is something I hope I will have the opportunity to put right, very soon. I'm going to miss you.'

She noticed that his hand was trembling, as he tried to work through this particular flurry of emotion. She'd seen him soften before. She'd seen him cry. But there was a tenderness, here, of which she was most uncertain.

'It brings me a little comfort to know that you have made yourself a new close friend in this hotel.'

She smiled. Evidently, Maynard saw and heard all, even until the very end.

'Mr Adams has been a welcome companion. He has shown me . . . that life doesn't have to grind to a halt, just because you've told yourself it does. And – perhaps there's a new life for you, too, Maynard?'

'Perhaps,' he murmured.

'I should like to think so.'

'And the young man you dined with on Christmas Day?' When there was silence, Maynard went on, 'Well, I should think I shall hear about him in due course. But until then . . .'

There was a little valise under the desk. Maynard was bowing down to take it up when, all at once, the office door burst open and a scramble of bodies burst through. Foremost among them were Frank and Billy, who seemed to have shepherded the rest to the door. But here was Raymond, and Nancy, holding her new husband's hand. Here, too, was Louis Kildare, Archie Adams and the chambermaids Rosa and Ruth.

'Out, out!' Mrs Moffatt cried, as if she was shooing away a stray cat. 'This is the hotel director's office, not the Candlelight Club! You can't just boulder in here and—'

'Emmeline, please,' Maynard said softly. 'Let them come.'

There had been no stopping them, in any case. Soon, with the door still hanging open behind them, Raymond had worked his way to the front of the crowd. He was clasping Nancy's hand when he said, 'It's true, then? You're leaving?'

'My dear man, I have no choice.'

'There's always a choice, Mr Charles. You can rescind the res-ignation.'

Maynard's eyes landed, fleetingly, on Frank and Billy, who had been listening at the Queen Mary's doors. He supposed he couldn't be too harsh on them for this; it was he, after all, who had taught them the subtle arts of the spy.

'There's a war coming, Mr Charles,' Raymond said. 'The Buckingham needs you.'

Maynard set his valise on his desk and took in, for the final time, the confines of his little office. Twenty years, he'd spent between these walls. It had been his life. His brandy decanter, his Olympia Elite typewriter, the files and ledgers and portraits – all the things by which he'd ordered his existence. And now here were the people of the Buckingham Hotel as well. He was going to miss them so very much.

'My friends,' he began, 'I believed I would be here for the war as well. I believed I would be walking these halls, to shepherd you all through it – wherever the next years take us. I believed that, one day, I might go to sleep in my suite here and never wake up. But it is not to be. You all know, by now, the truth about Herr Tobias Bauer. You all know the degree by which I surveyed him, and for whom I was working. My friends, I would do it over again, if I was asked. But in doing so, I have put the reputation of this hotel in jeopardy, and to set this right I must leave you now.

'Do not be sad for me,' he went on, though he could see it on their faces, 'for I did what I know to be right.' He stopped, faltered, looked at each of them in turn. 'The Buckingham must survive, so that you – each and every one of you – can survive. So that none of you fall into the cracks that open up in a country at war. So that none of you perish, for want of food in your bellies and roofs above your head. I could not see a soul among you cast into the wilderness, not on the eve of a war. But listen to me, and listen well – you can do this, together. You don't need your old hotel director, holding your hands. You have each other. Every porter and page, every dancer and chambermaid, every cocktail waiter and cleaner among you – you are as one. There is a thing I've learned, in my time at this hotel. Whether low-born or high, we are all a part of this world. Lord Edgerton and his fellows will understand it, soon enough. Not one of us gets to opt out of the war to come. But if you stand together, as I know you can – if you stay strong, remain united, hold your-selves to the very best standards . . . If you understand, in your very hearts, that the world out there is just like the world in this hotel – a world where commoners and gentry must work together if any are to survive – well, there's every chance we'll be raising a glass together on the other side of it – as friends, every last one of us, together.

'In time, there will be a new director in this office. I pray, for you, that John Hastings gets his way in making an appointment, and not Lord Edgerton. But whoever it is, they're going to need your help.'

He opened his valise, took out a pen and notepaper, scribbled out a message, signed it, and handed it over to Frank.

'Mr Nettleton, in my last act as director of his hotel, I am giv-ing you an audition as a hotel dancer. Let your talent speak for itself. Your fate, after that, young man, is in your own hands.'

He took another sheet of paper, hurried another note, and delivered this one to the hands of Nancy de Guise.

'My dear, consider this letter an assurance that your job here is not at risk, neither because you have become a married woman, nor because of the help you have afforded Miss Edgerton at the Daughters of Salvation. The Buckingham Hotel will need its talented female staff when war descends. You can be certain of that. Young lady, should you so desire, a career is waiting for you in these halls. I shall leave the rest to the ever-resourceful and excellent Mrs Moffatt to work out.'

He turned to Raymond, at last.

'Raymond,' he said, 'my friend. It took you some time, I know, to convince me of the wonders of that ballroom of ours – but, by God, you convinced me in the end. I have already sent a letter to Miss Marchmont. It is a matter of some regret that I could not protect her, too, in the end, although' – he flashed his eyes at Archie – 'she has friends to support her, all the same.' He paused. 'It is time, now, my friends, for me to leave.'

The crowd parted, revealing the office door, and as Maynard passed between them, he plucked his bowler hat from the stand and, placing it squarely on his head, stepped into the corridor. For a time, he did not hear the footfalls behind him. Then, as he reached the reception hall – where the board, still fevered from their hurried conversations in the Queen Mary, were themselves preparing to disappear into the growing dark – he looked back, and saw all of the familiar faces of the Buckingham Hotel gathered like a group of mourners, to make their goodbyes.

It was enough. He nodded once to them all, then ambled calmly beneath the boughs of the Norwegian fir, past the bank of faces of the board, and through the revolving brass door.

Berkeley Square was still cloaked in snow, and the street lamps just flickering to life. The doorman, who had no knowledge of the tragedy that had just unfolded inside the hotel, doffed his cap graciously to Maynard as he appeared, and in return Maynard gave him a smile of farewell. Then he tramped down into the snow.

What a thing was life! The December cold was soon working its way into Maynard's bones, but by power of will he managed not to look back at the old, familiar façade of the Buckingham.

Not one of them had asked him where he would spend the night. He was grateful for that. He did not want to have to lie.

He left Berkeley Square by one of the avenues leading south towards Piccadilly and Green Park – and there, in a pool of darkness between two street lights, sat a black Rolls-Royce. He approached it slowly, without breaking his stride, opened the passenger door and slipped inside without a word.

In the driver's seat, behind the wheel, the light of a single White Owl cigar flared.

'I didn't think it would be you,' Maynard began.

'I'm your man.' Mr Moorcock smiled. 'How does it feel, Maynard, to have torn up your life?'

'I feel light,' he whispered. 'I feel untethered. Floating away. But you told me I'd be provided for. You told me there were provisions.'

Moorcock said, 'We at the Office have no intention of leaving you to rot, Maynard. You and I have not always seen eye to eye, but you did good work for us at the Buckingham. Good work does not go unrewarded.'

'I want you to leave Billy Brogan out of it from now on. He may get away with it all and keep his job, if the board believes what I wrote. It will stymie his career, of that I've no doubt – but I should like it if he could keep his livelihood. He has a family that depend on him.'

'I'll speak to my superiors,' Moorcock said. 'But Brogan would be a useful asset.' He paused. 'And you, Mr Charles?'

'I want a bed for the night. I'll need to take stock. I'm not like my old friends in there. My family are long gone. My lover . . .'

445

There was silence in the Rolls-Royce, as Maynard dwelt, momentarily, upon things he could never get back.

'Mr Charles, I didn't come here to provide you board and lodging for the night. I think you understand that. You and I both know the scope of things to come. The Office is in the epicentre of the biggest recruitment drive in its history. Enemies, at home and abroad, need monitoring. Influencing, even. The British fascists remain on the rise. There is, we believe, the beginnings of a Nazi fifth column, right here in London. What I am saying is, there are uses for a man of your intellect. A man who has already marshalled the kind of army you had in the Buckingham. A man who, though he would not describe it as such, has already been running secret agents of his own.' He paused. 'There's a war to be fought. We're fighting it already. I'm authorised to ask you – what would it take for a man like you to enlist?'

Maynard said, 'To come and work for you—'

'*With* me,' Moorcock corrected, 'and many others embroiled in the same endeavour.'

'And that is?'

'The endeavour of saving Great Britain.'

In the Rolls-Royce, there was silence – until, at long last, Maynard Charles turned to his companion and, lifting one hand, said, 'Mr Moorcock, I think I should enjoy one of your White Owl cigars.'

Across the town houses outside, fat flakes of snow had started to fall.

The postman who trudged up Brixton Hill, the third day after Christmas, had red and ruddy cheeks, as befitted the labour of his day. It was already afternoon when he reached the snows of Sudbourne Road and knocked at the door of the basement flat. The elderly couple who lived inside were always cheery, and on this occasion they even gave him a quick glass of port to warm him on his way.

Inside the terrace, where tinsel garlanded the walls, Hélène Marchmont was on the hearthrug with Sybil, trying to assemble a wooden jigsaw puzzle that the Archers' youngest son, Joseph, had cut and painted himself. Christmas Day had been a cramped, chaotic – and completely jubilant affair. The sitting room had welcomed not only Maurice and Noelle, but Joseph, his sister Samantha and her husband Dickie as well. Samantha, who had helped with Sybil so much in the early days, had news of her own: a baby on the way by summer. So there were other things to toast beyond the Yuletide this year.

Other things to lament, as well.

Hélène had woken on Christmas morning and taken Sybil to the tree to find her stocking – but, even as the wrapping paper was torn and the new presents revealed, there had been a sadness in the air. It had barely been mentioned since Hélène arrived, but Chicago had been at the forefront of every mind in the house.

Noelle Archer came back from the front door, having foisted a mince pie on the postman before sending him on his way.

'It's for you, Hélène,' she said, and passed her a fat letter, its envelope imprinted with the copper crown crest of the Buckingham Hotel.

Inside the envelope lay a second envelope, and folded around that a letter in the hand of none other than Maynard Charles.

*Dear Miss Marchmont,*

*I am writing so that I can myself break the news that, as of this today, 26th December, 1938, I am no longer to be director of the Buckingham Hotel.*

*Formalities aside, I want you to know that I wish you all the best in your new life in Chicago. It was with great sadness that I watched events unfold for you this year; had it been in my power to preserve your position in the Grand for longer, I would gladly have done so. You have my utmost respect for the experiences you have lived through, and the person who has shone so vividly throughout it all. I have known secrets in my life, but few carried, like yours, with such grace and dignity. Would that there were more like you in the world, Miss Marchmont.*

*With the hope that, one day, the stories of our lives may intersect again.*

*Yours, with affection,*

*Maynard Charles*

*PS. Please find enclosed correspondence that arrived in the hotel post room before Christmas.*

Hélène had to take a moment, lingering over Mr Charles's news, before she turned her attention to the second letter. The Buckingham Hotel without Maynard Charles – it was as unthinkable as the Grand Ballroom without Raymond de Guise and Hélène Marchmont. But the century marched on apace. Time, like music, never stood still.

She recognised the writing, of course. It was this same writing that had undone her life in the last year: Aunt Lucy's handwriting, sent out into the world to destroy her. It was for this reason that Hélène did not open the letter, not at first. She returned to playing with Sybil, helped Noelle make the tea, straightened the blanket on Maurice's lap, where he slept in his armchair by the fire – and only then, because she could not ignore it any longer, did she sit down again and, with Sybil squirming in her lap, open it up.

Dearest Hélène,

It is Tuesday evening, 20th December, and I am writing to you, having been up to London to visit the offices of Messrs Lawton & Lawton, your father's solicitors since he was a young man. We laid your father to rest two days ago, and it was indeed a bleak midwinter day that saw him committed to the ground in the graveyard at Rye. That you were not there brings shame on us, Hélène, though not on you. Your mother and I carry this shame alone.

I had hoped to be writing to you with better tidings. I had thought – though you may think me a fool – that we would arrive at Lawton & Lawton to discover that my brother never truly wrote you out of his last will and testament. But, on the reading of this, it was revealed that your father left but two beneficiaries in his will: half the estate to your mother, and half to me, that it might exist in the Marchmont line a little longer. My brother died a stubborn man with a broken heart, breaking further hearts with his last breaths. I am sorry, Hélène.

Noelle had noticed that Hélène was shaking. From the other side of the room, she said, 'Hélène, is everything all right?'

Hélène just looked back, with shimmering eyes, and said, 'I don't know why she even wrote. The story's over. It's finished.'

Then she returned to the letter.

Hélène, my brother's death will echo in me for some years – but the sins of his life will echo in me further, unless I can do something to set them right. I had not expected to inherit much from my brother. Your grandparents left me their jewellery and some family heirlooms, but beyond that,

*I have had little. That he has bequeathed me half the Marchmont estate can only be because this was meant for you. And, Hélène, my dear, I have today instructed Lawton & Lawton to begin the process of gifting this, in its entirety, to you and your daughter Sybil – in the hope, my darling, that you might come home, and that (though I expect no forgiveness in return for the gift of something which should rightfully be yours), somehow we might be close again; and that, in time, I might walk with Sybil in the orchards as I once walked with you, might picnic with her on the sands, might read with her and teach her arithmetic, and be the auntie I once was, in a better time, to you. I should have fought for you, Hélène. I should have abandoned them when they did not see. But I did not, and this regret burns in me. I hope that there is a way we can begin to put this right.*

*I am sending this to the Buckingham Hotel, in the hope that it finds you this Christmas. But whether I see you or not, Hélène, your father's estate will be yours to do with as you wish; and my heart will be yours as well.*

*Yours with love, always,*

*Aunt Lucy*

As Hélène finished reading, Sybil was wrestling the letter out of her hands. She had little strength left to resist her. She was sitting there still, the heat of the fire crackling over her, when she realised that Noelle had taken the letter from Sybil and was herself reading its contents.

'Hélène,' she finally ventured, dropping down beside her. 'Oh, Hélène . . .'

'I know,' whispered Hélène.

'What will you do?'

Hélène fell against Noelle's shoulder. The year was rushing past her in fits and starts of colour: everything from that first

450

letter to this, from being cast out of the Grand to sitting here, with Maurice and Noelle, and telling them that there was no other option – that she was going to have to go to Chicago.

Now, she heaved a great sigh and let herself sink deeper into Noelle. The elder woman held her fast.

'I'm going to live,' she said, and smiled.

On New Year's Eve, the trains were running slowly into Rye, when they were running at all. Hélène and Sybil took the bus up out of town, with the little red sledge they'd borrowed from the Archers tucked under one arm, and then, once they had disembarked, Hélène towed Sybil behind her, the little girl cheering each time the sledge flew over a new hummock of ice.

The Marchmont manor: how it seemed to have changed, now that she knew her father was no longer here. She did not need to knock, for Lucy had seen her, at some distance, from one of the uppermost windows, and came to join them in the grounds before Hélène drew near.

They froze, ten yards distant from each other. Sybil, however, held no such reservations. She picked herself up from the sledge, staggered in the snow on the way to Lucy, hovered somewhere between them – and, in doing so, brought them together.

'I wasn't sure if you'd come,' Lucy began.

Hélène nodded. 'Thank you,' she started to say – but Lucy shook her head with the force of an impassioned mother and said, 'What's yours is yours. The rest is paperwork. Hélène, can you forgive me? Not yet. But – one day . . . ?'

'I had plans to leave. A job at a hotel in Chicago. Somewhere we could go and be together. It was tearing me in two, Lucy. I'd have had to take her from her grandparents. They might never have seen her again.' She paused. 'Is my mother inside?'

In fact, Marie had appeared in the open doorway. She was waving at Hélène, bracing herself against the December cold, uncertain if she should step out or not.

'She's nervous of you. She knows what she did. Your father was a strong man. She did it for him, Hélène – I think we both did – but ... There's still time, isn't there? In life, I mean. To write new stories. To remember new things. To – not forget the past, but to right it. To come together.'

It was Sybil who answered. Something was drawing her to Lucy. The little girl had her arms opened out like an acrobat as she danced across the top of the snow to meet her. A few moments later, Lucy had dared to crouch down and scoop the child into her arms. And Hélène remembered, then, what it had been like, to feel those hands close around her.

'We have time,' she said.

She turned on the spot – her mother was coming out to join them, at last – and took in the whole of the manor grounds. Though it was but a plain of undulating white, by springtime it would be green and verdant, and in the summer filled with the most unimaginable colours.

Her eyes landed on the little snow-capped folly on the other side of the orchards, and further on a single stone abode.

'Who's living in the old ground-keeper's cottage?' she asked, and when Lucy told her that nobody had lived there since Hélène was small, her mind flashed back to the Archers in their little Brixton terrace, and an idea started to form. If what the newspapers said was true, it might be wise to leave London soon.

Sometimes, life changes overnight. The revelation was that it didn't always have to be for the worse.

Hélène looked at Sybil being whirled through the air and allowed herself to *believe*.

On New Year's night, there was dancing in the Grand. The music spilled out across the reception hall, along the Buckingham's outermost reaches, and for a time it seemed that the whole hotel was luxuriating in the songs and simple joys of that night. But for Raymond and Nancy de Guise, all of that was a world away – for there they stood, on a snow-encrusted doorstep in Maida Vale.

Raymond had picked up the keys in the days after Christmas, while Nancy changed bed sheets in the hotel's uppermost suites. Now, each wrapped up in new winter coats, he placed them in the palm of her hand.

'It's all yours, Mrs de Guise.'

She was smiling as she slipped the key into the lock. It fitted perfectly – just, she caught herself thinking, like Raymond did her. What was it her mother used to say? Every old sock needs an old shoe. There were certainly more romantic ways of speaking about love, but none truer, as far as Nancy was concerned.

So she opened the door.

In the end, Raymond de Guise couldn't resist one more romantic gesture – so, before they passed through the doorway together, he put his arms around his new wife and carried her over the threshold. Inside, all was dark. But the building had been fitted with new electric lights, just as Raymond had instructed, and soon they were gliding from sitting room to study, through kitchen and bathroom, from first bedroom to second bedroom to third. This was not just a home for Mr and Mrs de Guise. One day – perhaps not soon, but one day – this was the home for a family.

'Empty rooms,' said Nancy, with a smile, 'but they won't be empty for long.'

They drifted together, back to the hall, speaking of the furniture they had to buy, and how all the manifold gifts from the wedding might make this house a living, breathing home – and how, as soon as they got back from their honeymoon in the north country (all of it courtesy of Vivienne), they would set about it with gusto.

Raymond's eyes drifted down. There, lying on the doormat, was a single envelope.

'Strange,' said Raymond, 'I haven't told a soul we're here yet – not except . . .'

He had stooped down to pick it up and, by the buzzing electric light, saw the names on the front – MR AND MRS RAYMOND DE GUISE – in an all too familiar hand.

'Nancy,' he whispered, and led her by the hand into the sitting room – where the house's single piece of furniture – a worn old armchair – invited them down.

'You know that writing, Raymond?'

Raymond nodded. 'It's Maynard Charles's.'

In the end, he left it to Nancy to open the letter. She drew out the single yellow leaf, across which Maynard's spidery hand had danced, and perched on the armchair's edge as she began to read.

*Dear Raymond, dear Nancy,*

*It would not do to leave you both without the fondest farewell.*

*I remember an age when I scorned music and dance as a distraction from the very real business of running the Buckingham Hotel. That age is* long gone, my friends, and good riddance to it. Raymond, you will know how my heart feels as I set down these words, but you will also know the joy in which I have spent my years, and the satisfaction I have gained from a life lived in such fine company. I do not mean the lords and ladies we have together served. I mean the good people who man the Buckingham Hotel – and, among them, the good souls I am writing to now: two of the finest people I have had the privilege to know.

Time is marching on. The world will not wait. I am preparing as I must, to look after my friends and colleagues once I am gone. I have today instructed the Queen Mary, French bistro and Candlelight Club that any excess food meant for the refuse will, from this moment on, instead find itself redirected to the Daughters of Salvation charitable organisation in Whitechapel. Let Lord Edgerton discover this, and make of it what he will, at his own pace. I will do what I can for Emmeline and Archie, for Billy and Frank, for all of those who I have come to think of as family over the years. Because, make no mistake, that is what the Buckingham has been to me – a family, where I have none of my own.

I would leave you with one word of advice before I sign off. It is, perhaps, advice you would not expect from the hotel director you have come to know. But, Raymond, Nancy, I implore you: keep dancing. Dance together, in the privacy of your home. Dance together, in the ballrooms and clubs. Dance together, when you wake in the morning and when you prepare for bed each night. Dance when you are weary, and dance when you are not. The world is going to need joy, and it is down to each of us to call that joy into being and keep it alive.

I have little doubt that, in two souls as perfectly matched as yours, there will be joys untold.

Yours, with love,

Maynard

After Nancy had read the letter out loud, she read it again, breathing the words under her breath. Then she shrank into Raymond's shoulder – somewhere along the way, his arm had curled behind her back – and said, 'It will be a strange hotel without Maynard Charles, won't it, Raymond?'

'It will be the strangest year for all of us,' he said, 'but every time there's an ending, there's a beginning. Just like this old house here. Imagine what it will be like this time next year, Nancy. A Christmas in our very own home. Maybe Artie and Vivienne will be here, along with the baby. Maybe Rosa and Frank. Because that's what Mr Charles is telling us, isn't it? That we can get through it, but only if we do it together. That's the Buckingham way.'

He stopped, left Nancy on the armchair and drifted to the window, where the hypnotic snow was still falling down.

'What a year it's been – but this year just started? Well, things are going to be different. I can feel it in my bones. If there's one thing a lifetime of dance has taught me, it's that good times are coming. You've got to keep dancing. All this talk of war – well, there's always another song. There's always a new refrain. And ... I'm glad to be dancing it with you, Nancy. This next year, it's going to be the dance of our lives. You'll see.' He smiled, turning back to face her: Nancy de Guise, in whom all of his future hopes and dreams were vested. She reached out her hands to him.

'I'll show you myself,' said Raymond. '1939 – it's going to be the making of us.'

# *Acknowledgements*

Just like my first love, dancing, writing and publishing a book is a partnership. It really is a team effort. I'm eternally grateful to all those who have helped bring the Buckingham Hotel and its characters to life. Thanks to my marvellous editorial team – Sarah Bauer, Katie Lumsden and Kate Parkin – who have been there every step of the way. Thanks for all your help shaping my ideas and stories into the wonderful finished product before us. It seemed like we'd never get there when we were planning out this book over Zoom during lockdown! I'm very lucky to have worked on all three of my novels with a wonderful writing collaborator; thank you for all your input and assistance over the last few years.

Thanks also to Steve O'Gorman and Laetitia Grant for their thorough copyediting and proofreading.

I'm so grateful to my wonderful publicist, Francesca Russell. We've not been able to travel all over the country together this year, but she's still worked just as hard to share my books far and wide. Thanks also to another terrific publicist, Clare Kelly, who has worked tirelessly on promoting my novels.

One of my favourite things about having a book published is seeing the stunning covers evolve. I'm so grateful to Alexandra Allden and Nick Stearn for all their beautiful work. I've dreamt of having a festive jacket but I never thought it could be as stunning as this.

So many people are involved in marketing and selling a book, so my heartfelt thanks go to Stephen Dumughn, Felice McKeown, Elise Burns, Mark Williams, Stuart Finglass, Andrea Tome, Carrie-Ann Pitt, Victoria Hart, Amanda Percival, Jearl Boatswain, Vincent Kelleher, Sophie Hamilton and Kate Griffiths.

My thanks as well to Alex May, Ella Holden and Eloise Angeline and the whole production department, without whom the book would be only a pdf on a computer.

I'm grateful also to Laura Makela and Jon Watt who organised and created the audiobook. I love audiobooks, and always have one on while driving, so every year I am thrilled that others will be listening to my book in the same manner. Thanks also to Thomas Judd for bringing the members of the Buckingham Hotel to life in the audiobook.

Thanks go to everyone else at Bonnier Books UK, including Ruth Logan, Stella Giatrakou, Ilaria Tarasconi, Saidah Graham and Shane Hegarty.

My gratitude to Melissa Chappell knows no bounds. I am so lucky to be able to call you my friend as well as my agent. Thank you as always for your insight and advice.

Thank you also to Hollie Paton Pratt for always being across everything, keeping me organised, and making sure I always know where I'm meant to be and when. Thanks, too, to Kerr MacRae, my literary agent, for his constant input and support.

Thank you to Scott Mycock at Bungalow Industries for all your support and hard work on this project.

Finally, thanks to you – my readers. Few things make me happier than hearing that somebody has read and loved my books, so thank you for welcoming the Buckingham Hotel and its many residents with open arms.

Hello my loves!

I feel as though we're getting into something of a rhythm here – a book a year! Well, none of this would be possible without the support and encouragement from you, my wonderful readers, so thank you for joining me for this, the third novel in my Buckingham Hotel series: *A Christmas to Remember*.

Many of you, I hope, will have become familiar with the world in and around the Buckingham Hotel from my first two books – *One Enchanted Evening* and *Moonlight Over Mayfair* (the former a *Sunday Times* bestseller, the latter shortlisted for the Historical Romantic Novel Award – do forgive me the plugs!). Well, it would have been rude of me to leave us all in the lurch without a book three – and, between you and me, our characters had begun to take on such a life of their own they'd have given me little peace if I hadn't continued telling their stories!

Now, I realise that this new book has a 'seasonal' title and it may feel a little strange if you're diving in at another time of year. It's no secret that I'm a big fan of Christmas, I'll not deny it! I love the pure magic of it – especially these days, seeing it through my family's eyes. But here, in our Buckingham world, the title celebrates that last Christmas before the outbreak of World War II and speaks of holding the good times dear while looking to an uncertain future with courage and hope. A time of great change, so much of which rings true today in our new world of lockdowns, quarantines and isolations. A little escapism to a ballroom in a bygone time is surely a welcome tonic – it has been for me – and I hope I've been able to whisk you away to share it with me, too.

The stage has now been set for a new period in the world of the Buckingham Hotel and the lives of all its characters (with some cliff-hangers too!) – hopefully you're as excited to read their ongoing stories as I am about telling them. Your messages, tweets and comments are always a thrill to receive, and your encouragement means the world. Best keep it coming – I've the next instalment to write!

In the meantime, keep in touch. You'll find all the links for the social media channels below – including my YouTube with dance lessons and keep fit classes – so we can all stay connected.

Keep reading, keep dancing, keep safe, and keep well, my loves!

Anton
xxx

P.S. Don't forget to follow me:
🐦 @TheAntonDuBeke
📷 @Mrantondubeke
📘 www.facebook.com/antondubeke
▶️ www.youtube.com/c/AntonDuBekeTV
www.antondubeke.tv

If you loved *A Christmas to Remember*,
find out where it all began with the previous
books in the Buckingham Hotel series . . .